Fiona Cooper was born in Bristol in 1955. Her first novel was *Rotary Spokes* (available in Black Swan) and she has also written *Heartbreak on the High Sierra*, *Not the Swiss Family Robinson* and *Jay Loves Lucy*, and has published numerous short stories. Fiona Cooper lives on Tyneside.

Author photograph by Julia Darling

D0532542

Also by Fiona Cooper

ROTARY SPOKES

and published by Black Swan

The Empress Of
The Seven Oceans

Fiona Cooper

BLACK SWAN

THE EMPRESS OF THE SEVEN OCEANS
A BLACK SWAN BOOK 0 552 99490 1

First publication in Great Britain

PRINTING HISTORY
Black Swan edition published 1992

Set in 11pt Linotype Melior by
County Typesetters, Margate, Kent.

Black Swan Books are published by Transworld Publishers Ltd,
61–63 Uxbridge Road, Ealing, London W5 5SA, in Australia
by Transworld Publishers (Australia) Pty Ltd, 15–23 Helles Avenue,
Moorebank, NSW 2170, and in New Zealand by Transworld
Publishers (NZ) Ltd, 3 William Pickering Drive, Albany, Auckland.

Made and printed in Great Britain by
Cox & Wyman Ltd, Reading, Berks.

With thanks to Evelyn and Roy, my parents,
for all their love and support

Part One

The River and the Woods

The Bells Are Ringing For Me And My Gal

Twenty feet below them, the river swirled. Lazy green spirals merged with a deep dash of bubbles; a muddy ripple catching on a stuck branch finally tugged it free, dashing it downstream with a triumphant tail of foam.

Their branch lay out over the deepest pool in this reach of the river – deep enough for swimming as they both knew from the times they'd tickled each other to a wonderful free-falling plunge. But this was a lazy afternoon, too hot inside the thick-leaved bower to move much beyond a lazy stretch and caress. Rowan did both, her hand stroking Esther's cheek, her body snuggling just that pleasantly impossible bit closer.

'Careful,' said Esther, 'We'll both tip off.'

'Won't be the first time,' said Rowan.

The leaves murmured around their giggles.

'This is bliss,' said Esther, putting the tip of her nose on the tip of Rowan's nose. 'Oh, my honey, you have at least five eyes, and they're all big and brown and swimming in freckles. I want to kiss every freckle you have.'

'That'd take for ever!'

'Well, I'd better start now,' said Esther, elf-lips fluttering round her lover's brow. And then she froze.

She froze, Rowan froze; their bodies in the bark-brown leaf-green clothes became another part of the branch; Esther's white-gold hair was a patch of sunlight lying smooth against the dark brown curls on

9

Rowan's head. Below them came the sound of bracken broken by young animals, sticks cracking under carelessly exuberant paws, then three splashes.

The women in the tree raised their necks so that they could look through a leafy peephole. Three soaking heads bobbed up, spitting jets of water and shrieking with laughter.

Six impertinent eyes scanned the branch high above them.

'We know where you're hiding!' shouted the biggest child.

Then the children all started to splash upwards as high as they could. The spray came nowhere near the branch, so the small heads drew together, whispered something and dived deep again.

'Do you think they really know we're up here?' whispered Esther.

'No. We came the long way, and mine have no patience at all. Let's just keep very still. It's nowhere near sundown yet . . . for Chrissake!'

A drenched child dived on top of them, whooping. Rowan tipped off the branch, Esther in her arms, and they bombshelled into the pool. The child swung along the branch, screeching with wicked delight.

'Wild and wicked!' yelled Rowan. 'You're a squirrel, not a girl!'

Two more children bobbed up and yanked her knees so that she sprawled in the water.

'Otters!' she shouted, grabbing them and tossing them clean over the other side of the pool.

'Water-rats!'

'I am not a rat,' said the smallest child, sitting on Esther's belly as she floated, 'Esther, I am not a rat.'

'Of course you're not, baby!'

'And I am not a baby!'

10

'Well, what are you?' She smudged the baby nose with her wet finger and thumb.

'I am a great big turtle,' said the child, drawing in her arms and legs and collapsing solidly on her mother's body, her shelly little head buried in Esther's breasts.

The wild and wicked squirrel girl reached the end of the branch and launched herself into flight. She flew slow and sure, drifted light as swansdown over the river surface, then gathered all her weight back with a mighty breath and exploded into the giggling group.

'Otter!' she screamed, diving and grabbing every leg within arm's reach.

They were making so much noise that they didn't notice the two demure grey figures staring pop-eyed from the far bank.

'Disgusting!' said Sister Charity.

'They're only children,' Sister Mercy protested. Her feet were shredded by the penitence pebbles in her heavy leather sandals, and she envied all their fun and freedom, the frolicking in the river. She knew that envy was wrong, of course, and she said a quick Ave Maria. The Blessed Virgin would understand, she was a mother herself.

'God forgive you,' Sister Charity said darkly. 'It's the Lord's Day. They should be at church, praying for forgiveness, not disporting themselves in this foul pagan manner.'

'They're only children,' said Sister Mercy again, softly. 'Their sweet innocent souls are worshipping His Creation as best they know how.'

Sister Charity clutched her arm and drew back.

'There are grown women there!' she hissed.

Rowan and Esther scrambled up the bank, shaking children off like puppies. The baby turtle stayed

11

floating, drifting with the current. The women pulled their clothes off and spread them on the bushes.

'Avert your eyes, Sister Mercy, this is devil's work! Nakedness . . .'

Both nuns stared. In the distance the church bell started to ring.

'We're late, Sister Mercy, late. May the Good Lord see our suffering and lend us His forgiveness!'

But as the bells began ringing, the naked women on the other bank covered their ears and shrieked. The children roared with laughter, and the biggest child leaped on to the bank, her high voice carrying clear across the river.

'We are gathered here in the name of Misery!'

'Alleluia!' came exploding from the other children.

'Because you're all BAD, WICKED and IRREDEEMABLE! On your knees and pray!'

'Mockery! Sacrilege!' whimpered Sister Charity.

Sister Mercy said nothing. The child was mimicking Father Dominic perfectly, from his rolling eyes and swaying stance to his sonorous speech, punctuated by accusations as heavy as a sledgehammer. She was afraid to speak for fear of laughing.

Then one of the naked women swooped on the chanting child and hurled her into the river. She skimmed the surface like a stone and back-flipped under the water.

Sister Charity crossed herself.

'Witchcraft!' she whispered. 'That child flew. God save and preserve all decent Christian folk! Mark this spot, Sister Mercy, mark it well. We shall be back with Matthew the Pricker and Father Dominic!'

'The child didn't actually fly,' murmured Sister Mercy.

'I wonder about you sometimes, Sister Mercy,' said

Sister Charity, and her eyes were as cold as the grey belly of a fish on the slab.

Sister Mercy's heart began to race. Matthew the Pricker was in the area? Her skin went cold. She'd heard about this Pricker. Lecherous, fanatical, hell-bent. She crossed herself.

'You do well to ask for Christ's protection,' said Sister Charity. 'We must make a report as soon as service is over.'

They scurried along the path towards the insistent bell.

Baby Big Turtle uncurled herself in the reeds. She had ears like a bat and she did *not like* the voices she'd picked up as she rocked against the far bank. She swam straight back to her sisters and mothers as soon as the heavy leather soles had clumped out of hearing.

'Rowan, Esther,' she said, 'what's a pricker?'

'Come and get dry, Big Turtle,' said Esther. 'Where d'you hear that word? Tell me all about it!'

Her eyes met Rowan's over the baby's head, and her hands rubbed the lovely little body dry as Big Turtle gave them the nuns' conversation word for word. Isabel, the middle child, said nothing, but her eyes were huge and smoky with feeling.

'Tell you what, girls,' said Rowan, 'we're going to sleep in a secret place tonight.'

'I want to sleep in the tree!' the Squirrel cried, stamping her foot.

'Tough,' said Rowan. 'Let's go. OK, Belle?'

The silent child nodded and stuffed her fist into Rowan's hand.

They vanished into the deepening shadows of the forest.

The Acrobat's Child

He flew out of the darkness overhead, a slice of high-speed sunset, his skintight white costume streaked with crimson and orange and gold from the flares around the circus ring. The faces in the crowd glowed red, as though they were sitting by a huge bonfire instead of muffled to the ears against the chill of the open air. Mouths gaped at the sight of the flying man: small children screamed as he vanished into darkness; they screamed again as he whirled back high above them. And now his body was the grisly green of a marsh ghost and the faces turned up towards him had the ghastly pallor of nightmare. He swung eerily slow and paused in midair like a swimmer taking breath. Agonizingly slow, he drew his body upright so that he seemed to be standing on an invisible platform, his arms raised as if poised to dive.

This was the best bit, and though Jen had seen it a million times, her heart raced with ecstasy and terror. She watched the faces of the crowd with glee. Now the flares were belching out mauve smoke, and the crowd seemed struck by plague. Their mouths were open, their eyes huge with disbelief, and she knew he'd started to tip forward with the supremely casual control that had earned him the name 'Dolphin of the Skies'.

'He's going to fall!' a child wailed. 'He's going to fall!'

14

That made Jen feel superior. Kids! She'd done the same when she was a kid; she just couldn't see how he could do anything but fall headfirst – but he never did. Now she was seven and sure of his skill. She smiled at the stupid child in a knowing way and looked back up at the sky, where the Dolphin was hanging like a fly caught against the blackness and the faraway stars.

A drum started somewhere behind the crowd, very deep and slow, filling the ring, picking up the heartbeat and speeding up as the air diver began to spin. The beat was deafening as his white figure became a blur: his head was a line of whirling eyes and mouth, distorted as his flight took him back into the dark, to return a split second later as the flares cracked and flashed and made him a phosphorescent streak of lightning. The smoke and flames died down, and he moved slower and nearer to the ground, as if treading the gracious curve of a spiral staircase.

His feet touched the ground and he tripped around the ring to applause and amazement. Then he cartwheeled through a gap in the crowd and was gone.

Jen scrambled to her feet and danced into the ring.

'Ladies and gentlemen, good folk all! I'm sure you'd all like to show your appreciation! My little fidget here will be passing among you . . . we'll be back with more magic and mysteries very shortly!'

Jethro the Magician, booming way over her head, dug his hard fingers into her shoulder. He made her an elaborate bow and took off his hat. She curtseyed the way they'd rehearsed, took the hat and went round, wearing a stupid doll smile just the way he'd told her. Coins rained into the hat. She went around three times before handing it back to him. He bowed and tapped her bottom, then ushered her and her fixed smile out of the ring.

God, how she hated him!

The flying man was sitting by the fire, stripped to the waist.

'How's my girl?' he asked, putting her on his knee.

'All those kids were screaming, Dad! Honestly, they thought you'd fall!'

'You used to think that, Jen,' he told her.

'Yes, but I'm not a kid any more,' she said. 'And you never do fall. Dad, will you tell me how you do it?'

Her father laughed and hugged her.

'Trade secret, Jen,' he said, 'I can't tell anyone that – there can't be two Dolphins of the Skies. Now, if I had a son, I could teach him, but since I haven't . . .'

Jethro came up close.

'You can't let the secret go with you,' he said, and Jen thought he sounded sly. 'You'll have to pass it on one day.'

'I learnt it from my father and I'll pass it on to my son or not at all,' said the flying man. 'Just call it magic, Jen.'

Jen sighed. It was great to have a dad who could fly, brilliant to have a dad who was magic, but she wished she was his son, not his daughter. Maybe she would change into a boy one day. Everyone told her she was young yet, and anything could happen. She wished Jethro would go away. But he sat beside them and pinched her knee.

'She's getting the idea with the money now, Tom. I told you I'd soon show her. Smile, smile, smile, little lady! She'll do even better when she grows a bit.'

God, she hated him! Him and his horrid smile under his moustache, him and his moustache like a great big caterpillar with a waxy horn at each end.

'She'll need sleep now.'

There was the one voice in the whole troupe that

16

no-one argued with. Granny didn't even have to raise her voice or sound angry. People just listened to her and did what she said. Even Jethro! He might sneer at her behind her back, and there was a grating, tinny sound to the way he said her name, but one word out of place in front of her earned him her Look, and got him mumbling his apologies, while his big ears reddened under his black curly hair and the blush went right down to his collar.

Granny lifted Jen from her dad's lap and held her close as she walked over to the caravan standing under the trees.

'You're getting a bit heavy for me, Jen love,' she said. 'I remember when I could sit you in my two hands . . .'

'And my face was the size of a goose-egg,' Jen giggled at the thought of a big yellow yolk behind her eyes.

'And your fingers were so small they just met round my little finger.'

Granny's voice got quieter and quieter, talked Jen smaller and smaller up the steps, then tucked her under the covers.

'I could put you into my apron pocket and take you everywhere with me. And when you got bigger I fastened you safe on my back, and we'd go through the woods together, to market together, do you remember? Then you could walk, you learned so fast I had to tie a length of ribbon round your wrist and mine or you'd have been halfway to London town before we'd noticed you missing. You were like a little elf . . .'

Jen snuggled deeper and wriggled her shoulder-blades. Once she'd felt that there were wings growing there, but twist and turn her head as she might, she could never quite see. She drifted into sleep with the rustle of her feet on autumn leaves, her wrist skipping

17

a scarlet ribbon between her and Granny. She was picking the leaves and shoots that Granny showed her, cutting the twigs that Granny couldn't quite reach. And the smells! Musky, minty, fresh young green, motherwort, fennel, wild garlic ... Granny smelt of herbs and flowers when she kissed her brow.

Sleep.

'She's learning!' Jethro called as he swaggered by the caravan next morning. Jen curled tight under her quilt. She hated what he said and the way he said it: was she an animal trained to perform? An animal he'd broken and terrorized tricks into like the sad and furious bear? Jen always wanted to stroke the bear's poor rubbed nose, her fur worn to bare skin by the iron ring round her neck: but she snarled and whimpered with fright at any human being who came too close. Jethro had done that. Jethro and his waxed cane and studded club. Granny came in muttering. Jen kept her eyes closed.

'You'd think he owned us all, curse him,' Granny said. 'Tom, there's tea for you. Tom, wake up, I want to talk to you, son.'

'What is it?' Jen's dad yawned.

'I'm not happy with that child being up so late, prancing around the ring.'

'It's always been that way in the family, Mam,' he said. 'I was up to all hours with Dad when I was half her age – you remember!'

'That was different. You had a skill to learn, and you were up with your dad besides. A better man never drew breath. This child is exhausted with Jethro worrying at her all afternoon. She was almost asleep by the fire when he came to get her last night.'

'Oh, you've got a bonnet full of hornets about

Jethro!' said Tom. 'Look what he's done for us. Remember the lean years, Mam, and let it be.'

'It takes more than money to live on,' said Granny. 'That little child shouldn't be skipping around to all hours in that flimsy costume Jethro got for her: there's no warmth in it.'

'Oh, I suppose you'd send her around in a shawl and leggings and clogs and a hat?' Tom replied sarcastically. 'Maybe folk'd take pity on my daughter done up like a beggar in winter. Don't fret and fuss, Mam. It's the way of things. She looks like a fairy princess, and Jethro says she charms the coins out of peoples' pockets like a real little professional.'

'If she had her mother here this wouldn't happen,' said Granny, 'but you men just laugh at everything I say. And you know nothing. You're just boys, the lot of you, boys with beards and big britches and bandages round your hearts and eyes.'

'If her mother was here!' Tom was furious. 'By, you're hard, Mam. If her mother was here I'd be twice the man I am! We'd never have had to take to the road, take up with this fleabag show to scratch a living!'

Granny glared at him.

'Oh, the truth will out! Fleabag show, is it now, and am I supposed to feel sorry for a fool who near as doomsday drank us to the gutter and burned his own talent? That child's in danger, Tom, I feel it!'

'She's cold first, then she's tired and now she's in danger? Tell me about it!' shouted Tom, flinging on his clothes in rage.

'I know what I know and I see what I see, and words will be spoken when they need to be heard,' Granny responded flatly.

'Moithering old blether!' roared Tom. 'Let's ask her what she thinks!'

'Let her rest!' Granny stormed as he swung over to Jen's bed and lifted her out. 'What does a child know?'

Jen sat petrified on her dad's knee. His hands were shaking and hard. She looked at Granny's set face, her blue eyes gone flint, her mouth gathered into a hard line. Her dad's cheeks were scarlet, and a vein on his brow stood out angrily. She felt sick, and too scared to tear herself out his grip and run to Granny.

'Now, Jen,' he said, voice on the edge of fury. 'What do you think about working, little maid? Do you like being with the big folk in the ring? Your granny thinks it's bad for you. Speak up, my princess, don't be frightened.'

Jen was speechless with terror. She shut her eyes. Yes, she did like it a bit: she felt beautiful and important with the crowd watching her the way they'd watched the acts; she liked them throwing coins and her catching them and feeling the hat grow heavier. Jethro's hat. There was the bit she didn't like. Jethro. He made her feel uncomfortable when he touched her, showing her how to dance and curtsey. She didn't like his touch. He called her Princess and Sweetheart the way her dad did, but there was something in the way he said it. Squirmy, she thought. Like his moustache when he smiled. He smiled a lot, he had more teeth and whiter than anyone she'd ever seen, but his eyes were always . . . squirmy.

'I like it in the ring,' she said as her dad shook her almost gently.

'SEE!' said Granny and her dad together, neither of them letting her finish. Granny's face was stone.

'We'll see,' she said.

'We must pack up and get a move on!' Jethro stuck his head over the half-door. Jen wrenched herself free and hid behind her grandmother. Next thing he'd

20

come in, all unasked, just walk in and sit down, maybe grab her and sit her on his knee like the speaking doll he advertised the shows with; clacketty-clack mouth and his red lips never moving. He was squirmy, like the pinky brown worms Granny shook so carefully back to the soil from the roots of plants she dug up in the forest. Jen hated them, felt a bubble of sick in her throat at the very thought of them. Granny had told her she was silly, and that the worms helped the plants grow. Slimy! Once Jen had tried to pick one up, had nerved herself for hours but just couldn't do it. She'd stamped the worm to bits in fury, then thrown up in the bushes for ages, tossed her shoes away and never told anyone.

'How's my little rising star?' Jethro's voice slid around Granny's skirts. She shut her eyes and held her breath. If he comes in here I'll . . . I'll bite him, I'll hit him, she thought, with mauve sparks stinging her eyelids. But he didn't come in, just blew a cloud of smoke into the caravan and then strode off, shouting orders to everyone in sight.

'I must get a move on,' her dad said. 'And no more nonsense about our Jen. She's said it herself: she loves the life! It's in her blood, Mam.'

'I fear what I fear,' Granny whispered, rubbing her hand through Jen's hair, 'and I'll draw blood if needs be.'

Torches Along The River

'There must be fifty of them!'

Night in the forest was a time of deep shadow, a darkness you could breathe and savour, sounds that bristled the hair on your arms and neck and made you glad for a warm body beside you. Night animals went about their business of preying, night birds were silent and deadly overhead. It was a time for Moon to silver everything which Sun had made golden all day long. People should sleep at night unless Moon invites them to join her, demands that their eyes should open, her light fingers coaxing sleepy heads and bodies into her world.

Tonight in the forest there were loud angry voices scaring sleeping animals, sending the hunters cowering into hiding, harsh torchlight singeing branches, men hacking with their sharp angry axes to make a path where there was none.

Rowan and Esther and three sleepless children huddled close, deep under the knitted muscle of tree roots on the opposite bank. The Squirrel was wide awake, shivering in her mother's arms. Esther cradled Baby Big Turtle close and safe.

'If you can't sleep, baby, then you must stay silent. And still. Those people with the torches are bad. They'd smash turtle shells just the way they're shredding bushes now.'

The baby nodded. Then she stiffened as the first of

the torchbearers broke through to the water's edge. She nudged Esther's throat with the back of her head.

'What?' Her mother put her ear down to her mouth.

'Those two – they were the ones I heard talking about the pricker.'

Esther looked. Goddess, they were women! Nuns! The flickering flames made their eye sockets like black holes, their mouths caves of darkness. They were at the head of the jangling column, beside a brown-robed man flourishing a cross like a pitchfork. Then there was a man with a dark hood veiling his eyes and drawing a savage line across his thin nose and whip-thread lips. Matthew the Pricker. Esther held the baby closer.

'They were here!' Sister Charity shrieked. 'Witches and goblins! I saw them!'

'And you saw them too?' the Pricker's voice stilettoed the dark towards Sister Mercy.

'I saw them . . . they looked like little children,' she said desperately.

The Pricker closed his bony hand round her elbow.

'She saw demons and you saw children? What of the witches?'

'I saw two women . . .'

'Naked as sin!'

The file of torchbearers made an ugly crowd around the nuns. With the smoke and orange-red light they looked like one of the pictures of Hell painted on the church walls. The cross above the priest's head became horns.

'It's this tree!' declaimed the Pricker, kicking the mighty trunk. 'They're in this tree!'

'Why no, sir,' said a voice from the branch overhead. 'We've been up this tree and there's no-one here at all.'

'Come down, come down,' hissed the Pricker. 'They

have come from this wicked tree and disappear here every night. Chop it down and we'll see witches' blood on the ground, not God's good green sap!'

Man's work! They rushed to it and buried their axes in the growing wood.

Rowan shuddered. Esther hid Big Turtle's face. The Squirrel quivered in agony as they murdered her living home, tears rolled down her face for every THUNK! of metal on wood.

'See!'

The Pricker howled as the beautiful tree listed towards the river, her trunk ragged. He drew his thumb over the gashes and a trickle of dark red liquid spurted from the naked white splinters. The axe-killers flew at their work now and a chant rose.

'Witch! Witch! Witch! Witch!'

Sister Mercy thought she would faint. So much hatred! But Matthew kept one bony hand round her elbow and she shuddered as his face turned towards her.

'You're in grave danger, Sister Mercy,' he murmured. 'I can help you. If the devil is out, there's no need to worry, you know. Say it with the rest: witch, witch, witch, witch!'

She could say nothing, and his arm went round her shoulders like a rope. He drew her into the shadows. Now his eyes glittered and he threw his hood back.

'The touch of a Holy Man, Sister Mercy,' he hissed, digging his fingers into her breast, and, 'She's feeling faint, Father Dominic!'

Her scream was lost as the tree thundered into the water and the men started to torch the roots. She tore herself from the stinking breath and grasping fingers and ran blindly into the darkness, headlong into the river.

'What?' Sister Charity was beside him immediately.

'Ah, the devil is driving her,' said the Pricker, watching the heavily robed figure flail around in the water.

The raggle-taggle mob cheered and crossed themselves as her body sank out of sight.

'It's God's work,' said the Pricker. 'God's work.'

They set off back to the village.

'Now tell me, Sister Charity,' said Matthew, his voice larded and low, 'you're touched by the Spirit, I can see. You know this village well? I want you to tell me everything.'

The hellish mob straggled back to their homes. Rowan stripped bare and slid into the midnight waters, swimming towards the inert and sodden body that turned like a log in the current. She lifted the heavy head and swam back to the deep hole under the roots.

'That's the one who didn't like what the other one said,' Big Turtle told them seriously. 'Will she be all right?'

'I hope so,' Rowan said grimly. 'There's been more than enough death this night.'

Esther stripped the soaking wool robe from the inert body as Rowan hustled her own clothes back on. They rubbed the chilled flesh with a blanket and Rowan turned the nun face downwards. She raised the thin shoulders up and back, up and back, as if she was rowing desperately upstream. Squirrel saw a thin trickle of water dribble from the mauve lips, and the pale eyelids fluttered like the wings of a butterfly caught in an invisible web. The bony throat worked a little and the nun coughed out a spurt of river water.

The cough hacked and jerked her whole body. Rowan rolled her over and sat her up, wrapping a dry blanket round her.

'It's all right, Sister,' she whispered. 'We fished you out. But we must be very still and quiet. They could be back any time.'

Sister Mercy shivered from head to toe. Her last memory was the nightmare rush through bushes and bracken, her feet blind, then the sickening feeling of falling, no more earth . . . a rush of cold water straight on to her face, her legs tangled in her heavy robes, her arms seized with cramp, a last glimpse of the lurching surface of moonlit river. And now she was dry, breathing again, with a soft voice telling her all was well?

'I must be dead or dreaming,' she hissed. 'Where am I?'

'You're on the other side of the river. I'm Rowan, this is Esther. We're the women and children they were looking for.'

Sister Mercy looked at the shadowed faces, the dark roots making a cave all round them. What if they were witches? What if they were devils? It was freezing, so she couldn't be in Hell. She crossed herself. Neither woman winced. And no witch could withstand the Sign of the Cross.

'I tried to stop them,' she said. 'I tried, but Sister Charity swore on the Bible that she'd seen a child flying, and women who couldn't stand to hear the sound of church bells. I tried to reason with her . . .'

'It's all right,' came a gruff little whisper, 'I heard you. I told Rowan and Esther. They're not cross with you.'

'Dear little thing,' whispered Sister Mercy as Big Turtle grasped her hand.

'I am not a deer,' the child growled.

'She's a Big Turtle,' said Esther.

Sister Mercy crossed herself. Maybe they were shape-changers, God forbid! A chuckle came out of the darkness.

'And I'm a Squirrel!'

The nun crossed herself again.

'Why do you do that?' asked the same voice. It was the older child, the one who'd caught Father Dominic's doom-laden preaching style so uncannily. Sister Mercy turned to her.

'Our Blessed Lord, Jesus Christ, died on a cross to save the world,' she said. 'I make the Sign of the Cross to remind myself of His love and forgiveness whenever I'm in any kind of worry or trouble.'

'Oh, that,' said the child. 'Well, you've just got out of trouble, you know. We're not going to hurt you. Rowan would never have bothered with rescuing you if she was going to do something awful to you, would she?'

'I suppose not,' said the nun. How could she explain to this wild child that there were more dangers than physical ones? How to share the revelations of His divine love with a young innocent who dismissed His glorious crucifixion as 'oh, that'?

'We'll need to sleep a while,' said Esther. 'I think they'll be back soon after dawn, and we must be gone. And they're going to want a body. They'll search everywhere in daylight.'

'God protect us all,' said the nun. 'What are we to do?'

'It's OK,' Rowan told her. 'We knew the forest wouldn't be safe for ever. We've got a raft well hidden. I won't sleep, and Squirrel will help me steer it down here when the moon reaches the third quarter of the sky. You are coming with us, Sister?'

'Where are you going? Perhaps I should go back to

27

the convent and sort this terrible mistake out. Reverend Mother will understand.'

'How come she let tonight happen? She couldn't keep a check on your friend Sister Charity. And no-one can keep a check on Matthew the bastard Pricker,' said Rowan.

Sister Mercy crossed herself against the obscenity. Squirrel snorted with laughter.

'Sorry,' she said when Esther kicked her.

'We'll sort out a body for them,' said Esther, 'one that'll start them gossiping!'

By now, all three children were awake, and any idea of snatching a couple of hours sleep was shrugged off. Rowan and Squirrel swung up to the bank from the roots and Esther had a conference with Isabel as quiet as the water's shrug against the bank. The silent child had no fear of darkness and vanished to collect material for the bogus body. Big Turtle began to pack up, bossing Sister Mercy as to what went where.

An owl call from the water told them Rowan and Squirrel were waiting with the raft, so they boarded carefully, gliding silently past the village, ditching the bogus body with its soaking grey habit as they went.

By cockcrow they were miles downstream. Rowan paddled up a thickly overhanging creek. The forest woke around them, birds flashing through the highest branches, welcoming the day with a riot of song, checking out the raft with its women and children and bags and bundles as it came to rest. When it was clear that all this odd bunch of humans was planning to do was lie still and sleep, the birds took no more notice of them than a rock in the river: no worms and insects or slingshots here!

*   *   *

'It's a terrible business, Sister Charity,' Matthew the Pricker said as they walked towards the church for morning service. 'The devil is cunning, he gets everywhere, even behind the sacred walls of a religious order.'

'I thought I knew Sister Mercy so well.' Sister Charity shook her head piously. Matthew clutched her arm and pointed at the river bank, towards a sandy spit of land where the women of the village gathered to pound the dirt from their families' clothes. A grey shape had landed there ... Sister Mercy! Nun and torturer ran towards the body and hauled it from the water. Sister Charity screamed as they turned it over: no human face this, but a tangle of grasses and twigs balled together, with broken birds' eggs where there should have been eyes, a jagged series of peeled sticks for teeth. Big Turtle and Isabel had snorted with laughter at this touch. Matthew ripped open the robe and leapt back: there was a body, certainly, but it was a crude affair of branches and bracken, bound with grasses at its twig wrists and ankles. Sister Charity fell to her knees and prayed aloud. Matthew waited until she'd finished, then helped her to her feet.

'We must take this *thing* back to the village,' he said. 'Let them see what witchcraft can do. And I must interview all the nuns of your order, Sister Charity. For Satan has been in their midst and who is to say who is free of his taint?'

'Sir, surely you can tell,' whimpered the nun.

'There are marks, Sister,' he said. 'The devil marks the flesh. And where he leaves it unblemished, he takes from it all natural feeling. God has given me the gift to prick out Satan, Sister. The innocent have nothing to fear.'

'God bless you in your work,' cried the nun. 'Why,

we all have a mole or a freckle or two, but that's not what you mean, is it?'

Matthew threw her a look from the burning core of his eyes.

'Ah, I suppose you will call a birthmark innocent, Sister, God forgive your ignorance. I have seen new-born children stamped with the sign of Beelzebub, Sister. And I have done my best to drive him out. But Satan would rather have the blood of an infant shed than a soul reclaimed for God.'

Sister Charity felt a trickle of sweat snail down her spine and gather in a chill pool in the small of her back, right around the smudged strawberry shape she'd had since her first breath on earth.

And The Bear Came Too

Jen grew slender and wiry. Her dad still wouldn't teach her the skills he'd have proudly passed on to a son, though it was her birthright as his only child. She had eyes and ears and a way of freezing by a tree or crouching by a bush so that she was invisible. She swung from high branches, she slung ropes to make her own trapeze: if he would keep her on the ground and say that pretty little maids weren't to do anything dangerous, well, to hell with him! This pretty little maid thought she wasn't pretty – Granny had told her she was beautiful. And as for little? She towered over all the circus women and some of the men. Not in height, but in stature. She carried herself with all the loving pride her Granny had nurtured her with for being a woman. She had fed and feasted on stories of her mother, and of how she and her father had danced together in midair like butterflies, like fireflies. She was her mother's child, and drew the knowledge into herself when she passed her father and Jethro and the men out-bragging each other and rosy with drink around the fire.

Her father's act had gone stale. She knew it, he knew it. She was afraid he would fall, not with the open-mouthed fear of a child, but with a weary despair as he stumbled where he should have flown, lurched and almost missed his footing: The Dolphin of the Skies had drunk his way into becoming a floundering porpoise, and Jethro had told him to create a new act. As a clown.

'Tommy boy,' he'd said, passing the bottle – there was always another bottle, 'see, you stick to the ground and clown around, you're not so young as you were and you make little slips. I don't want to see you with broken bones, my son. Be a clown. It's all part of the act, then.'

Tom, shrunk, grey-faced, drunk, scarlet with wounded pride, Tom, her broken dad, had swayed towards him and swung his fists. He looked like a little old man as Jethro caught his fists in one hand and slapped his head from side to side wearing his cold grin.

'Calm down, old man,' he'd said. 'We don't need you like we did.'

It was true. She watched Jethro push her dad, stumbling, to where he slept now, under the caravan. Granny wouldn't have him sleeping inside unless he was sober, and he had grumbled and raged and cursed at first. But he couldn't stand up to the tiny fiery figure with her foaming crown of pure white hair. She moved awkwardly with pain these days for all the remedies Jen brewed.

'My ears feel like sheep's wool,' she fretted. 'There's shadows on everything I look at. Oh Jen, I'm an old old woman and I fear I'll never see you grown.'

She sat up suddenly some nights and talked out loud. She talked to her own mother, dead for years; she talked to an Auntie Kitty; she quavered for help to her own granny; her voice cracked in anguish when she spoke with Jen's dead mother. She felt she'd betrayed her, she hadn't been able to keep Jen safe, she'd be dead and buried and then It would get Jen, some huge and powerful It that was after her. There were silences

32

between her words: the dead spoke to her and she wept at their words.

Jen had nightmares about this It, this Thing that Granny feared for her. She would be on a sunny woodland path, gathering herbs and fruits when a jagged shadow loomed around her and froze her to the spot although the rest of the wood was warm and breezy and full of birdsong. She'd run and the shadow would move with her, the shadow would laugh triumphantly around her, then she'd trip . . . and wake up screaming.

What was It?

It had the laugh and voice of Jethro, but she wasn't afraid of him. He'd found himself a young wife and spent all his time with her in their caravan. Or else he was boozing round the fire. The young wife was going to have a baby, and Jen was relieved. She wasn't sure of it, but he'd linked his arm in hers once, and looked at her. He wanted her. She'd stared straight back at him until he looked away and broke from her roughly. She'd told Granny, and kept right out of his way after that. And now he didn't even look at her. He'd got his wife very soon after that. No prizes for guessing what he was at most of the night! She despised him and pitied the slender little woman he'd trapped with a gold-coloured ring in some market town where they'd played.

The shadow. What was it? Sometimes she thought it was the thing infecting her dad, driving him to the joyless depths of any bottle he could get his shaking hands round. She refused to drink anything fermented. And Jethro got a lot of mileage out of that; she heard him muttering 'Pure as the driven snow, not a drop passes her lips tho' she's *his* daughter, virgin territory, boys!' Or something along those twisted lines, every time she was anywhere near him. His voice made her feel dirty. She itched furiously whenever she'd been near him; she wanted to plunge headfirst into an icy pool and feel clean.

Dawn was the best time for Jen. The rest of the camp was fast asleep, even Granny, who only slept peacefully in the first hours these days. Jen slipped out of bed and put on leggings and a shirt under her dress. She put a covered basket over her arm and went into the woods. The air was damp and chill, crushed leaves pricked her nose with a sharp smell; she heard a half-hearted twitter high above her, then a shrill cheeping. She smiled: was that a rowdy bird babe waking too early and being scolded back to sleep?

She ducked off the path, and wove a way to a clearing where a circle of beech trees made a cathedral of grey columns. Swathes of leaves flounced and flowed like the silk of an exotic tent. Her heart raced: she'd found this place so quickly and it was perfect. She shed her shoes and dress. Red Riding Hood carried cakes and preserves to her grandmama: Jen had coils of rope and dowels in her basket, and slung them across one shoulder. She squirrelled up the sheer bark to the first branches. Sitting on the silver limb, she considered. Better to go higher. She lashed one end of the first rope above her head and stood, swinging the heavy coils from one strong hand. Her eyes measured the distance to the next tree and she flung the rope to flip neatly around another branch. She tightroped along the dipping wood and leapt after the rope, landing one foot either side.

She lashed it securely, and took the end across the clearing. Good. Twenty minutes later she'd built a web touching every tree, and supporting two trapezes. She stretched, and started the agonizing work-out she'd watched her father practise for so many years.

She swung faster and faster until her body vaulted a whole circle around one rope, then flew at the trapeze, twisted on one hand, her feet already gripping the next place. That was the secret: to look as though you were completely involved in one series of movements and hold the fantastic pose they led up to, but to have your body ready and reaching for the next.

The sky was clearing to blue, and birds were calling in the first threads of warmth when she was finished. She took a deep draught of water and deftly took her web to pieces, stowed it in the basket once more and dressed like a woman. She grinned at the silent trees and made a gallant bow to each one. The circus would be here for at least a week!

On the way back to the camp she picked mushrooms and leaves and berries to camouflage the basket. She'd had a narrow escape a few weeks before, with Jethro strutting and yawning by the fire, trying to catch at her skirt and see what she'd been up to.

'I'll scream,' she told him very quietly, 'and what will your wife think?'

Now all was still; she curled up in bed again and slept until her dad's hangdog whine woke her, asking for breakfast.

Jethro was well gone late that night. Something was making him furious. He'd screamed at the grizzled and broken bear, taunting her until Jen had grabbed the switch from his hand and snapped it in two. He'd lumbered to the fire and sat drinking bitterly for hours. His wife hadn't been seen all evening.

'And where are you going?' he slurred at Jen.

'I'm taking your wife some food. It's nearly her time.'

'Bloody bitches of women,' raged Jethro. 'They want a man for one thing and then it's bye-bye puppy dog.'

He blubbered into a fresh bottle.

'Love the woman,' he maundered on, 'love her, you hear me, and she won't touch me. I'm her husband. Got the ring and everything.'

'She's near her time,' Granny said shrilly. Jethro turned. The old lady was usually in bed, and now she stood like judgement itself, pointing at him with one arm raised.

'You should be ashamed, Jethro! That woman's bearing your babbie and you're still wanting to be all over her!'

Jethro spat.

'Back to your bed, Granny,' he threatened, 'or . . .'

'What?' said Jen. 'Or what, Jethro? Don't you be threatening Granny. You should go and sleep it off – and not in your wife's bed with the skinful you've taken!'

'Another bitch!' Jethro shouted and stood up. 'Only a cold one this time!'

'Leave her alone!' Jen's dad said. 'You've gone too far, man, just sleep it off. It'll be better in the morning.'

Jethro blundered to his caravan and tripped on the first step. He sprawled there, snoring.

'Aye,' said Granny. 'Leave him there.'

But his wife came to the door and saw him. She moved with difficulty but started to drag him inside. She was weeping.

'Don't none of you help me,' she cried. 'You all hate him, but I know he's a good man, he's my man and you're all against him!'

'Think on that, lass,' Granny called. 'And you men, get on your feet and help the silly bairn if she's sure she wants him!'

Jen led her inside, then the two women sat and gazed at each other hopelessly.

'Did she eat, Jen?' said Granny.

'Yes, a bit. But she was fretting about Jethro: what would he eat, and how he was drinking too much and saying he hated the bairn.'

Granny sighed a gust of impatience. She muttered, and her thin hands made fists. Then she looked at Jen and sighed again.

'Jen, I've so many words inside me. So many years and so many places and so many people. I dream of them, Jen, I see your dad when he was a little child and full of sunshine and hope – and look at him now! A laughing stock! And you, pet, there's a cloud on your brow. So much sadness and so much life ahead of you. You watch out for Jethro.'

'Him! I can deal with him,' Jen said. 'I'm not afraid of him!'

'You've a good heart, Jen, and you're no fool. But I have my dreams. I'm afraid for you.'

'I can take care of myself,' Jen assured her. 'You worry about yourself, Granny, I can't be without you. Get some sleep. There's a lot of talk in the camp. We're not the only ones who've had enough of Jethro. Something'll have to be said and done about him. We'll sort it.'

'It must be soon,' said Granny. 'I won't last much longer and I'd like to breathe my last knowing you're safe, my little Jen. It's a bad world for a woman. You must take care of that silly child he's married. Women must take care of their own. The men are never there.'

Jen didn't sleep. She sat and held Granny's thin hand all night and tried to work out what to do. She had to leave this place, this grumbling angry unease. She tucked Granny's hand under the covers at dawn and escaped to the beech trees.

But Jethro was awake too. He glared at his sleeping wife and the mound of her belly. His head was cracking inside and he looked out of the window. Now where was that Miss High and Mighty taking herself off to so early? He waited until she was out of the clearing, then followed her. But she'd disappeared, so he set his jaw and hid behind a tree. She'd have to come back this way! And what business did she have running off? He'd made her what she was, a fine dancer and a good-looker, and how did she repay him? Haughty looks and bad words and trying to turn his own wife against him! He'd take her down a peg or three!

Jen set up the ropes mechanically, joylessly, meticulously. Then in mid-flight, she started to smile. Theirs was a good horse. They could just harness her and go it alone. Her father had started this way, and she could quell any nonsense about being his daughter and not his son. She'd show him her skill! He was afraid of Jethro's rage, grovelled to him in case he cut off the precious liquor. He'd be glad to get away.

Winding up the ropes again, she started. A hare was standing staring at her, huge eyes demanding what are you doing here?! She knew a hare was more than luck. Yes, it was a good idea to leave. She'd do it at night and take the shambling hulk of the bear with her. A dying Granny, a drunken father, a clapped-out bear and herself. Why not?

She was smiling at the crazy thought when Jethro stepped out in front of her. As she screamed he jammed his hand over her mouth and dragged her into the bushes.

'I knew it!' he growled into her ear. 'You walking along with that smile. I know you! You're hot for it, Jen, your body's raging for it!'

He scrabbled at her clothes and she bit his hand. He hit her face with his fist and she flung her thigh between his legs as hard as she could, grabbed his unshaven throat and pushed him away. Then she was on her feet and booted him with all the pent-up rage of the years she'd spent around him, kicked him and screamed at him, kicked him like she'd stamped that sickeningly untouchable worm when she was a child. He groaned and went limp. She grabbed her basket and tore back to the camp. There was no time to lose.

Granny was still asleep. Jen tied everything securely in the caravan and harnessed the sleepy horse. She dived under the steps and put her hand over her dad's mouth.

'Listen,' she whispered. 'It's Jen. I've killed Jethro. I'm leaving. Are you coming or not? We have to go now.'

Her dad stared at her.

'You're mad, Jen,' he hissed. 'You'll never get away with it?'

'We'll see,' she said grimly. 'Are you coming or not?'

He closed his eyes and shook his head. She was paralysed.

'If you're not coming, then lie about us. That's the least you can do.'

His weak, veined eyes flickered like a guttering candle. There was no time for this! She clicked her tongue at the horse and the caravan lurched out of the clearing. She stopped and ran to where the bear was chained and shivering.

'Come on,' she said, and led the animal to the back of the caravan, looping her chain in place. They probably

39

wouldn't get far. But what the hell, at least Jethro's wife was safe now. She urged the horse past where his body lay. It took for ever to reach the hard road, and there was nothing she could do about the tracks she left behind. She went west and stopped after a hundred yards, tearing back to kick the tell-tale mud from the stones. She threw some clods on the road east and smudged the tracks to make it seem she'd gone that way.

Granny was still asleep. She'd wake her later. The rising sun threw shadows ahead of her, and she shivered in the new day.

Isabel Finds The Falls

Isabel woke first and slitted her eyes, altered her breathing to sniff out any changes, any danger. She was snuggled against Rowan's body, a smell and touch that meant safety; her bare toes were against Esther's leg, skin that she knew and delighted in. Esther had been the second woman in the world to ever hold her, Esther was safe. And the four-armed, four-legged lump that was Squirrel and Baby Turtle, her sisters, her friends. There was a different smell: Sister Mercy. The nun smelled of anxiety, of fear, like Turtle had when she was ill once. Isabel stuck her head up and gazed at her.

She was so pale and strange. Her thin hands twitched as she slept, her mouth worked unhappily. Winter was months away and yet her whole body was covered with clothes – how was she planning to run or climb? Or even walk with all that cloth catching on bushes? Isabel was puzzled. Then Rowan stirred and she slid back into the curve of her body, pretending to be asleep. Rowan's arms went round her, her lips brushed the top of her head. Isabel loved waking up this way and kept her eyes shut long past when everyone else was awake and whispering.

'Old sleepy-head,' said Rowan. 'Belle, wake up, love, we've got to move soon. It's nearly sundown.'

'Let's tip into the river,' Esther suggested. 'No splashing. It'll wake us all up. Did you sleep all right, Sister?'

'I had awful dreams,' the nun fretted. 'Terrible! God save us all!'

Squirrel giggled. But Isabel stared at the nun's white face. The shadows of her nightmares were scored across her brow. She looked terrified, and closed her eyes as the women and children stripped off and slipped over the side of the raft. Her hands went to take her clothes off, but she couldn't.

She's scared of her body, Isabel thought, she thinks there's something wrong with having no clothes on. Why? We all saw her after they tried to drown her.

And the nun sat shivering while the river washed the rest of them clean and woke them.

'I must pray,' she said, as if challenging them. She climbed awkwardly on to the bank and went through the bushes. Isabel followed her like a shadow. The nun knelt down and put her hands together, closed her eyes and started muttering. Isabel squatted in the bushes and looked up at the great canopy of leaves, a lacy lattice against a pink-streaked sky. Here and there a branch was lumpy with a roosting bird; darkening flames of red squirrels licked around the tree trunks. Deeper in the bushes, a pale tan deer froze and melted into the first deep grey of the night, tree trunks shivered into columns, then the columns became a high wall of deep shadow.

'Amen,' said the nun firmly. Isabel disappeared back to the raft.

'What do you mean – bread and cheese, Esther, I'm starving!' said Squirrel.

'I mean if we make a fire people will know where we are. Maybe we'll eat something hot tomorrow.'

'I want soup!' demanded Baby Turtle.

'For Chrissake! Sorry, Sister,' exploded Rowan. 'Look, this isn't a game, you two. If those people get us,

42

they'll do awful things to us. Like they did to those rabbits and deer you found last week. They want to trap us.'

'People don't eat people,' Squirrel remarked scornfully. 'Why would they kill us? You said they wanted to eat the rabbits and deer.'

'Give me strength!' Rowan said. 'You know why we don't live with them? You were very small when we went into the forest, Squirrel, but they took our house away, they fenced off the woods we'd lived out of. They don't like us because we don't live like them. Do you want to have to go to church every day? Wear long skirts and a scarf over your hair and never climb a tree again? And that's only the start.'

'It's all her fault,' said Squirrel furiously, pointing at the nun. 'She's spoilt it all!'

'Enough,' Esther remonstrated. 'If it hadn't been her, it would have been someone else sooner or later.'

Esther didn't often say enough, and the two children went quiet. Isabel sat between them and Sister Mercy. She hadn't decided about the nun yet; all she knew was that the woman was scared and had bad dreams and didn't seem to see things that mattered. Fear and nightmare she understood only too well.

They guided the raft out on to the river and let the current take them where it would. Rowan would occasionally pole them around a dark rock or push them off a sandbank.

'In a few days we'll be able to go by day,' she told them. 'Just get clear of this bit of the country, just far enough from the gossip line.'

Isabel curled up and slept.

A few nights later, they took a chance on making a fire,

the raft tugging at a rope and ready to flee with a knife slash if any danger threatened. Sister Mercy went into the trees to pray and Isabel followed her. This time she let herself be seen, and the nun gave her an unhappy smile. The lips worked, but her eyes stayed anxious.

'You can pray with me, Isabel,' she said. 'Maybe the Lord will release your tongue in His own good time.'

Isabel pushed her tongue against her teeth. Release? She kept her lips together as she thought of her tongue flying out of her mouth somewhere vaguely upwards, the way the nun's gaze flitted upwards before she closed her eyes. She didn't want to pray, but she knelt by the nun and nudged her.

'What is it, child?'

Isabel pointed. Her hand said *Look!* Leaves edged with gold; a lizard just making it to the tree-bole before it got too cold to move; bats like bonfire shreds against the trees. Sister Mercy, do you know? There's a flower that closes when the sun goes down, and here's a flower that opens – smell it!

'Don't disturb me, child,' said the nun quite kindly.

Isabel shook her head and went back to her family.

Squirrel and Baby Turtle were ravingly ecstatic over hot food, and Esther giggled.

'You'd have turned your noses up at this a few weeks ago,' she told them. 'Any change is good in your books!'

But Isabel sat there and didn't notice what she ate. Sister Mercy couldn't see anything, and perhaps that's what made her look so unhappy. She prayed with her eyes shut, she had bad dreams, she had bad things in her head and she kept looking at them. And she never said anything worth saying, she just wittered and God-blessed, and God-save-us-all-ed, and treated Isabel like she was very young and simple. Just because of her not speaking? Isabel was a proud child and she shrugged.

I give up, she thought wearily.

The sun was high the next day when she heard a new sound, felt a wilder tugging from the heart of the river, and her body quivered with excitement. The noise was some way off still, and she wanted to know what it was. Anything that loud must be huge and wouldn't notice her. She stood as the raft lurched over the foamy edge thrown up along a ridge of shallow rocks on the riverbed. The other children shrieked.

'It's getting rough,' Rowan said. 'Maybe we'd better walk a while.'

Rough? Couldn't she *hear* it? If this was rough, then downstream was Monster, Isabel thought, eeling through the shallows on to the mossed slabs of ice-grey rock on the banks. She saw a dark line across the river – and then no more river. She had to get there first and fast, before a final no from Rowan, a kind be careful from Esther or some bloody stupid nonsense from Sister Mercy. She sure-footed it over the damp rocks, racing until her heart and breath could go no faster. She stopped still.

This was it. The big noise. The biggest noise she'd ever heard.

She gazed at the falls. Muscles of tawny water, lion shadowed, hot treacle brown and liquid at their heart, writhing over and around each other like ropes bigger than oak trees; lion muscle made water, butterfly bubbles skimming along the river to explode at the hurtling edge, drops erupting like sparks from a knotted piece of timber at the heart of the flames. Foam racing, tearing great white swathes and froth along the weight of a whole river dropping a hundred feet.

I am magnificent, said the river falls, *try pinning your eyes on one part of me, child, and forget it! I am faster than your eyes can see! You want to touch me, yes you do, but I'm so swift as I scythe through the air I'd take your fingertips clean off and weld you to my heart, I'd burn you close and hold you fast like frosted metal. You wouldn't believe the chill, child, as you plunge deep into me, no-one can swim in me, even the queen of all salmon would think many times before she tried flying this way . . .*

Isabel lay flat on the rocks, her head was spinning and the rocks were tipping and she wanted to dive deep. The water fell with swashbuckling rock-eroding abundance; this water sliced rock like crumbling cheese. She dragged her dizzy eyes away and up and saw the furthest stack of rock jutting into sheer air and she knew she must stand there. Now! Before she thought about it and got scared. She stood on the edge. Let them try and stop her! The proud loud voice of the river left no room for voices other than its own. Her toes gripped the edge of the rock and she gazed downstream, a hundred feet below to where the water was a silvered blue-blackness, where somehow a deep calm had grown from the wild waters that lashed the rocks piled like rough cut bread under her feet.

She opened her mouth wide, dragged in great balloons of the stinging cold air and pushed it out again from the depths of her stomach. And with the seventh breath came a high sound like a seagull hoarse after weeks away from land. A great power pulsed through her with a heat that brought a roar from her lungs, and Isabel the silent child roared all along the river.

'Mother of God!' screeched the nun, starting towards Isabel.

'Leave her!' Rowan grabbed Sister Mercy's arm. Her own face was white, her body shaking: her first child, her Isabel, her silent baby poised as if to fly over the raging sweep of water – one false move, one start of fear and she'd tumble down, and that dear little body would have the life drowned and crushed out of her.

'Shut up!' she screamed at Squirrel and Big Turtle as they shrieked with terror; Goddess, you'd think *they* were the ones in danger! She clutched the sky-blue crystal in her pocket: it had protected her when they'd driven them all from the village and scoured the woods with scythes and ropes and hatred and murder on their loud lips. Ice-cold in times of danger, it lay sharp and warm in her palm now. So Isabel was not in danger . . . though Rowan's eyes and heart howled that her daughter was on the edge of extinction.

But the old woman in the village had touched Isabel's lips when she was three years old, touched Rowan's ears with her other wise old hand and told her:

'You'll live to hear her speak, Rowan. When you've got something to say, eh, Belle?'

And the child had smiled hugely and laughed.

'See?' the old woman had said. 'She can make sounds – that laugh's pure water-magic, Rowan. She'll be one of the wise women, mark the words I'm saying to you, she'll be a water witch. And there'll be plenty of words when the time comes.'

Rowan's palms sweated. *Save my baby*, she said over and over inside her head. Isabel whirled on tiptoe and danced towards them, airy as thistledown in a breeze over a lake. Her eyes were sparkling like the sunshine on the river, her cheeks were a stinging rose – and her smile! A wild and wonderful grin proclaiming

47

freedom. She ran into Rowan's arms, laughing and wriggling with joy.

'Baby!' murmured Rowan, squashing the breath out of her.

Isabel pulled back and looked at her with raised eyebrows. Rowan nodded.

'I see,' she said. 'Not a baby any more. Witchling! Water witchling, and so precious to me!'

Isabel smiled slowly and butted her head under her mother's chin. Sister Mercy gasped. Her hand flew to her pale brow.

'Oh, don't cross yourself!' snapped Squirrel. 'You said it was to protect you in danger! What's the danger here?'

'You said . . . witchling,' whispered the nun.

'Sister, before we go any further, we need to talk,' said Esther. 'Let's go up into the trees and sort this out.'

She led the paralysed nun away; tugged her up the steep shale through the saplings and sat on the first piece of soft grass.

'Look,' she said. Rowan and the children had linked hands, kneeling in a circle on the rocks, 'That's witchcraft. Isabel's time has come to start learning her craft.'

'You mean Rowan's a *witch*?' whispered the nun.

'I think you know in your heart that we both are. I think you'd also better tell me what you think a witch is.'

The nun's eyes flickered like dying embers. She swallowed.

'We all know what witches are. I took you for good women, oh, unchristian, but good. Those poor children!'

'We are good,' said Esther. 'Tell me what you think you know about witches.'

'Evil!' hissed the nun, 'I've seen the tracts and heard people who've been at their devil-worshipping covens. Human sacrifices! Sacrifices of innocent babes! Shape-changers! They make waxen images of people and stick them with pins! They . . . *do* . . . the most disgusting things with young virgins! They use animals as familiars to spy on their neighbours and terrorize them! They fly on broomsticks to their evil meetings at full moon and cast curses on the land! They go into the house of Our Blessed Lord and desecrate holy relics! Oh, Lord save and preserve me, I should have gone back to the convent!'

'There was a man in our village,' Esther said. 'Listen to me. He used to sell short measures of corn and milk gone stale and eggs gone rotten. Finally they all got together and told him to mend his ways or leave. You know what he did?'

'What's a cheat and liar to do with this?' the nun whimpered desperately.

'He told the village elders that he started out from his farm with full measure, sweet milk and fresh eggs. He passed Rowan's cottage on his way and he said she put the evil eye on him. You know why? Because he lusted after her – a woman on her own with two children, well, she must be a loose woman! And she'd sent him packing! His wife said as much, his wife said he always started out with second-rate short-measure trash . . .'

'Well, then,' said the nun, 'the elders would have seen the truth of that!'

'They said his wife was a nag and a scold. They ducked her and chased her through the village half-naked, beating her with sticks and pelting her with rubbish.'

'Oh, get away with you! Gossip!' said Sister Mercy.

'That's not justice. Did you *see* all this? The elders always have a priest among their number, a man of God. I can't believe you.'

Esther stripped her shirt up at the back. The nun retched at the scarlet scars across her ribs and shoulders.

'I was his wife,' Esther said. 'They left me for dead in the woods, and Rowan came and found me and brought me back to life. More witchcraft, they said: she'd used herbs and poultices. So they boarded over her house when we were out, then burnt it down. They hunted us for three days and nights. Who's evil, Sister Mercy?'

The nun touched her scars with her fingertips.

'That's a wicked deed,' she said. 'But witches, Esther! There's no harm in curing people, that's not witchcraft. Every village has a wise woman. We know that.'

'You've been listening to lies,' said Esther. 'All that filth you just told me about witches – that's devil worship.'

'Well, if you don't worship God, you must worship the Devil. Unless you're a poor heathen, and there's always salvation if you repent.'

'We don't worship God,' Esther told her. 'And we don't worship the Devil. We don't worship, Sister Mercy, we love. We love this beautiful earth and everything that lives and grows in her beauty.'

Sister Mercy shook her head, dashed away tears of fear and bewilderment.

'What are they doing down there?' she said. 'Is that witchcraft?'

Big Turtle and Squirrel had gathered pebbles and sticks and leaves and placed them in the circle. Rowan was singing and Isabel knelt with a magnificent calm, swaying to the rhythm, the rhythm of her mother's voice and the sweeping ripples of the river.

'That's witchcraft,' said Esther. 'And I must join the circle. It's a great day, this waking to being a witchling.'

She squeezed the nun's icy hand, then joined her lover and their wonderful children on the river bank.

Rowan spread a piece of cloth the colour of moonbeams on the rock between them. Baby Big Turtle examined the pile of treasures she had collected, and picked out a half eggshell, ice blue like Rowan's crystal of safety and danger. She looked at it, then added the bleached skeleton of a bird's wing and an oval stone rippled grey and turquoise like shallow waves. She knelt back on her heels.

Squirrel curled a strand of deep green water weed into an I. For Isabel. She made a circle of seeds she'd scooped from the river: red, green, blackened, split and winged. She dripped wax from a candle stump on to the cloth and fixed the candle in its flow. She made a heap of honey-cakes and her eyes danced with Big Turtle's when she sat back beside her.

Rowan placed her dawn-blue crystal on the cloth. She poured a heap of sand beside it and balanced a shell full of river water on the top. She tinkled a scarlet thread of thirteen silver bells around the crystal, and took her knife from her belt, laying it due east. She looked at Isabel's sheer grin and raised her eyebrows in a question. Isabel giggled.

Rowan brought her hands from behind her back and put down a stick with silvered peeling bark to lie north and south.

'Your wand,' she said softly.

Esther joined them.

'I have to bring something to this circle,' she said. 'What beautiful things! All for Belle.'

She went to the river bank, touching Rowan's shoulder and the children's heads as she passed. She lay on the rock and dipped her hands into the river, and dashed back to flop a tiny silver fish into Rowan's shell. She made a fan of seven pure white downy feathers and a black and white wing feather straight as a blade. Then she knelt with the others and handed something shiny to Isabel. The child was delighted, and leapt to her feet. She unwound the ball of silver thread in seven circles round them.

'The circle's closed,' said Esther, reaching out to hold Big Turtle and Isabel by the hand. Isabel's other hand went to Rowan, Rowan's to Squirrel, Squirrel's to Big Turtle.

Up on the bank, Sister Mercy went to cross herself: the women and children had simply disappeared. But her hand wouldn't make the sign, just froze in front of her burning eyes, her stretched lips and silent howl.

'North,' said Rowan. 'N for new and N for now. Never fear or fail. Blessed be for all our bones and our bodies that take us over the earth that is her body. We are fields, we are seashores, we are hills, we are mountains. Mother of all fruits and trees and grains and grass, hail, Belili, welcome into our circle. For rivers flow through your earth like blood flows in our bodies.'

Isabel touched the heap of sand, the seeds, her letter in serpentine weed. She grasped her wand, then put it down again alongside Rowan's knife.

'Breathe deep,' Esther said, and her voice was a breeze. 'Feel how the air fills your body, how she tingles over your skin. Think of a still tree and the magic of wind in her leaves, think of a still pool and the way the winds turn her from black to silver and grey. Feel the wind in your thoughts and dreams, how she blows away the leaves in autumn, how she tosses dead branches into a river, how she drives the waves to the shore. O bright and beautiful Arida, goddess of the east, we greet you, we ask your clear clean sweeping power into our circle.'

Isabel ran her fingers over the knife-blade, stroked the down-nest with her knuckles, smoothed the feather-spine with a fingertip, spread her hand like the blanched wing-skeleton, grasped her wand with both hands and turned it to face south.

Rowan looked at Squirrel.

'Me?' asked Squirrel, dismayed and delighted. '*Me*?'

'It's south, my honey, and if ever anyone was south! Just say what you see, my Squirrel.'

'Sunshine!' Squirrel said, going crimson, 'the candle. It's like when I dream about flying, I'm really warm, I think it'll be cold but then the sun comes up and I can see flames round everything. Like a fire at night when my face is so hot it feels like it'll crack, and my back's so cold I can't feel it. And that star – the one that goes red and blue.'

Isabel smiled at her and flicked her hand through the candle flame. She touched the red berry and picked up the scarlet thread with its silver bells and rang them and rang them. Then she picked up her wand and stroked the shining wood where the bark had split. She kept hold of the wand now, holding it to face west.

'West for a water-witchling,' said Esther, squeezing Big Turtle's hand. 'We'll do this together, hey, Turtle, you know all about water.'

Turtle closed her eyes and thought of the river. Cold at first, then hot, like Squirrel's fire. When she opened her eyes and the water was clear she saw tiny fish clear as glass, creatures with shells coming out of the mud and disappearing again in a flurried brown cloud.

She always tried to stay under longer every time, she always swam a little further, she knew how to float if fear came when she looked back to the banks. But she felt suddenly shy and looked down. She shook her head.

'You haven't seen the sea yet,' said Esther. 'Where the river fans out in a great muddy sweep and fights with the ocean and tosses you back or tugs you on. The sea's like the falls, and grey and green and blue, and it comes in wave after wave. You run down the sand into the waves and they sweep you off your feet and throw you to the next wave, your mouth and nose get filled with foam and when you see a thousand white lion-manes of foam towering over you like a cliff, you can just go headfirst into the green wall of water and the wave will crash. Her sound is a hundred miles away and strokes your ears to silence. The falls are a promise of ocean. And the moon tugs the tides high on the shore, she draws them back to leave a swathe of white sand strewn with empty shells and seaweed: the sea'll pick them up again at high tide. Everywhere the waters are full of strange fish and serpents; rivers snake their way over the land, and oh, serpent of the waters, we welcome your power, your moonbeam moondreams, welcome, Tiamat!'

Isabel passed her wand over the shell and her tiny fish; she touched the rippled stone, the frozen ocean in the crystal, the half eggshell. She sat back and smiled.

Rowan wondered if she'd speak. Peace to the thought, she chided herself, there would be a time. She smiled at Esther and a laugh bubbled round the circle. Isabel picked up a piece of honey-cake and passed it on. She looked at Rowan pointedly.

'Don't understand,' said her mother. Isabel leant towards her and kissed her. Rowan passed the kiss with her warm lips to Squirrel who dashed it on to Turtle: Turtle liked this bit, and smooched her nose and face against Esther. Esther turned to Isabel and kissed her lips, her eyes clear and deep as a well.

Isabel bit into the honey-cake and closed her eyes.

I Will Remember Your Face

Jen saw a hamlet ahead, smoking chimneys meaning people up and doing with busy eyes to notice everything about her. Everybody knew everybody's business in a place like this. Before she passed the first house every last tongue would be busy with the stranger with a brightly coloured caravan and a bear in tow. She'd have a raggle-taggle string of children running behind her clamouring for the circus. She tugged the reins. The horse stopped and ambled towards the grass. She didn't know what to do. Stopping now would mean certain discovery. Going on would mean the same, just hours or a day later. She urged the horse well under the trees and covered her tracks.

The bear stared at her and growled, batting the air with her paws.

'You'll be all right if I can manage it.' The young woman did her best to keep her voice calm. 'There's no more Jethro to hurt you.'

The bear balanced on her haunches.

'Oh, don't do that!' Jen said softly. 'You'll get your food without having to do tricks for it. You've a right to food, it's not a reward!'

She went into the caravan: amazingly, Granny had slept through the journey. She dipped her hand in the honey pot and went out to the bear. That's how Jethro got her to lick his hand in the ring, and then all the people cooed and said he was a marvel to tame such a monster.

'Loving care and gentleness, ladies and gentlemen, that's all it takes,' he'd boom. 'Any animal is like a woman – treat her right and you'll have her eating out of your hand.'

The men in the audience always laughed at this. Jen had been outraged when she first heard it. Then she'd realized he treated everyone the way he treated the bear: frightening them with his loud voice and fists if they were women or smaller than him; threatening them if they had the guts to stand up to him. Her dad used to stand up to him until Jethro found he could use the drink to shut him up or have him begging. He tried to humiliate her with his lewd remarks and gestures, but all her life she'd seen Granny's clear gaze send him packing. She developed an unblinking calm around him, breathed her body into metal; she imagined a scarlet horseshoe plunged into icy water to hiss and smoke. She'd never have to do that again – well, not to Jethro. There would be no more of his lies now.

The bear cowered as she came near, then stood on her hind legs as she smelt the honey. Jen sat on the ground.

'Have your breakfast,' she said softly. 'Sit yourself beside me, it's all right.'

The bear's tongue was rough, wet and warm. The animal was incredibly delicate, for all her size. Her eyes were huge like gold-brown marbles, and her lips and gums were a childish pink around the sharp white teeth. She whined when Jen got up and nudged her palm for more.

'I've got a horse and Granny and me to feed as well,' said Jen. 'There'll be more later.'

The bear grumbled away and lapped at her teeth for

every last bit of sweetness. Jen wished she could take off the iron collar and swore that she would one day. If she lived that long. She unhitched the horse and put her on a long rein.

'Granny?'

The old woman was still. Jen sat on her bed and looked at the tiny caved-in face, white hair fine as sea foam against the pillow. Granny had been born by the sea and her blue eyes shifted grey and green when she talked about it. Her voice rose and fell like the tide. She'd been happy there and often said she'd like to go back.

'We'll get to the sea, Granny,' Jen said softly and picked up one hand. Dear God, no! The hand she cradled was icy, and so was Granny's cheek when she touched it.

When had she died? Was it the sudden jolting over the rough tracks? She'd been dead long enough to get cold. Jen's eyes blurred with tears; they soaked her cheeks and ran into her mouth. She wrapped herself round Granny's body and rocked her, rocked her with sobs tearing from her belly, shaking her like a sapling in a high wind.

'I don't think I can bear it,' she said out loud, then jeered herself upright, fists grinding into her temples.

You don't have any choices, my dear, she said grimly. *You're on your own now and if you don't manage then you'll be managed.*

That all sounded very fine. It was one of Granny's stock phrases. *When the door's bolted fast, there's always a window.* Another one. *Feed the belly though the heart be breaking.*

She made tea and sat by Granny again to drink it. Granny's body. She should be buried with all the love and mourning for a dear life that will never be again.

Her nearest relatives should compose a poem or song celebrating her life, and say it or sing it at the graveside. Women should wash the body, dress it in white and wrap a scarlet kerchief at wrists, throat and ankle. Granny said that was to trick the demon-dogs in the wandering time after death: they'd slink away, thinking one of their kind had already drained away the lifeblood with its claws and teeth. Every piece of gold the dead woman had owned should be buried with her, for bribes along the shadow-path.

The body should be buried as near to running water as possible, to help the spirit flee to the ocean and freedom in the open skies. There should be a tree whose roots would grow around the wooden box and bones and hold the spirit fast until the flesh was gone. A tree like the spirit of the dead one. Granny had told her that her mother was buried by a sycamore, with its abundance of keys that flew far and wide in autumn. The whole camp should be in mourning for at least a week – for someone like Granny, the mourning would never end and her family would be cared for unstintingly until they were ready to go on with living.

'Well, I'm all the women now,' Jen said out loud. 'And when there's no well, get water from the river. And when the river's dry, get water from the stream. And if the stream's dry, dig for it.'

She stood up and breathed long and deep. Scissors she needed, thread she needed, a spade and long box too. There was much to be done.

At midday, the time when shadows were shortest, she went walking in the woods, listening for water. She wanted to find a rowan tree for its silvery spry branches; its wiry roots that cling on against all the odds; its clusters of coral berries bursting from the sparse limbs. A rowan tree and a stream.

She walked a long way before she sensed water. The air was crisper and the trees thinned out enough for the velvet tread of grass underfoot. She slowed until she was sure no-one was about, then flitted from tree to tree, fitting her body close into each trunk for a moment. Now she could hear water rushing over stones, and a breeze shivered through the branches. The breeze blew stronger, giving her liquid trills of birdsong. She stepped from behind a gloriously muscled trunk and the earth shelved away in front of her: roots swung through empty air for ten feet where the earth had worn away. It was a river she'd found. She climbed down the woody cat's cradle and out of the wind to stand where the roots splayed their grip, cleft like a camel's hoof, strong as pillars.

The river banks caught the wind and tossed it lightly over the sparkling water. The river was wide and shallow over golden stones, the water swept busily downstream where it deepened and darkened. A heron flapped slowly away, wings like heavy paper. Jen sat and thought. She flung her head back on a gust of weeping and stared. The tree above her had a cave of roots and the trunk was curved like the thigh of a giant acrobat in mid-leap.

Yes. This was the place.

'I wanted a stream and a rowan tree,' she said, smiling and dizzy with loss. 'And I got a river and a heron; a giant beech, a goddess of a beech. She'll take care of you, Granny.'

She must be careful where she dug; not the sandy slipsoil at the water's edge; not so as to undermine the magnificent roots of the tree. She closed her eyes and whirled around until she stopped with her arm pointing just down the bank, where stones were only just damp; where strange clumps of stone-coloured lichen crumbled to powder in her hand.

Up by the tree she turned to face the wind. It was a wind that meant business and blasted into her open mouth as if she was biting on ice.

The bear was chewing her way through a rotten stump she'd smashed with her great paws and claws. Jen started talking to her from across the clearing – Jethro had taken cruel pleasure in stealing up on her and shouting, then slashing at her with his cane when she turned with a roar of outraged surprise.

'Have you found yourself a feast there, Miss Walnut? Lots of beetles and grubs? I've found my Granny's grave, and we'll be out of here by midnight.'

She drew the curtains in the caravan and lit candles. The soft flames made Granny's waxen skin pale gold. *Nearly there, old darling*, Jen thought, taking out the scarlet silk scarves and tying them softly around the stiff joints. They smelt of rosemary, and dust, and a hint of sandalwood from the box.

There was no way of getting a proper coffin, all shaped and sanded and waxed. Jen had decided to use the illusionist's casket, stowed away since her dad had got too shaky for any sleight of hand. He'd once been able to make someone disappear with such skill and flourish that his audiences crossed themselves against magic, and gasped when the person skipped back into the ring unharmed. But she could barely remember – it was so long ago. Ye Gods, the box was warped with years of sun and rain; thank heavens Granny was a featherweight. The faded paint on sides and lid read: MARVEL! MYSTERY! MAGIC! WATCH A LADY DISAPPEAR!

'I hope they can laugh on the shadow-path, Granny!'

Jen was back by the river before moonrise, the horse tethered to the giantess beech tree, the apology for a coffin on the ground beside her. She dug slantwise into the bank until she was sweating and her hands were blistered numb. Near the bottom of the hole, she hit a great cord of root and sighed with relief. Granny would stay at rest. She hauled and shoved the box into the hole. Then her knife flashed in the moonlight, and she closed her eyes.

'I've no gold to give you, Granny,' she said. 'Just this.'

She dropped her heavy blonde plait into the hole, tossed a handful of rosemary after it and dug all the earth back in, flattening it and packing it safe all over with stones.

Time drove her: the moon was racing past midnight. She packed in a frenzy; ropes, food, clothing, treasures, herbs. If she needed anything else, she'd have to buy or barter. She saddled the horse, and built a slow circle of fire around her home. The bear's rope looped round her hand, she waited in the shadows until the fire made a Catherine wheel of the wooden spokes and blistered up the sides of the caravan. The smoke caught her nose and eyes and she turned away, urging the horse through the trees, tugging the bear.

Their three-headed shadow scudded clumsily through the woods, catching branches, crushing bushes. The bear grumbled at so much haste; the horse felt Jen's fear through the reins. Only when they found the road again, a safe few miles from the hamlet, did she relax the pace.

She remembered a night when they'd been travelling, and she'd woken up and stumbled to Granny's bed to find it empty. The rocking caravan had thrown Jen from side to side as she screamed at the empty pillows, the cold sheets, the shadows staggering like monsters where her Granny should have been. Moments later, all was still and Granny was holding her, wrapping her in a shawl and taking her to sit with her and her dad as they jogged through the darkness.

'Granny'll never be far, mind, shh, shh, don't you cry now, it's all safe, my little darling, all safe, so safe, Granny's got you and I'm not letting you go, and there's nothing to be scared of. I won't let anything hurt you.'

Tell me a story, Granny.

'There was a dragon,' said Granny, 'a dragon who flew all round in the darkness before you or I were born, a million years ago, who knows? She was huge, this dragon, bigger than a horse, or a tree, or a three-masted ship with a hundred guns, or a mountain with its head in the clouds: she was bigger than anything. If you stood at her toes and looked up along her beautiful scaly neck, you wouldn't be able to see the sky. She was all colours, this dragon, she changed her colours like a dragonfly's wings. If you were the smallest flea on the smallest flea and looked at a dragonfly: why, that's how big she was. Only bigger. And one day as she was flying she grew sad at the sound of her lonely wings beating through the darkness, and she started to weep. Every teardrop was as wide and deep as the ocean and soon she was floating on salty water, her wings all wet at the tips. The sound of the waves soothed her, so she dragged herself up into the air again and flew high in the sky, scattering drops of water all over. Then she laid a silver egg in the midnight blackness and that's our moon. And all her tears sparkled in the light from the wonderful egg, and that's our stars.'

Jen looked at the night sky and remembered lying in Granny's arms trying to count all the stars before she fell asleep. She'd never done it.

Tell me a story, Granny. About the dragon.

'Well now. She was very tired when she'd laid the egg and she sank back down on the waters to drift awhile and rest. But she slept so deep she began to sink, and the waters crept over her back and she didn't wake up. Then the waters slip-slopped up her neck and still she didn't wake up. She didn't even wake up when the water crept along her mouth and past her nose and over her eyelids and closed over her head. She just kept sleeping and snoring away and sinking deeper and deeper until she slipped right through the other side of the water. She started falling so fast that cold great winds stung her awake. For a minute she didn't know where she was and she spat out a tongue of flame to see, but she was so soaked through it came out as smoke, and that's the mist and the clouds. She flapped her wings and huffed and puffed and wheezed and breathed, until little licks of flame appeared and finally she blew a great bubble of fire and flames and her mouth was dry. And that's our sun.'

Jen loved the dawn and the dragon-breath streaks of gold and orange licking along the horizon. The sun coming up all shades of fireglow and hovering just over the edge of the world until it popped up whole like a soap bubble. But there were many miles she needed to go this night before sunrise would be a welcome sight.

The road dipped through a ford, and she checked the horse. This was upstream from where Granny's body lay and she thought of the great beech tree, she thought

64

of the dragon and her silver egg. And as she looked at the moon and her light on the waters, she saw Granny's face clear as day, saw Granny smiling.

'And I will remember your face,' Jen sang down the river. 'I will remember your face.'

Wishes Beside The Mighty Falls

'We should think about what we want to do,' said Esther.

'I want to have a fire!' Squirrel cried.

'Me too,' said Turtle. 'A great big huge fire!'

'That's no problem,' Esther said. 'Though I was thinking a little further ahead.'

'We have to get this raft past the falls,' said Rowan, 'or ditch it. Depends where we're going, really.'

Isabel frowned and shook her head. That would mean being back on land and right now, wild water felt safe and sure of its direction. She had sensed the unease in Esther's question, and felt a stir of alarm when she realized that Rowan had no clear plan. Rowan always knew what to do. A chill finger of wind stirred the moonbeam silk between them.

'Yes,' said Rowan, 'you're right. The river's best for us now.'

'Surely if we found some deep woods,' Esther suggested. 'They can't get everywhere.'

'That's what we thought after the village,' said Rowan.

'I like the woods,' said Squirrel. 'And they've killed my tree.'

'Can we start the fire?' Turtle snuggled close to Esther.

'We're headed east now,' Rowan said. 'Maybe we should go north – only that would mean leaving the river. Anyone want to leave the river?'

'When it's safe,' said Squirrel.

'Anyone else?'

'Rowan, I'm cold, I want a fire!' Turtle's voice was on the edge of scared. 'I don't care about the raft! Let it get smashed to pieces over the falls. I'm COLD!'

'Soon, baby,' hushed Esther. 'OK. Who wants to stay with the river?'

They all nodded, except Turtle who was clamped round her mother's waist. Squirrel frowned.

'What about Sister Mercy?' she said. 'Have we got to ask her, too?'

'I think Sister Mercy'll make her own mind up,' said Rowan. 'She's a grown woman and we can't afford passengers. If she stays, it'll be fine. If she leaves, we'll have to make really good time. It won't be long before they get some kind of story out of her and set the district alight with lies and rumours. Goddess, I hate these times!'

'Let's open the circle and have a fire,' Esther said.

'The circle is open and never broken,' Rowan responded. Turtle and Squirrel dived for the trees. Isabel wound up the silver thread and gave it to Esther, who smiled and dug into her bag. She took out a smaller bag, beaded with silver and blue-sheened like a kingfisher's wing: she gave it and the thread back to Isabel.

'Magic bag,' she said. 'It's time to let that poor fish go free again, Belle. And choose everything that's yours from the magic cloth.'

Isabel picked up the shell and lay flat on the rocks as she dipped it in the river, watched the fish lie still for a moment then flick out of sight in the darkening water. She straightened up and looked towards the trees misting together up the bank, where she felt the nun still crouched and fearful. Her family heaped up sticks and branches for their fire, a careful distance from the magic altar. She ghosted into the shadows.

The nun was sitting like a stump blasted by lightning, her face haggard and petrified. Isabel sat with her back against a tree and watched her by sliding her eyes sideways. This was how she got rabbits to let her stroke them. It took hours, sometimes days, but then they were never scared of her again. The nun had neither seen nor heard her, and started rocking like a crazed beggar, muttering in a voice like a rusty bucket scraping down a well.

'Witches, for the love of God, and all disappeared, not even a puff of smoke, led me here to lose my soul and I've eaten their food, I'm lost. Oh, how could I doubt Reverend Mother? My own mother gave my life to Jesus when I was an innocent child as small as those three hobgoblins. But that man was evil. Evil! Is it pride that I judge a man of God as evil? Heaven give me a sign, is it pride and fear have brought me down this pagan path to damnation?'

She looked at the branches smudging into the twilight sky, then buried her head on her knees and sobbed as if an ill-made dam was bursting inside her. What kind of sign did the nun need? Isabel felt herself grow still as the tree trunk, her toes spreading like roots. She hummed inside her head, on one note at first, then clearly came the darting tune of the shallows, the joyful throaty choir of the waterfall. The tune dashed and flowed, the way Esther had talked about the sea, the notes flowed in Isabel's blood like a bolt of gossamer-fine silk rippled by a breeze. The music stirred her to rise and sit cross-legged in front of the nun, willing her to look up slowly, move her head gently, to *see* that this was a beautiful evening; to know that she, Isabel, was a good future woman; to trust that

Rowan and Esther were safe and wise, and that she could lose all her nightmares and over-the-shoulder terror-filled glances for ever if she came with them. If she wanted to.

It was an age before Sister Mercy looked up, and Isabel reached out her hand before she could start or call out or cross herself. The nun clasped her fingers: Isabel had thought she was cold, but the thin icy grip made her feel very deeply warm in her body.

'Child, you're alive!' whispered the nun, touching her cheek and brow with her other shaking hand. 'Here's me fearing human sacrifice and you're as real and warm as you ever were. It's a sign.'

Isabel heard the fire crackle down the bank and stood up, tugging the nun to her feet. Sacrifice! Mad! She saw Rowan and Esther and Turtle and Squirrel licked by a golden light and looking around. For her?

'Belle? Belle?' Rowan hollered: curiosity, not concern. For her.

She led Sister Mercy out of the trees.

'Are you with us, Sister?' Rowan asked, her face expressionless.

'If you'll have me with you,' the nun replied. Rowan met her eyes, unblinking, then she nodded. Esther smiled.

'Come into the fire circle and get warm,' she said.

Food and flames sent Turtle and Squirrel into a dozing lump, covered and tucked around by Esther. Isabel wrapped a blanket round herself and leaned against Rowan.

'A little wine for you, I think,' said Esther. 'And a little more for the big people.'

Sister Mercy stiffened. These people were known to

steal communion wine and sacred wafers for their wicked rituals. For all she knew she'd eaten blessed bread, desecrated the host and damned herself already.

'What wine is that?' she asked, and immediately felt ungrateful and ungracious.

'You're not obliged to drink it,' Rowan told her.

'This is wildwood and windy wine,' Esther said calmly, taking Rowan's hand. 'All the windberries we could find on Whitestone Common, apart from what the babies stuffed; blackberries, brambleberries.'

'It's just . . .' the nun said, close to tears.

'I know,' said Esther. 'But you'll have to let it go, Sister.'

She held out a cup of wine, her eyebrows raised with a query. The nun took the cup. A heady scent of sunshine and ripe fruit delighted her nose at once.

'Let's drink,' said Rowan. 'Drink to all our dreams coming true and our wishes being granted.'

Her brown eyes challenged the nun, and she and Esther clinked cups together, then with Isabel. The nun held hers out, waiting for God to strike her. The sound of the cups rang clear over the crackling wood and no lightning bolt rent the heavens. She was either safe or so far lost that her Maker had despaired of her.

'For all good things that we deserve,' she said, shakily.

'We deserve,' said Esther, with a deep giggle. 'We deserve everything.'

After they'd drunk, Isabel slid into sleep, Rowan's thigh her pillow.

'Well, Esther, that was a big one. What do we want? I want a safe place for me and you and the children to grow without fear and live happily.'

'Me too,' Esther said, 'but where? Downriver eventually we'll come to the sea. I've never been on a boat, even.'

'The sea!' said Rowan. 'I've got a funny feeling. Maybe things are better over the sea. Somewhere. I've never been to sea.'

'I crossed the sea many years ago,' Sister Mercy told them softly. 'With the Order, when I was just a child. I grew up by the sea. There were thirteen of us and no work. The land had gone sour for miles around. So my mother gave me to the nuns to take care of. I'd likely have starved otherwise.'

'What do you want, Sister?'

'I've never given it a thought. My whole life's been in the convent. Every hour of the day we had a prayer to say or a service to attend. Or a task to perform – gardening, cooking, cleaning. I'd just started to attend to the sick: Sister Charity was teaching me. The day I first saw you was my third trip outside the convent walls. I was so full of it – the sun and the trees and the river. Doing the work of the Lord and privileged and trusted to go out into the world. It all seemed so clear.'

'Maybe it'll sort out,' said Esther. 'You don't have to decide here and now.'

'Well, I need to set my mind to it,' the nun said. 'There's only twice I've really known that I want something. The first was when I was seven and given to the Order. When my mother walked out of the gates, I just wanted to run after her and be home with my family. I knew it was for the best, but that's nothing to do with what you want, is it? And I made myself forget about how much I wanted them all. You have to not want when you can't have.'

Rowan poured them more wine. The nun gulped.

'What's the other want, Sister?'

The nun's voice changed from its timid lilt to a wondering anger.

'When that Pricker came to your tree in the forest, he dragged me in the bushes and it was not the touch of a holy man I felt on my body. I wanted to get away from him. I didn't care what happened to me.'

'Well, we happened to you,' Esther said. 'Is this what you want?'

'I think – I don't know,' said the nun. 'I just want to live. Oh, and it'll be grand to see the sea again!'

Gentleman Jack Daw And His
Amber Princess

'Where's the circus at, bonny lad?'

Jen started. The voice was unexpected; she hadn't seen anyone.

'Who's asking?' she called with all the depth and bravado she could find.

A man sloped out of the trees, thumbs hitched into a string belt, a pipe curling blue smoke around his earth-brown hat. His coat was long and loose and brown over moleskin breeches and chestnut boots as glossy as a racehorse: as surprising as the glittering buttons ribbing his waistcoat and the elegant twist of his moustache. Jen stiffened: was there something of Jethro in his easy swagger? She looked him in the eyes. No, there was a gold-flecked humour there, and he made no move towards her. Jethro would have been at the horse's head by now, pawing her as if he owned her, greedy eyes weighing up a way of using her and her bear.

This man stood still. Curious, so he'd asked. But with a who-gives-a-damn nonchalance if she didn't choose to tell him her business.

The bear growled and tugged at her collar, batting the air with her great paws until Jen shushed her.

'You're all right, Miss Walnut. Don't do anything to startle her, she's fine when she's not frightened.'

'I wouldn't argue with a bear, bonny lad. Have you far to go?'

'As far as it takes,' she said. Jethro would have been cursing by now. The stranger just smiled.

'If you've a mind to rest, I've a fire close by. You're welcome to a warm and a wet.'

A warm and a wet. Granny used to say that to strangers with the same grace and courtesy, once she'd sized them up. They had felt as if royalty had invited them to dine at court. Jen considered. Dusk was clouding the trees and claiming the path. Besides, she'd had it in mind to stop soon.

'That's kind,' she said, slipping from the horse's back and following the brown-clad man through a tunnel of trees, then round and around a twisting labyrinth of bushes and bracken. She wondered at herself as they went deeper into the woods, and checked the dagger at her belt. She'd use it if she had to. The bear grumbled as one delicious tree stump after another went by out of reach. The stranger looked back, alarmed.

'Is she all right there, your Miss Walnut?'

He sounded as doubtful as she felt. Well, that was good.

By the time they reached his fire, she could barely make him out in the dusk. A horse whickered as he appeared and he crossed to pet the brilliant white-starred face.

'Hey now, Amber Princess, don't fret, I'm back and we've got company. Shush now. I told you you'd see more of the world with me than harnessed to my fine lord's carriage. We've got a bear and a lad and a horse for company.'

His horse was on a long rein, and the firelight picked out magnificent limbs and a proud arching neck. Jen tethered Auntie Clop, who looked like a stout peasant next to that russet leanness. Then she led the grouchy bear to the other side of the clearing, and settled her where she could claw up the ground and grub away without scaring the aristocratic Amber Princess.

'My name's Jack,' said the stranger, sitting on a log and pouring beer. For Granny a wet meant tea, and Jen reminded herself she was a man now. But what was her name? Her mind went blank. What was she? A runaway, a killer, an orphan as good as, a poor kind of man and on the run.

'Thank you, Jack. It's good of you. I'm Robin.'

'If we were south in bonny Sherwood, I'd take you for Robin Hood himself on some mad caper. I took you for a lass when I first saw you – you're ower young to be beating this track all alone, bonny lad. Mind, I was your age when the woods came calling. A beardless boy and bold as brass!'

All this was an invitation to explain herelf. Jen gulped her beer and stared into the fire.

'I've always been travelling,' she said. 'Set up on my own now.'

'You'll do well with a bear,' Jack commented. 'Does she dance?'

'Oh, aye. She's grand with a good tune.'

'I'll get my fiddle out when she's through shredding that tree,' Jack said.

'She'll sleep then,' said Jen. 'She only dances when she's hungry. I wouldn't have trained her that way. The man I bought her from kept her hungry most of the time. She's on a bit of rest for a while. She's not well.'

Miss Walnut crunched a grub-laden branch to pulp and mumbled happy bear sounds, unaware that she had suddenly become an invalid.

'You cannot be too soft, mind,' said Jack. 'It's a tough life on your own.'

'It's fine. No-one telling you what to do. You're a fiddler?'

Jack laughed pleasantly.

'I can play a tune,' he said. 'There's other ways of fiddling.'

He threw this in with bravado and refilled his mug. Did he think she'd ask him a lot of questions? Did he want her to? Well, she didn't want to – that way, she'd have to answer his.

'Where are you headed, Robin? Maybe we can throw in together for a mile or two?'

'The sea,' said Jen, reckoning that was vague enough. 'There's a lot of money comes in from the sea. I should do well.'

'You've many a long mile ahead then,' said Jack. 'Think on it. I could use some company. I've no mind for the sea, but there's a lot I can pick up on the way.'

Jen wrapped herself in her cape and a blanket and stretched out by the fire. Jack banked up the embers, whistling softly through his teeth before he lay on his back at the other side, his eyes shining under the moon. He wasn't one for prying, she thought, no doubt there were secrets behind him too. And if he knew the country, he could save her from stupid mistakes until she was over the hills and far away.

'Maybe we'll go together for a bit of a way,' she said in the morning. 'I've no wish to see towns and villages yet awhile. Children pestering me for a circus and that bear's not well. No point in tiring her.'

'We're of a mind then,' said Jack. 'I'm known round here, Jack Daw and his jumping fiddle, and they think a mug of ale pays for a night's work. Bugger all in the way of money in these parts. And I can see that bear needs rest. We'll head east and keep to the forest, eh, Robin?'

'Aye, Jack,' she said, meeting his mischievous eyes.

But where she was prepared to bluff out any passing interest if needs be, Jack Daw would melt into the trees when they heard any voices. She wondered what the truth was about him. He didn't want to be seen. It was four days before they came anywhere near houses. They paused at the brow of a rise and looked down. Whitton-le-Hole nestled smokily below them, a necklace of lit windows beside a wide road.

'If I'm not far wrong, there's an inn down there, Robin, and I could use a good meal and a night in a bed.'

He led them along the crest of the valley through the trees and they tethered the horses and the bear and walked back. This seemed a long way round to Jen, but Jack Daw had a twinkle in his eye and a flush in his cheeks and swore he knew what he was at.

'I've business here, bonny lad, and not a word at anything I say.'

Whitton-le-Hole was a clump of houses in a sleepy green dip of land. The scent of herbs and night blooms came from dusky gardens behind tumbledown walls. Trees and a dark spire loomed up the hill, and a stream flowed alongside the rutted road, giggling its way underground. This was sheep country, where sheep grazed themselves fat and the people sat outside and gazed at the strangers wordlessly. They walked into the Queen's Arms to a hush, and ordered wine and food.

'You'll be wanting the northern coach, masters?' said the landlord, as if he didn't care.

'Why no,' Jack Daw replied. 'We're going south to London town. My brother and I hear a singer and a player can pick up gold playing in the streets down there.'

News to Jen that they suddenly shared a mother, an ambition and a destination. And Jack Daw's face seemed as naive and young as the lie he'd just come out with. What the devil was he up to?

'You'll have a couple of days grace, masters,' the landlord told them. 'North you can get to tomorrow morning, if you're up with the birds. She's through here by five. Don't stop unless I leave out a lantern. South don't come in till the evening of the day after tomorrow. You'll be staying here tonight?'

'We will,' said Jack Daw.

'I've no wish to seem, that is, I'll need to see the colour of your money,' the landlord blustered.

Jack actually blushed and pulled a new leather pouch out of his shirt. Just like a fool who thought he could make a mint in London!

'We can pay,' he said loudly. The whole bar nodded to itself. Fool and his money soon parted and home wi' your tail down, broken-hearted. It was well known. Best to sleep wi' the sun and rise wi' the dawn and work hard to keep the devil away in between. The landlord took money for two nights and sent his daughter up to air the room.

'Don't take me wrong,' he said, generous now he was richer. 'Only we've heard of some strange doings out there. Outlaw bands and devil only knows what else in that forest. They've trained wolves to do their sheep-stealing, we've heard, and thank God they've let us be so far.'

Out there must be out of the valley, away from the nibbling ewes, the tales carried along the coach route and growing wilder and bloodier at every stop, scandal sheets bristling with woodcuts where robbers towered high as houses and murderers carried enough cold steel to make a suit of armour.

'Aye, these are terrible times,' an old shepherd said, poking Jen with a stick. 'When I was a lad you could sleep out in the woods and never think twice. You've to be careful.'

'We wouldn't dream of it, eh, Peter?' said Jack, nudging her.

'I'd be terrified,' said Jen. Damn it, what game was he playing? Now she was Peter – and who was he?

'Maybe you'd like to practise your street singing after your supper?' the landlord suggested. 'We've no gold to toss at your feet, masters, but you're good for ale for a sweet song or two.'

'I told you, didn't I, Peter. I said, they're warm friendly people in these parts, or my name's not Jonathan Pettifer!'

They sat against a wall, Jack smiling vaguely.

'We'll have to give them a tune or three, Peter,' he said softly. 'Do you know "The Gypsy Lad and the Moon"? That's a good 'un. And "The Ruin'd Shepherdess" – that'll get them going. You fall in with the chorus, bonny lad.'

Their supper was good mutton and potatoes. To Jen, it tasted like ambrosia, bread and cheese being all that had passed her lips since her helter-skelter flight from the camp and the ill-concealed corpse in the bracken. And not longer after, Jack let himself be persuaded to tune up his fiddle. This was an art in itself, and he drew all eyes as his hand flew over the strings, inclining his head like a faun so his ear almost rested on the swan neck of the fiddle.

'There once was a gypsy lad, bonny and brown,
Loved a lady so fine in the city,

79

But she'd have none of his loving looks,
Ah me, his heart ached, 'twas a pity.

Gypsy lad wandering sad by the stream,
Heart full of pain and sweet sorrow,
Gaze at the moon and dream on, aye, dream,
Love will be yours and it may be tomorrow.'

Jack had been modest when he said he could play a tune. He could draw tears with his fiddle and his voice was wild and soft and *strange*. Jen found herself humming after the first line, and the chorus came as sweet and natural to her as breathing. Children darted out to tell the village, and the inn was full by the fifth verse. The landlord smiled as coins rattled over the bar, and poured two mugs of the best for these handsome easy strangers.

'Oh, gypsy lad, wander the world and be free,
She's married another, a lord and a loon,
If you want a true love, lad, then let it be me,
Sang the beautiful face on the silvery moon.'

The landlord bustled over as Jack put his fiddle down.

'Maybe you'll get your gold in London, masters,' he said. 'Will you give us another?'

'Let me wet my whistle first, man,' Jack said, and as he sat down again, Jen saw a darker look in his eyes.

'That was a lovely song,' she told him.

'Should be, Peter, bonny lad, I wrote it myself,' said Jack.

And although he seemed sad, he launched into song after song, raucous ballads all, until the midnight church bells rang and he insisted on going to bed. Jen felt light-headed: she'd drunk most of the beer after a while, and she stumbled up the stairs, trying to think clearly how to get to bed without Jack knowing her for a woman. Part of her didn't care, the slow-swimming heady ale and sitting next to Jack most of the evening, she knew she liked him in a way she hadn't liked a man before. What will be . . .

But she slept almost immediately and didn't see the tragi-comic look on Jack Daw's face as he slid an arm round her and felt the breathing heat of her breasts. She didn't feel the chaste kiss he gave her brow, nor the way he turned his back to her and banged his head on the pillow four times. And if a tear glistened in his moonlit eyes, no-one saw it but the lofty moon herself.

High up in the woods, the bear growled in her sleep as a coach went clattering past on the valley road. Amber Princess started awake and whickered around, looking for Jack Daw. She could hear him whistle and in moments he appeared, lean and dashing in black from head to toe.

'Hush now, beauty,' he said, stepping over to her. 'I hadn't forgotten you. Now, these are strange times, strange indeed. Down in that inn, we've a lad asleep that isn't a lad, snuggled up with a bolster that isn't a body. Is that bear a bear, Amber, and are you a horse? What a riddle!'

As he talked he rubbed some russet stain into the white flash on her face, then he saddled her up and swung on to her back. He urged her through the dawn-sodden grass, keeping to the ridge, the road barely a twist in the pre-dawn grey far below them. Far away he could see a whisper of clear light over night-blue hills, but the valley was floating in mist like a dream.

81

The church spire stuck up like a rock in the ocean, and the tree tops lay like treacherous tussocks in a marsh. After a mile or so they flew down the wooded hill sure as sunlight. Indignant birds screeched at them: we'll be up at sunrise, quit your noise! I've got six chicks asleep here, I don't know what the woods are coming to!

They slowed down as soon as he could see the road. He reined in behind a huge oak tree, whose rippling trunk and branches were solid enough to hide a half a dozen men. Here the road rose and straightened for a hundred yards or so. Jack Daw grinned.

He tied a mask round his eyes and set a three-cornered hat on his head. He pulled his scarf up over his mouth, and balanced a pistol on the saddle horn, waiting and listening, whistling quietly.

Amber Princess's ears twitched, and her rider sat forward. First the sound of hoofbeats, then the iron clatter and wooden creak of coach wheels. He tightened the rein for a count of thirteen, which he'd laughingly taken as his lucky number years ago, then urged his majestic horse into the middle of the road.

'Stand and deliver!' He rolled out the words with all the arrogance of cannon-fire.

The coach came to a halt.

He rode hard at it and seized the coachman by the waist, wheeled round and stood in front of the horses. Jabbing his pistol behind the man's ear. He spoke again.

'Step out of the coach, good sirs and ladies!'

A sleep-tousled bucolic head stuck out of the window.

'What's this? Why are we stopped? Oh, blessed saints! A highwayman!'

'You won't get away with this!'

'Pray silence,' said Jack Daw smoothly. 'It's too early

82

in the morning for arguments and I have the advantage. My pistols are loaded and cocked, and your coachman's brains will be breakfasting on lead if there's any trouble. All of you, out! At once!'

Out stumbled six prosperously dressed travellers, four men struggling with satin waistcoats and ruffled shirts, the reddest-faced of them bursting with rage and straightening his crushed wig. The women were powdered and dishevelled, one clutching a bag as if her life depended on it.

'What's your name?' Jack asked the terrified coachman.

'Elias, your honour,' he gasped.

'Well, good morning to you, Elias. I shall tell you exactly what to do, and do you do it slowly. Mine's a nervous hand and a quick-tempered profession and I've no tolerance for trickery. I shall set you on the ground and hand you a bag. You're to get the ladies and gentlemen to put all their gew-gaws and gold in the bag. Every ring and every watch and every shining diamond buckle. Then you're to come back and hand it to me. And I'll have milady's bag too. To guard it that close, it must be worth something.'

The red-faced man started to bluster and protest as Jack dropped the coachman to the ground. He turned the horse and snapped a whip to cut the mud at the traveller's feet.

'I've no wish to hear it!' he said imperiously.

'We'd best go along with this,' one of the women said. 'I've heard about these dirty highwaymen. A woman's virtue isn't safe with them!'

The other woman sank to the ground around her bag.

'A nice thought, madam,' called Jack cheerfully. 'My compliments to your maidenhead, wherever she may lie! Pick up your good friend's bag, I'd not have a dirty coachman fumbling with her!'

The coachman stumbled back to Jack and handed him both bags.

'Many thanks,' he said civilly. 'Now, there's a little task further for you. Do you unhitch the horses. Gentlemen, I'd have you unstrap your cases and bags from the roof and check your packing.'

They stood, irresolute, until his whip sent cold air stinging around their cheeks. Then they scrambled for the luggage and threw it to the ground. Dresses and breeches and shoes were flung everywhere, Jack's eagle eyes spotting any sparkle and commandeering ownership immediately.

'And one last thing,' he said smoothly.

'I'm ruined!' gasped the red-faced man.

'You'll recover,' Jack said. 'Now stand well back. I've no wish to hurt you! And you can live to tell your grandchildren that you had the honour of being robbed by Gentleman Jack Daw!'

They fell back against the trees.

He shot both pistols full at the coach wheels, and the carriage crashed to the ground, sending the freed horses tearing up the road. Jack Daw hurtled after them, diving up into the woods as soon as they cleared the bend. He rode like fury, Amber Princess sweating under him. As he rode, he stripped off hat, mask and scarf, bundled them and his cape into the bag and tied it to the saddle.

He leapt from the horse just up the hill from the inn, and Amber Princess galloped on, true as an arrow. Jack raced through the sleeping yard silent as a great cat. With a spring and a bound he was through the window where Jen lay sleeping, her arms round the bolster. He smiled and took several deep breaths

84

before stripping off his black clothes and hiding them. He had a nightshirt on underneath. Then he slid under the covers and eeled into Jen's embrace without waking her. Apart from the belting tattoo of his heart and his flaming cheeks, he seemed to be asleep at once. Jen stirred and realized where she was and who she was with. And just how hot he was, and how rosy and handsome. And she'd spent the whole night with him! She rolled over at once.

'There's lovely walking round here,' the landlord's daughter told them as they breakfasted some hours later. 'And father says we should have a dance tonight, if you'll play.'

'I don't want paying for your food,' boomed the landlord. 'That fiddle of yours is worth its weight in gold, master, worth its weight.'

'Kind of you,' said Jack Daw, wiping his lips. 'Peter and I'll take a walk around today, and no doubt we'll make merry this evening.'

There was a hammering at the door then, and the landlord bellowed that noon was soon enough, wasn't it, Lord love us all. Grumbling and smiling at Jack and Jen, he unbolted the door and the coachman burst in, breathless and wild.

'Highwayman!' he shouted. 'All my passengers have been robbed of everything, and the horses fled north with the highwayman!'

The landlord poured him aquavit and sat him down.

'Jack Daw!' the coachman said bitterly. 'He's never been known this far north. He's a villain, masters, all in black from head to toe, and his wicked eyes gleaming like steel. I was sitting this close to him with a bloody great gun in me ear'ole, and him laughing. Shot the blasted wheels off of the coach and had all the luggage scattered over the road like a pawnshop! My ladies and gentlemen are sitting out there now. What's to be done!'

Jack nudged Jen.

'These two young gents are waiting to go south,' the landlord said. 'Mercy, what terrible times we do live in!'

'Will he strike again?' Jen asked.

'He's got the cheek of Satan, young sir. Devil knows how he gets about, he does over one coach in the morning and another a hundred miles away in the afternoon, Then you hear nothing of him for months, while he's wenching and squandering it all somewhere, no doubt. Then, ho, thinks Gentleman Jack Daw, I've only a dozen diamonds left, I'd better go and get some more. Treats the blasted coaches like he was going shopping, damn him!'

'Oh, the world is a terrible place,' said the landlord, 'if all folks say do be true, masters!'

'Amen to that!' Jack Daw nudged Jen again.

'You never feel safe these days,' said Jen. 'Oh, Jonathan, I don't trust the coaches. We've nothing to steal but your fiddle and the clothes on our backs! He'd cut our throats!'

'He's not known for killing,' the coachman assured them. 'Take the teeth out of your head, mind, if he could make money out of them!'

'Do you sit there, man,' said the landlord. 'We'll get a horse and cart up to fetch your ladies and gentlemen. They can stay here while we fix your coach and get word to York.'

He was already reckoning up board for six for at least three days. And with Jonathan Pettifer to play fiddle, he was quids in!

Jack and Jen tutted a little more, then strolled into the street. They were hardly noticed – the magic fiddler and his brother were yesterday's news beside the evil glamour of Gentleman Jack Daw, who was whistling as they passed the last house and took a track leading uphill.

Neither had spoken since they left the inn. Jen was waiting for Jack to say something, and his eyes danced away from her, teasing and bold. When they reached the horses and the bear, she nodded.

'Walnut?' she asked, pointing to the horse's nose.

The bear growled at her name. Jen meant honey, Jen meant sugar, and she'd loved dozing in the warmth of the early morning after the relentless dawn to dusk they'd done since leaving the camp.

'Walnut,' said Jack, rubbing a sticky substance into the horse's face until her white star was clear again. 'That's why I said come with me, once I knew your bear's name. Walnut's always been lucky.'

'So have you,' Jen said drily, 'if what folk say do be true, masters!'

Jack laughed and punched her arm.

'Gentleman Jack Daw?' she said, and shook her head. 'I've spent the night with an outlaw.'

'Hard to tell who you're spending the night with sometimes,' said Jack, unsaddling the horse and rubbing her down. 'Why, I had a friend who travelled the roads in a similar line of business to mine. He picked up with a lad and they went together.'

Jen glanced at him. He was concentrating on the horse, and chatted on, lightly, lightly, but her skin prickled.

'This lad had a dancing bear and was riding a horse that was made for pulling a heavy load. Like a cart or even a caravan. A lovely lad he was.'

87

'Is that so?' Jen said, turning away and suddenly busy with Auntie Clop.

'This bonny lad never said a word of his business, and that made my friend curious. One night they were in an inn. Rather like the one we slept in only last night. The bonny lad was sleeping like a dream, and the moon was out. My friend woke up and looked at him and it seemed he was too bonny for a lad. And then my friend had business to do and he crept out before cockcrow. When he came back, the lad was holding the bolster to his breast like a lover. And a bonny breast it was – for a lad. And he wondered, my friend, he wondered what to say to this close-mouthed lad. And what do you think of that, Peter Robin?'

'I think your friend would have done best to keep his questions to himself,' said Jen. 'The lad may have had secrets it's best not to share.'

She whirled around, and Jack Daw found himself pinned flat on his back with a knife at his throat.

'You see,' Jen said softly, 'the lad could have been a murderer. And they do say that a murderer never strikes just the once.'

'And this lad was too bonny for a lad, and ower strong for a lass,' said Jack Daw evenly. 'So my friend decided, since he was a nick away from death, that he should mind his business and forget he'd ever seen the lad. He decided it had all been a dream. But he'd taken a liking to him, you see.'

Jen stood over him.

'Maybe your friend was wise after all,' she said. 'What happened to him?'

Jack sat up and dragged a bag towards him.

'He gave the lad some jewels and cautioned him not to sell them for a good few weeks. The lad was set on going to sea. So they journeyed together for another day, and in the evening, he told the lad how to flit like midnight from county to county, to keep himself quiet in the woods hugging the river bank and that would take him to the sea.'

He stood up and dropped a fistful of glittering jewels into Jen's hand.

All day they kept to the high ridges, stopping at the windy heights to see another sweep of plain, pausing at streams for the horses to drink and the bear to plunge in and flail around scratching in ecstasy.

The sun was a burning orange and the sky blushing pink when Jack Daw stopped and spoke again.

'I'll make a camp here, bonny lad,' he said. 'Your way's down this hill and over the next. You'll hear the river. Follow her the way she flows, and she'll take you to the sea.'

'Thank you, Jack Daw,' Jen said, and shook his hand. Their eyes met, unblinking, as if they'd known each other for years. Jack stepped back and waved his arm as if giving her the whole world.

'And,' said he, laughing, 'if my friend's lad had been a lad, they'd have had some fun together. Only it turned out he was a lass, and my friend had a liking for lads . . . love go with you, Peter Robin.'

Jen nodded and walked away from him.

Down the hill, restless mists will o' the wisped the land, and the clouds were fantastic dragons and horses rearing in smoky indigo. Evening wrapped the distant hills in scarves of grey and white and when she looked back, Jack and his Amber Princess were invisible. Jen tugged the tired bear along, coaxing her the last hour's walk until she heard the river. She could see its wide glittering path hundreds of feet below, and she settled among dark trees whose branches interlaced like a circle of full moon dancers caught in flight.

An Ambush In The Woods

Rowan woke early, and eased her body around Esther's back, brushed her neck with her lips. Esther's hand clasped hers in the heat of sleep, then curled up round its own palm, soft with its heat-sleep dreams. Esther woke up slowly, as slowly as a riot of starving Turtle and Squirrel allowed. Those two were locked round each other, the way they always slept, Turtle's arm pinned by Squirrel's and sticking straight up in the air. Dear babies!

Rowan was wide awake at once. She inched her body slowly apart from her lover, and tucked the blanket round Esther to keep her snug while she sat up. Isabel was sprawled across her legs and sat up suddenly, eyes wide and bright. They tiptoed together down the bank to the falls. The water was a dawn-dragon's nest, surging with muscled life, glittering grey vanishing into mist right along the river.

'There's no way the raft can ride this, my Belle,' said Rowan.

The river bank was cut off like a knife slash where Isabel had stood and shouted, unheard. The rock shelf dropped as sheer as the falls, and maybe a nimble child could elf-hop down the jutting slivers, but no-one bigger, and no-one carrying anything. Perhaps they'd have to take the raft to pieces and take it piece by piece through the woods and put it back together again a hundred feet below. It would mean at least a morning and maybe a day of exhaustion. Even though she didn't know where they were going, Rowan wanted to get there fast.

She looked up at the woods. The bank swooped up, wild and sheer from the riverbed, trees balanced on one powerful root against the wall of earth and maze of rocks. Isabel went ahead of her up the steep bank, disappearing round rocks as tall as her mother, slipping on mud sticky with night dew, ferns batting her head and gold-legged spiders racing out to see what monster fly had bungled into their web so cold and so early. They had to struggle up a long way before the earth flattened at the top of a dizzy cliff, and both were breathless and sweating.

Suddenly, Isabel reached behind her and grabbed Rowan's hand, and they both froze. Isabel turned her head as slowly as a leaf caught in the spindrift of a still pool. Rowan followed her flicker of fear. There in the smoky mist of a glade was a strange sight indeed. A huge furry lump, heaving up and down with deep breaths, a horse splashed brown and white and snorting sleep into the jewelled grass, and a young man sprawled around the ashes of a fire. The last two were unremarkable, but the first made Rowan's skin prickle cold. Foxes she'd seen and laughed silently at their play, she'd turned to stone for deer, delighting in their delicate browsing: but this furred creature was massive.

Isabel threw her an eyebrowed question, and Rowan shrugged as imperceptibly as a bird stirring in its sleep. Isabel was all at once a hundred years wise, and squatted on a bowl of a rock with the grace of wine poured into fine crystal. Rowan's body flowed to the same position.

They didn't have to wait long amid the cold rocks

91

and icy mist. The first chill fingers of dawn light made the huge furry shape shudder and raise a massive arm and paw, etched at the tip with lethal black spikes. Isabel became a flattened rock, Rowan was poised to flee. Then the young man stretched and muttered. Moments later, he was awake and slumped to a sitting position.

'Hey there, Miss Walnut, not long to go now, what do you think?'

He crossed to the furred lump and ruffled a huge head. Rowan and Isabel heard grunts of pleasure, and their hands instinctively reached for each other. Finger-tip on palm was a warm sensation. The young man dug a jar from his pack and stuffed a fist into it. The furry head dipped and rose around his fist. The horse flicked an eyelid, and her intelligent brown eyes fixed straight on the women in hiding. She snorted and rose to her feet at once. The young man unclipped her bridle and shushed her in the direction of spring green shoots.

'Whey ah there, Auntie Clop, go fill yourself.'

Isabel's fingers tightened. Rowan felt better too. Whatever the monstrous shape was, it had been calmed in the presence of a human. Rowan had her own hard-learned opinions of men, but one on his own was usually at least to be reasoned with – at first. She didn't know what Isabel was thinking. She knew there was no fear there, and she waited for her marvellous child to let her feelings show however she wished.

And Isabel was deeply thrilled. She loved all creatures that lived and breathed, she'd been teased for her passionately defended ant roads and the way she'd make the Squirrel and Turtle find another tree if woodlice were clearly busy with the one they wanted to climb. She'd seen many a silk-skirted centipede to safety and commanded silent adoration when a chrysalis had elected to shed her skin and become a creature winged and magic. The sheer bulk of this massive furred creature fired her the way the monster falls had woken her to ecstasy.

The young man followed the still brown gaze of his horse, and frowned as if to see clearer. He patted the horse's nose and shook his head. But she snorted and wouldn't look away.

'What's your trouble, Auntie? Are you seeing things? Dawn and dusk are great for changing things. I've seen tree stumps that look like people, and people for all the world like boulders. I'll take a walk through these trees and find us a path for the river.'

He strolled out of sight.

Isabel touched her eyes and looked at her mother.

'I think he's seen us too,' Rowan mouthed. They inched backwards as quick and silent as adders on a heath with an eagle shadow flicking over them. They waited behind an overhanging rock. Where was he?

Jen looked down from the tree tops. She hadn't been sure the shapes were people, but since they'd vanished, they must be. Damn! After Jack Daw, she'd decided to travel alone: she'd been more than lucky there and she knew it. If they were gypsy folk they'd be happy to leave her be and expect the same. She leaned against the tree trunk and waited.

Something hit the back of her neck – and it was too early for nuts and berries to fall. A whole shower of tiny sharp missiles rained round her shoulders. Her hand slid to her dagger.

As she looked up, something hit her right on the nose, and she heard a screech of triumph streaking from the leaves above. Pellets rained against her shirt, her back, her legs: they came from every direction, and she covered her eyes. There was no telling how many attackers there were, leaping from tree to tree and manic with laughter.

'You'd better put that knife down!' shrieked a very young voice. 'You're surrounded!'

'For Chrissake, Squirrel!' a woman's voice came from the rocks. 'Stop it!'

'We're all armed to the teeth!' shouted the child, bold and boisterous. 'He's in the tree and he's really good at climbing. And he's got a knife!'

Maybe it was all children. Maybe not. Either way, Jen decided to stick her knife back in her belt. She sprang to the ground and held her arms away from her sides.

'Throw that knife away!' the same voice ordered from on high. Jen tossed the blade to quiver in the ground where she could grab it with a dive, if she had to.

A woman and child stepped from behind the rock, and another child shot down the tree trunk and stood beside them. The woman had a thick plait of deep auburn hair, and all three wore shades of green and brown, their skin tanned and rosy as if they lived outside. They seemed to be a part of the woods, a tree and two saplings made human. The woman looked at her with the same peaty eyes as the climbing child, while the other child held her with a cool grey stare.

'I'm Jen,' she said to their silence, and saw the woman relax just slightly.

'I'm Rowan,' she said. 'This is Belle. This is Squirrel. I'm sorry if she pelted you to death.'

'I'm not!' shouted Squirrel. 'You were spying on us.'

'We were spying on her too,' Rowan said. 'We didn't know you were here until we came up this morning.'

'I got here late last night,' Jen told her.

Rowan considered. A woman, for all her short hair and swagger and well used to the woods from the easy way she'd disappeared into the trees. Isabel tugged her hand as a complaining roar came through the trees.

'What's the creature you have with you?' Rowan asked.

'She's a bear. Miss Walnut.'

'I've never seen a bear before, you see,' said Rowan. 'Would she mind if Belle met her? Me too. And Squirrel, I dare say.'

'Don't make any sudden noises,' Jen advised.

Squirrel picked up her knife and gave it back to her, handle first.

'Thank you,' Jen said, then led them to her camp. She started talking to the bear before she could see her.

'Visitors, Miss Walnut. Squirrel's a climber, just like me, and Auntie Clop, you were right, our tree stump and boulder are Rowan and Belle.'

The bear was sitting upright and bared her teeth, waving her front paws.

'That's good morning,' said Jen. 'And more honey and owt else that's going, I'd think.'

Squirrel stood still, considering. She'd fallen in love with Jen the moment she'd sprung straight up to grab the first branch of the tree. She was amazed at her surefootedness. She'd said *Squirrel's a climber, just like me!* And now she had this mountain of fur and claws and teeth as well and wasn't a bit afraid. Isabel let go of Rowan's hand and squatted. It could be weeks before something this big trusted you.

'It's bloody big,' Squirrel said loudly. 'Bigger than the last bloody bear I saw. Bloody bloody big, isn't it, Rowan?'

'She bloody well is,' Rowan agreed, laughing.

Squirrel stepped backwards and swaggered away, calling:

'I'm bloody getting bloody Turtle, Rowan. She's only little and she's never seen a bloody bear before!'

'My Squirrel gets very bloody when she's a bit nervous,' said Rowan.

'Quite bloody right!' said Jen. 'Will you share a brew? And what's a bloody Turtle?'

'Our youngest – so far,' said Rowan, sitting easily and stretching.

Isabel inched towards Miss Walnut, humming as softly as a bumble bee. The bear watched her until she sat still again and then lay on one side, itching her great pelt against the rough ground. Isabel copied her and then sat pretending to eat sticks when the bear went back to gnawing her tree stump.

Jen built up the fire and tossed sage into the flames. Rowan smiled and nodded: it was an ancient welcome between women of the craft.

The sun was almost down, painting swathes of turquoise and pink along the damp sands, rippling fine gold lace along the waves as they swept back under the froth of the next breaker. A woman was bent double, skirts hoicked up over bare legs and feet, her hands busy at the sand, clattering what she picked into a tin bucket. A baby tied in a blanket made her look like a hunchback.

Children darted away from her along the beach and back again, tugged like kites, light as the dippers skating the swirling face of the ocean. They tossed handfuls of shells into the bucket and the woman straightened and stood with her hands on her aching hips.

'*John, Sean, Michael, Kerry, Nick, there's enough! Come here now!*' *she called, and her voice rang out like a song. The children flew at her.*

'*Where's Kerry got to? Kerry!*'

Kerry was hiding behind a rock and let her mam call her name three times before she scrambled out and pelted towards her. She just saw her lips and the lovely smile and leapt . . .

Sister Mercy woke up. The rushing music of the river kept her dizzy in her dream a moment longer before she was drenched with loss. No hug, no mam, no seashore, no sunset, no buckies for tea . . . She sat up and felt every bone keen at the memory.

'You snore!' Turtle told her with an impish grin.

'Give me a cuddle!' said the nun. Turtle shook her head and scampered away down the river where Squirrel had exploded through the trees and was screaming at her to hurry. The nun wrapped her arms round her knees.

Esther stretched and reached her arm over to rub Sister Mercy's shoulders.

'Dreams?' she asked softly.

'It was all that talk of the sea,' the nun said brusquely. Esther's warm touch moved her to tears and she shifted away, although she didn't want to.

'Where's Turtle gone?'

The nun sniffed and pointed.

'Peace!' murmured Esther as she rolled over again.

Sister Mercy went stiffly into the woods. It was well past time to rise, and she was flooded with guilt at the awful thoughts she'd had about the convent the night before. Questioning the Good Lord and swilling wine like a heathen! She chose to kneel on rocks so sharp they cut into her knees and ordered herself to stay there until her thoughts were pure and clean again. For

97

all she closed her eyes tight, tears poured down her cheeks; birdsong rang in her ears like a wild free dance and all the scents of river and trees filled her senses. She clenched her fists and drove her nails into her palms. It was no good. She slumped on the ground and her body wriggled away from the punishing stones then lay still, shuddering with gut-wrenching sobs. She beat her fists against the earth until they were numb.

Maybe she'd just lie there, really quiet, lie like a stone or a fallen tree, lie so still that no-one could find her and she'd never have to get up again. She'd fasted for forty days every year and if she didn't drink any water either, surely the end would come, just creep over her like the rising tide. It was a wicked thought, and she knew it, but it sat in her mind, calm and immobile, impersonal and relentless. Only now, when she closed her eyes, she could see the beach from her dream, her mother's floating smile, and the pain was too much. She forced her eyes open.

An ant was having a hard time with a sliver of neatly chewed leaf three times as big as itself. It had just reached a twig it considered to be the size of a cathedral and was running backwards and forwards. Stumped, it put the leaf down and ran up the bark, ran back for the leaf, climbed again and fell back. Again and again.

She was about to move the twig when she heard the women and children calling from the river bank. For her? She went leaden.

'Sister Mercy! Breakfast!'

She wouldn't feed the wicked flesh, nor did she want to be among their kindness and questions. She lifted the twig and the ant rushed underneath, its leaf a bright green sail bowling along the ridges of bare earth.

Bare? The ground was as busy as a market. A beetle crawled along, black and glossy, a ladybird settled on a leaf then flew away, a silvery creature with dozens of legs as fine as gossamer undulated around seeds and over leaves. Busy, busy! God only knew what chaos she'd caused, flinging her huge body down on the ground with never a thought!

With a rustle, ten bare toes appeared an arm's length from her. Isabel, her eyes polite and anxious, holding out bread and a cup. Sister Mercy took both and tried a smile. It wouldn't come.

'See here,' she said shakily, to distract that unwavering look, and pointed at the ground. The child bent close, then looked at her with a grin and sparkle. She nodded down to the river. The nun looked. Gracious Heavens, more than the riot of them! A wild looking young man and a – great hairy creature on a leash, bigger than a dog, and taller than a man on its back legs.

Isabel squeezed her hand and skipped away.

Sister Mercy ate and drank. A dancing bear? She'd seen one when the gypsies came tumbling through her village, and she'd raced to hide behind her mother. She'd had nightmares for weeks about the teeth and claws and being smothered in its shaggy arms. Her brothers had dared each other to go close and Sean had even stroked its nose. He said it was lovely, and that its eyes weren't red and flashing like she thought, but honey brown and puzzled. Then she'd wanted to touch the bear too, but the gypsies had gone and it was too late. Of course, those women had no fear, and the children would be just the same.

She couldn't hide for ever.

She sidled through the trees and splashed her face in the icy water and joined them. Lord above, it wasn't a young man, but another woman boldly clad in breeches and boots and a shirt, her hair cut short as a lad's.

'Good morning!' said Rowan. 'Sister Mercy, this is Jen and Miss Walnut.'

'Good day to you,' said the nun, aware of Squirrel's insolent gaze and be bothered if she'd give her the satisfaction!

'What a beautiful bear,' she said. 'Would she mind if I was to stroke her?'

'She's not scared!' Squirrel was frankly disappointed.

'I dare say Sister Mercy's used to bears,' Esther commented. 'She's from over the sea, you know, Squirrel, and I expect they have bears over there.'

Jen took Sister Mercy by the hand and ruffled the bear's thick pelt with their clasp. The bear nudged the nun's arm and snickered. It was true, Sean was right, her eyes were like pools of amber. Jen let go of the nun's hand as she rubbed deep into the bear's neck and scratched her. Suddenly Sister Mercy saw that they were all staring at her and she stopped. Miss Walnut butted her for more, and she sat down hard with the force of that massive head. The bear grunted and sat beside her, leaning close for more scratching, snuffling with pleasure.

'She'll be after you all day now,' Jen told her. 'Your arms'll be aching by nightfall. Lazy old bear.'

Squirrel was awed. She hadn't actually had the nerve to *touch* the bear yet. She decided not to care and tried to draw Turtle into a game in the shallows. Turtle just sat and stared. Isabel sat by the nun, amazed as the bear patted her, wriggled full-length then lay with her head in her lap.

'Sister Mercy's from beside the sea,' Rowan said.

'And that's where we're aiming – the river will take us there. Jen, what do you think?'

'You don't travel light,' Jen said slowly. 'Mind, there's six of you. Of course, *I* only have a pack and a horse and a bear. It's the raft you're worried about?'

Rowan nodded. She was convinced that there was no way other than dismantling it and rebuilding it. And that would wreck the resin seal between the logs. There just wouldn't be time to do that again properly.

Jen stood up and walked down to the falls, Squirrel sauntering six paces behind, as if she was going that way anyway. She stopped and looked at the incredible falls, then swept her gaze up the sheer banks.

'What do you reckon, Squirrel? Ride it over the falls and take a chance? Or . . .'

'We need wings,' Squirrel said.

'Sure. Only . . . we haven't got wings *as such*. What would the wings do?'

'Make the raft fly!'

'Fly through the air,' murmured Jen. 'Do you see that tree up there, roots like a nest of snakes? Yes? And the next one . . . silvery, branch as thick as your body . . . hmm.'

Squirrel saw the trees she meant, the oldest and strongest ones.

'Ropes,' said Jen. 'What would you say to some bloody strong ropes? We could try swinging the raft from those trees. You and I could tie the ropes in place – if Rowan'll let you help.'

'Rowan can climb a bit. She's not as good as me. Or you,' said Squirrel. 'But I never fall. Not once.'

'Me neither,' said Jen, and they strolled back to the others.

'We've worked it out,' she said. 'It's dangerous: not for us, but if it breaks . . .'

She made a plan out of grass and sticks on the rocks while she was talking.

'I don't see a choice,' said Rowan. 'Esther?'

'I just don't want to watch,' she replied. 'Squirrel gives me seizures in the woods as it is. With a drop like that! I know you won't fall, Squirrel, I just can't convince my knees. We'll shift the rest of the stuff, hey, Turtle? Belle? Sister Mercy?'

'Miss Walnut is not about to let you get up,' Jen told the nun. 'You're the best back-scratching pillow she's ever found. Maybe you'd keep an eye on her?'

Sister Mercy nodded, and patted the hairy head lying across her breasts, gazing into her eyes in bliss.

'You're a big, soft lump,' she told the bear, and got a faceful of warm tongue in return.

Jen and Rowan and Squirrel went up through the rocks and started to plait ropes together, to weave an impossible web high over the river.

Flying Over The Falls

The sun made a noon-high dazzle on the river by the time they were ready. Esther couldn't bear to look, and couldn't bear to look away. She settled for peeking through her hands. Turtle was buried in her lap and just wanted to know when it was all over. The loudest yell was drowned in the roar of the falls, and all Rowan could do was wave at her lover and the children and the nun and the bear.

'I know your opinion of Our Lord and Maker,' Sister Mercy said. 'But I'm telling you, I'm praying every second!'

'Sister, I'm sure the Goddess will take your goodwill. Even if you can only see her wearing a long beard,' Esther responded drily.

But for the bear's arm pinning her down, Sister Mercy would have flounced away. Forced to stay, she met Esther's laughing eyes and shook her head to stop herself smiling back. That would be heresy.

'We'd better test it out first with something heavy,' Jen said. 'No not you, Squirrel, what if . . . ?'

Squirrel was crouched on a branch too high to reach and too thin for either one of the two women to stand on. She lashed a rope around her waist and wrapped her arms and legs around another.

'Squirrel, I'm warning you!' Rowan said, but the child laughed and kicked against the tree trunk, launching herself into midair to spin slowly over the falls, fly down the precipice and land like a bird near the others. She untied herself and scrambled back up to Jen and Rowan.

'It's fine,' she said, 'only you twist a bit just where the rocks end.'

Jen laughed with relief.

'The raft won't twist,' she said. 'It'll be in the net.'

'There's no flying from fate,' Rowan said. 'Let's hope fate flies with us.'

Esther couldn't see anything, and it seemed an age after Squirrel vanished back up the bank before a shape jerked into view above the bluffs. Rowan and Jen were both clinging with one arm to the trees, moving along the web of ropes, and guiding the raft with ropes and poles, setting their own weight against the unwieldy mass. The wind caught the raft at one point as easily as a sail and it seemed to be lurching out of control, but then it swung majestically back along its aerial path. The women were filthy and sweating, their hands torn and scratched, by the time the ropes creaked slack and laid the raft carefully on the lower bank.

Esther wrapped her arms around Rowan and sank her face into her neck. Squirrel flew from the trees and clamped herself around Jen's body. Isabel hugged Turtle and Sister Mercy.

'You did it, oh my darling, you did it!'

'We did it,' said Rowan, kissing Esther's mouth. Which seemed a bit strange to Sister Mercy. You'd think they were sweethearts! But pagans were known for excess, she told herself. Moments later, they were dancing and whooping in a circle, and Miss Walnut jerked her to her feet to dance with them. You cannot be a wallflower when a bear demands a waltz, and it was glorious to be flung around in the sunshine. God forgive me, Sister Mercy thought.

'We'll get the ropes and get going,' Jen said. 'Auntie Clop can join us up the way a bit, when the banks smooth out.'

Sunset found them camped downstream. Turtle had seen a huge white bird with bright black eyes and a yellow beak: Esther told her it was a seagull and Sister Mercy said it meant that the sea would only be days away now.

The children were sleeping, and Jen was dozing against the flank of her horse. The nun's eyes were closed, her pillow huge and furry, when she heard Rowan and Esther giggle.

'I think we could,' Rowan said.

'Too right. Only we'd better go into the woods,' Esther said, and they slipped away from the fire.

What heathen rite was so important that it kept them awake when they must be exhausted? How could they leave their children in the middle of the night? The nun was wide awake and indignant. She ducked into the shadows and followed them.

She stopped when they stopped, and shut her eyes when they kissed and the kiss went on longer than any kiss should. But she froze when Esther loosened Rowan's shirt and stripped her silvery naked in the moonlight and knelt in front of her. As if she was worshipping her!

But there was such a languorous tenderness in their embrace, so much gentleness as Rowan's hand traced Esther's shoulders and back . . .

'My darling woman,' said Esther. 'My love. My lover.'

Each word was a delighted caress, and Rowan's head buried into Esther's breasts and belly as if they were one creature. The nun couldn't look away, though she knew she should, for this was sin if ever she'd seen it. But it was so beautiful! Only when Esther lay spreadeagled on the ground and splayed her hands in her lover's hair, moonlight blurring the way she turned her head and cried out, did the nun flit back to the fire. She had to. This was private. She wanted to say *disgusting!* She wanted to say *filthy!* But she was filled with wonder and longing, and drifted into sleep alight with dreams. She was running into someone's arms and it wasn't her mother; she could feel lips on her lips and it was wonderful. She'd only ever kissed the crucifix and the priest's hand, and this kiss was an all-night miracle.

'Every bit of your body, goddess, I worship you,' said Rowan's mouth to Esther's knee, to her thigh, words lost as she buried her mouth in the nectar and hot petals of womanflesh, spiralling Esther along galaxies, flying with her through constellations of sheer delight.

'We'll sail away,' said Esther, 'sail away and find an island no-one's ever lived on.'

'My honey,' said Rowan. 'If there are any left on earth, we'll find them.'

Part Two

The Coast

Last Words Before Dying

She haunted the docks like a scrimshank moggy. She cursed the sailors when they kicked her away from pilfering, she wheedled compliments at them if there was a spit of drink or crust of bread likely to come her way. She moved like a tattered spider, veined hands clutching parcels, her rags lumpy with what she called her treasure. She slept in the bleached sheds unless they slung her out and she always came back, whining and muttering.

'She seems harmless enough,' said a young salt. 'Leave her be!'

'Auld witch! I caught her trying to steal on board last week. 'Tis bad enough having a woman aboard, but that woman, makes your guts run green!'

The young sailor spat and walked over to where the woman had ended up against a coil of rope.

'Have some food, mother,' he said, squatting beside her. 'I saw you gowking at wor snap.'

She stuffed the bread and cheese in her mouth, red eyes glaring at him.

'Not your mother, boy!' she snarled.

'Ah, plague take you!' He was indignant and sat back with his friend. 'You're right – you can't even be kind to one like that.'

'It's like dogs,' the older man said. 'Some are born plain mean and some get kicked so bad they go that

109

way. With an auld bitch like that who cares? She's bad luck, that one.'

The old woman skittered away out of sight, between a wall and a shed. Mebbes they'd leave her be a while here. She started and swore silently at every footstep, flattening herself against the stone, head ducked down between her bony knees. Sleep may have come, she couldn't tell; nightmare shadows and her waking life were indistinguishable. But it was quiet and dark except for a knife-blade of moonlight that rippled over her bundles.

She clutched at her bony chest and swallowed a burning pain rather than cough and have them hunt her out again. It was still there. Her treasure. The slip of paper that had brought her to the docks although now she couldn't remember what it was about. She had to do something with it. What? She rocked until her shoulders were aching but nothing came.

It was months later before she remembered. It was a map. Ach, where had she got it from? It had been years ago. And what was she to do with it? No way could her bag of bones take her on any journey. The docks would see her last days.

She stood like the carcass of a crow wired to a fence for a warning. She snuffed. Sawdust! Her ears led her to the dry dock and her eyes slid sideways as she passed the construction of a new ship.

'Get out of it! Keep your evil eyes away from here, grandma. Be off with you!'

They set the dog loose, and tongue lolling, barking like fury, it bounded towards her, then suddenly flattened against the ground seven feet from her, whining and trembling.

'See her off, you useless mutt! See her off!'

She smiled and tottered away. Dogs! She could sort them!

The moon was full and the dry dock empty when she ghosted back to the fresh-cut timbers. She wished for a cloud and when it came, she flitted on to the bare deck and lumped herself invisible by the great oak mast. She drew out a nail-thin blade and cut into the wood, scrabbled in her clothes and finally sat back, shallow gasps of air rattling her throat like wire.

She'd been so busy she hadn't noticed the feet creeping up on her. A shape stood there, blotting out the moon.

'What are you doing?'

'No harm, young sir,' she twittered. 'Pity a poor old woman.'

'I'm no young sir, you old faker.' The shape sat next to her. 'I'm as welcome here as you are, if they but knew it. Though they've never had anything but good luck from me being on board! Call me Patience like my mother. What are you doing here?'

'This ship has a voyage to make, Patience,' hissed the old woman. 'Give me a pipe. She'll make a thousand first, but then she'll go on the strangest voyage ever. Happen you'll be aboard, Patience, happen you won't.'

'Are you there, Simon Quint? Why aye, lad, show yourself!'

Patience stood up.

'I'm not sleeping. All's well and quiet.'

'You shout us if you need help! It's quiet the night.'

'Aye,' Patience said, and sat down again.

She waited until the men had gone.

'Tell me about this voyage, grandma,' she said.

'Stranger voyage you'll never hear of,' the old

woman told her. 'Maybe to Davy Jones's locker, maybe – I can't tell.'

She tapped the mast with the side of her hand.

'Go on, tell me more,' Patience said. Mad as the birds! But the old woman said nothing, and Patience took her hand. It was still warm but there was nothing beating at the wrist. What a thing! She scooped up the featherweight body and her bundles and dumped them down on the dock.

The sky cleared and she looked to where the old woman had tapped at the mighty oak. She wondered. But then she heard the men come back and swaggered to her feet.

'All reet, Quint?'

'Reeter than you'd know or guess,' she said.

The Queen Of The Quayside Holds Court

The good folk of Newcastle had heard enough about Queenie's quay to pass on scandals that snowballed, until people who'd never seen her would have sworn she lay somewhere between Lucifer and Lucrezia Borgia.

'Go down to Queenie's quay? Not for a hundred pounds!'

Which suited Patrick Monplaisir very well. He had swaggered off a ship, loaded with coins and jewels, and needed a place to disappear for a while, cool his heels. As usual, he was in that delicate position, a half step out of the frying pan and damned if he'd put his nimble feet into any fire.

Come down here at your peril. He strutted past the deep-sea stench of fish and brine-soaked ropes, trampling over ends of rope knotted into salty fists bunched on wrists of frayed hemp. He stepped over chains as big as his waist, lashed around iron posts and sliding heavily through the air to dip into the slapping waters. He watched the heavy links sliding out again like sea snakes rattling across hulls bubbling with rust and salt crusted like dripping paint. Yeah, he'd get another ship at the right time. He picked his way carefully as the soles of his shoes slipped on a skin of fish scales and his heels caught between worn stones filmed with green slime.

At the end of the quay, the last bit of land between

here and Norway, he found the human dregs and debris of the oceans. Men who walk uneasily on the unmoving earth, men in rags of many faded colours, toothless, gold-toothed, eyes bleary or twinkling in a scrawl of wind-woven lines. They'd sign on board for food and drink alone and call themselves lucky, their glory days as faded as the tattoos smudging and darkening on their skin.

Free and easy with words and money, Patrick Monplaisir bought himself a place among them, and two weeks later they could all have sworn he'd been there for ever.

Except Queenie. She knew his sort, she'd seen them come and go. They came glib and generous and left handcuffed to bailiffs, protesting their innocence, prepared to swear away anyone else's life other than their own. She hadn't dealt with this Monplaisir yet and sometimes late at night he would feel her eyes burning into him, taking the full measure of his rotten soul.

This grey dawn they all lay asleep, Queenie sprawled on a coil of rope above them like an ancient tribal queen. No-one knew where she'd come from or when. She was just there, ragged and regal, a muscled sagging hill of a woman. To outsiders she was outlandish, in weathered trousers, a scarlet cloth wound around her waist, threadbare shirt and a flapping waistcoat with hints of rich gold embroidery. The gold embroidery didn't fit with the rest and neither did her fine hands, brown as her neck and face; her eyes were unblinking and her hair showed only wisps of raven-black and grey under a rough silk cloth knotted at the nape of her neck.

She woke herself up with a snore louder than cannon-fire and booted the calf of the nearest slumped body. He groaned and rolled away to sit up as she kicked him again.

'Get your idle arse up the dock, you dish of lubberwort,' she said. 'Queenie's got the thirst of a whale this morning!'

'Give me the money,' he whined, rubbing his leg. She wheezed with laughter.

'It's a good thing I've got a moonshine memory, Jackie-boy,' she said. 'I won your lousy pants off you last night, and by christ, if I wasn't a lady, I'd strip you naked. I told you I'd let you off for two penn'orth. So it's up to you, bonny lad!'

She pulled out her knife and surged towards him, and away he went, yelping, crashing over crates and chains with the seagulls jeering him on.

'You're a bloody hard case,' Patrick said. 'Poor sod's not even awake yet.'

'Shite to that, Mr High and Mighty,' Queenie said scornfully, cutting a plug of tobacco. 'He shouldn't play a natural born woman at cards when his pockets are empty.'

'You're no bloody woman, Queenie, and you were never born natural or otherwise,' Patrick said with a dangerous familiarity. 'They got you out of a furnace in one piece cuz the heat couldn't melt you into nothing useful. Goddamighty, here's me with a bloody shark thrashing round my brains from that bloody drink, and you're shouting for more! They'll never bury you, woman, you'll be pickled upright and sold to a freak show.'

Queenie considered him. Mouthy bastard, cocky sod, he'd only been here a fortnight or so and he was getting on her nerves.

'Oh, I had a mother,' she said. 'I had a lovely mother – the sort of woman who'd cross the street if she saw

115

me coming now. Not a drop ever passed her lips. She'd never have sat around with the likes of any of us. I remember it like yesterday. We lived out in the countryside, in the hills – hell, I could take you there and show you . . .'

'Yeah, yeah, yeah,' he sneered. 'I heard it all yesterday too. I heard all about your sainted mother and the rose trees and – what did you say – you had an orchard and a cow? Hens? Let's go there and see it. Today. Right now. Only I never heard about your father, Queenie. What was it, a virgin birth?'

'Step over here and say that, Mister Monplaisir,' she said. 'Come over here and say that!'

'You come over here and make me, Your Highness,' he mocked.

Queenie rocked on her heels and stood up, towering over him like the wrath of God. She swayed towards him and grabbed two handfuls of his shirt, hauling him to his feet.

'Oh, come off it, Queenie,' he whined. 'Can't you take a joke?'

'You can joke me from here to kingdom come,' she spat at him. 'And you do, your sort, fools that you are. But no-one says a word about my mother, good or bad. You've done it before and I've heard you when you thought I was asleep or sleeping it off. You've got a lot to learn. I sleep with one eye and one ear open and I see and hear every word and every deed. And what I don't see or hear gets back to me, you can be sure, *Mister* Monplaisir.'

She had lifted him up so that his toes were just trailing the ground. She straightened her mighty arms and carried him like a puppet to the edge of the quay and hung him out over the slow greasy tide. She started to laugh.

'There's only one way with your kind,' she said as he tried to grab at her arm. 'You stink and I can't get the smell of you out of my nostrils. Get yourself clean!'

She hurled him outwards, and roared with laughter as he hit the water. She nodded to herself; he could swim like an eel and for all she cared he could keep swimming until he drowned. She strolled back to the rest of the waking mob.

'You've got to tell them,' she said, stuffing her pipe with tobacco and puffing peacefully into the pale sunrise.

No-one said a word. The reluctant bather had had it coming. They'd seen it for days now. He'd been pushing Queenie ever since he arrived. She'd thrown them all in at one time or another, and even jumped in after Jackie-boy when she saw he couldn't swim.

'I've thrown better than him in seas worse than this,' she said, her eyes oceans and years away. 'Captain John Drinkwater was the first, and he was a bloody drink of water, I can tell you. First ship I ever sailed on, and I'd passed myself off as a boy. Captain Bastard John got ideas on the high seas when he found I was a young woman. They all did. I thought to myself, Queenie, tho' I had a different name then, I thought, start at the top or it's curtains for you. Straight over the side with Captain John and I never had another word of rubbish from the scabby lot of them. Did you know, did you, my first voyage and every man on board asking for my hand?'

They knew. It was one of her favourite stories and she liked to start the day with a good one.

'Here's your chef, Queenie,' said Sim, chuckling as Jackie-boy came hurrying back with a bottle wrapped in waxed paper. She took a huge swig, re-corked it firmly and stowed it in her shirt.

117

She felt warmer almost at once, and looked around at her verminous court. As bad a bunch as you'd find anywhere and she was proud of that. She felt like a buccaneer out here. They were all headed nowhere, their only maps a tangle of memories coloured and distorted by drink and bravado. But today . . . something was going to happen today. She had a feeling.

'What day is it, Sim?'

He scratched his bald head. Bald as an egg and addled with it, Queenie swore.

'How should I know, Queenie, eh? It isn't Sunday or the preacher'd be down here trying to save our souls. Can't be Saturday or them bloody kids'd be down here making trouble. But it's early yet. Could be Monday, I suppose. Then there's Tuesday, Queenie, what if it was Tuesday? Or else . . .'

'Give me bloody patience!' yelled Queenie. 'I know the days of the blasted week, Sim. I just don't know what *today* is. Our smartboy swimmer would know. Hey, Jackie-boy, earn yourself a drink. Go see if *The Mermaid's Eye*'s due back yet.'

He glared at her.

'You get the drink when you come back,' she said sternly. 'And you'd better make it sharp, my laddio. This bottle won't last all morning.'

Jackie rushed away like a rat down a drain.

'I get it,' said Sim. 'You've got a real soft spot for Hjalmar Gustaffson, haven't you? I've seen the love-light in your eyes, oh Queenie!'

He sang the last bit and gave her a lopsided bow. She took another drink and considered belting him one. What the Hell. She *had* got a soft spot for Hjalmar. He was as tall as her for a start. And he wasn't afraid of her tongue or her fists. He could match her drink for drink, and never goaded her on to the sky-high braggadocio she couldn't resist from the quayside scum when she was too drunk to slap them silent. He was the one equal she'd found in a world of rats and worms. And he was the skipper of *The Mermaid's Eye*.

A dripping figure hauled itself over the edge of the dock.

'Enjoy your swim, Mister Monplaisir?' she asked lightly.

He glared at her.

'You think you run this place,' he said. 'You think you can tell everyone what to do.'

'Patrick,' she said, warningly, 'learn something. I never wanted to be in charge here or anywhere. But if you're not in charge, there's always someone telling you what to do. And I won't have it.'

Sim held out a shirt for Patrick and he peeled off his sodden clothes.

'Queenie!' called Jackie-boy, '*The Mermaid's Eye*'s due in at noon.'

She handed him the bottle and grabbed it back as soon as he'd drunk.

Hjalmar Gustaffson! She'd shipped with him years before and even told him she was a woman when no-one else on board knew. And he'd done nothing about it, although they were sharing a bunk. Yes, it was high time *The Mermaid's Eye* came back into port, and she fancied hustling her way on board. A sea trip would do her the world of good. Of late she'd been spending the odd night in gaol for brawling and drunkenness, and she knew the law was out to get her. It was becoming a regular sport. Go and pick up Queenie, she's always doing something wrong.

Yes, she was just a little uneasy. And worse than that, she was bored.

She turned her back on the scruffy crew and gazed

119

out to sea. Keeping a weather eye, she thought. The dawn mists hung in shifting folds. She'd be lucky if *The Mermaid's Eye* made it by noon. Still, that ship always had been lucky. She was rumoured to have skirted ice floes in total darkness, flown like a sand-marten at high tide through the fanged jaws of rocks swilled invisible by boiling waves. The worst storms had devoured dozens of ships like fire ripping through matchwood, and calm would find *The Mermaid's Eye* with no more damage than a shredded rigging or a torn sail. Queenie had seen her built.

Oh, she'd seen her built, and she smiled with a glorious secret. She never smiled that way facing land. The sun fingered a pale path through the damp grey cloud and stroked a line of sheer beauty along her cheekbones. She'd sail out with her this time. She knew it.

Miles away, she started as Sim's voice babbled through to her, his hand plucking at her waistcoat.

'Queenie, there's someone here says she knows you.'

Plague take her whoever she was! How was she to will *The Mermaid's Eye* to port if she was to be forever interrupted? She turned with a frown. Jesus! There was a face she never thought she'd see again. She was torn between a bellow of joy and sheer rage. She steeled herself against either, just rocked on her heels until the frown became a scowl.

'So, Alice Yeldham, you've found your way down here after all these years. What do you want?' she sneered.

'Nothing changes with you,' said the other woman. 'You've got a chip stuck in your heart and your brain, Queenie, but I'll tell you something to shift both. Here – it's my best.'

She held out a bottle. Queenie let her hold it for a full

minute, while her eyes ran over the flashy figure. Alice copied the latest styles but used outrageously gaudy fabric that turned heads. One row of lace at the bosom? Alice had six. A pretty pink muslin hooped and ribboned? Alice wore vermilion caught with chrysanthemums of satin. A daring ankle showing a glimpse of rosebud embroidered stockings? Alice hoicked her skirts to mid-calf and her legs were a riot of jewelled peonies. The good folk took her for a whore on sight and so did the customers at her dockside bar, El Dorado. But they never made that mistake twice.

Alice was a brewer; she'd learnt her trade from Battling Jack Yeldham, her father. He'd raised her alone when her mother died. He had been proud of his daughter and then dismayed when it was clear that her only wish was to carry on his business. He'd had ideas about grandchildren and a good marriage, but by the time it came to it, he was too old to better her in a fight. The El Dorado had flourished in his lifetime and continued just the same with Alice in charge: good ale, heady wine and spirits that took you far away to dreamland after you'd lurched and tottered to your doorway bed.

Alice would have no robbery and no brawling on her premises. What the girls did after hours was no affair of hers. She'd been in the El Dorado all her life, except for two years when things had come to a head with Battling Jack. Then she'd thrown in her lot with Queenie, and the pair had scandalized the whole region by travelling round fairs. Two women alone and seeming to like it that way? They dealt in gold and silver curiosities, no trash and no questions asked. Queenie had gone sour on Alice when she announced she was going to marry a packman, and when he evaporated overnight, she'd seen her friend right until the baby was born, installed them back with Battling Jack and taken to the high seas again.

She nodded and took the bottle. Alice sat beside her as she drank, both looking at the veiled horizon.

'Well?' asked Queenie.

'They've taken my Princess,' Alice said, shivering.

'Who?' Queenie became massive with rage. Princess was Alice's daughter and the child Queenie had never had.

'There was a bunch of them in the El Dorado last week. I didn't like their looks. All grey and brown robes and eyes that click over everything, remembering. Jonah the potman was for throwing them out, but I know better. Treat their sort nice and there's no trouble. I thought they were bailiffs, fool that I am, but he knew different. Well, one of them took a shine to Princess and she'd have nothing to do with him. She's her mother's daughter. He started to grab at her and before I know what's what, she's tipped their ale over them, upturned the table and I've got a riot. So they came and got her today.'

'They? I've had the bloody sheriff and his miserable lot down here more times than I can say. She'll get a few days locked up and out again. They've got bugger all else to do than come and make our lives a misery.'

'I know about the sheriff, Queenie, give me strength! I pay him and his snivelling hangers-on to leave me be. These were foreigners, some of them, and churchmen. Come to seek out the wicked. Witchfinders!'

Queenie laughed.

'Oh, I heard about them when they last locked me up. It's a flash in the pan. They'll not be here long . . . Alice Yeldham, you're scared. I've never known you scared. Tell me.'

'The sheriff and the council and the church have

hired them. Twenty guineas for every witch they catch. They've got Princess for a witch, Queenie. They won't even let me see her. It's been three days now.'

'How is Princess a witch?'

'She's supposed to trap men with her beauty. Steal their souls for Satan. Queenie, the same men burnt thirty-five women in Yorkshire.'

Queenie frowned and put her warm arm round Alice's shoulder.

'They won't get Princess, by thunder!' she said with fire. 'I can get my way in and out of that blasted gaol!'

'Then what?' said Alice. 'You think they'll leave her be at the El Dorado? They've got Judith, the baker's wife too. And Katherine – the carpenter's widow. Who's next?'

'You and me,' said Queenie. 'They'll swear you sell the devil's brew and me, well, they'll find something on me. That bedswerving baker's been lusting after a new wife for months! And Widow Katherine, mouth like a chicken's arse – she wouldn't look at another man. I'm glad you came down, Alice. We'll find a way through this one. I knew something would happen today. My bones, my aching bones, they're never wrong.'

She turned to the ragged bunch of men.

'We've got work to do, boys. And the booze is on Alice, isn't that right, bonny lass?'

'No question,' said Alice, shifting close to the solid raging heat of Queenie's body.

Midnight on the quay, and Queenie's crew were juiced up for the next day. Alice had been recklessly liberal with liquor at any word of dissent, and there was plenty stashed under Queenie's rope-coiled throne to souse the dawn stragglers.

123

The misty day had revealed no *Mermaid's Eye*. Under starlight and a moon verging on full, Queenie's eyes were still glazed open in her vigil for the ship.

'Do you remember Meldon?' Alice said.

Queenie stiffened and turned to her with drunken dignity.

'Meldon?' she said, disguising the stabbing joy the name fired through her body. For that night of delirious power had been trumped by Alice and her quick-tongued packman. She'd preferred to dismiss it as a dream.

'I know I was a fool, Queenie,' Alice said. Tough for a woman like her to admit to any regrets. 'But what do you do when your body goes wild and won't hear a word of reason?'

'You tell me,' Queenie said roughly. 'Meldon was when *my* body went wild, and never since. It's been the oceans and the bottle for me. Oh, I don't blame you. I'm too old for that. But I remember.'

Alice clasped her hand. Queenie closed her eyes.

It must have been twenty years ago. They'd done Meldon Fair and cleaned up; there was enough money to buy a title between them, or so it felt. The sun had kissed the sky with gold at dawn, painted the clouds like a chalice and warmed them all day. At sunset, they'd sat by their fire out of the village, and the light had burned like iron in a forge, molten crimson lavish over the horizon. Then Alice had dug a straw-wrapped bottle from their cart, one she'd been saving . . .

'For a special occasion.'

Queenie heard her voice again, rough as a fiddler tuning up for a wild dance. The liquid tasted like raspberries and sea foam, cream and dew drops. Who had touched first? Whose fingertips had crept forwards first, bringing a shimmering web of desire, whose lips had dared to move against the other's first? Queenie would never know.

But suddenly, they were so deep and thrillingly inside their flesh that they had left the earth and they were flying. Over a lake, where her fingertips trailed the chill water so fast it was like a burn, around the church spire widdershins, laughing like starlight; they had perched in a tree like owls, seen all the tiny grey quicksilver creatures rustling from dry leaves; their speed was the exuberance of water creatures nose-diving, bubble-skinned against the current.

The next dawn they woke in each other's arms, naked and hot with dreams and ecstasy. There was just a moment when they could have spoken, but neither did. They made breakfast in silence and talked about the daily nothing as they packed up.

A week later, Queenie had stayed up by the fire and fallen asleep before Alice came back. A week after that, Alice had blurted out that she was in love with the packman, and Queenie had said:

'Never tell me his name. I couldn't help but curse him.'

Alice Yeldham sighed now into the chill dockside darkness.

'Do you think we could do that again?'

Queenie shuddered. That moment was gone for ever. But she kept Alice's hand loosely in her own. Her thumb found a life of its own and caressed the achingly soft inner wrist. Her wind-blasted face flickered to warm life as Alice traced her cheekbones and nose.

'I'm worried about *The Mermaid's Eye*,' she said.

They drifted off the quay. There was a second when

they faltered high above the waves, but their eyes met and they flew onwards. It could have been moments or hours later when they saw a curve of lights on the shifting waters. They swooped downwards, salt water icing their faces with fine spray.

The crew of *The Mermaid's Eye* were having a high old time, banging down hands of cards and draining bottles, reckless with laughter, less than a day short of land. Queenie and Alice breathed deep and landed on the deck like feathers, velvet-glided below deck and ghosted the third door open. A man sat on his bunk there, a half empty bottle and a candle his only company. His blond mane was ruffled by silver, his beard tousled and tawny.

'You!' he said with a great gust of breath.

'Think of this as a dream,' Queenie told him. 'You'll be in port within the day, Hjalmar, never fear.'

'And when your ship comes in,' Alice crooned, 'there'll be a party, Hjalmar, a welcoming party you can talk about for the rest of your life.'

He lumbered to his feet and came towards them. Alice squeezed Queenie's hand and they fled along the corridor, up the stairs to the night air.

'Wait!'

They stood, poised at the foot of the mast. Queenie ran her hand over that well-known trunk and they gusted up into the darkness, flew round the mast three times – widdershins, widdershins – and were gone.

Back on the quay, the cold seized their guts and rattled them like a starving dog. Alice took out another bottle. They did it justice and when they woke, they were close and warm as chicks under the feathered breast of a mother thrush.

*   *   *

Queenie swaggered into the El Dorado, and her arrogant grey stare swept the room, knocking hostile glances and whispers aside like ninepins. Jonah the potman squared up to her until Alice pushed him aside.

'I thought you'd died, it's been so long. What do you want?' she asked, loud and cold.

'I want a drink,' Queenie said, slurring. 'Last time I came in here I was almost poisoned. Maybe you've learnt your trade by now.'

She roared with laughter and leant over the bar to pinch Alice's cheek.

'Alice, we shouldn't serve her,' Jonah said.

'Oh, you take your orders from a potman now, do you?' Queenie grinned. 'I wonder if that's all you take from him!'

'Have your drink and get out,' Alice said, going crimson.

'Well, now,' Queenie replied, as the doors burst open and her mob came straggling and cursing towards the bar, 'that's a nice decent way to treat an old friend. You know what she said to me, boys? "*Have your drink and get out*," she said.'

'No manners, some people,' Jackie-boy said.

'I think she should apologize,' Queenie said. 'I think a drink on the house for me and my friends would be a good way of making me feel better. What about it, Alice Yeldham?'

'No-one gets free liquor in my bar,' Alice told her. 'Let's see the colour of your money, Queenie.'

Queenie swayed and stared at her.

'I've heard there are those who can drink free in the El Dorado. And there's one or two can sleep free here. It's all over town. Alice Yeldham and her precious Princess! You can't call them whores cuz they don't sell it, they *give* it away! And they give it away because who would buy it? *No-one!* That's who!'

'You've gone too far this time!' Alice screamed, tearing a copper ladle down from the wall and swinging it at Queenie's head. 'Jonah, get the sheriff!'

For a big woman loaded to the gills, Queenie was surprisingly canny and nimble. She danced out of Alice's reach, goading her to follow.

'I told you she'd be trouble!' one of the regulars muttered and earned himself a grimy knuckle sandwich from Sim. Jackie-boy pitched in behind him, and stools and mugs and tables met skulls and ribs and shoulders to a cacophony of curses and taunts.

The sheriff burst in, and all the room froze – except for Queenie, who strode up to him.

'I'm glad you got here,' she said, clapping him on the shoulder. 'This woman's running a bawdy house and there's some strange stuff going into the pisswater she serves for ale. I want her charged. I want this terrible place closed down. She's giving the docks a bad name!'

The sheriff was speechless.

'Have you gone stark raving mad, Queenie? I'm taking you in for a start. What's going on, Alice?'

'She came strutting in here, sir, blind drunk and asking for free booze. I said no and she started miscalling me and my daughter. She's got a mind like a hog wallowing in its own filth. I want her arrested. You're barred from here, Queenie, barred for the rest of your miserable life! Which won't be long the way you're going!'

'Oh?' Queenie loaded the one syllable with total scorn. 'Then why have they arrested your precious daughter, Alice Yeldham, tell me that!'

Alice glared at her.

128

'We haven't arrested your daughter,' said the sheriff. 'What's she moithering on about?'

'It was the king's men and some spanish priest, Sheriff, three days back. She's in your goal now and they won't let me see her. This slop-bucket tramp knows everyone's business!'

The sheriff looked shifty.

'I don't know anything about Princess,' he said. 'If it's the king's men and the bishop's, then it's out of my hands. But they deal with . . . *witchcraft* . . .'

'Whoring!' bellowed Queenie. 'Where's the witchcraft in that, eh? It's the oldest sin in the book, Sheriff. A whore for a mother, and the daughter goes the same way! Get me up to that gaol and I'll tell your fancy cardinal what Princess Yeldham does! Bugger all to do with witchcraft! Hah!'

The sheriff stared at her. Why couldn't they have taken her instead? And what if she knew about the backhanders he took so freely from Alice and every other bar on the quayside?

'I'm taking the lot of you in,' he blustered. 'And the El Dorado is closed until further notice.'

Everyone rushed for the door: too late. The sheriff's men stood in a great phalanx beside the carts and cheerfully clubbed and cuffed the lot of them inside.

Oh, what a welcome sight through the respectable thoroughfares: three loads of quayside scoundrels bound for prison, and two of them women. Queenie! The name flew from malevolent lips like a poisoned dart as she passed by, hurling obscenities and curses at the top of her powerful voice.

Patrick Monplaisir had not been at the El Dorado. Queenie had given him a special task. She'd let him believe that she knew he was different from the rabble, and that his value and price were naturally higher. So he was lounging on the dock when *The Mermaid's Eye* bobbed into sight, and he attached himself to the huge Norwegian skipper as soon as his foot touched dry land.

'I've got a message from Queenie,' he murmured.

Hjalmar looked deeply suspicious: why would she be using a slippery customer like this? But he remembered his dream, and when the man showed him her dragon-head ring, he listened, nodded and finally grinned.

'Moonrise?' he asked.

'And moonshine,' Patrick said with quiet triumph.

It had not taken long to find Princess. Queenie's crew were roaring out every song they knew and nothing would shut them up. Finally the gaoler had appealed to her to do something and she bellowed:

'SHUT IT!'

Immediately there was silence.

'But, my fine laddio,' she added, 'they'll start up again any time I say, and then who'll be walking the streets looking for work?'

'What do you want?' he asked surlily.

'I want to see the whore!' she shouted. 'The one they've got for a witch! I want justice on Alice Yeldham and her whoring bastard!'

'You don't go near Princess,' snarled Alice. 'If I can't, you can't.'

'No-one gets in there except the king's men and the bishop's men,' the gaoler said.

'Take it away, boys!' ordered Queenie.

The mob began to bellow a song.

'There once was a goaler with a fistful of keys
Loved a lass whose locks were all gold
But none of his keys could open her door,
For the right one was rusted and old!

Though he fiddled for hours at her little keyhole,
Though he oiled it and tried every play,
Her door stayed shut tight all day and all night.
The gaoler could not find the way!'

'Oh, blast you!' said the gaoler as the walls rang with shrieks and laughter. 'All right, you can see her. Five minutes, mind. I'm not running a bedlam here! And you both walk ahead of me. I've got a pistol here.'

'And is it all cocked and loaded?' jeered Jackie-boy.

'Shut it!' said Queenie.

She and Alice jostled and cursed each other all the way down to the dungeon.

'We're past the stacks now, Queenie,' said Alice.

'Time for some games, boys,' Queenie roared, smiling hugely at the half-sozzled mob around the captain's table. Patrick Monplaisir smirking and randy alongside Hjalmar and his shipmates, and Princess and the carpenter's widow carousing like good 'uns. The gaoler was going to have a hard time explaining what he was doing mother naked in the deepest dungeon. Curse him! Call it witchcraft, thought Queenie, call it a big fool of a man who doesn't believe a woman can deck and strip him in less time than it takes to turn a key.

She felt a bit bad about Hjalmar. The big Norwegian had fallen in with the idea of a party run by her immediately.

'We'll only borrow the ship for the night, back by dawn and none the wiser, but all the happier,' she'd told him. Another big fool tricked by the gleam in her eye. He read her twinkling *I want* as I want *you*: she wanted his ship. And was about to take it.

'Games,' she said, standing up and snapping her fingers at Princess. Alice grabbed a tambourine and rang out a rhythm through the smoke. Her daughter teased one of the brilliant scarves from her neck amid roars and leers. She tied it round the flesh-greedy eyes of Patrick Monplaisir. The scarlet and black folds sat above his grin. He thought she had chosen him. But she flourished another scarf and lashed it tight to blind the old sailor on her other side. She darted round the table like a quayside goodtime girl, pinching cheeks and squealing at pinches, silk fabric flying from her neck and shoulders like crazy snakes, until all the sailors were blindfolded and Alice tarantella-ed her tambourine.

'Come along, boys,' said Queenie, and led the stumbling dance round the table three times and out on to the deck. Alice brought up the rear and Princess darted the other way. Alice and her tambourine were almost drowned by the raucous shanties the sailors bellowed, and over the decks and around the mast they went.

'Queenie, I'm dizzy!' puffed Hjalmar. 'Where am I?'

'You'll be lying down soon enough,' Queenie said throatily, and speeded up the lurching line. She swung her arm high and flung Hjalmar ahead into the darkness. The line of sailors jigged and jostled through the gap in the railing where there should have been a gangplank. But there was no gangplank, just a drop to the breakers, knitting their heads together around the north and south stack rocks.

132

Queenie flew to the sails, firing orders at the other women. It was mad to take a boat out this way, but there was no choice. And this boat was *The Mermaid's Eye*.

Clouds gusted the moon free and full, silvering the lines of the ship, and made the flapping sails ghastly for a moment. Then, as they filled with wind, they were the fierce curve of a swan's breast rising over her cygnets. Queenie took the helm and *The Mermaid's Eye* sped out into the open sea.

The Mermaid's Eye *Weathers A Storm*

The moon was a sliver short of full, and Queenie decided to leave the sails unreefed and see which way the winds shivered the compass. She'd broken laws and paid the penalty; stealing *The Mermaid's Eye* took her into a different league. No magistrate alive could do anything but hang her if she was ever fool enough to set foot in England again.

And she was filled with a reckless gladness that was better than strong drink. She'd faked the slur and weaving walk that had had them all arrested in the El Dorado, and she'd been so heart-racingly busy from then on that there'd been no time to sag and swill the way she'd found all too easy and familiar amid the hopeless debris of the dock. Her mind was washed clean and clear – and that was a novelty. She liked it.

The wind crept over her cheeks and ruffled her hair. She grinned into the starlight.

'Are you all right up there, bonny lass?' Alice, leaning beside her.

'I should have done this years ago,' Queenie said, staring straight ahead. 'You go and sleep, Alice.'

'Want some company?'

Queenie stiffened. That lilting murmur still got her hot and wistful.

'Nah,' she said gruffly. 'You sleep, Alice.'

Alice kissed her cheek and walked away down the dock, the moon beams curving a lazy silhouette from her love-learned and lovely shape. Queenie gripped the worn spindles of the tiller until her hands hurt. She sucked in her lower lip and bit just short of drawing blood.

Some things you just don't forget, and the last three days with Alice – flying out to find their ship, play-acting a brawl, tricking the idiot gaoler, making drunken blindfold fools of the sailors – such zest, magic and danger had all relit the fire of her feelings like careful breathing on last night's embers. Who's to know when a spark lurks among the ash? Queenie's spark had never died; after nigh on twenty years of a hard time, you'd have thought, she jeered at herself, you'd have thought pride alone would have doused the damned thing called a heart. The seat of the emotions, she told hereslf now, fighting tears, the damned thing starts us awake every morning and goes beating beating beating through the darkest night. Sober and sozzled she'd talked herself well out of what she felt about Alice. Words!

The wise and distant words meant as much as a sailor's wedding vow.

She batted her cheek where Alice's lips had been seconds before. She could still feel them. And, curse it, nothing could cure it, she could feel Alice's lips on hers from twenty years before. Her booze-battered body still thrilled with the sweet touch of Alice's fingers, her heart and breasts and belly burnt with a furnace blast of heat where Alice had lain so close to her.

Seven rolling seas in between, twenty years in between; hours, days and weeks lost in drink and exhaustion and the damn body still remembered everything. Not even like a bleary yesterday. Like it was happening now this minute. There was only one thing for it.

'Alice!' she called.

Alice turned.

'Bring me a bottle,' Queenie said gruffly. 'This night's a cold bitch.'

Damnation, what else could she do? Bring on the harridan, bring on the shite-kicking Queenie they all laughed with. And at, for all she cared. Which was nothing. She sweated tears while Alice brought her a bottle.

'You'll be all right?' Alice asked.

'No bother,' Queenie said, and wrenched the bottle open with her teeth, spit the cork clear over the side – she knew how to spit! 'Me and Lady Moonshine, we'll while the hours away.'

'I wonder where we'll end up,' said Alice, lounging on the rail.

'Davy Jones' locker, ha ha!' said Queenie, swallowing the brain-numbing liquor, one hand locked around wood, one around glass. 'Go to bed, Alice, you cost too much!'

'Ah, we'll survive,' Alice said. 'You're as tough as old boots, Queenie. You'll get us somewhere. Good night, I'm dead.'

She walked away again and Queenie's jaw locked on a silent howl. *I'm dead.* Would it be easier if she was? She forced her eyes away from Alice's dark figure, and looked down the path of moonbeams.

The drink relaxed her, slurred her thoughts through shanties and wild scenes of celebration on every deck she'd ever shipped on.

Alice.

And then we were on an island with sand as white as the Virgin Mary's tits, sorry, Queenie, there's a lady present, boys, but you don't mind, do you, Queenie, you don't mind?

I diven't give a tinker's curse.

The native girls were all over us, by Christ, not a stitch on them, boys, and one of them even put flowers round your neck, you old salt bitch you're cunning, no offence eh, Queenie?

No offence.

But the best was that little spit of coral, bugger knows where we were, and the hospitality, boys, I'm a Christian gent and can say no more. I want to know what our Queenie was up to ... diven't ye slap me, Queenie, it's all meant in fun, are ye humpty with me, ye auld soak? By, she's touchy the night, boys!

I'm not humpty with ye, boys. And I'm not touchy. Just the moonlight and the moonshine. Sends me back, boys, send me back, send me overboard. I cannot move, for all I'd like to throw this aching flesh ten fathoms deep and no more words and breathing.

They had voices like singing canaries, boys, voices to charm the heart out of your breast, eh, Queenie?

I've heard a voice, boys, a voice that's made me deaf to everything else.

Oh, Queenie, Queenie, Queenie's in love! And who's the lucky fella, Queenie?

The rowdy shadows nudged each other in her memory. She closed her eyes.

Alice.

Queenie existed in a vile hangover after that first night at sea. She wouldn't move from the helm unless her roars for another bottle brought no response. She'd cursed at Alice; she'd shocked Katherine, the carpenter's widow, with a lecherous wink when the good woman had brought food; she'd glared straight through her the next time she tried the same useless

137

mission. She sang crude songs at the top of her voice and cursed a stream of names in between times.

'Perhaps I should talk to her,' Princess said. 'She's got a soft spot for me, and she *is* my godmother.'

Alice shook her head. Below decks, the four women had improvised some order. Katherine had kept her house spick and span all her life, had even found a wordless comfort in the rigours of housework when her husband had died. Her door was closed against gossip and the lechers who leap on a widow like blow-flies as if she was dead meat. Any tears she shed came hard, when she was alone and reached out to an empty pillow, half-asleep and dreaming. For some people virtue is a term of scorn, and for others a woman still capable of bearing children and taking care of a husband should be doing just that. Katherine had been a good wife, and the only difference between the lechers and the respectable bachelors was that the latter were prepared to allow her a time of mourning before they pestered her. But months and years passed, and her door stayed shut. The rumours grew, fed by lust and anger, until the witchhunters burst in on her and wrecked the house like bandits, dragged her half-clad through the streets and stripped her naked in prison.

One man said under oath: 'She drove me mad with her beauty. She sent her spirit to torment my dreams and think of wicked deeds of the flesh.'

Another upright citizen had sworn: 'She scorned my offer of marriage and said she would do very nicely on her own, her and her cat. Her eyes looked strange, enchanted, as if she was somewhere else. I thank God I realized how close I was to selling my soul! A witch and her familiar! I was bewitched!'

They had said these things with one hand on Holy Writ, a scribe had written them down, a priest had witnessed them: evidence enough to have her arrested. The graphic stories on the woodcut scandal sheets made no bones about what happened to witches. A confession of guilt – and they had licence to use any methods they chose to get such a confession – meant merciful strangulation before burning. If somehow, denying the sworn testimony of Christian men and the agony and humiliation of the inquisitors, a woman still maintained her innocence, then God's chosen torturers were free to act out on her body any abominable fantasy they could think of. And then she would be burnt alive.

Katherine knew all this, and where she would have kept well away from the likes of Alice Yeldham, and even more from the outrageous swaggerings of one as notorious as Queenie, when the two of them had burst into the airless cell and cut her free, she had fled with them with no thought but FREEDOM!

On *The Mermaid's Eye*, she was taking a room and a task at a time. With all the salt water in the world a rope-haul away, there was no excuse for dirt and disorder. And she had developed a wary respect for Alice Yeldham. She was coarse but decent, given her haphazard quayside life. Queenie was living up to her reputation. Katherine had decided to have nothing to do with her. The idea that such a woman could be a *god*mother!

'I don't think you should do anything,' she told Princess sharply now. 'It'll do no good. You wouldn't even be talking to her, just to the drink. *Drink and the devil went out a-walking, when drink could walk no more, the devil started talking.* If Queenie didn't have that helm to hold on to, she'd be flat on her back. Or her face. Someone else should be steering this ship. She's not capable.'

'Where do you think you'd be without Queenie?' Princess asked indignantly. 'Where would I be? Or you?'

Judith, the baker's wife, refused to listen. For years she'd denied all the gossip about her prosperous baker husband and his wenching: she'd had him swear on the Bible that the stories weren't true and that he was. She'd believed him and dismissed all the tales as vicious jealousy. And then one day he'd brought strangers into the house where she was sewing a doll for their little girl. She jumped up and stuck the needle and thread in her work and offered them cakes and ale. The smile on his face made her sick with terror. He had a red face from the huge ovens, and a clean floury skin. His lips were indecently rosy, people said: now she saw it herself, like an obscenity.

'You see,' he'd said, unctuous and triumphant. 'Caught in the act!'

He'd always joked about almost everything she did, and she smiled placatingly. But he tore the unfinished toy from her hands and brandished it as if he was holding a hot coal, and the men had dragged her towards the door without a word. She'd screamed at him to help her and he just stood with the same smile and flung the doll into the fire. Not one neighbour had said a word or stepped forward to help her as they shoved and kicked her down the street: she read fear on all their faces. Only when they flung her into a cell did she realize that her husband wasn't going to help her, and talking in whispers to Katherine and Princess, she realized he'd condemned her to a death beyond all imagining. She vomited constantly and banged her head against the stones to stop the agony. When the women had virtually carried her away on to the boat, she was past all caring. During the desperate mummery

140

with the deluded sailors she'd remained catatonic, smiling glassily and unable to speak. She never wanted to trust a word to anyone again and only spoke at the thought of her little girl alone with her murderous father and god knows who else. Then she cried, she cried out, *Ruth, Ruth, my baby.*

'That mad old souse up there is my best friend in this life,' Alice told Katherine now. 'You know nothing about her. She's got a heart of gold – and there's many haven't got any kind of heart at all, as we all know. Aye, Princess, go and talk to her. It may do no good, but I'd rather do a thousand times too much to sort things than look back in my life and wish I'd done more. I'll talk to her later myself. Take her a drink.'

Princess went to talk to her godmother, and Alice glared at Katherine.

'Are all your lugs clagged up with sleeping? Can you not hear that wind? I might as well be shipping with a nest of land crabs!' screamed Queenie. 'Look at you all, scuttled off to dreamland like this was a bloody pleasure cruise! I'm captain, master, master's mate, pilot, bo's'n and cabin boy, me! I've had enough!'

She slammed her lantern down on the table, spilling oil, then froze at the sudden ripple of fire. She stood hypnotized and suddenly bleary while Alice leapt out of her bunk and stuffed a cushion over the flames.

'It's the middle of the flaming night, Queenie,' she said sharply. 'And it damn near was a flaming night. You and your boozing! You kept us awake singing – I've heard better from tomcats! What the hell's wrong with you?'

'Drink,' said Katherine bitterly from her bunk. 'Drink!'

Queenie turned her heavy head to stare at the woman in the shadows. She spat.

'I know your sort, my fine lass,' she said. 'Know you? I've had your sort for breakfast and been sick to my guts for a week after! D'you think this bloody heap of timber keeps afloat by magic? There's a tiller to steer her, and I'm dizzy and blind with turning it! There's a hundred ropes to lash and loose and it's my hands growing horns doing it! Have you heard that canny flapping, pet? That's canvas, bonny lass, canvas sails, and I've nigh had my head slapped flat the night reefing the bastards and not one of you up there with a word of can I help keep myself alive? No! Nobody's raised a finger.'

'Let me tune my fiddle and we'll have a wake,' Alice snorted. 'You've been clarting on worse than a nest of hornets ever since we started out. Who the hell'd risk their head offering you a hand? Not me! I've had my ears shaved by the rough side of your tongue for offering you a shive of bread!'

Queenie looked at her and started a maudlin shoulder-shaking wail.

'Even you, Alice!'

'I came and asked you what needed doing,' said Princess indignantly. 'You said you didn't need any help, you were more woman than the rest of us put together.'

'I couldn't let *you* help,' said Queenie. 'My little Princess!'

'Oh, be buggered with that name!' cried Princess. 'There's no space for ladies and idlers on this ship, Queenie. And there's no point wasting words with you right now. You're drunk. And don't waste words giving me no – I've thrown more drunks out of the El Dorado than there are days in a twelvemonth.'

She leapt out of bed, wide awake and furious.

'Water,' she said firmly. 'Queenie, if it's the last thing you do and the shock of it kills you, you're going to drink water till your brain's thinking clear again.'

'Haven't I drunk enough, my little darling?' Queenie said tragically.

'Doesn't the high and mighty Pope of Rome father bastards! And I'm nobody's little darling! Drink!' Princess put a cup in front of Queenie and stood with her arms folded while her godmother grumbled and drank.

'Shouldn't we be saving that water – oh, excuse me for drawing breath,' said Katherine, sitting neatly out of the way.

'Gangway! My bladder's at danger point!' Queenie yelled suddenly and charged out on deck. The night wind slapped her face as she pissed copiously over the side. Her unsteady bulk balanced precariously and she wondered what tight-arsed Mrs Katherine did for pissing. She'd be the type to shit needles! Damn Princess! Was she trying to drown her with water? But as she hoisted herself back to the deck, she found that her eyes were clearer. It was a relief to see one mast instead of the towering vision of three that had driven her raging in panic down to the sleeping women.

That and a sixth sense, she now realized. The clouds were shifting at a fair old lick, and *The Mermaid's Eye* had started a slow pitch and roll among waves that threatened trouble, building up dark and menacing. If they grew evenly higher and higher, slapping the bows like a taunt, it could be just a warning, the edge of some spent skirmish. But if they built up like a mountain then dropped deep as a well, they were in for a storm. Queenie had sailed many a ship with a handful of crew, but that handful had all known what

143

to do, each man racing from one task to another as they did the work of three. They had moved as surely and deftly as a piper's fingers dancing to a blur over a wild tune.

She couldn't imagine the women below catching on fast enough – if it was a storm. Alice would have a go, she was one of her own kind. She was a good 'un, no question – but the rest of them! As much real use on a ship in a storm as a toasting fork made of lard.

She leaned into the wind. No doubt in her bones that it would be a big one.

She wrapped one arm around the mast and hauled in huge cold sobering breaths. The wind ripped at her hair, and she braced herself against the dip and pitch of the deck as she tightened her scarf to keep the damn thing from stinging her eyes. A great black ox of a wave drove at the poop, high back ridged with licks of white foam. She stood stock still. The ship shuddered, then toppled into the kickback glass trough. The next wave ripped out of nowhere, a glossy dune sousing the bowsprit, twisting the craft so that every spar shrieked.

She strode back to the best she'd got for crew.

'Reet,' she said firmly, 'the sea's a nest of serpents out there, and we'll need to be canny and sprite to wriggle through. You'll need both the hands you've got and a dozen more.'

'This is madness!' cried Katherine. 'I'm not taking orders from a drunk: we'll all be drowned!'

'Who's drunk?' bellowed Queenie. 'If you're not with us, keep your useless mouth locked and bolted and we'll do without you. And we will do without you, my fine madam, you're for shore as soon as we find one.'

'I'll do my bit,' Katherine protested. 'But what was

144

all that back there? Cursing and shouting like a madwoman? Were you play-acting drunk? You sound sober enough now! You're an evil woman!'

Queenie half stood as the whole ship shivered the things from the table and Katherine tottered backwards into her bunk.

'Are we going to get a lesson in sailing?' Alice flung this in brightly. 'Only I think it had better start soon, cuz I'm slow at learning and mighty eager to live out the rest of my natural puff. Save your sermons and scrapping, Miss Katherine. You may find your lips using other words to Queenie if we see another sunrise.'

'By, someone's got sense!' Queenie shouted. 'Now there's divil a point in me giving a lesson: we've got a storm here and she's just warming up to her worst. We'll need to drop every sail on every spar and ride her out. You'll need to lash ropes with knots that'll hold and tie every blasted thing on deck down as fast as a duchess's turd.'

Alice stood up.

'Me, I'm game for owt,' she said. 'But I'm not going mother-naked on deck, and I'm as much use a dancer on crutches in this dress.'

'Those lads must have left their kecks behind,' said Princess. 'We didn't exactly give them a chance to pack. Open that trunk!'

Queenie roared with laughter when the women had changed. They were the spit of the salt-ragged quayside mob she'd left floundering off the stacks; except for their hands and faces. They looked wonderful. Even Judith had made to rise and join them, but Alice had sat her down again firmly, and told her to watch the lantern: their lives depended on it. Queenie paired the rest of them off and issued a final warning:

'Divent none of you take a step without you're holding fast to something that's fixed tight!'

She dropped to all fours until she reached the mainmast, Princess in her wake. Best to keep her close where she could save her if needs be. She grabbed her goddaughter's arm and clamped her hand to the wood.

'UP!' she shouted through the rain slapping her cheeks and filling her mouth. She reached the first spar and sat astride it, hauling her darling child up to sit beside her. The canvas was possessed by a thousand demons, the ropes swelled and stiff with salt and rain. A loose rope caught her cheek and she almost lost her grip. Princess eeled ahead of her, numbed fingers working knots loose, lashing in new knots after a back-breaking tug.

'UP!' Queenie roared.

Princess gripped the sodden timber with her thighs and forced herself to climb, eyes closed. With the wind, the rain, the thunder-clouded night, she was best going by touch.

Finally the massive sheet was lashed to impotence and *The Mermaid's Eye* slowed her bucking nightmare ride to destruction. Queenie and Princess gained the deck.

'Do you go down!' Queenie yelled, and pushed her towards safety out of the storm. But Princess clutched her arm and shouted 'NO!' Queenie's curse was whipped to silence, and she inched her way aft along the deck. Alice was a sodden mass glued to a crude nest of ropes and Queenie dived towards her, damning and blasting the beginner's mess she'd made and she'd have to do over.

But for all its cat's cradle appearance, the roping was effective and Queenie shooed her friend back below decks.

Swimming around the mizzen mast, hand over fist, two steps forwards, three steps back, she and Princess made it to the bowsprit, and Katherine. She'd rolled the sprit-sail like a bolt of cloth, but had tied it fast enough.

'Enough!' Queenie hollered into the younger woman's ear.

When she'd clawed her way to the tiller, she found Princess still close beside her. She roared her rage into the careless jaws of the storm and lashed a rope around her own waist and the eel-slippery spindles. For all she yelled at Princess, the girl wouldn't leave her, so she twisted and roped her securely to the railing. Buggered if the waves would grow fat and sleek on either of their bodies!

Princess tore her hair back off her face where the elements had wound it tight as cheesewire to cut her brow and cheek and neck. But so cold and numb was she that the cuts hardly stung. The tilting deck threw her back against the drenched rope, firm as the metal links of an anchor chain. She gripped the handrail and gazed at Queenie's storm-lit face.

For as far back as she could remember, there was Queenie. Louder than her mother. Bigger. So solid that as a child she'd run full pelt at those mighty legs and land her head full in Queenie's belly and never shift her; Queenie's hands round her ribs, strong and sure, her forearm a warm shelf where she'd swing her to sit. Queenie's gold tooth, her gold-threaded scarf, the shining hoop in her ear, her voice rocking out a story and a song to send her squirming and screaming with joy. Queenie was as big as a horse to the child and she climbed all over her, tugged her arms and legs every way there was, then collapsed against the huge warmth. She'd ride along, calling out insults at the top of her voice, knowing Queenie was a lioness who adored her and that she was completely safe.

Later, she'd seen Alice and Queenie argue, and had wanted to rush down the stairs out of hiding to stop them: it was hideous and frightening to see Queenie's eyes blaze like a dagger in the sun and hear her mother's voice grow shrill and scornful. That was in the days before Alice would let her into the bar of the El Dorado, and all she knew was what she could pick up through the crack in the upstairs door. One awful night after a cold and final row, Queenie just disappeared. Princess had pestered Alice asking where she'd gone.

All her mother would say was: 'Queenie's a strange one, Princess. She's taken another boat and hell knows when she'll be back. Or *if* she'll be back. Don't bother me.'

She'd run away down the docks to meet every ship until she was sick with each one of them being empty. She gave up on Queenie and could only remember the glint of gold in her big smile, or the warmth of her arms when she woke on a summer's morning all snug in the sun and wrapped round her pillow. She'd forgotten the way Queenie could light up their back room in minutes and have Alice smiling and sparkling no matter what gobshite drunks she'd had to deal with that day.

Queenie became a legend in the bar: do you mind the time she hobbled the sheriff's carriage horses when the king came to town? And what about when she tied the bishop's robes round the cathedral bell clappers, 'cos she couldn't sleep on a Sunday for the ringing? They'd all laugh and toast her as if she was dead and gone.

Princess had been serving in the bar for eighteen

months when the doors burst open and in roared an unmistakable presence, sozzled and swaggering, bags full of strange coins and carvings, mouth racing on rum and adventures so tall and wide that Alice was laughing like she hadn't for years. Queenie? Princess stood back, suddenly shy.

Queenie was a hundred years older than she remembered and smaller. But there was the gold gleam in her smile; her hand drawing extravagant sketches as she talked.

'And where's my bonny lass, Alice? Where's my Princess? Ee!'

She looked at Princess, and her eyes lit up like a summer sea. She moved forward hesitantly, her hands at a sudden loss. Princess came up to her and all at once she was buried in those arms, safe against that warm body, wrapped in the scent of tobacco and spice she'd forgotten until that moment. Only now her head was at Queenie's shoulder, not her waist.

Since that hug, there had been an awkwardness between them; Queenie had seen Princess as a beautiful young woman where she remembered a giggling rough-and-tumble tyke; she'd seen her elegant dress and had become aware of her own wild garments; she'd searched Princess's face and found something in her eyes that she read as dismay. She thought Princess was embarrassed by her and being polite. The young woman was sure that Queenie had lost all interest in her so she held back – and so it went and the distance grew. Some nights she cried about it, her little-girl-so-loved wanting her fierce protector back.

Queenie didn't feel comfortable drinking in front of what she took as disapproval, and she had stopped using the El Dorado. Princess felt abandoned.

Then came the ugly day when the bastard in church

cloth had run his hand up her skirt and she'd soaked him in good ale. Within hours she was in the gaol, clouted, cuffed, stripped, the men of God making it clear they could do whatever they wanted to her in the name of their God and mauling her in the name of their truth until she knew there was no way out of this dungeon except to a witch's stake. Nightmare. She had heard Alice screaming outside the goal on the first day. And the second. Then nothing. Nightmare and darkness.

Until the key turned and she cowered against the wall for terror of what they'd do to her this time. And then – incredible! – the strength only Queenie had holding her close and cursing like fury, lifting her – and then waking on board ship with Alice bathing her face and Queenie laying out a plan so bold and wild for escape! And with none of her usual throwaway panache, oh no. Her voice was sure and deadly as cold steel. The night they'd drifted past the stacks, Queenie had sat on her bunk and held her close till she slept, soothed her and sworn nothing would ever hurt her again. Princess knew that that mighty heart would beat between her and danger for the rest of her life.

Damned if she'd let Queenie out of her sight! She was sure this storm would do for them and they'd go down together. She was thrown against Queenie's wall of a body and wrapped her arm tight round her waist. Queenie threw her a wild grin.

So maybe they weren't done for! From all Queenie's stories, she'd had storms like this for breakfast and spit them out by way of supper. But she'd never mentioned the sheer cold and the fear. Perhaps her furnace of a heart didn't feel them? Queenie squeezed her bone-cold hand and shouted something the wind ripped away with a shriek of scorn. Princess looked at her

150

serene face and proud smile. If they weathered the storm, maybe she'd get to see the islands where the trees were full of scarlet parrots like autumn leaves! Where crabs the size of cats did a pas de deux with bright blue claws raised like flags! And best of all, her favourite dream, lush forests where silver monkeys flew like butteflies and ate apples the colour of moonlight.

The Mermaid's Eye hauled into port with the defiant dignity of a lady going up her front path in tattered evening dress with a Cinderella hobble at eight in the morning. Damned if she'll give the neighbours the satisfaction of a glance! Beyond Queenie tossing the water rats some coins as they rushed to tie her fast, there was no sign of life, and the ship was only one of many other battered craft limping in for rest and repair. The storm had cleared the skies to a crazy blue, and the shops along the wharf were thronged with cursing and bartering.

Besides, today was the Festival of the Nets, when Our Lady of The Oceans was paraded along the streets in all her gilded glory, the infant Jesus in one hand, and a herring in the other. Grazeby Cove was alive with masked revellers, jugglers, hawkers, cutpurses; every street had its players and tumblers, and the air was filled with noise and smoke as a fire-eater swept a circle clear in the crowd.

'It's a good place to disappear,' Queenie told Katherine. 'Only you're not leaving this ship until I have your Bible oath for silence. I know you hold by what they call the good book.'

'Oh, you've got my silence,' Katherine assured her. 'Am I likely to give myself away? I've you to thank for

151

my life, and I'll never forget that. Nor what brought me to you all. A woman's not safe on her own in this land. Give me the book!'

'What will you do?' Alice asked after she'd sworn.

'What's it to you?' Katherine asked. 'Have I leave to go?'

'Take the book with you,' Queenie said. 'We've no use for it here. It'll be a souvenir, Mistress Katherine.'

She swept from the cabin, Alice a step behind her.

'She'll not be single long,' Alice said. 'The name of a good man and a house to fuss over. I can see it now.'

They settled Judith on deck, telling her to count the seagulls and talk to no-one.

'Not that she would,' Princess said.

'We'll not be long, bonny lass,' Queenie said. 'Just fetching stores and making her shipshape, then we'll hoy ourselves out on to the seven oceans.'

It was impossible to stay together in the holiday crowd, and Alice shouted *food* over the head of a horned clown before disappearing behind a masked demon. Princess clutched Queenie's arm.

'Water!' she screamed, as a line of eels and lobsters danced her away.

Queenie strode through the throng, batting a dancing sun to one side, lifting a drunken Neptune on to a pile of crates, cutting through a wrestling ring by pulling the greased bodies apart as if she was tearing paper.

'Will you take us both on?' said one as the crowd tossed coins and roared with laughter, thinking her outlandish figure part of the show.

'Mebbe later, boys,' she said, banging their heads together.

She dived into the brown cave of the chandler's and

stood a moment. The place was crowded and impatient, and she looked over the heads to the counter. She spat as she saw the man standing there and zigzagged to stand behind him, arms folded and waiting. He was rattling out a volley of broken English and sending the chandler mad with pulling down ropes, emptying drawers and slashing sacks open. Nothing seemed to please him. Queenie smiled slowly.

'Mucchio di Rottami di Roba di Scarto!' she said as he paused for breath.

'Bless us, do you speak his lingo, sir?' gasped the chandler. 'He do seem to be mortal choosy.'

The man swept around, and his face went ashen.

'Quint!' he muttered. 'What brings you here, in my back like a shadow?'

'Oh, sod it, if you're together!' spluttered the chandler. 'Sort yourselves out and I'll do some regular business.'

Queenie's glare drew the man towards her sure as a whirlpool. He barely came up to her shoulder, and his eyes flickered under a landslide frown. She caught his arm and pushed him ahead of her, using his body to carve through the crowd and into a side street inn. She bounced him down the steps ahead of her, ordered ale and sat him in a corner, fenced in by the wall, a table and her long legs propped on an upright barrel. The landlord asked for money, and she nodded at her prisoner, who paid without a word.

'Up to your dirty tricks as usual?' she said coolly.

'I make business,' he said.

'I know your business,' she told him. 'We've some to finish. Thought you could rook a woman, didn't you?'

'I was young, Quint, how was I to know . . .'

'You were born old and crooked, di Scarto, don't

give me that. I'm just working out how to end the business between us.'

She emptied her tankard and took out her knife, digging at her nails with the gleaming point.

'More ale!' she shouted, banging one fist on the table so that the mugs and her prisoner jumped.

'I've got a cargo,' he said eagerly. 'When I come back, I can pay you three times over.'

She looked at him while he babbled, and laughed.

'You don't change,' she said. 'If I let your little rat-hide out of my sight, I'll never see you again. What's it been, fifteen years? Mind, I've changed. No-one's ever fooled me twice, and these days there's no fool would try it the first time. Of course, if your little rat-hide sprung a leak or three, you'd never see your cargo again, and the seas would be a mite cleaner and clearer.'

'Now, Quint, no, you're joking,' he said. 'I can give you a part now, you know how it is.'

'Where's Lola?' said Queenie, drawing a crude, but unmistakable noose in spilt ale.

'Lola? Who's Lola?'

'You tell me.'

'*Madre di Dio*, Quint, that was . . . what did you say, fifteen years ago? A man like me, women come and go, you know? A woman like Lola, I can tell you what happened to her without knowing. What happens to women like her? You're no fool, Quint, whatever else you might be. *Sangre di Cristo!*'

'*Sangre di* Lola, *sangre* di Scarto,' Queenie said quietly. 'There's a lot on your hands, you cheap poplolly.'

'I didn't say Lola was dead!' he hissed.

'What's the difference? Dead or in a dockyard cat-house? Some life, di Scarto, some life you let her choose.'

'I treated her right for the kind of woman she was.' His hands fluttered in the sign of the cross as he saw Queenie's face darken.

'She said you loved her, and she believed you. Fool that I was, I could have sworn you'd be back to pay me, and back with her, once she'd worked out what love is to a shite like you. Never hide nor hair of the pair of you since. I missed seven good berths out of Port au Prince on your account, you oily bastard! You owe me, and you'll pay, and you owe Lola. I'll take hers.'

'What are you going to do?' His eyes had stopped flicking from side to side. This slow mountain of a woman sat like Nemesis, whistling and staring at him like the trapped vermin he was.

'Well, I'm going to fit out my ship at your expense for a start,' she said. 'Then I'll have a root through your cargo and borrow anything I think might come in handy. Then I'll have your hoof print on a bill of sale. That's what you owe me. As for Lola, well, di Scarto, you've always been one for the ladies by your own account. I'll see to it you take a long holiday from raping and seducing. Maybe for ever.'

She swilled the last of her ale and stood up.

'I'm all over this town,' she said. 'I'm five steps behind you, two steps in front, and my knife flies like an eagle. By sundown, that ship of mine'll be trim, and yours'll float a little lighter. Double-cross me this time and I'll introduce you to Davy Jones. Personally.'

She walked out whistling.

She bought some white heather for luck and a bottle of spirits for happiness and let the crowd carry her along. She'd had years to think what she'd do to di Scarto if she ever caught up with him, and right now his terror was as sweet as strong mead.

'Alms, for the love of God!' screeched a beggar, hobbling beside her on a crutch.

'If I'd a leg to spare it'd do you more good!' she roared, and gave him a coin.

She found herself dancing from the cloth-scaled arms of a dragon to a tin armoured St George, arm-wrestling a tattooed drunk who soon gave it up, and then she was swept along in a tide of painted mermaids. She stood stock still to take a swig and the mermaids rushed past her. She turned and found herself eye to eye with a bear.

'I'd be honoured,' she shouted, catching the out-swept paw and whirling around in a reel. By, the lad inside this skin was a tough 'un!

'You're all feet, you great galloon,' she shouted, as he rocked her out of rhythm so that even her muscles couldn't pull him the other way. The crowd was laughing and she went with the laughter, catching the eye of a tall blond lad.

'You have the next one!' she panted, tossing her partner's heavy hairy arm his way. And the lad went into a clinch and shrieked at her as they rollocked down the street.

'She's a *real* bear!'

By Christ! Queenie followed the insult, boozily sure of her prowess. A beardless scallywag, she'd have him kissing the cobblestones in a second! If she could catch him and his nimble partner! She'd take on the both of them!

They burst through the crowd on to the square and the lad skeetered to a halt. A tightrope was suspended from the alehouse to a mast, and a moustachioed man leaning on a cane was cracking a whip as he roared out promises of flying acrobats and tumbling clowns and jugglers . . . a taster for the evening. Blast! Queenie had lost the lad and the 'bear'! No – her eye caught them flitting up the alley between the chandler's and the alehouse, and she stormed after them.

'Wait up there, lad! I want words with you!'

They only raced faster, and she shrugged: this was a blind alley and she'd find them soon enough. She did. They were crouched in a doorway, and she drew back at the scent of fear and the sight of naked steel in the lad's clenched fist.

'Who are you calling a real bear, bonny lad?' she mocked.

'This is a real bear, my bear, you great fool!' the lad gasped.

'So I was dancing with a real bear, was I? And that makes me a great fool? Put your blade away and use your naked fists!'

'I'm not going back to Jethro!' the lad said fiercely.

'Who the hell's Jethro? I don't give a monkey's shite who you're running from. But I'll not be insulted!'

Even through the haze, Queenie could see the lad was in mortal fear. She sat heavily on the doorstep opposite him and took a drink. She looked at him, considering. Hell, she'd met a few that would have called themselves her master, and it was a long time since the last bitter fight to lose the last one of them.

'Are you with that circus in the square?'

Jen looked at her. If ever she'd seen fearless, this woman was it. Now she was sitting like a queen on her doorstep throne, her rough voice softened and strong. And she was a woman: Jen had an instinct to trust her.

'I've a need not to be seen by the bastard running the circus.'

Poor lad! He'd no doubt taken the bear for an afternoon's sport and was shitting himself about how to return her unnoticed.

'We'll get the bear back, feller-me-lad, and the circus'll be gone by tomorrow sundown. You lay low and leave it to me. Diven't ye worry. I've had worse tasks before breakfast many a day. That swaggering gimp!'

'Look,' Jen said. 'I left that smirking turd for dead not a month back. You can guess why. I'm not giving the bear back: she's staying with me. He'd horsewhip her every day, just like he used to. I've got to get away. And I'm not a lad: this is just to make it easier to get around. I'm Jen.'

'I'm Queenie,' she said, crossing the alley and holding out her hand.

She sat and thought. Jen had a story and she'd get it out of her one day.

'And what did you do in this circus, Jen?'

'Oh, women could do nothing but curtsey and simper and collect money. My dad's The Flying Dolphin, an acrobat, the best; if I'd been his son, he'd have taught me. But I've taught myself.'

'And now you need to get away? Far far away?'

'I do. As far as possible.'

'We can't sit here cracking on all day, Jen. Give me your bear. I'll get her past Mister Moustache and the six lives left to him. I'm sailing out at moonrise on *The Mermaid's Eye*. Meet me there and you can sail with us, you and the bear. Or you can have her back and make your own way.'

She stood and held out one strong arm. Jen handed her the bear's chain.

'Take good care of her, Queenie. And if I come with you . . . well, I may not be travelling alone.'

'We'll see who's with us come moonrise,' Queenie said grandly, leading the bear down the alley into the carnival roar.

Any passer-by would have taken Queenie and di Scarto for old friends as they strolled arm in arm along the quay. No-one but the small man knew of the dagger point snagging a jagged hole in his shirt or the blood-stopping grip of Queenie's fist on his upper arm.

'We'll have a drink on it,' Queenie said loudly, and propelled him up the gangplank and on to *The Mermaid's Eye*. Once below decks, she shoved him ahead of her and shook her hands free as if she'd been contaminated. He cowered in a chair while she took out parchment and a quill and sat at the table, whistling.

'What's this? You said you'd got crew, Queenie, but *this*?'

Princess stood at the door, frowning. The man had cheapster, trickster, hustler and pimp engraved in every line. Alice would not have allowed him more than one foot inside the El Dorado.

'It's old business, Princess,' Queenie said, writing with great flourishes. 'Business as well finished before we leave this shore. I wouldn't sail with this no more I would than a barrel of swill, and I doubt he'll be sailing with many come the dawn. Put your blasted name here, di Scarto, it's our bill of sale.'

He signed, trembling as Queenie started a fresh sheet of writing.

'What's that? Haven't you had enough from me?'

'It's the story of your life, *bocca de culo de galina*: it's what you owe to Lola and Jesus Christ knows who else. A full confession, in case you were thinking of

159

singing my praises one day. Every word in here is a noose, *stronzo di cane*, and I can pull it tight any second I choose to. Sign!'

His pallid face went ashen as he read the page.

'*Madre de Dio!* I could be hanged!'

'And the seas would flow cleaner as the crows plucked your bones clean! Sign!'

'Surely there's something I can offer you . . .' he pleaded.

Queenie drew her dagger and nicked the hardwood table.

He signed and stood up.

'You'll let me go now?'

'Sit!'

'Ah, Quint, what more? You've got my fortune and my life in your hands, what else is there?'

'Your quicksilver tongue, laddy-boy. You'll talk yourself into someone else's pockets by dawn. You've done that once too often.'

His eyes bulged and he clasped one hand over his mouth. Princess rushed on to the deck. Queenie laughed and tied his limp body to the chair, then blindfolded him. She ripped his shirt to the waist.

'What the hell's going on here?' Alice demanded, her daughter at her heels babbling mutilation and murder. 'Don't we have enough to run from, Queenie? Let him live!'

'This is di Scarto, Alice. I've told you about him.'

Queenie winked at her and started to sharpen her knife against a stone. She mouthed one word and Alice grinned.

'Perhaps you're right,' she said and took Princess's arm.

'Think again, Quint!' squeaked the blindfolded man. 'You'll never get away with this!'

'I've thought as long as you thought about Lola,' said Queenie. 'My mind's made up. Sing your loudest, *buzzuro!*'

Alice came back with a bowl of steaming suds and lathered them all over the man's head and chest.

'It's only tar,' said Queenie. 'And here come the feathers!'

He squealed like a stuck pig and jerked around in the chair until Alice and Princess held it still.

'He's mighty noisy and tuneless with it,' Alice said sadly. 'We'll need to teach him a different song. What about it, Princess?'

But Queenie sang:

> 'Don't I know you, bonny laddy?
> Are ye not my babby's daddy?
> Are ye not the one who swore
> To wed me when ye came to shore?'

She drew her knife along the foam covered cheek and dropped half his beard in the bowl.

> 'My babby sweet has eyes of blue,
> I love him and I love you too,
> Ah, let me go to sea with you,
> And keep your promises so true!'

She scraped away one eyebrow and made a line through the soap on his scalp. This done, she stood back, smiling and cut away the hair on the opposite side from his newly shaved cheek. Alice and Princess belted out the chorus.

> 'Ah, my dear I love you so,
> The tide is high and I must go.

161

For you cannot go to sea,
With a babby on your knee!'

Queenie whistled the tune as she stripped the hair from his chest, tutting when her knife caught on his gold medallion. She snapped the chain with a twist of her wrist and tossed it to the floor.

The three of them stood back.

'What do you think, Alice? Will I make a barber, do you suppose?'

'Hard to tell with all that soap on him. Here.'

Alice tossed a can of cold water over him and peeled the blindfold from his eyes. He looked ridiculous and with one eyebrow gone, his bulging eyes looked mad.

'He's no beauty, but then, you make your face. He looks more like the man he is now than ever in his life, I'd say.'

Di Scarto glared at them, spitting soap and hair from his half-shaved lips.

'You're not women!' he hissed. 'You're devils! What have you done to me?'

'You rawhead bogy!' sneered Queenie. 'Get yourself a ladylove looking like that! Get yourself a fool to back your trip now, you chiseller!'

She ripped the ropes from his arms and hauled him to his feet, booting him up the stairs like an old sack. His screams and curses were lost in the shouting and songs on the quayside. She saw the moon drift clear from low cloud and nodded.

'East, west, home's best,' she said soothingly, tossing him overboard.

'Trouble?'

She turned. It was Jen.

Jen and three others: no, six, including three small

162

people. Circus midgets? Queenie stared at them, then at the flailing figure in the water.

'Man overboard and that's the best place for him,' she said calmly. 'Time enough for who's who and what's what and fancy introductions later. Hoy in that plank, Alice, and Jen, do you unstitch those great ropes from shore. You! Haul away at this until she's tight!'

Sister Mercy hauled, muttering a breathless novena for those in peril on the sea.

'Reel in this here, and double hitch it there!'

Rowan reeled.

'Let that bugger free 'til your knuckles are trailing the deck, then lash her tight as a pig's squeal!'

Esther leapt on the loose rope and did what she could.

'Leap aboard, Jen!'

Jen landed on the deck as sure as a cat, and *The Mermaid's Eye* lifted out on the tide as sweet as a song. Out of the harbour, Queenie remembered her first order, and strode over to where a robed figure was hanging on like grim death. She took the taut rope from her.

'Whip her round here, I'll show you,' she said. 'Christ, I'll do it for you, woman!'

Queenie was everywhere, Princess her shadow, and the great sails unfolded in the night breeze like slow wings. Finally she was at the tiller, grumbling at the sextant and the tilting horizon.

'And that's the crew?' asked Princess when she seemed to have set a course.

'It is,' Queenie said grandly, 'We've a whole circus by the looks of it: she said she had company. And there's a bear in the hold.'

She threw the last in casually.

'I put her down there so as not to alarm Judith,' she

163

said, as if explaining. 'That one starts at shadows, Christ knows what she'd do meeting a real live bear.'

Princess stared at her. No point asking questions when Queenie had that grim teasing gleam in her eyes. She'd knit it all into a story so tall and wide it'd fit anyone's curiosity. When she was good and ready and not a second sooner.

'Do you go below, Princess, and tell Jen I could use a word or two.'

In the cabin, Judith was sitting upright with more light in her eyes than they'd ever seen. She was smiling shyly at a solemn grey-eyed child. There was a woman with a wiry child wrapped round her neck like a monkey. A bewildered nun sat at the table, clutching a string of rosary beads. Two other strangers sat with yet another child draped between them, and there were bundles and bags everywhere. Alice stood among the chattering explosion and shrugged as Princess came down.

'Food,' she said briskly. 'I'm gutfoundered with the day I've had!'

'I'll give you a hand,' one of the women said, sliding the child on to her friend's lap.

'Queenie wants to see Jen – whoever she is,' Princess said, and the woman with the monkey-child stood up.

'Where's Miss Walnut?' she asked. 'The bear? I'd best feed her.'

'Below decks, according to Queenie,' said Princess. 'That way. Only you'd best see Queenie first.'

Jen raised her eyebrows.

'I'll see to the bear,' she stated. 'Talking can wait a bit, hey Squirrel.'

Princess stared. Queenie didn't like to be kept waiting, but this woman seemed very sure of what she was about. Princess felt a twinge of anger, as if she'd been challenged by Jen's confidence. Didn't the woman know what a privilege it was to be here at all? And to be summoned by Queenie? Just who did she think she was?

'We'll see,' thought Princess. 'We'll see.'

Part Three

Out To Sea

One For All And All For A Nun

'What does that do?'

Queenie shook herself. By, she'd better start watching the brew: she was hearing voices in the cold light of day!

'What does that DO?' The words were gruff and seemed to come from around her knees. She looked down and almost lost her grip on the tiller: seeing things too! She looked around the empty deck. It was best to humour anything that appeared out at sea, she knew, ships had been lost for less. So she smiled at the small leaf-clad creature with the huge brown eyes.

'It steers the ship, my little water-sprite!'

'I am not a water-sprite,' it said, frowning.

'And what might you be, then?' she asked.

'I'm a Turtle,' said Turtle. 'They can go in the sea as well, you know.'

'I do,' said Queenie. 'I've seen turtles as big as a horse.'

And eaten them in a stew or two, she thought. Shut your mouth, Queenie, and close your memory, they can read your thoughts! Never again!

'How does it steer the ship?'

'Buggered if I know,' Queenie said. *Mind your manners, woman, since you haven't any at all!* 'Let's think: it goes down through the deck and then there's a great paddle under the ship.'

'We had paddles on the raft,' said Turtle.

'Whey aye, did you now?' Queenie responded carefully.

Alice appeared with a dish of food and grinned at them both.

'You've met Turtle then,' she said. 'She's a canny little lass.'

'Ee, I'm relieved,' Queenie laughed. 'I thought I was seeing things. Will you take the tiller while I have some snap, Turtle?'

She lifted the child and put her hands on the worn spindles.

'Just hold her steady,' she said. Turtle gripped and nodded seriously. She'd been watching Queenie for an hour before she had the nerve to speak: the woman looked so huge and fierce and angry. And then she'd smiled as the sun broke through the clouds on the horizon, and her face looked completely different, happy, beautiful even. Turtle had been ready to run if she'd been shouted at, and it had taken a lot to repeat her question. But when the giant woman had picked her up, she was so gentle! And now she was letting her steer the ship. And the other woman with the loud laugh and wonderful bright clothes had said she was a canny little lass. She didn't know canny but it sounded like something to be proud of.

'You can stay up here if you want,' Queenie said. Turtle grinned. If she wanted! There was nothing she wanted more.

'Alice, we should all meet on deck in an hour or so. We've covered a fair lick of salt water and the wind's with us. We'll need to set a course.'

'Bonny lass, that'll be up to you,' Alice said. 'We're all at sixes and sevens down there, not a one of us knowing where to go, and I think they'll be looking to you.'

'More fools they,' Queenie said. 'I'd sail for ever, me.'

'And I'll stay with you,' Alice told her softly.

Queenie swallowed and watched her teasing walk down the deck. Ah, Alice Yeldham, if you only knew what I hear when you look at me that way! And never a chance of that, she thought grimly, never go back.

They dropped sail and Queenie slung out a sheet anchor. There was nothing in sight from tipping horizon to horizon, and *The Mermaid's Eye* rode the smooth swells, tugging impatiently for a clean white foam bone between her teeth and a fair wind behind her.

'Well, Dame Fortune has flung us together,' Queenie told the assembled company. 'Buggered if I know what for, but here we are and everyone of you thinking where are we going, I'll be bound.'

The women and children looked at her expectantly. Turtle was sitting cross-legged between her knees, and grinned at Rowan and Esther.

'Well, divent ye stare at me for answers,' Queenie said. 'I'm happy to bide on board and take what comes. Mebbes you'd give me a few answers.'

'I'm for adventure,' said Princess. 'I want to see some of the places you told me about when I was a child. Nights I'd stay awake dreaming of turquoise seas and white beaches ... when I slept I dreamed of parrots and palm trees as tall as a house.'

'I think I have to find this bear a home,' said Jen. 'After that, well, I don't know, Queenie. I've no wish to see England again for the rest of my life. There's nothing there for me.'

'You'll maybe change your tune,' said Queenie. 'I

mind the first time I put out to sea and spat on the shores of England. It was years before I found myself missing the green and the rain and every voice using words I understood. Years.'

Rowan smiled and stroked Esther's hair.

'We've spent a long time on this one, haven't we?' she said. 'We thought the woods were a good place after the village. The river was fine. It's when you get houses and hamlets and towns that it gets difficult. We just want a safe place for us and the children. Somewhere we can be outside most of the time, grow our food, and just get on with loving and living.'

'Somewhere safe?' Alice asked.

'You've got it,' said Esther.

'Oh, how you all talk!' said Sister Mercy. 'Somewhere exciting, somewhere safe! What do you think you were put on this earth for? To hear you, you'd think life was nothing but a heathen junket! I was brought up to be of service to people, to help them and myself to save our souls. That's the sort of love sanctified by God. Your sort . . . well, I know what I know. There's no safe place on this earth, surely you know that?'

'Heathen junket?' said Rowan. 'Sister Mercy, you know how to make a good thing sound bad!'

'And what about you, Alice?' Queenie asked.

'I'm easy,' said Alice. 'It's good not to be working every hour under the sun. It's good to have my daughter safe. It's good to be with my oldest and dearest friend. I'll take what comes. And it's time I saw more of this world. I've been in that blasted bar too long. I'll be brewing because it's what I know best, and I can make the sort of wine you'll all sing for. And now I'll have time for some of those *when I can find the time* things I've been wanting to do for years.'

'Like what?' said Princess. 'I didn't know you weren't happy.'

'Oh, I was happy, my lovely,' Alice reassured her. 'I'm always happy. Only I've been restless for a change for a good while, and wondering what to do about it. Now the change has come and I'm not young and daft any more. I'd be hankering for home if I was. I'll just be old and daft, hey, Queenie?'

'I've been old and daft for ever,' Queenie said. 'Born that way. Here's to it!'

'Well, yes,' said Esther. 'Here's to it. But Sister Mercy isn't happy, are you? There's no point in sitting all tight-lipped and miserable, Sister, you've said what you don't want. What *do* you want?'

'I'm just not accustomed to that as a way of thinking,' the nun said severely. 'I've always been taught to ask God for guidance in this vale of tears. I want the time to pray for His guidance. I'd like to be in a religious order again. That's the path He guided me to. Perhaps I could go to Spain or France or Italy, and do His work there.'

Jen leaned on one elbow, Squirrel wrapped round her back. She raised her eyebrows.

'You said it was the witch-hunters who drove you away,' she said slowly. 'They're racing through Europe like a forest-fire, Sister. We had a troupe of acrobats travel with us last year. The Inquisition had destroyed a whole village, burned every woman there as a witch. There's no safety for women in Europe until they're stopped. And there's no stopping them.'

Judith twitched at the words *witch-hunters* and *Inquisition*. Isabel moved closer to her and held both pale hands.

Queenie looked around at every face and lit her pipe.

'There's worlds out there you couldn't dream of,' she

said softly. 'There's islands where no human foot has ever walked, where the fruit falls out of the trees and you and the monkeys can gorge yourselves. You can bathe in sparkling waterfalls clear as diamonds and sleep under the trees when the nights are so dark you could reach out and touch the stars. You can see right to the edge of the world and any ship that's coming you know about five days before she lands. Plenty of time to hide until she's gone. And if they decide to stay, then you can slip away by moonlight and find another island. There's always another island, always some-where safe if you keep moving.'

'Will we set a course then?' said Alice.

'Sou' sou'west?' said Queenie.

The women nodded, the children nodded – only the nun shrugged and said she supposed so.

For Jen and Squirrel, the masts and ropes and rigging became a giant climbing frame. Queenie scented the wind and bellowed from below for the bonnet atop the foremast, and they flew together to fix it. Squirrel's muscles hardened with hauling ropes, and her fingers grew smooth and hard with making knots. But wher-ever they climbed, working or playing, the crow's nest drew them like a magnet. The air was warmer as the ship skimmed southwards, and they lounged in the crow's nest planning their next aerial chase, waiting for the next hoarse command.

'I get a feeling up here,' Jen said. 'There's something I can't quite put my finger on.'

She stood and ran her hands over the mighty mast and shook her head. Squirrel watched her.

'Why's it a crow's nest, Jen?'

'Because it's high up, like a crow builds her nest,' Jen

174

told her, frowning. 'But there's old wisdom here, too. Do you think I'm crazy?'

Squirrel sighed. Jen – the amazing acrobat – crazy? She'd kill anyone for saying that!

'Of course not!' she exploded. 'But you should ask Rowan to come up here. She knows all about wisdom, and she could climb up here if we showed her how.'

'Ask her,' Jen said, and the child flipped over the rail and hurtled to the deck, fingertips and toes just grazing ropes and spars.

It was true. Just the way that Granny's caravan spoke to her: Jen knew she was safe the moment she was inside the scarlet doors. She'd put it down to her Granny's presence. And there was the same indefinable *something* here. It was more than the mast being solid oak, radiating years of salt breezes and sunshine, years of storms well-ridden . . . the crow's nest held a magic stillness even in the wildest winds.

Squirrel found Rowan lying on the orlop deck, with Esther asleep in her arms.

'She's always sleeping,' the child hissed.

Rowan shushed her.

'She's been far too busy far too long,' she whispered. 'Isn't she beautiful?'

'Course she is!' said Squirrel. 'Me and Jen want you to come up to the crow's nest. She says it's old wisdom. I think she means magic, but I don't know if she knows about magic.'

Rowan nodded. They'd told all three children to be very careful who they talked to about magic; even Turtle remembered the terror of the village and the woods, although she'd barely started walking when their lives were turned upside down and nearly ended.

'I'll be up soon,' she said.

'You know how to get up there?' Squirrel asked. 'You have to climb . . .'

'Child of mine,' Rowan said, twinkling. 'I know I'm not the genius Jen, but I would just remind you that I am at least one of your mothers, and I used to be quite good at climbing in your book.'

'Oh, you are quite good at climbing,' Squirrel said hastily. 'It's just that, well, Jen's just *brilliant*!'

'Ungrateful brat! Scat!' Rowan told her, giggling. 'I'll totter up and see you very soon. If I get stuck I'll holler for help.'

Esther opened her eyes as Squirrel scampered away. She snuggled closer.

'What was that?'

'I think it was my Squirrel,' Rowan said. 'Torn herself away from the fabulous Jen for five minutes. Jen's sensed magic up in the crow's nest.'

Esther sat up.

'Old magic? Yes. I sensed it too. There's old woman magic in the wood of this ship. She seems to know where she's going, and she's mighty eager to get there. It's as if she's just humouring Queenie by following her course.'

They looked to where the pirate queen figure stood at the helm, Turtle in front of her. On the deck, Alice was sitting in a tumble of brilliant cloths with Judith and Isabel.

'You do realize,' Esther commented dreamily, 'that our three wonderful children don't have a lot of use for us at the moment. Thank the Goddess for Jen and Queenie and Judith – it's been years since we could just be together like this.'

'What's Belle doing?'

'Well, aside from guessing to a T exactly what Judith wants before Judith knows it herself, Alice has started

176

on one of her when-I-have-the-times: she's making a quilt, and got our Belle cutting and stitching.'

'Perfect!' Rowan said. 'She can keep us clothed in our old age. I'd better go and see the crow's nest.'

'I'm going to go and organize some food,' Esther said. 'Rowan – the crone's nest, I think.'

'The crone's nest,' Rowan repeated. 'I like it.'

She liked it even more when she swung herself in beside Jen and Squirrel. It was like walking through quiet woods on a sunny day, perfectly happy with the rustles off the path and scents rising from the ground: then suddenly stepping into a clearing. A clearing where the grass is as green as the dawn of time, and every slanted column of sunlight dances with flying creatures as clear and light as thistledown. The sort of place where you stand in wonder with every woman who has ever stood there wondering.

High as a rooftop, high as a tree-top, the windblown crow's nest felt safer than houses; Rowan squatted and reached out to touch the mast, as strong and warm as a mother's spine to the anxious arms of a child troubled by nightmare.

'Magic?' Jen asked.

Squirrel gazed at her adoringly – of course Jen would know about magic. Rowan nodded and took her crystal from her pocket. Up here, the surfaces glowed like sunlight edging a cloud, and she cupped it in her palm as she walked slowly round the mast.

'Here, especially,' she said, as the crystal glowed with fire. The fire showed them a rough square part of the mast. Someone had carved here, carved a line so fine only fingertips could trace it. Squirrel took out her knife.

'It's a secret place,' she said firmly. 'Only we've been shown where it is so we can share the secret.'

177

Rowan nodded as the child drew the blade carefully round the crack and eased out a chunk of wood the size of a fist. There was a packet behind it. Squirrel took it out, then tapped the wood back into place. They sat as she opened it, and shook out a roll of parchment sealed with a lavender ribbon of watered silk.

'It's not just ours,' Squirrel said doubtfully. 'We ought to open it all together – do you think?'

'Yes,' Jen said, standing up. 'Oh, Christ!'

'What?' Rowan asked.

Jen pointed. Way to the west, but near enough to be sure! Squirrel hid the packet in her shirt and they swung down to the deck.

'Queenie, there's a ship!' Jen said.

Queenie shinned up to the crow's nest, pulled out her telescope and squinted down it for a long time.

'It's a blasted frigate from the King's Navy!' she shouted. 'Damn it to Hell and back again, we divent need this!'

'What's to do?' Alice asked, folding away the cloths she'd been working on.

'We could run before them, try and lose them, only then they'd be sure to give chase. Nosy bastards make every ship on the ocean their business. She's built with the blood and sweat of the working people of old England, and bristling with cannon worse than a hen-hedgehog. They could blow us to buggery a good way off. And there'll be some gold-medalled prick of a milord strutting on the poop and greedy for glory. Shoot first and find your lying answers later!'

She paced the deck, muttering and shaking her head. Then she stopped.

'I'm not promising,' she said. 'But I sailed with Blackbeard once and learnt a canny few dodges from that one, I'll tell you! I helped myself to a furl of flags

178

and pennons from that Italian gobshite while I was rifling him to ruination. We'll need to do a bit of play-acting. Hoy, Sister Mercy, you said you wanted to be useful, my sweetheart? There's a bit of deception required, but you've the face for it. You could sell cow-shite to farmers, and they'd think they were getting a bargain!'

'I'll have nothing to do with piratical shenanigans!' the nun said, blenching.

'No choice, my hinney,' said Queenie, deadly serious. 'It's bend the truth a little or swing for it. The King's Navy have no respect for women, nuns or virgins or mothers or spinsters.'

'Why me?' the nun asked.

'It's true, you've an honest face, Sister,' Alice said.

'And you'll work your blasted ticket!' Queenie told her. 'Do you have Latin?'

'A little,' said the bewildered nun. 'But I don't know what to do!'

'Ah, you're a good 'un,' said Queenie. 'Do just what I tell you! And here's the plan!'

'Ship ahoy, Cap'n!' sang out Jim Beam, the look-out on H.M.S. *Gallant*.

Captain John Wilshire removed his monocle and fitted the telescope to his eye.

'Dash it,' he muttered. 'She's flying some deuced strange colours! Mister Rigby, would you do me the goodness of stepping up here a moment?'

The master's mate took a good long look at the distant ship and crossed himself. How to tell the land-rich landlubber captain what the pennons meant, without letting him know that he knew that he hadn't a clue?

'We should give her a wide berth, Cap'n,' he said.

'Lord knows what plague is on 'em, with two yellow spots in the wind!'

'You are aware of Admiralty rules, Mister Rigby,' said the captain. 'One is obliged to offer reasonable assistance to a fellow voyager in trouble, as the captain deems suitable.'

'By the book, Cap'n,' said Mr Rigby. 'Only when she shows the plague flag 'tis a sign to keep well away. You'll not get the men within shouting distance, sir. 'Tes been a long trip and we're but three days from shore, sir, the men has done you proud over many a long week, sir.'

'That is their duty,' the captain replied coldly. 'Heave her to and go alongside that unfortunate vessel. We must at least ensure that she has fresh water. No Christian would do less. And if there are any dissenters, Mister Rigby, no matter who they be, I shall flog them personally.'

'Heave to!' roared the master's mate.

'Ah, what ails his Lordship?' grumbled Jack Daniels, scurrying to obey. 'Haven't we slaved enough this trip? That's a cruel bastard!'

'Shut your trap, Daniels!' roared Mr Rigby. 'Look lively!'

The *Gallant* wallowed around to take her new path. The sails sagged for a moment, then bellied out over her crew swarming the deck and rigging like demented ants. As they drew nearer to *The Mermaid's Eye*, Jim Beam crossed himself and let out an oath.

'She's flying fever flags, lads!' he shouted.

The crew glared at the immaculate figure of their captain, standing over them, stiff as a painted figurehead.

'We shall board her if I judge it necessary!' His icepick tones carried the length of the vessel.

To a man, the crew growled uneasily.

'I shall require volunteers to row over with fresh water.'

The wave-weary crew cast villainous looks at the aristocratic profile. Volunteers! You, you and you, that was the way with Captain John Wilshire. And a gutful of the cat for a sideways glance. Off the Azores he'd had a man force-fed with seawater and tied down in the sun all day for questioning an order. The same man was a gibbering skeleton below decks in irons to this day.

So the men had worked out a crazy system to beat the monstrous dictator. They straightened up as one and roared:

'Aye, aye, Captain Wiltshire! I'm your man!'

Curse them! A tic started in the captain's left cheek. *Wiltshire!* The filthy dogs! It was the one thing he couldn't stand, and a red cloud raged in front of his bloodshot eyes.

'Take over, Mister Rigby!' he spluttered.

Mr Rigby allowed himself an inner smile and blessed the day he'd eavesdropped on a maudlin Captain Wilshire, blubbering his secret weakness into the bosom of a whore in Haiti. Wiltshire!

'The fourth watch will row over in the event of rowing over!' he ordered. 'And you'll not stand watch the night – in the event!'

Well, that was fair enough, though the captain would never have made such an offer, and indeed was apoplectic below decks as he heard it. Why must the men be bribed to do their duty? He stalked back to the poop deck and struck a pose intended to be dignified as he inspected the plague ship.

Great Heavens, she was in a bad way! Her decks were white with age or neglect, and there were but two figures to be seen. One, a shapeless wreck of a man, was leaning on the tiller like a corpse. The other, a hooded priest, stood in the prows like Death itself, pale fingers working a rosary. No, there was a third soul on board. The captain crossed himself, for the priest was saying the last rites over a canvas-wrapped something at his feet.

They were close now, and the thin voice carried across the oily swells.

'*Nunc dimitis servum tuum*,' Sister Mercy said frantically.

'Keep it up, Sister,' Alice hissed from inside the canvas.

'*Mehercule, Iesu Criste, Domine nostrum, qui es in coelis*, I think I'm going to pass out, Alice! *Domine libera nos qui* . . . they're awful close!'

'The bell, Sister!' hissed Alice.

The nun looked over at the *Gallant* underneath her hood. Lord save us, the captain had a cruel hard face! The crew were gazing at her with horror, and she flashed back to the night on the river bank when she'd realized the mob would hack her down the way they'd axed the tree! One word from Matthew the Pricker – and now, one word from the captain!

And to think she'd meant to give herself up to the King's Navy and fling them all on the mercy of church and state! The icy arrogance of Captain John Wilshire whipped this thought away like a gust of arctic air. She bent down and picked up the heavy bell, and rang it slowly and solemnly, the way Queenie had told her to. Speak deep and slow, Squirrel had urged, you know, just like Father Dominic.

'Can you not see the flag?' she intoned. 'Go, while

182

you can! Go to safety! We're all doomed aboard *The Mermaid's Eye*! Save yourselves!'

'Captain John Wilshire at your service, Father. Do you need fresh water, what?'

Sister Mercy started to laugh hysterically.

'God bless you, Captain Wilshire. The dead don't need to drink! We've water a-plenty, only no lips that'll part to take it, beyond myself and the captain! Leave us, for it's an airborne infection!'

The crew of the *Gallant* covered their mouths.

'I'll have the chaplain say Mass for you! God go with you!' bellowed their captain. Good God, the man's face was twitching like one possessed!

'Amen to that, Captain!' the nun said sonorously. 'Now go! Go swiftly from our cursed presence!'

'Heave to!' ordered the captain, sweeping his hat to his spangled breast.

The crew of the *Gallant* flung themselves into action like men possessed, and the mighty ship ploughed through the waves like a frightened cow plunging through an orchard.

Sister Mercy collapsed next to Alice, shaking with relief. *The Mermaid's Eye* drifted on in total silence until the other ship was out of sight.

'Ah, you were champion!' Queenie said, hugging the nun. 'Come out of the bag now, Alice, it's safe. We'll get her shipshape and running with the wind, and treat ourselves to the fine cellar Signor di Scarto was generous enough to part with!

'For the time being,' she went on, 'we'll let the plague flags flutter. As well use the same trick till we're clear of these waters. In case we stumble on the likes of the *Gallant* again. Now look lively! Sister Mercy, you divent need to raise a finger. You've done a lifetime's work the day.'

The nun went below decks, her shocked face a whiter shade than its usual pallor.

They scrubbed the deck fore and aft, they rummaged the bilges, they washed the gunnels, they trimmed the sails, they sweated salt that dried to powder in the salty breezes on their skin. Came sundown and a to-the-bone weariness as they flung their clothes into a tub of water and soaked themselves cool in another. Queenie stomped her clothes cleaner and wrung them out.

'It's like a blasted laundry!' she said cheerfully, reaching up to peg the dripping cloth to a rope.

Alice smiled at Queenie and looked at her magnificent naked flesh. By, she was some woman, big and heavy and powerful: a giantess. Her raised arms gave her body the lines of a goddess statue, from the times when women were revered for wisdom and strength, not simpering submission. Everything about her was Woman, golden in the sun, radiating heat like a furnace. As she caught Alice's look she felt shy. Then an impish smile came and she gazed boldly back.

By all the powers, Alice's body was something to celebrate! In song, in dance, in wine, on land, on sea, in bed! That curving belly had held Princess safe inside as she grew, her strong spine and thighs had arched as if to tear apart giving her birth. Her legs were saplings splayed on feet with a grip of the earth in every toe. Her belly was a tree bole, her navel a pucker of flesh-bark. Ribs swooped like a bird landing under her breasts, and the muscle rode to her strong shoulders sure as a smooth-grassed hill. Her hair thundered around her face in wild corkscrews, splashed by the sun and sparkling like her eyes.

Queenie's body was a peachy hibiscus, unfurling all its petals and leaping for the sun. When her arms went round Alice, she gasped with a stab of memory and

184

yearning, rubbing her cheek in the electric lunacy of her hair, feeling Alice's lips on her neck.

'Bonny lass, I'd almost given up,' Alice said, wrapping her close.

'You?' Queenie was amazed.

'*You!*' whispered Alice, kissing her like a humming-bird.

'We'd best get dressed,' she mumbled. 'Everybody's – everywhere!'

'For now,' said Alice, teasing a hand across her belly. 'Only for now, my love.'

Queenie had made free with the merchandise in the hold of di Scarto's luckless trader. As well as stores and liquor, she had seized bales of velvet and silk, rolls of lace lavish with silver and gold, organdie and grosgraine spattered with seed pearls; brocade weskits and breeches of heavy silk, feathers and farthingales: enough fal-de-lal and frippery to please an entire court of blue bloods. Alice had already magpied the brightest and best for her quilt, and now they ransacked the scented chests together, tricking themselves out as fine as any crowned heads on earth.

'What about me?' giggled Turtle as Alice egged Queenie on to improvise a glittering turban.

'Ah, we'll fit you out, little lass,' Queenie said, swinging her into the air.

'Now, let's sort out the vittles!' Alice said. 'Leave the rest of them some space to dress for dinner, my lovely ones.'

'Sister Mercy said we thought life was a heathen junket,' Rowan said, grinning at the riotous pageantry on the bone-clean boards.

Alice was scarlet and gold, Queenie was silver and white, with a buttercup-sheened Turtle between them. Isabel had found every shade of sea-blue for herself and Judith. Autumn flame and tree-brown linked Squirrel with her beloved Jen. Esther and Rowan were twinned in elegant viridian spring foliage. Princess glowed in ianthine velvet, plum satin draped across her shoulders.

'Well, where is she?' Alice asked. 'We've got to toast her health and bravery first. We'd all be in irons without her, and no two ways about it.'

'I'll find her,' Princess said, rustling below decks.

There was no sign of the nun in any of the cabins, and Princess began to feel alarmed. She called her name, and a growl came from under her feet. In the cool darkness of the hold, she found the exhausted grey-clad shape lying asleep across the bear, held safe by one furry brown arm.

Sister Mercy woke and said, 'How long have I been sleeping?'

'Long enough for us to get shipshape and ready to eat, but we won't start without you.'

The nun turned over and groaned.

'Come on now,' Princess coaxed. 'You can't spend all night down here, Sister, there's ten women up there want to drink your health.'

The nun looked bewildered and closed her eyes again.

'We've all dressed up and we're waiting for you. Do you come with me and I'll find you some clothes a duchess would kill for!'

'Oh, perish the thought!' the nun said severely. 'I've worn this habit for twenty years, well, not this particular one, you understand, and it's good enough for me and my Saviour. Gorging and drinking and fine clothes! The idea!'

'Well, I'll let you off the clothes. But if you don't come up now, Queenie'll be down and sling the pair of you over her shoulders to get you on deck!'

'She would too,' said the nun.' That's a monster of a woman and no mistake. I'll not have her carry me off like a child to be laughed at! Come along now, Miss Walnut, we could do with the fresh air and a little food.'

Princess sailed splendidly ahead of the hairy brown creature, Sister Mercy a grumbling grey-robed shadow in her wake.

The nun was not prepared for the cheers that greeted her, still less for the bear rearing up on her hind legs to waltz her from the mizzen mast to the orlop and sweep her off her feet in a huge hug. And when Queenie grabbed both her hands and took her reeling around the mainmast, skipping up to the poop and back again, she was too much out of breath to protest. Dancing! Whatever next?

A goblet, full to the brim, was pressed into her hand by Alice.

'What's this?' she managed.

'It's a toast to your very good self, woman of the cloth though you are,' Queenie said. 'I thought you'd get some cackle-headed notion of turning us all in to their hacky highnesses, the King's Nay-veee! when you had the chance today!'

'The gob on you, madam!' Alice cried. 'This is a good 'un we've got in our midst, and let's drink to your health, Sister Mercy. You saved our lives today, and I for one will never forget it.'

'You were really brave,' Squirrel said awkwardly. She'd watched the whole thing from the crone's nest, and her scornful impatience had been knocked aside by sheer admiration.

'I thought you were really funny,' Turtle said, wriggling into Queenie's lap. 'You were just like Father Dominic.'

The nun blushed as twenty eyes appreciated her with glowing thanks. It had been a wicked thing to do, but not to have done it would have been wickeder. She'd never make sense of it! She gulped the wine down, and leant against the bear for safety. Safety! There was another puzzle – her, a Christian, feeling safest next to the heartbeat of a savage beast.

'Ee, this is better than boiled haddock and frumenty!' said Queenie, biting into the miracle she and Alice had concocted. 'I mind the time I saw ice floes and great bears like your Miss Walnut, only white as snow. I thought that trip would be my last. We were down to a half-barrel of salt fish and a thimbleful of water twice a day.'

Squirrel nudged Jen and whispered to her.

'My mother taught me that it was bad manners to whisper,' Alice said primly. She leant over, laughing, to Queenie, and spoke into her ear as soft as smoke. Whatever she said, it made Queenie's neck flush crimson, and Alice's eyes danced with glee.

'Unless it's a secret,' she added and filled all their glasses again.

'We found something in the mast,' Squirrel said. 'Only then that other ship came. I think it was a secret, but now it isn't any more.'

Rowan looked around. It was only Sister Mercy she was worried about, but there was no priest for her to go tattling to. Whatever that parchment said, it held deep magic and had been there for so long that clearly now was the time for it to be opened.

Squirrel handed it to Queenie, who gave it back.

'No, bonny lass,' she said. 'You found it – it's yours to open.'

Isabel leant forward and handed Squirrel her silver witch's blade.

'I don't want to break the seal,' Squirrel said.

'It's time for it to be broken,' Rowan and Esther said together.

Their eyes met Queenie's: she knew about the Power too. And Alice. Only Judith and Princess and the nun missed the signs.

Squirrel smoothed out the parchment, weighting it down with four pebbles that Isabel handed her.

'It's a map,' Princess said. 'What does it mean?'

'You found it in the mast,' Queenie mused. 'So *that's* what she was doing.'

'Who?' Turtle asked.

'Oh, many years back, when I was slender enough to pass for a lad, I stood guard over the timbers that built this ship. Simon Quint, tough as flint! One night, when the moon was full, and the wind was high and the sky was all a tatter with clouds like ghosts that can find no rest. On a night like that, you see shadows move at the edge of your sight and nothing there so be you turn quick as a flash. I was jumpy, I can tell you. Then over by the sheds I saw a shadow change its shape, grow a raggy bit that froze still as I looked. Aye, aye, I think to myself and stroll away a bit like I've seen nowt. The shadow moves slow, then darts, then stops . . . all the way down to the fresh timbers of the deck, the very deck we're standing on now. Like a lodestone, it fetches up by the mast and gets swallowed by the shadow lying all along her bonny length. I can move like the soul of a cat when I need to, and back I go. What do I find?'

She paused and swigged.

'There on the deck of the half-built ship, scrabbling away at the wood of the mast like a thing possessed – was an old woman. Old? There was little blood flowing through those veins and little spark left to keep her heart awake. She had no fear of me once I let on I wasn't the brave lad I looked, and she told me stuff I took for raving. She said I'd travel on this ship, and here I am. She said it would be the strangest voyage ever sailed. I said to her, where? Where's this strange voyage going to take me? She was silent a long time.'

Queenie paused and swigged again.

'What did she *say*?' Squirrel burst out.

Queenie smiled.

'She died while I was speaking, little lass, and to this day my question's had no answer. She must have hidden this map before I spoke to her. Let me look and see where it is. I mind most of the coasts and islands you can sail, me.'

But her brow creased as she traced the sepia lines and sworls. She shrugged.

'I can't tell for certain. Any of you have an idea? Sister, you're educated.'

The chart meant nothing to any of them. As they pored over it, Isabel gave it one brief searching glance, as if she was just checking something. She sat back and nodded very slightly. Of course, she thought, what else? And no-one but Judith noticed her expression. Their eyes met and they nodded with their quiet secret.

Part Four

Beyond The South Seas

The Mermaid's Tale

What draws them along the whale road? How do they know to glide their great grey magnificence through the trackless deep? In silent mystery they move away from the abundance of crystalline ice floes, carving their stately path below the water. They rise through the waves, mighty exuberant silver balloons, their sleek obsidian brows breaking the silver sliding sea-sky with boisterous fountains of foam. South they go, sure of coast and ocean, making melody by moonlight, plunging to invisible depths, southwards, ever southwards. Can such creatures play? Does a cathedral spin cartwheels? But they delight in each other, in head-butting waves that send mariners skittering for shore and safety, they nudge and nuzzle their babes and lead them through rich acres of living pasture, grinning hugely as they feed.

And near a nameless rock far out in one of the seven oceans, every thirteenth moon, the waves froth and heave, and any watcher knows that all is well, for the lovely Leviathans have found their timeless way once more and all of Nature salutes their passing . . .

'Oh, it really is too much!' Countess Constanza cried, as a school of whales surfaced in an exuberant wash of foam. 'How is an artiste to practise if she cannot hear herself sing?'

She lashed her ample tail furiously. It always happened! No sooner had she found her pitch, no sooner had she led her choir in a chorus or two than up popped some speechless shoal of piscine hoi polloi!

'Another audience full of the oversized armless!' snorted Duchess Demelza, breaking off in the middle of an aria.

Mermaids love to sing, they sing as humans breathe: music flows in their pale turquoise blood. They sing when they swim, flicking their fabulous tails in rhythm; they dive and harmonize. They lounge on rocks improvising oratorios, and even in their sleep they hum along with the sighing of the ocean. They do it to please themselves and to impress other choirs of mermaids. But they always draw a crowd, though this is never their intention. As for luring mariners to their deaths! They preferred not to talk about that. The odd merman is . . . necessary, after all.

The whales were the worst, thought Countess Constanza, crowding the sea around the rocks, their great tails throwing up waves that ruined her careful coiffure. And no doubt they would have the cheek to join in, huffing and puffing what they liked to think of as music, once they'd finished their vulgar spouting. So, they could blow water out of a hole in their heads? Surely that was something to keep to oneself? Exhibitionists! Merciful Mermother, they even gave great gallumphing birth *in public!* No self-respecting mermaid would even mention such a thing. She merely disappeared for a few days and swam back with a new merbabe.

'Calm down, Constanza,' murmured Marchioness Martina, running a comb through her daughter's hair. 'They do have a wonderful gift of harmony.'

'Of course, your family knows a great deal about

harmony,' sneered Constanza. 'As young Lametta showed us only too well!'

Martina placed one arm around her merchild. Seven years old – a new mermaid now! What a conger the woman was! For it has to be said that not all mermaids are good singers, and Lametta was living proof of this. She had been a beautiful merbabe, her huge sea-grey eyes promising her a tidal wave of romantic involvements; as she grew, her mouth was irresistibly kissable, and by the age of seven meryears she had a strikingly gorgeous tail of which she was very proud. Its silvery-turquoise scales shimmered like dawn, its soft pink and grey circles were perfectly round, the size of pinheads at the tip, and peacock lustred doubloons towards her perfect waist.

But until a few days before, Lametta had never sung a note in the hearing of her choir. Now they were a rather unusual choir, who had inadvertently caused a particularly well-heeled ship to founder some decades before. This ship had borne the doomed souls of a royal household to their death, and the choir had used the privilege of their femininity to bond with the spirits of the women on board, titles and all.

Marchioness Martina had defended Lametta's refusal to sing for years. After all, the dear child was always diving for pearls and scouring treasure ships for gold and silver trinkets. But the choir had become adamant. She was seven years old, and quite frankly, her silence was embarrassing. She must sing – or leave!

Lametta had taken herself off to a volcanic island for the afternoon to practise. Giant turtles and iguanas had flocked around her, and joined in with her. She felt this was a good omen. The very island had lit up with scarlet flames and a hail of sparking rocks to applaud

195

her! She swam back to her choir and sat shyly on the edge of the rock. Martina felt a flush of maternal anxiety and crossed her tail.

Lametta parted her sensational lips and sang.

When she had finished, she looked around expectantly.

'Thank you, darling,' her mother said. 'Give us an hour or so to have a talk.'

She slid obediently into the foaming waves and went to watch the grand and fiery finale on the island.

'Well, ladies, I'm speechless,' Constanza snapped.

'One does wonder *where* you found her,' sneered Demelza.

'I am mortified,' Martina burst into tears. 'She sings – if I can use that sacred word – like the Scandinavian shrikenhammer, and my spirit reminds me that it is law to shoot such a creature on sight.'

'My dear, your Lametta could make lemmings swim for the shore!' sniggered Constanza.

'She is my child,' Martina said dolefully. 'There must be a way!'

And they greeted the bright-eyed Lametta with a row of shark-smiles when she returned.

'Lametta,' said Constanza warmly. 'We've reached a decision, my little finny one. You can join the choir. You may swim with us, you may dive with us, you may bask on the rocks beside us. You may even comb your hair with us. But when it comes to singing, you just mime!'

Lametta nodded silently as she felt her tail grow grey and heavy.

She had endured the humiliation of mouthing along with her choir for just three weeks. The day the whales came she couldn't take any more. She thought their singing was sensational, and began to despise

196

Constanza and her squid's cloud of verbal superiority. So that night she slipped into the sea, and by dawn she was an ocean away. She swam alone and sang her head off and sang her unhappy heart out whenever she wanted to. She developed a devoted following among sea turtles and octopi. Most of them kept a respectful distance, but she was growing uneasy about a persistent and infatuated octopus named Spinks.

Truth to tell, she was rather fascinated by the octopus, and a little afraid of the fascination. She'd been brought up to condescend to or despise every sea creature that was not a mermaid. They were so obviously inferior! Their lack of hair, for example, yawned Duchess Demelza, combing and plaiting. Diving deep, Lametta had seen creatures with feathery fronds waving in the current: swirling plumes in green, scarlet, indigo, and as fine as hair. Constanza had affected a sneer at their lack of speech. Lametta thought the gift of speech was a wonderful thing, wasted in Constanza's bitching and her own mother's tired disappointment: the whole choir spoke constantly as if life was not treating them quite as well as it should.

Besides, she had heard the voices of the deep. Oh, they didn't use words, but they didn't need to. The sea horses whickered with a delicate dash of silver bubbles, vaulting from a floating cave of liquid green to the russet veins of sea-trees. Shoals of flying fish whooshed through the water, tails slapping out a ready-steady-let's GO!, eyes laughing at their own daring as they shimmered through the air. Sea-dragons, her favourite, clattered their scales like armour, and chuntered along the sea-bed in a smoky trail of sand and bubbles.

Every sea-creature – speechless and armless, my tail! thought Lametta – was alive with sound: I'm here, I'm going, I'm going up, I'm coming down. The only time there was an uneasy silence in the shifting tides was when the big noises came – the sharks and barracudas with their crude cavernous jaws and the stench of death, carving through the water with a jeering bully-boy *We're going to get you, just you see!*

To confuse her further, Spinks the octopus had arms. Not just two, split into five fingers, but eight. Eight swirling, dancing arms spattered with suckers as perfectly round and beautiful as the spots on her tail, and strong enough to grip a rock in the wildest tides. Spinks had eyes that blinked and pleaded and adored and were always fixed on Lametta. And Spinks could climb out of the water and lie on the rock beside her, sighing hopeless salt-water breaths while she sang and pretended she hadn't noticed.

'Spinks, stop that!' she grumbled one morning, slapping the passionate tentacles that were caressing her brow, her ears, her nose, her lips, her chin, her neck, her shoulders. She sat up and glared into the hurt and humble eyes. Honestly! She'd forbidden it to come near her rock until lunchtime.

But the sun was high and here was the octopus bearing oysters, shrimp and krill, all Lametta's favourite foods.

The night before, Spinks had lingered beside her while the moon rose and trembled with longing. One tentative tentacle had inched along Lametta's tail until her song grew languorous and wild, and she seized the creature and flung her as far away as she could. But Spinks had swum back and bobbed below the surface until Lametta's sweet breathing grew even. One silent

198

arm crept on to the neck and eased its suckers to a silent grip. Then the next, and so on until her whole body slid out of the salt water and into the presence of her goddess. It was enough to see her, enough for her grateful cephalopod eyes to drink in the contours of her face, for her beaky little mouth to gasp silently at the memory of touching her.

In the morning the sun kissed Lametta's brow and shoulder, and Spinks couldn't resist. Sliding into the water, collecting the finest foods, parachuting back to the marvellous mermaid ... her first caress went unrebuffed, then the next, and Spinks dared to hope, to dream, to touch and go on touching and never stop ...

She hit the water some twenty yards away and sank to a beautiful piece of coral, dizzy with ecstasy. There was enough tingling in her cells to last for ever, or at least until the next time she could catch Lametta unawares.

Lametta stretched in the tendrils of heat and light. Blast that octopus! There was nothing for it: she'd have to move to another rock right now. A rock that the octopus knew nothing about, so far away that by the time the besotted creature knew where she was, she'd have moved on again. She dived exquisitely through the dawn and hightailed it due east.

Twenty yards below her, the octopus followed, arms now a star, now an eight-tongued flame, arms pulsing through the water and all for the love of Lametta.

'Oh,' thought Spinks, 'oh, Lametta, be mine! My tentacles will be tendrils of tenderness and joy upon your scales. I will tease and tangle you like the careless waves that caress you without feeling the fleshy warmth of your neck. Oh, if I were sea foam exploring the pearl shell of your ear! Let me be the heedless rock where your tail curves and rests! Let me be a broken strand of seaweed nestling between your breasts!'

Lametta floated above her, looking back. No sign of Spinks! She was both pleased and a little miffed. She swam on, singing loud and tunelessly, exasperated when a flock of mindless mullet rose from the coral clouds below, staring at her in frank admiration. Spinks used the flapping finny fans as camouflage, and allowed herself glimpses of the peacock-lustred perfection of Lametta's tail.

'Let me be more than I am, or less,' thought Spinks. 'If I am more, she'll maybe care for me, and if I am less then I won't mind.'

The mullet meandered away towards sunset and the octopus sank out of sight, hiding in bales of floating weeds, dodging deeper if Lametta seemed likely to dive.

Well after moonrise, Lametta draped her lovely body on what was the tip of a sunken mountain. Spinks lurked on the foothills and waited.

'Oh that she was wordless and touch could be our language,' she mourned. 'Or that I had words to sway her!'

Drawn upwards by dizzy dreams, she saw Lametta gazing at the moon, the silver surface making a shifting mirror around her. Lametta was singing, and Spinks shivered with desire, clamping herself out of the water yet out of sight under the rock.

Lametta sang:

'Oh what is love, I asked my mother.
My mother turned away!
Is it sun on my scales

200

Or the music of whales,
Or the foam in my hair.
Oh, what is love, I asked my mother.
My mother turned away.'

Spinks felt every cell in her body become liquid. Before she knew it, she was at Lametta's side, bracing herself for the brief ecstasy of being able to hold her body – only to be thrown away.

'Oh, it's you,' the mermaid said. 'Just don't touch me. I'm moon-communing.'

The octopus sighed as a wave washed over their bodies. Ah, the same water had touched them both. It was enough.

'I don't know what you're thinking,' Lametta said. 'You look at me so strangely. I know you like me. But there's something else.'

Spinks exhaled a poem of briny bubbles, which burst like stardust in the silvery light.

'You see, I hear you,' Lametta said. 'I know your sounds, Spinks. I heard you all day today, very faint, the welling of water as you followed me, the eight-stroke rhythm of your swimming. I knew you were under those moronic mullet, my tail felt your eyes . . . but I don't *know* what your sounds mean. No! Don't touch me!'

Then how am I to tell you? thought Spinks.

Lametta reached out, and one finger caressed the delicate tip of one outstretched tentacle. She watched, fascinated as the whole body rippled with joy, shivered with fire. Lametta turned away. She lay back on the rock and sang again.

'Oh, what is love, can anyone tell me?
Can you taste it,

Can you touch it?
Can you hear it?'

Spinks edged round the mermaid, slid a dizzy arm through her golden hair and touched her ear as gently as the breeze; another arm stole across her brow and snuggled into her other ear. The octopus closed her eyes and sent all her feelings into the quivering tips. Lametta closed her eyes and let her ears listen to the touch.

If this is love . . . Her skin shut the words out.

Feel me, said the touch, feel me from your earlobes to your lovely lips, feel *me*, feel the beat of my blood against your heart, know my touch from your navel to your nose . . .

Lametta stretched, and the delicious sensation shimmered along her spine and curled like a slow breaker around her waist. Now the octopus was coiled around her breasts, shifting, stroking, sending lava through her heart.

Know me, said the touching, let me know you, let me live in your skin.

Her tail stirred, and she felt every scale lift, the way they did when she played in the waves along the white sandy shore.

Spinks shuddered and teased her splendid fin, spread like the tail of a peacock. Lametta felt every gleaming spine become fronded like a sea-dragon, she sensed her tail fanning out, weightless, the shivering touch and her being were a wordless unity, and she slid into the silken water, the waves and currents and caresses and cool and heat all around and inside her.

It was as if her eyes were wide open for the first time at night. Her body was a froth of scintillating stars, and

202

she felt the octopus grip on her waist like a band of sunshine, pinning her with a heat so strong it was almost ... too much? It was perfect, bliss, wild and halcyon haven.

And the dawn rose as they floated free of each other. Then swam together for the rosy horizon with no need for words.

The Night Has A Thousand Rainbows

An ocean away, the sun slid into the sea and Queenie
gave up on the map for the night. Gulls settled on the
spars, and Squirrel fell asleep mid-bite.

'We'll sleep on the deck,' Jen said, covering the child
with a fold of her improvised cape.

Turtle wanted the same: only she wanted to fall
asleep on Queenie's lap in the massive heat of her
arms. But she was wide awake and couldn't stop
wriggling. And Queenie was talking to Alice all the
time, a deep murmur that she couldn't make any sense
of. She looked up and they were kissing. Honestly! She
went over to Rowan and Esther and stood uncertainly
by them.

'Oh, my Turtle,' Esther said, stroking her cheek. 'I
haven't seen you for ages! Has Queenie shown you
how to steer the ship?'

'Yes,' she said. 'Can I show you? The wheel's lashed
tight at the moment so no bugger alive can shift it, but I
can still show you.'

'Is that what Queenie says?' Esther asked, standing
up.

'Yes, and she says I haven't but two more feet to
grow and she can leave me at the helm alone and
proud as Cleopatra!'

Judith walked away with Isabel her serious shadow,
and they paused next to Rowan.

'Bedtime?' Rowan asked.

Isabel shook her head and pointed at the rising moon. The inky shadows delighted her and Judith; they were off for a moonbath. Judith rocked with the slipping mirrors of the sea while Isabel beat out quiet rhythms on the deck. Sometimes Judith would hum a tune so quiet Isabel couldn't be sure she heard it at all, and once she'd said the name *Ruth*, like a question, searching Isabel's eyes until understanding dawned and both nodded seriously.

Alice and Queenie stood up with a great show of clearing plates and goblets and food. When Esther came back with Turtle they were gone, and the child shrugged and snuggled down with her mothers. They were both so quiet compared with Queenie, quiet and restful, and she drifted off almost at once.

Princess had noticed the looks that burned through the air between her mother and Queenie, and she was glad. She'd seen those looks before, years ago when she was a child, and had forgotten them when Queenie had gone away. She'd been part of those loving looks too; either her mother's arms were open to her, or Queenie's. Alice became distant after she'd gone, and Princess had done a hard bit of growing up fast without the warmth of being hugged when she needed it. She'd stopped calling out when she hurt herself, she sweated her own way back to life after nightmares: all very useful when she came to work in the bar and had to deal with the repulsive leers and comments of the clientèle. Dockside scum one and all, losers and weepers who believed themselves God's gift to any woman after a couple of shots of rum.

Here on *The Mermaid's Eye*, her distance was getting in the way. She wanted to be easy with the children, but she resented their confidence and closeness to Rowan and Esther, to Queenie, to Alice even.

Alice treated them like untrained puppies, with a careless warmth she'd never shown Princess. The night Queenie had held her close until she slept was a sweet memory, but all the women on board assumed that her aloofness was real, to be respected, and she was helpless to break out of it. Oh, Christ, wouldn't someone break in?

'I'm for turning in,' she said. She said it quietly, wanting someone to hear. Only the nun turned to her, and Princess didn't like the nun: her robes and sermonizing were a shadow of the inquisitors who jeered and chased her every night in her sleep. And the nun put herself outside the rest of them: her crucifix hung round her neck like a leper's bell.

'Would you walk me down the stairs, Princess?' Sister Mercy asked. 'I've a terrible fear of the dark and with a drink taken I couldn't trust my feet.'

Why couldn't *she* have said that? It was simple enough to say you were afraid ... as well expect herself to fly, she jeered. They went below, the bear padding behind them making sleepy bear noises. Sister Mercy had set up her bed in a narrow alcove in the corridor and Princess found herself alone in the shared cabin. She looked in the mirror and practised a smile. It was no good. The need in her eyes was painfully sharp, a dark void, a mummer's scream.

Queenie and Alice were blissful. Full of bliss and unaware of their grown child's agony, fighting sleep and its monsters in her lonely bed.

They were in the cabin where they'd visited Hjalmar all those days before. Alice had thought to bring in a fresh bottle, suddenly shy and worried: would her ageing body please Queenie? Would she disappoint her lion-hearted lover? Hell, Queenie had been all over the world with her broken heart and a body made for love. Some people mourn a lost love in solitude, some roar and booze and whore their memories to oblivion – and Alice was no fool: her Queenie was no anchorite. Her memories of their lovemaking were all of Queenie; she'd forgotten that it takes two to tangle the flesh and spirit to ecstasy.

Queenie was shaking with fear. Curse all the drunken evenings and the morning's blighted crop of nameless strangers she'd found in her bed! She wished herself whole and new, young and supple – her body seemed to her a wrecked hulk and she couldn't imagine that Alice would really want her. How could she?

And so they stood, these two magnificent women in their middle years, as nervous as virgins and each wishing they were virgins for the other.

'I feel like a new bride,' Alice said, giggling anxiously. 'Only . . . oh, Queenie, hold me!'

Queenie slowly wrapped her arms round Alice, and drew her close with great tenderness. Alice's palms rubbed into her shoulders and her face snuggled into her warm neck, lips smudging into the heartbeat of her pulse.

'I can't stand up while you're holding me,' Queenie said, and they sank on to the wide bunk.

'Lie with me,' Alice said, drawing her lover's body down beside her. They lay, breathing the scent of each other's skin, fingertips shakily tracing each other's face, eyes searching deep in the lamplight. Tears came first to Queenie, and Alice nuzzled her weary eyes, shushed her with a cadenza of kisses, held her safe in one strong arm while her other hand worked at the clumsy armour of clothes masking that beloved body from her.

'Let me,' she whispered as Queenie started to fumble at the buttons and hooks on her pirate queen dress. She stripped Queenie naked and glorious in the golden glow, then slid from the bed and stood a moment, smiling. Her own clothes came away slower and she gazed at Queenie without blinking until the last petticoat had sighed to the floor. *This is what I am,* said her timid body, tossing her mane of hair defiantly, *this is all of me.*

Queenie stretched her arms wide, offering Alice the living heat of her breasts, the curved strength of her shoulders, the luscious balm of her limbs. Alice dived into her embrace, a land-heavy seal become elegant in the grandiose ocean. Rolled into a quilt nest, their lips spun a golden thread with every light kiss, their mouths knotted a golden love-web as tongues lingered on teeth and gums and each other.

Alice's hand grew to a soft fist to knead her lover's gorgeous belly, her fingers spread to a fluttering wing on the slopes of her thighs, closed on one knee like an explorer finally grasping sweat-won treasure. And Queenie? She felt every rich cell of her big body singing. Her palms curved over Alice's opulent breasts and drew her lips to the intimate softness of her nipple; she buried her face in Alice's breasts and made a wish to live here, to love here, to die here if she had to die. And for the first time in years, every part of her wished fiercely that it would never die while there was life like this.

'I need a drink,' Alice said. 'Don't move.'

'Bonny lass, beautiful woman, my love, I never want to be away from you,' Queenie said. 'I need a drink too, and a smoke.'

'It must be our age,' Alice laughed. 'The spirit is willing but the flesh, well, she's a tired old bitch.'

Queenie's shoulder was puckered with the livid line of an old wound. Another crossed her ribs, and a white line snaked across her belly. Alice smoothed each scar with her fingers, then with her tongue.

'You're indestructible,' she said.

'There's many that have tried it,' Queenie said quietly. 'I didn't give a shite at the time. One bad word to me and I'd wade in. I didn't know it would matter to me ever again.'

Alice thought about the series of deadbeats she'd allowed into her bed over the years. Black eyes, bruised ribs, robbery and blackmail: she'd sworn never again, until the next time, when loneliness betrayed her into the lies of a good-looking waster.

'We've all run our silly heads into a wall to stop the pain sometimes,' she said. 'Drink with me, lover woman, let's be warm. And here's your pipe. No hot ash on the good sheets, mind.'

'Oh, I'm a real lady in bed,' Queenie said. 'When I'm with a real lady, that is.'

Now they were beautifully comfortable together in the timeless glow. Toes nudged each other, calves and thighs found each other's curving weight in a shifting delight. Alice set her cup down and eased her body against Queenie, her flesh fitting like a root that's grown all its life around a rock, hair-fine roots prizing the slenderest cracks in the cool smoothness to make them one.

Queenie let her tobacco die, and stretched out to free both hands from cup and pipe. A rip-tide of yearning stirred her belly and her mouth sucked sweet secrets from Alice's lips. Her hands shifted their longing from breast to throat to a languorous lilting drift; her fingers followed the dazzling play of light in Alice's eyes, moving gently with each breath until breath

209

became sigh; sigh rose to a delicious gasp of primeval desire. Their bodies lost flesh and time and space, so full was every cell, leaping into the trackless time *close* becomes one and nothing can come between. Hands are dancers, wave to shore, spines are flame-lipped serpents and the sheer muscle of passionate celebration unfurls her wildest love, wrapping true lovers in an eternity of now.

Lametta Moonlighte Is Not Amused

'Is that Queenie singing?' Princess asked.

Alice looked modest, and her neck flushed like the scarlet silk on her lap.

'I just wanted to say I'm glad,' Princess said.

'Oh, my lass,' Alice told her dreamily, 'I'd forgotten what glad was. I thought the best I'd have for glad was making a really good wine. And being glad for you while you grew. Ee, I've not been the best of mothers, have I now? Divent be Lady Madam good mannered with me, Princess, you've had the Hell of a time one way or another.'

'I'm all right,' Princess said. 'I hated it when Queenie went away, but you get used to anything.'

'Buggered if you do!' Alice responded fiercely. 'Oh, you can put on a show, and I think we had the world fooled, you and me. There were times I'd cry myself to sleep, and I wanted to come through to you and tell you all my troubles. Only I was supposed to be your mother and tough as old leather.'

'I wish you had,' Princess said. 'Maybe then I could have told you mine.'

'Never too late, sweetheart,' said Alice. 'You go and take that lovely pirate some food. Go on. She loves you, you know.'

'It's in everything she does,' said Princess and surprised Jen as she passed her on the way to the galley. She didn't know that Princess could smile.

Alice licked her fingertips and threaded her needle, smiling too, smiling at her fingers' secrets. She spread the quilt out. It was going to be an orgy of blossoms: roses and lilies spilling around luxuriant buttercups the size of plates; forget-me-nots and dragonflies and purple daisies rioting among morning glories blazing like a high summer sky.

'Like it?' she asked Isabel and Judith.

Both nodded. Isabel pointed to the pinned garland of forget-me-nots and her eyes said *May I?* Alice handed her a needle.

'Certainly, little lass. It's a wonderful flower, forget-me-not. I had acres of it back home. Would you like to give a hand, Judith? This is the quilt I'm making for me and my true love to sleep under. It'll be like waking up in the garden of paradise and no half-wit Adam to spoil it!'

Judith giggled and shook her finger in mock scolding.

'Divent you start on me, madam!' Alice said. 'You know well there's nothing like it. And I don't mean that streak of piss you were married to. Ah, don't upset yourself now. You're best off without the bastard, and here's Belle thinks the sun shines out of your eyes. She's a knowing one.'

Judith sighed and wiped away her tears.

'Ruth,' she said, pointing at Isabel.

Alice hid her surprise. It was the first time she'd heard Judith's voice.

'Ruth?' she said. 'Was she your little girl? Ah, don't fret, Judith. I haven't said it before, but I knew the bastard you called husband. Wenching and wining every night there is, aye, and lying to you and you believing him: it's no shame to hope for what should be true.'

Judith raised her tortured eyes to Alice.

'I know the lass he was after,' Alice said. 'She's a bad wench for letting him. But she's not a bad wench, apart from that. She's got a bairn of her own, and I can't see Master Miller doing 'owt but giving over your Ruth to her. He was nothing as a dad when you were there, am I right?'

Judith was distressed and shook her head.

'Do you think he'll have the town call him a bad father? Not him! He'll have your little lass with his woman and her bairn. She's good to her bairn and she'll be good to yours.'

She took Judith's hands and looked into her eyes.

'Oh, my honey,' she said. 'It's not the best, and don't I know it. But your Ruth will understand as she grows up. Mebbes we'll even go back to the bonny Tyne before we're dead and find her. She'd rather know you're alive than live with the tale of her mother burnt as a witch. You had no choice, Judith, and there's not a speck of blame lies with you. You know in your heart it's true.'

Judith nodded, more to silence Alice than in agreement. So many words for so many things she couldn't yet think about without floods of tears or worse, a dry-eyed burning in her heart and helpless hands.

Up in the crone's nest, Squirrel was carving at a piece of wood. She was cross. Bloody cross, she thought. Jen wasn't much bloody help, either. Grown-ups!

'What's the matter?' Jen asked.

'What bloody use is a bloody map if no-one knows what it's a map *of*?' she exploded. 'Oh go on, shrug! I thought it was magic! Bloody stupid magic!'

'Oh, come off it,' Jen said. 'Queenie's going to check it out with all the charts.'

'When? She's too busy playing with bloody Turtle and bloody *kissing* Alice all the time. They're worse than Rowan and Esther.'

Jen stood up.

'I'm going to feed Miss Walnut before she takes a chunk out of Sister Mercy,' she said. 'Coming?'

Even the idea of the bear eating the nun didn't stop Squirrel's fury.

'Go and feed the bloody bear,' she snapped, and turned her back.

Jen resisted the urge to grab the child and tickle her out of it. She swung down to the deck, grinning with pleasure when she saw Alice and her helpers. Even Judith looked less pale. She strolled to the love nest on the orlop deck.

'Rowan, Esther,' she said softly. 'Squirrel's up there in the crone's nest, and she's bloody angry about the map. She's not daft, but she's out for danger. You know?'

Rowan nodded.

'Best to leave her to it,' she said. Jen went to feed the bear.

A piece of wood flew out of nowhere and bit into the deck at her feet.

'Bloody angry,' said Rowan. 'Who'd be a mother?'

She closed her eyes and roared: 'Squirrel! Get down here NOW!'

'NO!' screamed the child.

'You've got ten seconds!' bellowed Rowan.

Squirrel mocked her, giving a high-speed count of ten, then she sat down again out of sight.

Rowan looked at Esther and sighed.

Squirrel was as mad as a disturbed magpie. How dare

214

Rowan start ordering her around. So, she'd chucked a chunk of wood her way: it hadn't hit her, had it? She hurled a rain of wood chunks at Rowan as she dodged through the ropes towards her. Most of them flew wide and wild over the side of the ship. Bloody Hell, she didn't want to *hit* Rowan, not that much, anyway.

'Squirrel, what the blazes do you think you're doing?' Rowan asked, glaring at the girl.

'Stop that at once, you split-tailed mutants!'

The words rolled out with outraged authority. It wasn't a voice they knew, and they both looked down in alarm. Rowan gasped.

There in the water, silvery tail lashing in imperious fury, was a – *mermaid*? She lobbed a piece of wood back at them with such force that it stung the air between them and stuck in the mast quivering like a blade.

'What's to do?' called Queenie, for the sudden silence from above startled her. She hadn't seen either woman let rip, and wanted to see how they dealt with their children being anything other than their usual wild and wonderful selves.

'It's a mermaid,' said Rowan, awe-struck.

'Mannerless mortals!' shrieked the mermaid. 'It's a, IT is a nothing. *She* is a mermaid, *I* am a mermaid and I warn you, there'll be storms on the way unless you get mer-wise!'

Queenie lashed the tiller in place and leapt to the side of the ship. By all the goddesses, a mermaid! She knew for sure that they were in the South Seas now, shifting into a zone where anything was possible. She'd heard tales, of course, all her seafaring life; and the one twister she'd seen was blamed on the wrath of a mermaid. Once, she thought she'd heard the mermaids singing, on a late and lonely watch. But she was in a cloud of brew at the time, and never said a word to her shipmates.

And here she was, captain of her own ship, sober and stunned, and there was a mermaid, large as life and challenging her with grey eyes blazing vengeance.

'Good day to you,' she managed.

'It was a good day until one of you split-tails started pelting us,' the mermaid spat. 'We are not amused.'

She placed a regal arm in the water and a strange creature emerged, a dome-headed thing with eight arms, one of them wandering round the mermaid's proud shoulders.

'I'm more than sorry,' Queenie said. 'We've a bairn on board that doesn't know better.'

'Well, you should teach her,' sneered Lametta Moonlighte, finding it hard to concentrate her rage for the delicious warmth that was thrilling her spine. She shoved Spinks a little further away. There was a time and a place! The octopus thought *always* and *everywhere* when it came to loving Lametta. Even eating was an erotic ritual between them.

'You could have injured me or my octopus,' she said sternly. Spinks blinked. *My* octopus! She sank slowly and concentrated on Lametta's tail.

'Tell me what to do to set it right,' Queenie said.

'I shall return at moonrise,' said Lametta, catching her breath and unable to resist her leggy lover a moment longer. 'Be prepared!'

She glided below the waves with as much pre-orgasmic dignity as she could. A cloud of congers made dark question marks in her wake.

Queenie was shaking as she sat next to Alice. They all gathered on the deck, Squirrel subdued and more penitent than even Sister Mercy could possibly be.

'It *is* a mermaid?' Alice asked.

216

'*She* is a mermaid and don't you forget it!' Queenie said. 'She can raise storms by singing and we'd all be matchwood by morning. And she's got an eight-legged monster at her beck and call.'

'I thought mermaids were just a story,' Princess said.

'Every story starts with a truth,' Queenie replied. 'And if you say something here in the South Seas, the wind catches the words and they'll turn into something real – though you may never know it.'

'What do mermaids *do*?' Turtle asked.

'Ah, they can do anything they want to, little lass. They can make your wishes come true, only there's always a price to pay. There was a fisherman in Scotland years ago, and he was caught up in a tempest like you wouldn't believe. Twenty miles from shore and never a bit of shelter in sight! His whole catch was washed overboard, and him clinging to the mast sure it was his last moment. A mermaid bobbed up beside him and he shouted at her to save him, for God's sake. Mermaids don't hold with God and she said would he promise to do one thing for her in return for his life. Well, only a fool would think twice, so he promised, and a moment later he was on dry land, with his boat beside him, safe as houses. The mermaid was lying in the surf and she said: "Now for your part of the bargain. Every year you must spend six months living under the sea with me." Well, your man had a wife and bairns on land and he didn't want to do that at all. The mermaid said that was fine, she'd just put him and his boat back into the storm where she'd found him, and he could leave his wife a widow and his babbies orphans. So he had to agree.'

'And did he do it?' asked Princess, reluctant to get caught up in the story as more than a story.

'He did, and the six months below the waves his wife

would walk the shore calling him. Until the mermaid appeared with a string of sea-babies beside her and said she'd be back every day of the six months he was on land and call him back. Mermaids can sing sweet enough to have you leap off your ship in mid-ocean, stone mad for them.'

'I heard that,' Alice said. 'Ee, Queenie, what shall we do?'

And while the crew were all a-dither and full of doom, Lametta was full fathom five, her bones a frisson of fulfilment, her scales a seismic seesaw of sensuality. Is it possible, she wondered, drifting in an eight-petalled embrace, can it be possible that one day I'll have had enough of love? Her mother's one coy allusion to love had implied that it was an illusion, an irresistible urge that wore off after a while. Lametta hadn't counted the days or noticed the tides or even the waxing and waning of the moon since she'd been in love. For now she knew it was what she wanted – for ever.

With intervals. Like she had to return to the surface this moonrise and demand recompense for the aerial assault on her Dignity. She had no idea what to ask for: her choir had never lowered themselves to change words with dry-land split-tails. What could they possibly give her, the mermaid with the most beautiful tail and a lover whose tenderness and attention were total? What did split-tails *do*? What did they *have*?

For the first time since she'd left the choir, she wished there was someone around who used words. Demelza would want golden combs, Constanza would want servants and adulation, her own mother would demand a chest of sparkling jewels to stash somewhere and sneak away to.

There's something about letting diamonds and

rubies run through your fingers, she'd told Lametta dreamily, *just knowing that you are the reason that rainbows play through the coral, darling: it's divine!*

Lametta was not short of vanity, but had no wish to burden herself with possessions. She toyed with the idea of slaves. To do what? Spinks anticipated her every wish. Closing her eyes, she hummed a meditative berceuse, and shook a swarm of starfish from her shoulders with irritation. That would be something! To be able to keep the rag, tag and bobtail at a respectful distance.

Now, how could the split-tails help her? She and Spinks were bound for the Blessed Isles, where she planned to ask the Great Mermother to give the octopus immortality, for the thought of losing such a love was unbearable. The clear waters already thronged with a myriad marine creatures, and the warmer it became, the more there would be, a glorious galore became a grasping gallery of followers the moment she opened her mouth.

The ship! Lametta looked up. The curved timbers looked like the scarred belly of a great shark, and her shadow sent fish scuttling away. If she travelled with the ship, she was guaranteed the space she required. She'd have to bluff them into agreeing: there *was* a storm song, but she didn't know the tune. Such secrets were only shared after seven years in a choir, and she hadn't even had seven minutes! She swam serenely, practising mighty tail-flips and frowns.

Now, what was the ship called? That had annoyed her too! *The Mermaid's Eye*, for Ocean's sake! As if a mermaid had but one eye, and as if that were her best feature! She'd make them rename it in her honour – *The Mermaid's Tail*? No, that could be celebrating any mermaid's tail. *Lametta's Tail*? It didn't have the panache she craved. It should be something that would make her abandoned choir pink with envy suppose their paths ever crossed again. Damn their bourgeois posturing: she'd show them!

The moon rose, and with it, the mermaid's golden hair parted the waves and she looked up: the split-tails were waiting at the ship's rail. For the superb bluff she was about to pull, *they* should be looking up at *her*.

'Bring me aboard!' she commanded.

Queenie had been racking her brains all day as to what the mermaid would demand. Old tales came back to her about the curiosity a mermaid had about dry-landers, and she'd devised a rope cradle for just this purpose. They lowered away and hauled Lametta aboard, with her octopus clinging to the webbing and glaring balefully. Alice had thought to fill a barrel with salt water to keep the mermaid from drying out, and Lametta nodded graciously as she sprinkled her tail.

'I could raise a typhoon,' she said severely, 'but I have another use for you. You will follow me, and the Great Mermother will decide your fate.'

'Where are you going?' said Queenie.

'Follow me,' said Lametta, who was rather vague on exactly where the Blessed Isles were. 'The paths of the seven oceans are written in my blood.'

'Perhaps she'd know what the map is!' said Squirrel.

Lametta looked at the parchment and laughed.

'Naturally,' she said. 'That seems to be a crude split-tail version of my own journey. It was a lucky day for you when you met me.'

'You really know where this is?' Squirrel was over-joyed.

'Of course,' Lametta said. 'And there's one more thing.'

Now we come to it, thought Rowan, thought Esther, she's going to want one of the children. Come Hell or high water, they'd stop that.

'The name of your ship is offensive,' the mermaid said imperiously. 'You will rename her in my honour.'

'And what are you called?' said Jen.

'*The Empress of The Seven Oceans*,' Lametta announced, sweeping her steely gaze over them. By all the breakers! Not one face even looked doubtful. They'd bought it!

'We have spoken,' she said. 'Return us to the waters: we leave at dawn.'

'There's something not quite right about that mermaid,' Jen said as she and Squirrel and Squirrel's re-adopted mothers lay on the deck halfway to sleeping.

'She's brilliant!' Squirrel said fiercely. '*She* knows about the map. You're so silly.'

Rowan chuckled.

'You're demoted, Jen,' she said when the child was asleep. 'Oh, my passionate babe! When I first knew Esther I was afraid Squirrel wouldn't like her. It took two weeks of scowls and scorn and then one morning, she hopped out of bed and hugged Esther.'

'I was all right because Rowan loved me,' Esther said. 'Useless at climbing, a real bonehead. Squirrel couldn't work out what I was good for, until she realized that someone did the cooking and I had a whole load of new stories to tell. This mermaid's got the lot, really: none of us can compete with a tail and a tame octopus.'

'What is it about her?' Jen was thinking out loud.

221

'Maybe she just reminds me of all the sideshows I've seen. You know, the two-headed woman, the human serpent. There's always a trick and it's always clever enough to fool people. We had the Queen of the Fairies once. She was the same height as Turtle and sat on a throne with a great swathe of ermine and a golden crown, glistening with diamonds and rubies – they were made of glass. The ermine was a rabbit skin, and the gold got re-painted every couple of weeks. No-one ever asked what the fairy kingdom was doing with its queen in a side-show. I don't know. I kept expecting to see stitching in that mermaid's tail . . . but there wasn't any.'

'Oh, she's a real mermaid all right,' Esther said. 'What do you think, Rowan?'

'I'm just a little puzzled about how fast she knew what the map was,' Rowan said. 'She just glanced at it, and I saw Isabel and Judith look at each other. They don't believe her. And we may never know why.'

'I think I'll read the cards,' Esther decided. 'They know everything.'

She took her tarot from their scarlet silk pouch and shuffled.

'Some of us have work to do,' Queenie said self-righteously as she and Alice paused beside them and dumped down two buckets.

'We're off to scrape that name off before Her Imperial Swaggerado decides there's something else she wants from us poor human split-tails. Split-tails! I've been called some things in my life and not many of them polite. This beats all!'

'Whey aye, Alice, it could be worse,' Queenie said. 'Mermaids have been known to take a fancy to a human child, you know. I was expecting that, with Squirrel having started the whole carry on. Over my dead body!'

'Aye, bonny lass,' Alice said. 'Besides, there's no telling how fast news travels, and *The Mermaid's Eye* was spotted for a plague ship.'

'Nothing wrong with changing names,' Queenie said cheerfully. 'I've had dozens, me. Come on now, precious, or we'll never see our bed the night.'

'Aye, aye!' Alice said smartly, with a salute that would have earned a seafaring man six lashes for impudence.

'Anyway,' Esther said. 'At least we'll have no more arguments about where we're going.'

Below decks, Sister Mercy lay rigid in her cubby hole, one hand gripped in the bear's ruff. She had seen the mermaid, and had fled at once. If ever there was a manifestation of The Evil One! She told herself her eyes were playing tricks, and made herself frantically busy with supper. But while they ate, all the talk was of the mermaid, and she did her best to block it out by running a full Gregorian Mass through her mind. Try though she might to conjure up candles and incense, her eyes opened to the stars above, all of them in the wrong place, as if it was the end of the world: her nose brought her the smell of brine and sun-baked timber and heady wine. Queenie reckoned naming a ship new was the same as launching a new ship, and planned on doing it in the finest style the pilfered cellar could bring.

There are no such things as mermaids!

Said Sister Mercy's lifelong religion and her natural reason.

Turtle had exclaimed over a shimmering disc she found on the deck: one of the mermaid's glittering scales. Sister Mercy refused to touch it as it was passed from hand to hand. The whole thing smelt of witchcraft, and what was the use of saying that here. Witchcraft was a way of life to these women, at least to

Rowan and Esther and those poor lost children. And Queenie! You'd have thought she'd have a lick of sense, but no, she and Alice had been acting strangely all day, laughing at nothing at all and nudging against each other at any excuse.

She went on to the deck, crossing herself at the sight of the pagan card party and flitted up to the prow. Merciful Lord! Her eyes told her a truth to make her bewildered mind stagger towards the thin edge of insanity.

Queenie and Alice were bobbing beside the ship, only their heads in view. They were smiling, they even kissed each other the same way she'd seen Rowan and Esther kiss in the woods, the kiss that had sent her dreams from Satan! They were scraping away at the painted name on the timbers as casually as you might wash a table. And big and heavy the pair of them may have been, but they were suspended in midair without a rope or platform in sight to hold them!

Sister Mercy clutched her crucifix and whimpered before she fled back to the blessed darkness, chasing a peace of mind she feared would never be hers again.

Lametta freed herself from the tender tangle of her love-drugged darling. So sweet in slumber, a smile playing over her bliss-bearing lips! She straightened up and smoothed her dishevelled tail back into an orderly pattern of scales. Just touching the iridescent crescent of gold dots around her seventh centre of desire made her shudder with the recent memory of dizzy dissolve. Perhaps they could . . . just quickly? No! Quick and Spinks and love didn't belong in the same tide. She had to become severe and mistressful when she addressed the split-tails. It had been easy to bamboozle them into following her: she was on edge in case they called her bluff and demanded hard evidence by way of typhoons.

Lametta didn't even know how to make waves!

And the dry-skinned simpletons imagined they were following a map! The lines on the parchment meant nothing to her, but she'd keep them fooled somehow. She surfaced and looked up. Good. They were watching and waiting for her. She swam to the ship's prow and smirked gleefully: there was her new name emblazoned in gold.

The Empress of the Seven Oceans.

She swallowed the smirk and turned back to her split-tail entourage, borrowing a sneer from her memories of Duchess Demelza.

'That's a start!' she snapped. 'Reel me up, Queenie!'

They stood around her on the deck, gawping. She inspected them in awesome silence. Well, they did have arms, although these were wrapped in tatters like beached seaweed. And they had speech. It was only their scaleless and crudely split tails that marked their humanity. At least they had done something to conceal the fleshy nakedness, more dried seaweed in many colours. Some of their faces showed the ravages of perpetual dry air, as wrinkled as the Great Mermother's cheeks after a million years undersea. Their double tail-fins were most unsightly; bad enough for them to be split apart, but to allow a row of polyps to grow there! Or perhaps, since each fin sported five fleshy lumps in varying sizes, they regarded it as ornamentation. Poor mutants, what a pathetic attempt at disguise! *Never draw attention to a defect!* Martina's maternal advice flitted through her mind.

But one of them didn't show any sign of her split tail, and was swathed from neck to deck in something the colour and texture of a dead shark. Lametta felt vague unease. It took great magic to kill sharks, and even her choir had forgotten their languid dignity and raced for dry land at the sight or smell of them. Apart from the stiff shark hide, this one had hold of a gilt gewgaw shaped like a spar lashed to a mast. It was a piece of treasure! Lametta had seen hundreds like it deepsea. Had this hidden-tail dived seabed to find it? She decided to be very wary around her.

Sister Mercy's fingers were stiff around her crucifix. Merciful Mary, here was the Godless nightmare in broad daylight, naked to the waist and shameless! And *down below*! You could hardly consider a tail to be decent clothing, particularly this one which seemed to have a life of its own, undulating in a most suggestive manner before her very eyes!

'We shall go south,' ordered the mermaid. 'Follow me.'

'Would you be able to show us where on the map?' whispered one of the smaller ones.

'Of course!' snapped Lametta and took the parchment as if it were a bouquet of royal lilies. Curse it! There were swirls like anemones and dots all over it. She stabbed one elegant nail dead centre of one of the anemones.

'We shall reach there before sundown,' she said imperiously.

'What's it called?' the same creature asked.

'Atlantis,' Lametta told her firmly.

'*Atlantis?*' Queenie said. 'By, it's a good day we met you, Empress. That'll be a cracker of a tale to tell. We're ready when you are!'

'Of course,' said Lametta. 'Return me to my ocean, *one* of my oceans, and I shall summon my eight-armed minion. My bodyguard.'

Queenie and Alice lowered away.

'How old is she?' Esther wondered.

'Hard to ever tell with mermaids,' said Queenie solemnly, then on a burst of laughter. 'Here's me the expert, bonny lass!'

'Mermaids are immortal,' said Jen. 'She could be a thousand years old, she could be the same age as Squirrel. Or me. Or even Queenie.'

'Ee, God, is it possible?' Queenie said sarcastically. 'There can't be a creature living on this planet as old as me, surely!'

'You're blooming like a teenager,' Alice said. 'Is she not bonny, this auld wreck of a woman I love?'

'Ah, get away with you,' Queenie said, blushing. 'Let's be rigged and ready to fly behind Her Haughtiness the minute she says.'

'I want to hear the mermaid sing!' said Turtle. 'Rowan said there's nothing as beautiful as a mermaid's song.'

'Maybe she'll sing to us once she's got over her huff,' Esther said.

'There are some that live in a huff,' Princess said. 'I can keep up a real huff for weeks, me, can't I, Alice?'

'A huff and a puff and a scowl and a stomp to shake the house down,' Alice agreed. 'You were a holy terror, my Princess. If you hadn't been my own little child, I'd have sold you to the circus many a time.'

Squirrel looked at Princess wide-eyed. Princess was Alice's daughter? How could a grown-up person be a little child? And Princess had a temper? She'd never seen it.

'Do you get cross?' she asked in disbelief.

'I do,' Princess said. 'There's a lot you don't know about me.'

227

Part Five

Another Horizon

A Treadmill Of Hell

The chains around her ankles weighed more than her gaol-starved body. Another chain yanked her legs first to cramp, then to numbness, and its rusty links bit into an iron band around her waist. A short chain pulled her spine down fit to rip her discs apart where it linked with the band round her neck. Her arms were dead from the metal chafing her neck and binding both wrists between her shoulder blades. She was carrying enough metal to forge a dozen muskets: on her it made running sores. Between vomiting the rancid food they pushed into her torn mouth and the way the rutted track flung her about on the boards of the cart, she had given herself up as dead and her last life-wish was for total oblivion.

The cart stopped, but they wouldn't let her just lie on the dung-stinking straw. The sky was black above her when they booted her on to the ground and left her there, cursing the chill of night and building a fire to warm themselves.

Dawn dragged shades of grey over the horizon, and tattered clouds hung like shrouds. She registered a smoky line far away and focused on the dull pewter ocean.

So they were going to throw her off a cliff. She'd always loved the sea, and now the sea would flood her lungs and release her. She moved her head and the tears that gushed were at the needle-sharp agony as the scabs on her neck split and opened raw flesh to filthy rust. She knew what to do, and jerked her head against the collar so hard that the pain put her out.

Vomit woke her, and her eyes told her she was nowhere. A strange dark woollen back was rowing somewhere above her, and she screamed: was this the river of death? A hand reached down and felt for her face, then swung back and clouted her to deafness.

So she was going to Hell. The sun was suddenly scarlet through the mist and she thought of fire, her tortured back screaming its memories of flame and brands. Would it never end?

Hell seemed civilized. At first.

In a delirium she was bundled from the boat by the man with the clouting fist; another delirium and her chains were unlocked. Her legs and spine and arms wailed the agony of blood passing through parched veins, and she felt herself being carried.

The men were saying her name:

'Eva and a devil with knives!'

She burst into a sweat: was she to be penned up with a devil with knives for all eternity?

'She'll have no blades here.'

Defenceless against a devil with knives for all eternity? Then she knew they meant that *she* was a devil, for the killing she'd done to keep her own life.

Then someone was rubbing something greasy and warm on to her wounds. Someone was feeding her hot liquids. Someone bathed her stinking flesh and lay her down in clean cloths. She slept and tore awake with a nightmare of shrouds. And someone fed her more warm liquid, and she slept as deep as the North Sea.

'We don't get many women here.'

She'd heard that tone of voice before and kept her eyes shut.

'Only Mad Hattie, and that's hardly woman. Evil witch, I steer clear of her. Mainland and she'd be burning. God rot her!'

In spite of herself, Eva's flesh gushed sweat. Goddess knows she'd seen burnings. Women whose husbands were too weak or scared to protect them; women whose husbands were glad to hand them over; women who lived alone and would not fuck the witchfinder; women who would do anything through fear of death until he grew contemptuous and arrogant enough to send them for a travesty of trial: torture, the nightmare unreality of 'confession', and then the stake. So this wasn't Hell? It was earth, bloody earth and as dangerous as ever.

'This one's young.'

She made herself limp as a shadow crossed her closed lids and a male hand took the covers off her. A male throat laughed.

'Scarred, but that'll mend. Young and eager, I'll be bound. Look at the tits on her!'

'Better than that filthy faggot.'

'He likes it. He'll miss us.'

'She'll be pliant. Just a slip of a girl!'

'Pliant or she'll starve.'

So food was the currency of Hell.

Eva, the devil with knives, took herself out of her body and into the stone wall, lying passive as the man turned her body over and unbuckled his belt. She did not move. High in the wall, she closed her eyes and took herself to a piece of sweet music she'd heard in a drawing room once while she plundered the trinkets of the fine lady's bedroom above. The man who kept her cringing with his sharp blade had hit her then for daydreaming, but the music had stayed with her.

'Cunt! Fucking cunt!' The man gasped and stood up again.

And then the next man turned her body over.

She floated through the wall.

It was a bleak island, rocks and pale grass and outcrops of stone in the shape of houses. She skimmed the air above them, noted the inhabitants, grey and brown clad men, white-haired, shambling, bearded, rambling, mad as the breeze at spring equinox, muttering, dancing like marionettes.

Hell.

She ghosted over these derelicts to where the grass was greener, a dip in the land out of wind's reach, and turned, although the horizon beckoned her like a lover. In the sweet green dip there was a dwelling made of wood and moss. There she drifted down, painless and suddenly wide-eyed. There was the solid shadow of a woman in the doorway . . .

With a snap she was back in her body, some man pushing something into her anus while another pushed something into her vagina and the two sweated and howled like wild dogs, crushing her body between them. Still she refused to open her eyes, and a million years later they got up, spat on her and went away.

She'll have no blades here.

She begged her eyes not to weep, her fingers not to kill, but to be ready for every sight and touch of metal.

It would not be safe to defend herself until she could kill them if necessary. That or flight. So she simply removed her self from what they did to her body, and wished herself safe in the mossy green dip where the wooden hut snuggled around the woman they called Mad Hattie. Nights she flew beyond and looked for cliffs to jump from. On the west of the island, the cliffs lurched down in bulging slopes, and her body would be bruised and broken in the fall. Hell, she might even survive, survive Hell, survive crippled and so never be

234

able to run from them. To the east lay overhung shadowed beaches scarred with broken stumps of rock like rotten teeth. Even the high tide didn't cover them. The south, where her boat had landed was a bleak danger point, and the men kept burning night and day a stinking fire of seaweed and rotten timber that the sea spat out. They could see the whole south side from where they sat.

But on the fourth night of Hell, Eva tore herself through the stone walls and hurtled out due north under the stars. She glanced down at the dark safe dip of the wooden hut where she'd seen the woman's shape in the doorway, and the wind gusted her onwards. Suddenly the moon rode from behind the clouds, as bold and glittering as the masked eyes of a highway robber, and she was suspended above sheer white cliffs that plummeted straight down into the silver path of moonlight. If she stepped from the sharp edge into the air she would hit the waves eating away at the cliffs and it would be over.

Here lay oblivion. If she had to. They could hunt her body, drive her aching limbs this way and she could simply take a step further and be free.

They had decided that she was pliant, and once the novelty of a cunt had worn off, they hit her body for not responding to their rape. They told her she wanted it, was asking for it. She said nothing. She wasn't there. They cursed her for being broken-spirited, and decided to have her wash the plates they ate from, the cloth they sweated into. They put her in a dress that touched the ground and tied a rope round the waist. One of the men would lead her to the stream on a chain and lie smoking while she worked. She walked with small steps and thought of the nuns she'd seen. But on her knees at the stream, back bowed to wash their dirt, she would drag in deep breaths and tighten her muscles all over, pick up each plate with the strength needed to shift a great stone, pick up the spoons as if they were lead weights, and scour the surfaces with sand the way she'd grind their bloody faces against rocks as soon as she had her knife. And she banged the stinking cloth against the rocks the way she would shatter their skulls. *One day* . . .

The plates were tin. The spoons were tin. And the tin was thin. One day she tried to sharpen the bent handle of a spoon and found that the weak metal merely curled and sheered off like paper or rags. She dropped the frowzy evidence to rust in the stream bed and the men hit her for clumsiness in losing a spoon. She had to eat with her hands to their mockery after that.

They made her darn the holes her strength made in their clothes. After that, she would wring the rough stuff dry the way she'd choke the breath from their unshaven necks. *One dark night* . . .

Days blurred to weeks. The sores on her body healed in salt water, and her muscles rediscovered a panther power. Toiling up the path she would make the sheer strength look like lumpy solid awkwardness, and they jibed at her for getting fat. Every mouthful of food went straight to muscle on her and they couldn't see it, since she chose to hide it from them.

Weeks blurred. They stopped leading her to the stream, just lay around and jeered while she picked her feignedly clumsy way. She couldn't have shoes: only the gaolers, her rapists, had shoes. The soles of her feet learned every curve of the path, and thickened themselves against the flints. Her eyes darted quicker than the slender snakes eeling out of her way on the dusty track. At the stream, she washed the plates and her power surged through her with a rage that was so

clean and cold that she used it like a steel tightrope
tethered to the horizon.

One day . . .

And a day came when she was floating in the
waves, a rapist sitting by her clothes on the shore,
and she floated further than ever before. She had given
up the dream of swimming to freedom: there was no
land to be seen from Hell apart from the land she had
come from. And Eva does not go back. There was a
sting across her shoulder blades and she hurtled
round, snarling at the pain. She'd drifted as far as the
teeth of the mouth they called the Bay. The teeth, the
boat breaking rocks, had bitten her to the bone. She
caught sight of a swirl of pink in the water and found
her shoulder stinging like fire as she made for the
shore.

The men laughed at her scar and her lockjawed
silence. Used their belts and buckles on her skin to
make her scream. But her mouth was glittering with an
unearthly smile as she circled the Cliffs of Annihil-
ation, and only the bruises she found in the dawn told
her what had happened to her body. For as she
watched the cliffs, hypnotized like a cobra's prey, a
blade of white stone detached itself from the edge of
the cliff and fell slow as a feather to stab the waves.

Eva and a devil with knives.

She had been so fixed on a knife being gleaming
metal, parting flesh and stopping the hate-filled heart-
beats, that she had been blind, all those days of
drudging down to the stream.

A small round stone was slingshot. A heavy round
stone was a skull-shattering club. A stone honed on
stone would be a thin and deadly blade. Eva washed
the men's dishes and found her stone. It was twice the
size of her fist, rough at one end and as pointed as a

wild bird's egg at the other. She was alone. She took the stone in her hand from the heart of the icy stream bed. She held it in her hands and it was warm.

'Free me, Lady Stone,' she whispered. 'Free me!'

She looked around. Then dashed the smoothed end against the rock where she was kneeling, and a shard flew off to show its heart of flint, hard with a newborn deep blue baby eye milkiness. Seven times she struck the kneeling rock, and the stone lost her smooth white shell.

The next day she stowed Lady Stone of Freedom under her nun's habit, and her neck felt the sharpness under the straw pillow. In the morning she was allowed to bathe, and Lady Stone nestled in her armpit as she floated beyond the breakers, right to the rock that had let her blood. She clung with one hand and honed the midnight moon blade.

Weeks.

One day . . .

One fine day she pulled the stone from her loathed scratchy dress, and the sun struck clear through the edge of the blade the way she fires her blinding light along a sunset cloud. Fire over indigo. One fine day.

That night, or maybe the next, Eva lay in bed with Lady Blade Freedom a hand's grasp away. She steeled herself to stay in her bruised, angry, frightened body while one of the men came into the hut and threw his clothes on the floor. His breath reeked of the alcohol they made in Hell. Vomit rose as his fist pushed her thighs apart and he lay on top of her, the same fists digging into her back. He bit her neck while he raped her. It was the pain of his teeth that sent her arm snaking down sinuous as Queen Cobra to clasp her hand around the flinty handle of Lady Bladestone Freedom. She sent the strength of flint through his ribs and his mouth gasped, his teeth opened on the last gasp and he was a dead weight.

Her body gushed sweat as another shadow appeared in the doorway.

'Ah, let's leave him to it! The cunt's got her arm round him! We've finally got our log of wood to have feelings! I'll have the bitch in the morning! We'll go and give the faggot some fun!'

The door creaked shut. She waited for hours under the chilling flesh until the howling they called singing had died down. Then she shoved the dead rapist on to the floor. Lady Stone slashed at his penis, and Eva stuffed the cold flesh into his rigidly open jaw.

Outside the hut, the air was clean, stars bright as ice crystals.

The night was hers alone.

A Dance By The Ocean;
A Flight By The Light Of The Moon

She knew where she had to go for safety. Maybe even for escape. *Escape? Escape?* Her fears jeered and gibbered. *Mad Hattie, Mad Hattie.* Her heartbeat thumped with the name of male mockery as her talisman. But to go straight there would mean sneaking past the madmen's huts, maybe walking straight into one of the rapists . . . she sweated at the thought and clutched Lady Bladestone Freedom until her hand was moulded numb to the rough handle.

She'd seen most of the island on her night flights, escaping from the men and their terror/power/hatred. But now her body was with her, and whimpered its fears. Could she trust her spirit visions? She cursed the fear in her flesh, then slowed in a shadow. Her flesh had taken all the vile abuse, her body had carried her safely through what passed as life so far. It was her snivelling and fainting that had saved her from the gibbet. That and a swollen belly that had turned out to be nothing but a racking gush of blood months later. It would have been the bastard of the man she'd murdered, and how she'd hated the thought, sick every day at her treacherous womb. But it had saved her life, this tricksy body, always knowing how to survive, when her headlong spirit would have cursed and spat with no compromise and she would have been dead. She shut out memories of how her child body had learned to smile and please the thing called father in fear of her own death. Too much to think about in the face of present extinction.

Crouched like a stone in the shadows, she clasped her hands round her knees, and rubbed her thumbs into the acid-frozen muscles of her calves. Peace.

OK, Lady Body, she told her flesh, *we're in this together.*

There would be a time when she would so strengthen the fearful sinews and veins that she, body and spirit, would never need half measures again. She closed her eyes. Now, if she stole past the loathed washing stream, she could grope her way to the snaggle-toothed beaches to the east. It would not be safe to travel by day, and she felt sure of a cave to hide in there. Her cursed dark skin – the thing called father had once sold her to a freak show – would now be a cloak of invisibility. Her callused soles glided along the path silent as an owl's wings – and suddenly she stopped, gasped, for they had hit the chill stream water. So soon! There was work to be done with this running water. She plunged Lady Bladestone Freedom into the flow and rubbed her every surface clean, the numbness in her drowned hand washing her clean of the lifesaving murder. No, murders. The one that had brought her to Hell and the one that would free her.

She hacked at her stupid dress with her blade, cut it away from hem to knee and tucked the hampering wool against her thundering heart.

Then on was spirit memory. She banged against rocks, tumbled into ruts and dips, caught her bare flesh on sea thistles and sucked in breath for a curse. Her body tingled after the thistles and she fell to all fours, inching her palms through grass as sharp as a scourge, wriggling like a serpent. Her palms crumbled earth ahead of her and she knew she was right at the

241

edge of the jagged downward slope to the beach. She lay flat. Lady Body goosebumped with fear, Lady Spirit goaded her on, knowing what paralysed fear would mean with the men in the morning.

Her fingers clenched around the wiredrawn clumps of grass and neither terror nor exasperated coaxing would shift them. Her spine eeled past and sent her solid thighs and calves and strong feet over the edge, toes became metalled insects sensing for a place to grip. They settled firmly and jolted her frozen fingers downwards to bury themselves in earth. Toes scrabbled, fingers followed as the cliff soil crumbled and loosened, her spine pressed her aching flesh to the lumps of stone and dry clay. Feet found a ledge, and her hands flooded with heat and strength as their palms smoothed away any trace of her escape. She was clamped to the cliff like a limpet.

Winds ripped at her and tore away the strands and tatters of cloud from in front of the nail thin moon; the sky was filled with her misty silver sails and she flooded the night with her unearthly light. Eva looked down. The beach was a ghostly spit between the glittering waves and the gut-lurching darkness between her feet. She closed her eyes on the horror of falling and gave herself, body and spirit, to this tumble down route to freedom.

Crab shell rigid and ice-bound with cramp, suddenly the soles of her feet stopped searching as they met damp chill sand and she knew she'd reached the beach. Then she opened her eyes, twisting to face the sea, for all the world a rock, a shadow, so still was she.

A breeze scudding over the sand brought her the sharp scent of salt and damp green seaweed. Her back was cold with drying sweat, and the deep chill from the sunless shelf scooped inwards at the cliff bottom. A pistol shot rang out and sent her into a thing of metal-muscled stone. More shots – but not shots. The crackling sounds came from rocks to her left. Ghosts? Demons? Some fool man playing target practice? But nothing moved save the black and blue bands riding over the sea and her eternal waves.

Eva breathed the pungent air and listened to the suck and slap of waves against rocks, the muffled rattle of shells against pebbles against sand. The foam wave-heads broke into skeins of tattered lace and bubbles, bursting with a moon-glitter into grey nothing.

Her eyes picked out shades of black and told her how far one jagged monolith stood behind another. Her body eased itself to crouch on her heels.

Footprints would be a mistake, and call a dawn *hulloo!* from the ratpack gaolers. She needed her cave. It was impossible to know how far away dawn was – her rapists had taken from her all sense of time: darkness meant humiliation, fear, pain, and flying the night skies to be free; daytime brought curses and fists and drudgery and bad food. Shit! The sun could come bursting up over the horizon any moment now!

But the moon rode serenely into a deep blue lagoon of starry sky high above her. Cloud made an eerie white atoll round the clear night waters, and she knew time was hers until the silver crescent beached herself way across the spangled sky.

She arched her feet to smudge the smallest toeprints in the sand and stuck close to the cliff. She swallowed spit on a curse when she stubbed her toe in deep shadow and felt a rock shelf jagging at her knees. Here the shadow held a solid emptiness and she wriggled inside it on all fours, sniffing the dankness of Cave. She turned to face the night, spine bristling with unease.

243

'This could be my last,' she said quietly to the sky in its cavemouth frame. The moon was a whisker away from her fluffy white shore, and as one sharp horn began to be muffled out of sight, a slice of rainbow appeared on the whiteness. The coloured band grew to a perfect circle against the cloud, and Eva watched it, with a sure knowledge that the cave was right, that the moon would be back next night to guide her just where she needed to go.

Deep in the cave she scabbed hands and knees on sharp and slimy surfaces. But she was so tired the hurt was numbed, and she climbed high, braced against rock-strength she couldn't see until there was a ledge wide enough for her to lie on with no fear of rolling off. She pulled the hated deep hem of the dress from her heart and bundled it under her head.

Sleep, deep sleep in the womb of the cave.

She woke in blackness from a dreamless sleep, or at least one whose dreams eluded her memory. Her body ached from the path she'd taken, but there were no other aches, no dull bruises on her thighs from rape, no male-clawed gashes on her breasts or shoulders. It had been the first night she'd ever spent by herself. Brothers and sisters and father and terrified mother and the first man, the next man, the man she'd killed, the stinking shared gaol pallets, the male bodies: she had never just stretched out in the morning by herself in her life before.

Hers was a terror of darkness, but here she felt safe, ran her hands over her belly and thighs and curled up with her self, aching and at peace. Until her heart started thumping as she heard voices muffled and echoed from outside her safety.

'Fucking bitch! I hope the tides have washed her away . . . away . . . away!'

Small creatures die of fright, and her heartbeat tore at her like an autumn storm against bare twigs. But at the same time, her fists clenched, arm muscles settled solid like steel and she slowed her breath to almost nothing, like the Living Dead in the freak show. They'd taught her how to do it, and her heartbeat took its cue and slowed down.

If they only knew how she wished to be away!

For now she stayed still, cursed her hunger, cramp, need to piss, and then soothed her body with hopes of *not long now, my lovely.* Just the words her mother told her when she screamed that she wanted the thing called Father to GO! DIE! DISAPPEAR! Now as then, she simply slept in the embrace of the rock as she'd slept in her mother's thin and anxious arms.

Waking later, she hung her body as far as she dared over the ledge. Nothing but darkness. She slipped silently down the rock and padded forwards, wary in case there was a sudden burst of sunlight and the men sitting waiting for her. When the light came it was rosy and gentle, a grey-pink sky whirled all across with white and silver cloud like a loose skein of wool. Sunset was on the way.

She saw the foot-tracks in the sand, up to the cave mouth and away again. Silence. And then a richochet of gunshot sent her scuttling back to her bed. Wait! Last night there had been the same cracking and no man there to make it. Eva knew about the demons and ghosts and evil creatures of darkness who'd kill any human fool enough to intrude into the night.

They were shape-changers, they could make things seem to be there that weren't. Paths that led out across water and disappeared. That was Agatah Marsh.

They'd been travelling one late dusk on a path by a lake. The lake had been beautiful in the sun, but the cloudy night made it look treacherous.

'Agatah Marsh,' her mother had said quietly. 'She lived here. She told travellers there was a bridge and guided them there. Horses and carts and men and women would pay her silver for her help and set out across the bridge. But halfway, the horse would fall forward and drag the people and all the load deep into the cold waters. They would all drown. No-one ever caught Agatah Marsh. She could change herself into a tree stump or a stone or an owl. And it's not so long ago . . .'

Eva shivered, remembering that fearful night, where every dark tree seemed to have mad wild fingers to grab at her, where boulders leered and grinned in the darkness, and the lake was misted over with the phantasm of a bridge and people screaming as the waters closed over their heads. The wind made the branches dance like a madwoman on the shore, dancing with delight at her wickedness. And what had her father done? Hit her for crying, hit her mother for telling the story . . . he always had a reason to hit them both.

She spat into the sand.

The silence built up again, and she crept to the cavemouth as all colours merged to grey. The men had been there. Her senses told her they had gone, the moon confirmed it with a sudden flow of silver lapping waves, rocks and sand. Moon was safe.

'If there's a ring around the moon when you make a wish, it will come true.'

Her mother had told her that too. It was one night when they'd run from her father. He'd caught up with them though, and she'd never believed it. Perhaps her mother hadn't wished hard enough. Last night, Eva had wished for escape and safety with her whole being. She gazed fiercely at the moon, now as fat as a slice of apple. A faint watery rainbow glimmered, and she wished it and herself to life. The rainbow glowed, then burned.

She leapt into the scuffed sand of the rapist searcher's first footsteps and kicked and stamped. Then she danced along keeping time with the waves. The father thing had taught her to dance and collected money in the street as her feet and arms flew and she smiled, smiled, smiled. Now she grinned, teeth biting the air, dancing for herself and the Moon, as wild as she'd always wanted to be.

Suddenly the broken-toothed beach was a stage and she cartwheeled. So much nearer to Mad Hattie. And, she thought, cat-springing into stillness, if not Mad Hattie, then the white sheer cliffs of the splintering stone. Oh-blivion!

There was one more thing to do beside the ocean. She stripped off her clothes and dumped them on a rock. Lady Body shivered, Lady Spirit sweet-talked her: *we're going to feel much better afterwards.* She laid her knife by her clothes and walked into waves so icy that they numbed her. She washed her whole body, let the salty water flow between her thighs and cleanse her. Gazing at the moon she swore there would be no more filth for her body, then stumbled back to the sand, her drying skin on fire. She licked her hand and swallowed the briny taste deep into her. Clean inside and out. The hated rough robe was comforting now.

Moonlight buzzed along a damp loose zigzag of sand. She followed it, followed the glittering white stones up the far cliff, grabbed at wiry bushes when her feet slipped and once screamed as roots came loose, let her body fall, to be caught by the steep slope of rocky ground. She was panicked by the scudding urgency of clouds overhead, and made herself lie still. As if pawed by a gentle giant hand, she rolled over and watched the sky.

The clouds were making pictures, come and gone in a second. Huge faces of women laughing free, whose parted lips became an eye; the shadow of a chin became a serious strong mouth, patches of sheer white cheek split to become the brow of a wise woman. The night sky was alive with their faces, and every one smiled on her, gazed deep into her eyes with their own, held a strength and wisdom that held her. Then a perfect face formed and stars twinkled in the deep pools of her eyes.

It was time to move.

Hitting the stream so soon had made her realize just how small this island was, little more than an outcrop of stone topped with grass, far enough from anywhere else to dump devils like her. Recklessly she decided to make straight for Mad Hattie and her house of wood and moss. The men would have gone there first and she shuddered at what they might have been bold enough to do to her, bold enough from their loss of pliant easy fuck: her disempowered self. She glanced at the sky. Now her whole moonlit cloud face was a wrinkled crone laughing deep from the belly bowl of the horizon.

Let them do their worst! She wriggled over the cliff edge on to the tabletop of the island. It was comfortable to crawl through mud and grass and drop flat whenever she heard a pore-pricking sound. She closed her eyes to see and feel where she was and where she could go.

You can fly.

She balked at that.

Lady Body would have none of it – afraid she'd be left behind? So it was belly and knees and elbows and thighs on the earth. And Lady Bladestone Freedom digging in to tug her forward when the ground softened and scared her.

She felt herself pulled to follow the dimples of moonlight on pools and glittering rocks. She had to keep slowing from frantic, tossing a look over her shoulder to her guiding goddess. Moon. Moon. She was always on the right track.

The cry of a sea bird dagger-slashed the air. She paused by a rock, and put her lips to the earth to breathe silently, for an anguish had risen in her and tore at her every cell. Oh shit, oh shit, oh Jesus, Mary, shit, Hell, damn, there was more than grass in the dark patch of grass ahead of her! Her eyes slitted and her hand closed on the clump of murderous flint-heart stone by her breast.

A dark shape sat up from the grass, and her spine and thighs and calves and ankles coiled to strike.

'It's Eva, isn't it?'

The voice came from a hand span below where the top of the head made a rough dark line against the sky. She sprang for the throat and dug the moonlit venom of her knife into neck flesh quivering over life-pulse.

'One word above a whisper and your blood goes to feed the seagulls,' she hissed. 'Who the hell are you?'

She smelt the sweat of fear. Not hers. She was exultant.

'I'm the faggot,' whispered the dark shape. 'The one they raped before you came. I'm the one who wishes he'd burned with his beloved, rather than what's called living in this Hell.'

'Then it's Hell for you? Hell for a *man*?'

Her hand clenched in his hair, she felt hot wetness gush down her wrist. The man was weeping.

'Hell, Eva. Hell for a man like me. No fallen angel could have devised what they've done to me, and to you from what I've heard.'

He didn't ask her to let him up and she loosened her grip on his hair. They lay side by side.

'So how come you're here?' her voice rasped, even in a whisper, and her hand didn't shift from its grip on the stone against his throat. When his voice came, it held no treacherous honey, no lying fright.

'The Mistress sent me. They went to challenge her this morning: where were you? They ransacked her home for you. They won't be back. She told me to find you and bring you to her. It's all right, Eva, she trusts me: she said to give you this, so you'd know.'

He pulled a stone from his shirt and put it in her palm. The Moon ran gently across the surfaces, like tender flames caressing a thin edge of wood. The heart of the stone held milk blue and gold like dawn. Her hand closed around it and she stowed Lady Bladestone Freedom in her clothes.

'The Mistress. The one they call Mad Hattie?'

'Yes.'

'Take me there.'

Sometimes it seemed they were turning back on themselves, and she gritted her teeth and grasped the Moonstone. Then they would go ahead and she trusted his shifting shadow close to the ground. He stopped suddenly sometimes and her fear gushed sweat. What if he was lying? Well, she'd stab him first and fall on her blade second. They would never take her alive.

He twisted his body and hissed in her ear:

'Nearly there. Listen.'

She listened. Birds of night, an uneasy wind-whisper

through the grass, the distant sea-sigh waves lapping the shore, the savage roar of breakers smiting the rocks softened by distance. The faggot clasped her hand. It was curious for a male hand to clasp hers and be strong and warm and asking nothing.

And then came an owl cry.

'We're clear,' he breathed. 'That's the signal.'

'Owls on an island?' she hissed.

'The Mistress will explain everything,' he murmured. 'Follow me.'

Two jagged dips and dells later and they flattened against a ridge. There was a fire-glow and smell of slow-burning turf; her eyes picked out a doorway: they were on the crest of the dip where Mad Hattie, the Mistress, lived.

The faggot went first, crouching at first then gradually upright, hooting softly as he stood. Eva shadowed him, flesh still fearing betrayal. And then the shadow of a great bulky woman, a bulwark of a woman, filled the glowing doorway.

'Have you found her, Gilbert, is she with you?'

His hand reached back and she clasped it; he drew her into the amber glow and she searched for a face, for eyes, in the silhouette in front of her. She caught a glimpse of the woman as Mad Hattie stood sideways and welcomed them into her home.

Heat. A blast of heat that sent chill scurrying into the trackless dark. Heat like a furnace with all its blacksmith glow, radiating from the hearth at the centre of the far wall. Gilbert, the faggot, led her to a pile of cloths and sat her down, one hand passing over her shoulders, before he too sat down facing her. Mad Hattie, the Mistress, her bulk and shadow moved between them and she filled cups with boiling liquid, then sat on the floor facing the fire. She sat down the

251

way an ancient oak would sit, with a massive magnificence, speaking solid trunk, speaking of a canopy of a million leaves settling.

'Drink,' she said.

Eva drank. In the liquid was the green of wild herbs and sun-stroked leaves; the sweetness of nuts; the tartness of berries; the kick of quayside moonshine. She drank thirstily, felt she was drinking the essence of the earth herself, and when the clay cup was dry, she looked up.

Mad Hattie?

The Mistress?

A woman who had stolen, robbed, murdered, torched, witched . . . what had she done to be cast out on the high seas to Hell? Who survived and lived in this dark bad time?

She saw.

A woman like no other she had ever seen or heard of.

Face?

First, foremost, fabulous, her Eyes. She didn't blink, this woman, just fixed Eva's eyes in those deep pools of visioning. If she'd had anything to hide, Eva would have been squirming. Her mother had told her a story of a woman from the Northern Lands whose eyes stopped the rivers' rushing torrent, stopped the leaves from growing, stopped men in their foolish tracks. To kill her, they'd had to blindfold men to go and blindfold her, bind her to the ground and drive wild horses over her body. To kill her. Rather, of course, than to gaze deep into her magic Eyes and maybe – maybe – *learn*?

Eva felt her rage and murder and rape and tears burst their banks, and those unblinking eyes watched the torrent of stinking shit go by, into the shifting

252

landscape of wood and fire and flame and simply disappear in the smoke puffing and curling through the hole in the turf roof.

Stripped to the cell and bone, more naked than birth, she fixed on those eyes, those scrying eyes. Brown, like hers? Blue? Green? Hazel? Eyes, eyes, eyes. Then the woman blinked and freed her with the slow closing of lined lids. Freed her only to look at her face. Everything this woman had ever done or felt or seen was written on the skin of her Face. Laugh? A thousand lines were a web starting at the dark centre of her eyes, a skein that had cast its joy down her wide cheeks to lift her mouth into laughter.

Tears? A million had scored their track down the valley of flesh under her eyes, spilled over her cheeks, gushed around her mouth held wide or tight-closed with sheer pain.

Worry? Between the greying brows a line rose sure and wavery as smoke, cast its distress along her brow to the silvered temples etched with lines like distant waves on the ocean. Worry had eroded the flesh above her lips into cave-crumbling rivulets.

And anger! Anger, rage, fury, sparks in the firelight snapped from her eyes and settled into slashes along her jawbone and chin.

Love? In those deep eyes, all at once still, like a calm purple cloud after a storm and before the freedom of a rainbow, love? Such love that Eva didn't know if her heart should race or stop. Love like a smoky river haze at dawn, fleeing before the proud and scarlet banners of sun claim the sky.

Love.

Warmed by whatever the drink was, swept into total relaxation by those moments given to contemplate the eyes and face of Mad Hattie, the Mistress, tough Eva the knife wielder and murderess was wholly open to the Love pouring from those eyes. She saw everything without words to explain it, she wanted to use all the words to tell this woman her life, not to be told what she should have done, not to be sympathized with, but simply for the first time ever, to hear herself, to be Heard.

She told Mad Hattie her life. Everything. Bursting out with a volcano of outrage, pouring out with an ocean of tears; halting memories of fear and anger whispered in painful spurts like a weeping wound.

Her back cringed as she closed her eyes and felt again the terror of night and the endless mindless blows her father used to numb and terrorize her into nightmare and silence. She crouched the way she had in the cage when the owner of the freak-show stood over her with his whip; her body writhed recalling all the men, her partners in crime, her gaolers, her rapists. Each bone in her body raged with its remembered pain and her eyes burnt in an ocean of blinding, scalding tears.

Mad Hattie sat unblinking and nodded like judgement itself. But there was no judgement in her eyes. Slow and massive, her head took all the pain and spread it smooth like a cliff calming the worst that waves can throw at it.

Eva trembled as she came to the murder she'd committed; her hand clenched into the self-saving stab wound that had sold the rest of her life to this sterile island. She beat her furious fist against her head and bit her palm for the shame of tears. Eva does not cry. Eva's as tough as old boots and kicks back!

Mad Hattie raised one hand and silenced her.

'Murder,' she said, and her voice held the word suspended between them. 'Let those who've never had a knife at their throat talk about murder. Those who've never had a man at them when he's not wanted. Those whose throats have never felt hands close about them: let them say murder and talk of turning the other cheek. Ah, if it's a slap and the man's in drink, then maybe you turn the other cheek until he's passed out. It's called staying alive; is that a crime? Turn the other cheek and then you get out and never cross that doorstep again. Keep running. But what if there's a knife keeping you from the door? If murder is standing in front of you, Eva, it's you or him.'

Eva stared at her and felt as if she was breathing clean for the first time in her life. The air rushed to her brain and made her dizzy, made her see Mad Hattie in a chaos of stars, her face blanked out except for her eternal eyes. She felt like she'd been half-floundering, half-drowning, and this solid woman and her slow voice were a floating tree to cling to when she'd gulped so much salt water she was crazed and sick with it.

'You mean—?'

'Yes,' said Mad Hattie. 'I know. You know. We've no need to speak of it. I did what I had to, and there was never a flicker of choice. And you had no choice. I'd like to put my judges where I was and see what they'd do with it. They said I'd have a lifetime to repent. Fools! I've got nothing to repent of.'

'How long have you been in Hell then? I call this place Hell. The devils are running it, you know? Sticking you with their dicks like pitchforks, twenty thousand horns on their stupid heads!' said Eva.

Mad Hattie smiled.

'That's what they'd like you to think,' she said slowly. 'They'd like to break you. Well, Eva, I've been

255

here long enough. Long enough to make what poor wine you can from the shivering scraps of green in this place. I've had time to get used to a pipe stuffed with seaweed foul enough to make me howl for tobacco on bad nights. Long enough that I've earned the title of Mad and glad of it. It keeps them away from me. They think I'm a witch and I am, but not how they mean. Long enough that I've seen beardless boys come and leave as white-haired ancients with their bones blue and shining through their flesh.'

'You mean people get away from here?' Eva's eyes blazed with hope. 'Then let's go!'

'Sewn in canvas with a stone for a footstool,' Mad Hattie told her. 'No-one's ever left this place alive. Yes, I've been here long enough.'

Eva looked at her. There was not a note of resignation in her voice or a line of acceptance written on her marvellous face. Her eyes burnt as steady as the peats in the hearth, and her hands held the cup like a chalice. Should she tell her about flying out of her body and ghosting the jagged fortress of the coastline? About her dream of free falling from the cliff to escape? Yah, shut it, Eva, maybe you're a crazy woman. Maybe you've caught it from being here. But if she was, how would she know? Christ!

'Long enough,' Mad Hattie said. 'I swore in my dreams that if ever a woman came to this island, it'd give me the strength to escape. And always the picture I got was so shadowy I thought my dreams were warning me from even thinking about it. But my spirit has planned and flown and schemed and had me a thousand miles away a thousand and one times. I wasn't to know the woman who was coming was you. Eva with the brown satin skin.'

It was the first time anyone had said her skin was

satin. Everyone in her life had felt free to jeer and point at her colour, poking her with wet fingers to see if it was a stain, stripping her naked to see was she brown all over. *Dipped in shit, art thou, maidie?* Bastards! *Thy father must have lain with a she-devil to get thee!* She'd hated her skin. Here, by the fire, every pore in her body purred at the thought of being satin. For satin was special. Satin was beautiful. Eva is beautiful? Even if it took a so-called madwoman to notice it?

'The only way off this island is off the white cliffs,' she said. 'The cliffs to the north. If the tide was in, we could float and swim and see where the sea took us. The waves for a pillow, you know?'

'No,' Mad Hattie said. 'If that could be done, not a soul would be left on this island. The tides would just take us back to the mainland and the gallows. The other way, there's no land for a thousand miles or more. You're right about the northern cliffs, however.'

She passed Eva a pipe stuffed with shreds of weed and herbs. Eva lit it and grimaced.

'We're going to have to get out,' she said, 'if this is all the smoke I can look forward to from here to eternity. It's disgusting!'

'Now,' Mad Hattie said, smiling dangerously. 'Who's free to leave this place?'

'The bastard gaolers in their rotten little boat!'

'And? When you were dream-falling over the cliffs . . .'

'I wasn't falling,' Eva said. 'And who told you, anyway – don't answer, my brain's spinning mad already. It was weird, I'll tell you. It was like I was flying.'

'Yes,' said the monumental woman solemnly. 'The birds. They can fly anywhere they please. And so shall we.'

'Oh, leave me out!' Eva snapped. 'The only place we'll fly is straight down to the bottom of the sea. Which happened to be full of water last time I looked. I've got this funny thing, you see. I like breathing. And I've found it's best with air, you know? Tastes better and all that.'

Mad Hattie yawned and grinned.

'You're good for me, Eva,' she said. 'It's wings we need.'

'Wings,' said Eva, 'You mean like sticking feathers on our arms and flap sort of wings?'

'Wings like sails,' Mad Hattie told her. 'Wings of cloth soaked in seaweed water to seal all the holes. Giant wings that we harness ourselves to. With the winds we stand a chance of getting blown beyond the tides and then it's luck or loss.'

'I don't have anything to lose,' Eva said. 'Let's do it.'

'Good,' Mad Hattie said. 'How?'

'You're good,' said Eva. 'You've been here long enough to have found your way round the markets and the shops. Which emporium would you recommend, mistress? What fabric shall we choose? A gold brocade? A shot velvet? Ah, no, let's have a look at that bolt of scarlet cambric? Shall we have it delivered, your Highness?'

'Exactly.' Mad Hattie's eyes were twinkling and her shoulders shaking with laughter. 'In all my years here I've never been visited by a dressmaker. The wool we wear is too heavy. The only kind of material light and fine enough on this island for what we want is what the gaolers wear. We'll need their shirts and breeches.'

'Problem,' said Eva. 'Those stinking turds only changed their clothes when I was there to wash them. How do we get them naked now?'

'I shall have it put about that you had a plague that drove you to jump in the sea with fever. I'll have Gilbert rumour how the devils live in dirty clothes and the body needs air to fight them off.'

'Who's going to buy that?'

'All of them,' Mad Hattie said. 'It's enough that I'm a woman, a witch and mad with it. They fear my knowledge and my power – why else do you think I'm still alive and able to live as I please? As much as I can in this place. Give it two days and I'll wager we'll find our cloth. And we'll have a night to cut and stitch, then dawn will see us fly away.'

Eva dreamed of a rushing wind that tore the grass from the earth with its roots; a wind that ripped the ramshackle roofs apart; a wind that swept clean across the island to the north cliffs.

There she stood with Mad Hattie, cloth like folded bats wings heavy behind them. She could hear furious baying and laughed aloud as their gaolers stumbled towards them in all their ugly nakedness. The wind stirred their wings taut and lifted them clean across the ocean.

The Island Of The Silver Monkey

A world away, in a warm and wild ocean, Queenie and all her crew were dazzled by seas that were the dashing blue of a kingfisher's wing and as clear as glass. The mermaid swam sure as a swift at sunset, and *The Empress of The Seven Oceans* skimmed along in her wake.

'Atlantis!' Lametta thought desperately. 'Atlantis! Why did I have to promise them Atlantis?'

Because of course she knew where Atlantis was.

> Let the wind bring a ship without a sail,
> Let a mermaid swim without a tail,
> Walk on the sand on the arm of a whale,
> Bring me the blood from a patch of kale,
> And I'll show you Atlantis!

It was a favourite rhyme of her mother's, guaranteed to silence the thousand whys and hows Lametta could find between rising and breakfast. But the split-tails didn't know that! Any old undersea city would satisfy them and keep them to fin for a while longer. As soon as she got wave of an island, she'd steer them there, and amaze them with the cathedrals and boulevards of coral flanking the sheer white sands.

She swam tirelessly, and noticed with pleasure that the irritating confetti of carp and crayfish scattered clear of her path with frantic glances at the looming bulk of her tame ship. She could sing as loud and long as she liked, and celebrated her freedom with a rousing chorus of her favourite coarse ballad.

What shall we do with the boiled egg water?
The sailor leered at the mermaid's daughter.
What shall we do with the boiled egg water,
Early in the morning.

The women aboard the ship listened uneasily.

'There'll be a storm!' Alice fretted. 'Can you not hear?'

'Aye, it's a shrike,' Queenie said. 'Makes your blood run cold. It almost sounds human, doesn't it? The first time I heard that was in the Bay of Storms and I could have sworn someone had tossed a baby overboard and the poor drownded thing was crying for mercy!'

She scanned the empty blue skies and frowned.

'Not a cloud in sight, Alice. And I cannot see the blasted creature that's caterwauling either. It sets my teeth on edge.

The sound stopped as they listened.

'These are strange seas, bonny lass. That was maybe the echo of a ship swallowed up here long since.'

Lametta dived, clutching a bleached strand of grass that promised land within the day. She wouldn't have them see it first! But she had reckoned without the four curious and piercing eyes high in the crone's nest. Jen and Squirrel were up there, and Jen was teaching Squirrel how to turn a piece of wood into anything she wanted to, nicking and scoring with a sickle moon of a blade. They had heard the cacophonous chorus Queenie had taken for a shrike and Jen had muffled hysterical laughter when she realized it was the mermaid singing. Squirrel had scowled; her perfect passion for Lametta would not admit faults. She'd heard Sister

261

Mercy singing and hated it, although Rowan and Esther had said it was very good *church* singing.

She turned a little away from Jen. That was probably bloody brilliant sea-singing!

When she first saw a different shade of blue shimmering on the horizon, she said nothing. The light here was so different from even the sunniest day in the forest or on the sparkling river that had taken them to the sea. Shadows were solid black and sunlit surfaces so sharp that they dazzled your eyes to squinting. The sea was a silver sheen that left brilliant dots of colour dancing inside your eyes when you closed them.

All aboard were kissed brown by the sunshine, hands gloriously dark when held against the inner wrist, calves turned rich coffee, and the golden faces made all their eyes searingly bright; apart from Sister Mercy who remained head-to-toe grey and hooded from the delicious heat at all times.

But the distant shimmer stayed there, and Squirrel nudged Jen and pointed.

'What d'you think?' Jen asked evenly. She wanted to stand up and shout *Land ahoy!* But she was very wary since the mermaid had started lording it over them. What she had told Esther and Rowan about sideshow trickery was true; she hadn't told them about the Chicken Lady and the Living Skeleton and the Dog-headed Man who came to cluck and clatter and snarl at her in nightmare though it was years since she'd first seen them. They had been with a one-eyed scoundrel who cracked a whip at them and said he owned them. He threw potato peelings and cabbage stalks through their bars when people came to see them, and laughed as they scrabbled for the swill.

Granny had swept Jen away from the filthy cages, and railed at Jethro to be rid of them; the next day their keeper had driven away cursing, dark sheets covering their bars like a funeral cortège. Jen had felt sick at the sight of them, nauseous and outraged at the way they were treated. Granny had told her to save her pity for the living; the keeper, she said, was evil, and no blood flowed in the veins of his creatures. Shape-changers, she said, casting salt around the camp. How did she know? She knew. It was the one time Granny had used that tone of voice and her word was deep wisdom and law. Jen had never forgotten them.

She feared that the mermaid was tainted with the same evil, for all her proud posturing and loveliness.

And if she was, then anything connected with her was dangerous. The distant smudge of blue might be an illusion, a trick to draw them over the edge of the world into an unreality with no way back.

'I think it's land, Jen,' said Squirrel. 'It looks like when we first sailed away and I looked for the town and the river next day. Alice said squeeze your eyes up and you'll just see it slip over where the sky meets the sea.'

'I think it's a secret,' said Jen. 'Because no-one else has seen it, have they? It's a secret for us two, up in the crone's nest.'

Well, Squirrel knew that was rubbish. Hadn't Jen told her that the crone's nest was the eyes of a ship? That she must sing out loud and clear if she saw anything? She'd hollered everything from *Waves ahoy!* to *'Ware, seaweed to starboard!* until the novelty wore off. She looked at Jen, puzzled. *She* knew it was land, surely! But there was a line scored deep on Jen's brow and her lips were drawn thin.

'OK, it's a secret,' Squirrel said.

Jen smiled briefly and squeezed her hand.

Lametta brushed a twig aside and squinted at a pair

of seagulls with scarlet beaks curved like a cutlass. They were plump and glossy, a sure sign of shore. She balanced on a wave-crest for a moment, and held Spinks aloft to see. An island! The octopus stretched out one tentacle following Lametta's pointing arm.

At that moment, Sister Mercy ventured to the prow and took the gesture to be magic most foul: by pointing her unholy finger, the creature and her familiar had conjured up land where there was none before.

'Land!' she screeched hysterically. 'Land!'

Lametta thrashed round to see which split-tail had the nerve to steal her thunder and swallowed her rage when she saw the Shark Slayer high above her. For a moment their eyes met and Sister Mercy held her crucifix in front of her. Lametta dived in a huff and swore she'd ransack every wreck between here and the Blessed Isles and find a bigger and better mast-and-spar treasure to hang round her neck. That would impress the Shark Slayer!

Who was unaware of her envied status, who had fallen to her knees to thank God that he was merciful and had rid them of the satanic siren. Who was then doubly dismayed when the whole crew rushed to her cry of *Land!* just as Lametta surfaced.

She looked at the crucifix as if it were a treasured timepiece that had just struck thirteen and muttered a desperate garble involving a steadfast faith and heart and things sent to try us and the patience of Job. Casting her eyes to Heaven, she caught sight of the gulls inspecting them with their crimson-ringed eyes. She caught her breath at their bold beaks, hooked like the Devil's claw and as scarlet as sin: what circle of Hell was this that they had come upon?

'Yonder lies Atlantis!' cried Lametta. 'Follow me to her fabled courts and fountains!'

'Aye, aye, your Empressness!' sang out Queenie, and strode back to the tiller with a strange twist of a smile.

Your *Empressness!* Better than a dozen Marchionesses and Duchesses put together! Lametta smirked and preened.

It was late afternoon when they could pick out tiny palm trees clearly etched against the gold-blue blur of the island. Lobsters scuttled to coral safety from the flickering shadow of Lametta's tail and the majestic bulk in her wake. Electric blue and silver sprays of fish flew through the water like leaves in an autumn wind. Queenie had Jen and Rowan hanging over the side, sounding the shallows as they manoeuvred between the garish pink and white jaws of the reef. Eee, this ship handled as light as a skiff, she skated sweet as a lily leaf until Queenie judged it was time to drop anchor in the pellucid lagoon.

Lametta and Spinks splashed in the shallows while the women rowed the ship's boat ashore and hauled it above the tide-line.

'I'll show you the sunken city tomorrow,' Lametta promised, her rampant libido demanding immediate attention from the irresistible Spinks. She managed to swim with haughty dignity until they were out of sight beyond the reef, then clamped into the embrace she'd missed like breathing for almost twelve hours: a lifetime of celibacy!

Princess flung her head back in the hot salt breeze and dug her toes into the pearly sand. Her eyes feasted on the lush palm fronds, and drank in the artless perfection of a waterfall tumbling between the trees and across the beach. Until that moment, she'd expected the reality of a South Sea island to be a shadow of Queenie's sumptuous bravado. The heat was incredible, perfect, lifted by soft breezes. The honey smell of fruit and a salt tang laced the air like good brandy. Discarded shells lay everywhere, whorled and spiky, painted with amber stripes and sworls, carved with pyramids of purple and green, perfect, opal-sheened.

She caught a flash of ruby and diamond in the trees and ran towards it: the jewels took hectic wing over her head and vanished into the next tree with a pizzicato ringing as pure as crystal. She stood still and searched the trees. Spring-green fronds, bleached trunks peeling and tattered, a deep dappled shade enticed her with a whisk of something white; a silver monkey? She shook her hair loose from its braid and ran into the trees.

Sister Mercy had refused to go ashore. She didn't believe in any of it; not the sand nor the reef nor the trees. For a moment she had wavered; it would be sweet to touch dry land again! But who was to say that the land wouldn't melt under their feet and the trees disappear in a crack of satanic scorn? She had watched them land and nearly called out to them to come back for her: it all seemed solid enough.

Seemed! That was the word! For how long would they walk in that unearthly beauty before it melted and left them floundering in the deeps?

She mentally scourged herself and decided that a fast was called for. Her flesh was getting altogether too demanding. Why, she'd almost cast aside her habit this morning, as she sweated and itched in the harsh wool. Yes, she'd thought of decking herself out in unholy cotton – and on this ship that would mean the immodesty of breeches. It was time to take herself in hand. Just as that poor bear had to suffer in a fur coat, so she would suffer in the garments of her order. Listen to her! *Suffer!* The garments chosen for her by God, and her thinking them a burden!

She forced her swollen feet into her heavy sandals, wincing at the split peas she was using in the absence of good grit. A little penance was called for: oh, God forgive her, a lifetime of penance! She bared her head in the sunshine and sank to her knees on a coil of tarred twine.

As she raised her sweating brow from clenched fists, she saw the fish-tailed abomination and her monster plunge past the reef. Good God, was the creature trying to drown her? She gazed at the pair and saw a look of such unholy joy on Lametta's face that she stood upright and raised her crucifix high.

'The Shark Slayer!' gasped Lametta. 'We've got to go deepsea, Spinks: she's the only one who'll see through me unless I get a mast-and-spar too! I'm doing this for us, you know. Oh, squid shit!'

Spinks looked mournful as she wrapped herself round the mermaid's throbbing shoulders and they plunged out of sight.

'Well, here's your desert island, my hearty hinneys,' said Queenie. 'Fresh water and fruit and crabs as sweet as nuts and daft with it. Look at them!'

A phalanx of crabs was waltzing towards them, each with a blue claw held aloft and clacking a warning. Turtle clutched Queenie's thigh. The big woman just laughed and swung her shoulder high.

'Divent ye fret about crabs,' she said. 'Do you know how to confuse a crab, do you? Well, here it is. See how they go sideways in a little circle? Why, all you've to do is dance round them the opposite way and wait till they catch on and start following, then back round you go: look!'

She took on the boldest crab, which was waving with all its crustacean menace at her bare toes.

'Round we go!' roared Queenie and true enough, after a twirl or two, the crab stopped with a baleful blink and scuttled the other way.

'What next?' called Esther as she and Rowan reeled on the hot sand.

'Ah, they give up after a while. Not before you're dizzy and right out of puff, the blue-clawed bastards!' cried Queenie.

Sister Mercy stared in horror. Thank the Lord she'd refused to go with them, they were dancing as if possessed, whooping like Bedlam. But what would happen if they never came back? Or came back stone mad? The Lord will provide, she thought frantically. Ah, she was parched with thirst, her body oozing sour sweat. It was the first test on a fast, that dry burning in the throat. Three days without water and then a half-cup at noon and the same in the evening. As if to mock her resolve, Jen and the bear broke away from the Hellish fandango and ran to a silver glitter between the palm trees. Fresh water! Sister Mercy swayed.

Well, they might be taken in by this infernal mockery, but *she* shuddered at the thought of the contamination in that water. They'd lose their immortal souls if they took the fruits of Satan into the temple of their bodies. Sister Mercy licked her cracked lips and knelt again, closing her eyes and clutching at the humid beads of her rosary.

The crabs gave up on chunks of toe and ankle. Besides, it was nearly the time when the red-bills swooped out of the sky and flipped over any blue-claw in sight, razoring the shell open as if it was paper. Turtle watched open-mouthed as the crabs scuttled away to the damp sand and vanished, only a briny bubble exploding to show where they'd sunk.

'Will they come back, Queenie?'

'Who's that, pet?'

'The blue-clawed bastards!' shrieked Squirrel. 'I'm a crab, I'm a crab!'

She snapped one hand round Jen's knee and wrestled her to the ground. A heap of sopping wet bear joined in and sent Squirrel skimming into the waves. Then the bear stood up and shook herself all over Jen.

'I give up on decency,' Jen said, stripping her sandy wet clothes off and laughing. 'Don't you think we should get Sister Mercy to come ashore? I'd like to rip that manky old robe off her and give it a decent wash. I thought cleanliness was next to godliness.'

'Ah, the hacky holy woman,' said Alice drily. 'By, she has her moments, and I almost like her. Then she snaps as tight as a clam again, and it's all I can do not to shake some sense into her.'

'She's better with a drink inside her, I have noticed,' said Queenie. 'I feel like a lump of shite with the way she looks at me. I know I've a bad gob on me, but she gets offended at every frigging word I say. I cannot be doing with it! She did us proud with the King's Navy, and I'd hoped that'd loosen her up a bit.'

'She talked to me about that,' Esther said. 'That was a mortal sin, in her book – the Good Book. Lying.'

'Well, I'm damned for one then!' Queenie roared with laughter. 'Or does one lie cancel out another? Can you not lie to a liar? That dogsbreath captain called himself a Christian and you could tell by looking what ruled on his ship. The lash!'

'She doesn't see it that way,' Esther said. 'She's had Evil and Satan pushed down her throat with her mother's milk so she thinks it's food, not poison. I don't know what we're going to do with her.'

'Well, tonight we're doing nothing,' Alice said decisively. 'Let's sleep here, out under the stars.'

'We'll need a fire,' Queenie decided. 'The sun goes out like a blink in these parts, and it's cold as a witch's tit in half an hour. Not that I've ever come across a witch with cold tits, mind!'

Rowan drew a sign in the sand and gave her a questioning look. Queenie nodded and drew another, Alice yet another.

'Not something we broadcast,' she said. 'Christ, when those holy horrors took Princess I wanted to scream at them – take me if you want a witch! And I would have done, only then they'd have had both of us.'

'Then let's have the night for a ritual,' Rowan said. 'Let's bond and bind our strength and get some clarity. We couldn't do that with Sister Mercy around, and I think we need it.'

'And so do I,' said Jen. 'I'm not happy about this mermaid, the Empress of The Seven Oceans.'

'Oh, divent ye fret about her,' said Queenie. 'I've got her number.'

'Oh aye, lover? Well, you would have,' said Alice, snuggling into Queenie's beautiful arms. 'Don't kick me, Turtle, there's room for the both of us. And what's her number?'

Queenie smiled benevolently, all eyes on her.

'I'll wet me whistle,' she said, twinkling.

'Why do I love an auld soak like you?' Alice wondered. 'Maybe because it gives me a guinea pig for my latest brew, and one with guts of steel too!'

'Ah, you'll never kill me off,' Queenie told her. 'Anyways, this mermaid. She's a mermaid all right. Only by rights she'd have drowned us by now if she could. One, I made excuses for your Squirrel being a bairn and she took them. Would a high and mighty Empress give a damn whether it was a child or a dotard had lobbed owt at her? No, she would not. And then she wants us to go with her where she's going so that the Great Mermother can decide our fate. Now if we'd dropped an anchor on her head or fired a fizgig her way, you're talking serious. But what did we do? Chuck a couple of knobs of wood that didn't even hit her? What's to stop her deciding for herself?'

'Well, I've thought that,' said Rowan. 'But then I thought some more. Perhaps she's got something in mind for us and this is just a cover.'

'True enough, or mebbes,' said Queenie. 'But what did I call her today – your Empressness? And I'll swear the silly bairn was pleased!'

'Bairn?' said Alice.

'Aye, bairn,' said Queenie. 'What grown person has a daft great lump of a pet octopus draped all over her like a kitten – think about it. I divent know how old a mermaid is if she's a bairn, but that one I call a bairn. Now what she wants us for is anyone's guess, and I'm not tampering with mermaids that can raise storms as easy as blink. But I'm more empress than she'll ever be. Ah, divent ye giggle that way, Alice Yeldham. I know bluebloods. Not to speak to, even I couldn't get that one past you, but I've been in courts and palaces the world over and this I do know. Bluebloods don't ever have to prove it by swaggering and showing off. They know they're the most important people on earth, whether it's a gold-skinned Highness in silk from head to toe, or a brown-skinned Majesty with nothing but feathers and shells. They just divent see the likes of us as walking on the same ground. They only notice us if we give them no, and then it's off with your head and no quarter. That Empressness there – she's no blueblood!'

'Queenie, my honey,' said Esther. 'You're wrong about the octopus. That's no kitten. Haven't you noticed, it's got some kind of power over our mermaid? It's only got to appear and touch her and she disappears really fast.'

Squirrel squirmed out of Jen's arms and burst out:

'At least she knows what the map is! I don't care if she's a bairn, Queenie, I'm a bairn and I'm not stupid! None of you could read that map!'

'I'll row you out to the ship right now,' said Queenie. 'I can show you where we've gone today unless the stars above are lying in their twinkling teeth. This isn't Atlantis! This is one of a little necklace of islands discovered by Capitano Hoja di Coca. A reet rapscallion, that one, never furled in the skull and crossbones once in thirty years and knew every cove and island in the oceans! All of the Blood use his charts, and he even made charts for the King of Spain – leaving out all the hideaways, mind. That gave us pickings for years after! The mighty galleons sailing west for treasure – and sailing back home to be picked off like birds on a fence!'

Squirrel scowled. She couldn't argue with Queenie.

'I know you like that mermaid, bonny lass,' said Queenie. 'But you've a deal to learn. You can like someone and know they're not perfect, you know.'

Squirrel frowned. Could you? *How* could you?

'And the thing with that, pet,' Queenie went on soothingly. 'Then you know they can like you and you not always be on your best behaviour. Ee, if I thought I had to stay sober and never curse with Alice around, well, we'd be through liking each other in a week, cuz I couldn't do it. It's pretending to be something you're not, and if someone likes the act you're putting on, it's hard graft to keep it up, is it not? Look at me round Sister Mercy!'

It was a lot to take in. Squirrel frowned.

'See what I mean? Sister Mercy'll never like me till I mind my mouth and manners and join her in praying and churchifying,' Queenie said, wishing she'd never started. 'So is it me she likes? Or just folk who'll follow all her rules?'

Squirrel sat next to Jen.

'I like you and you've let fly at me,' said Jen.

'We've shouted at each other from the day you were born,' said Rowan. 'And I even love you.'

'Anyway,' said Esther, 'maybe the mermaid isn't an empress. It sounds like she's pulling some kind of trick on us. So far I like it. If it gets dangerous we've enough power between us – what are we? Women or witches? There's ten of us and the power of the Holy Church too if that'll impress her!'

The nun fainted dead away as Queenie and Alice flew aboard to a rousing cheer from the shore to collect blankets and pillows and food and candles.

'Ah, she's asleep,' Alice said maternally. 'It'll do her good.'

Princess chased the slipping streak of silver into the heart of the island. Breathless, her head throbbing from the heat, she sat against soft white bark in deep shade. Waxy leaves spread as wide as waggon wheels, midnight blue against the sapphire sky. On the ground lay dry pods the shape of garden pea pods, but as long as a prize marrow and with the rich chestnut sheen of buffed leather. There was a disreputable-looking clump of trees in front of her, leaves hanging in bleached shreds, trunks as thin as her arm and skewed every which way. Here and there, clusters of glistening scarlet berries were the only sign that there was life in the brittle shreds. Life within and – she froze – lovely life itself and almost invisible: her silver monkey was sitting in the spindly branches, its fur the same chalky shade in the sunlight. Even its unblinking eyes could have been points of sepia shade.

Oh, it was a beautiful creature! Princess stayed still and unblinking herself, poring over its delicate fingers and the neat way they fastened round a stem. Its long tail lay neatly along a trunk, just the tip curling to grip tight. And it was staring at her, this great clumsy rushing thing that had crashed along behind it and now sat still and quiet.

It broke the gaze in a slow blink, and raised one perfect paw up to scratch its head briskly. The same paw reached out and picked a berry in its tiny fingers, brought it to its mouth as the other hand picked the next one, and its lips pursed as it spat out the stones in between. Not a movement was wasted; it fed briskly and shifted along the branch just enough to reach another cluster when all the first was gone.

Princess swallowed and her thoughts turned to food and drink. She didn't want to move and disturb the creature, but she was getting stiff. And hungry. And thirsty. All the sounds of the island came to her with carnival bravado: parrots sang as harsh as trumpets; somewhere above her an invisible bird gurgled and chimed like a bell under water. A screech of outraged scorn flew from a treetop, and something made a great clatter of leaves and cracking branches as it fled.

The monkey froze as Princess stood up slowly. She looked away from it, and sauntered through the trees to the sound of rushing water. The river carved a deep gully through the fine silty soil, so she slid down the overhang, clutching at roots as hard as stone and arched like spider legs. Her feet gloried in the racing cool shallows, and she edged herself into a swirling pool. On the opposite bank a forest of primeval rhubarb shook great tureens of green leaves in the airstream. A scarlet feather zigzagged to the river surface and caught against her bare legs: she stuck it in her hair. Winged seeds and crazy dragonflies, gleaming metal rainbows dashed along the river: birds swooped in a blur at the silver flow and vanished in the treetops.

Something silver flickered at the edge of her sight, and her skin prickled from her belly along her spine and numbed her fingertips. Instinctively she knew not to look, just to listen to the sounds of bold splashing. Only when a rain of water landed in her ear did she turn to meet the brash amber gaze and grin of the silver monkey. Its exquisite paws scooped up water and dumped it on its head; a wild blow to the river sent a spindrift of spray all over her. She flicked a stream of water back and the creature danced away, clapping its paws. They played until Princess was drenched and delighted: the monkey stopped and looked at her quizzically.

She felt ravenous!

She got up slowly and heavily and sloshed along the current: *follow the rivers, hinney, and they'll always get you back to shore!* She was itching to see if the monkey was following her, but knew not to look back. Tiny fish flew around her toes like gnats; from time to time she ducked under a smooth fallen trunk as thick as the mast of *The Mermaid's Eye*. No, *The Empress of The Seven Oceans*. A much better name for their ship, she thought. She thought the mermaid was sensationally beautiful and envied her arrogance. Well, she *was* Princess Yeldham and had been all her life.

She jumped at a screech of alarm from behind her

and leapt on to the strong fallen trunk bridging the river before she knew what she was doing. The monkey was behind her screeching in mid-flight to a lofty branch. The river surged below her as a metallic row of brown studs burst its surface. Her blood ran cold as two yellow eyes ran over her and passed on, and the creature went under her log: its body went on and on and on, as sure as the powerful cogs driven by a mill wheel. There was a flash of a thousand teeth, the flicker of a fish and a pink stain in the water. Then the creature sank out of sight.

Princess was frozen until she started shaking, scanning the river ahead, toes curling in fear, and nausea filling her throat. Suddenly the garden of eden forest was full of menacing shadows: the creepers overhead swished like snakes, the undergrowth shifted with god alone knew what, and she swallowed a scream.

The silver monkey swung down to the naked roots of her tree and groomed itself nonchalantly. So the danger was over. She ran her fingers shakily through her hair and found a great comfort in her own touch, massaged her trembling skull until she felt calmer. The monkey yawned and tiptoed waist deep into the river. Princess felt the water was still treacherous, and made her way along the bank while the silver creature laughed her to scorn all the way down to the beach, glorious and golden in the late sunset.

'My bonny lass!' Alice called to Princess the moment she appeared.

Princess ran over the sand and held her mother tight. Alice stroked her hair and rubbed her shoulders, murmuring comfort until her daughter's grip loosened a little and her heartbeat stopped hammering her body breathless.

'We were going to start worrying about you at

sunset,' she said gently. 'Queenie was frantic. Hell, I was too, but you're a grown lass now – who's your friend?'

Princess looked over her shoulder to where the silver monkey was sitting solemnly staring at them.

'Saved my life, Alice, there was a creature in the river, it was as big as a boat and had hundreds of teeth and it would have got me. Only the monkey screamed out a warning. I was terrified.'

'I'd never have forgiven myself,' Queenie said, squashing them both to her. 'I was cursing all the tales I told you when you were a bairn. I left out the scary bits, pet, you see – and then you'd disappeared. There's snakes that look like a pile of stones, snakes that you'd take for part of a tree; there's fish that lie on the riverbed under the mud and you never know until their blasted poison spines have spiked your foot good and true. There's snakes that swim in the cloudy waters and you never know until they've sunk their fangs into your ankle. Ah, sweetheart, you're safe!'

'I'd never have gone exploring if I'd known the half of it,' said Princess. 'Anyways, I met the silver monkey and she took care of me.'

'There's sailors that keep monkeys for pets,' Queenie told them. 'Dress them up like a maharajah and have then dance on a fine gold chain . . .'

'This is no pet,' said Princess. 'This is . . . well, I don't know. Only all my life I've dreamed of a silver monkey and this one's let me be close. She lives here! How could you take her away somewhere strange? You could never put her on a chain, it'd be like prison.'

'I always thought that,' said Queenie. 'I had a parrot once. She took to my shoulder for nigh on a year and the beak on her! Cut my ear and neck to shreds, and she learnt to talk. Mind, she learned from me, and that's enough to make most folk blush. She flew away one time we'd landed and I never saw her again. I had to laugh though, thinking of her sitting in a tree somewhere cursing a blue streak and roaring for ale!'

'Sit down with me, Princess,' said Alice. 'I've been a lady of leisure all afternoon, sewing a fine seam. I had it in my mind to finish this quilt of ours by sundown. And I will, only it won't be this sundown. And I'm having second thoughts about the pattern, sitting here.'

Princess sprawled beside her and rubbed the silky petals of the rose between her fingers.

'All these are English flowers,' she said. 'There's something else you need, Alice. Look.'

She spread the quilt out and they walked round it.

'It's the heat,' she said suddenly. 'By, in England, you're so glad for a bit of sun you go out and bask in it. I never knew heat like here, the shade's a blessing. You need to put some leaves in – d'you think?'

'Mebbes,' said Alice, squinting. 'I can't picture it.'

'All round the edge,' Princess said. 'Like the leaves I saw today before the river monster. There were some as big as cartwheels, some as fine as lace. Some of them had the sun on them like polished glass. There were leathery ones shaped like giant hands; some of them were closed up like a fist in a fur glove. I think you should make a border of them. Look!'

She grabbed a stick and drew in the sand.

'Ah,' said Alice. 'I could do them in velvet, couldn't I? And some of that pearly material we've got in the hold. I can see it now. Oh, blast you, my darling, you've given me months of work.'

'It's where we'll sleep for our lifetime,' Queenie said. 'Who cares how long it takes?'

'See you with a needle in your hand!' Alice laughed scornfully.

'I'll keep our sails trig,' Queenie said. 'These old paws of mine are fine for twine – I don't even need a thimble to push a needle through sailcloth.'

She strode up the beach, with Turtle her adoring shadow. Alice and Princess sewed, glancing at each other when the silver monkey skedaddled over and sat on the quilt, picking at the fabric with her delicate fingers, sniffing the gaudy blossoms. She high-stepped her way to Princess and sat beside her, teasing her loose hair ferociously and scolding every tangle free.

'I've never seen such shells,' Rowan said. 'I don't know half their names. I can say witch's hat, oyster, scallop, razor. But what can we call the new shells? They're simply magic. Silver purse, baby's nose, sleeping snake, arrow-flight, mountain ridge, star-wheel ... Oh, my Belle, I can see why you don't bother with words.'

Isabel looked up with a smile. She was arranging the shells on a smooth stretch of sand. Big ones in the outer circle, smaller ones starting a spiral, trailing down to sea-pearled fingernail size at the centre. Just beautiful, thought Isabel, squatting and drinking them all in.

Judith sat a few yards from her, a peaceful smile on her lips, her eyes following the child's every movement.

Esther gathered fruits, frowning a little at their unfamiliarity. How to tell what was good to eat and what might be poison! She figured that anything without spines must be fine: the spines were a guard against animals and anything animals ate women could eat too. One bite would make sure of that: trust your tongue! Then there were fleshy fruits in shiny suncolours. Her nose said yes to these before she even saw them. She dithered over bruised gourds and rejected their bitter metal scent. Her fingertips sensed drums of deep green rind, and thrilled at the solid coolness. She saw a clan of russet monkeys gorging bunches of yellow pods and took their word for it. Finally she found primrose-yellow waxen star-shaped fruits. Edible or not, they were irresistible. She heaped them on a fibrous leaf the size of a child's boat.

Queenie and Turtle combed the shore line for wood and swathes of dry leaves for the bonfire. The child dragged branches as long as she was tall, and staggered along with bales of dusty sea-grass up to her nose. Queenie gave her an excuse to stop with every trip, but Turtle pursed her lips and refused to rest. Anything her heroine could do! And Queenie took it a little easier than usual, treating herself gentler than her usual hell-for-leather self-punishing pace.

Out on the reef, Squirrel sat scowling at the universe. There was no sign of the mermaid-empress. It was all very well, bonfires and feasting and at least the nun wasn't there. BUT. But surely, now they knew what the map was they should sail day and night following it. Even the mermaid-empress had no sense of urgency. What had she said – she'd be back *tomorrow*? Squirrel fretted at the idea of a whole evening and night messing around.

She glared over her shoulder. Jen had asked her to go fishing, but she hadn't even bothered answering that one. Fishing! You did that on a lazy afternoon, not when you had oceans to conquer! And there was Jen, lounging on a rock, gazing into the water. Probably whistling. Probably hadn't even noticed she wasn't there. Squirrel had flung herself into the nearest tree in a fit of pique and almost fallen: the stupid tree hadn't got any branches and she'd grazed her thighs climbing to the huge clump of leaves at the top. Then she'd seen a brilliant green thread whiplash through the leaves, a vicious arrow-head with scarlet lips and eyes glittering like ripe blackberries. Danger was written into every wiry curve and she'd backed down the trunk, heart racing. No-one had noticed. Huh! She'd swaggered away, kicking up sand and only stopped when she ran out of reef. And she was planning to stay there until someone gave her a bloody good reason for moving.

Queenie sat and wondered, her back against the shaggy pelt of a sand palm, her arms and body a nest for Turtle, lying on her lap and getting heavier as she slept. Her toes squeezed the cooling sand, and she shifted to fetch out her pipe without waking the dear babe.

Her gaze travelled to the last pennons and furls of sun-set and swept the melding horizon, the silver-pathed ink of the sea; she focused on the trim silhouette of her ship, riding safe in the limpid lagoon. Her eyes creased with a smile at the sight of Squirrel determinedly facing out to sea at the farthest point of coral. That was a right little bugger, and she loved her. Loved too that no-one had ever shouted and clouted her spirit to fear.

But she knew that back-to-you-all anger. It would be up to her to draw Squirrel back without losing face: up to her and Turtle she thought with surprise, registering the solid warmth of the sleeping child.

And there was Jen's tall and easy walk, a pole across her shoulders, sure-footed on the rocks. The black lump of the bear lumbered at her heels. Jen carried a good catch of fish, and paused at the edge of the sand to turn to Squirrel, then she shrugged and walked on.

Aye, it would be up to her.

Her eyes lingered on the palm trees, precise black stitches against the sky. Her whole face mellowed, breathing easy as she came to Alice and Princess. Her family, her lover still sewing in the twilight and all for their love; her grown woman child happy with the silver monkey caressing her head, grooming her like one of its own.

Such peace she had never known. She knew she was loved, she knew she loved, she knew she was alive.

Devil take the silly mermaid: suddenly Queenie wasn't worried. That was tomorrow and this is tonight. This is now, and time to light the fire and raise the power. Not even the thought of the nun and her bitter God could cast a ripple across her happiness.

Queenie sat in wonder a while longer, then stood in a slow curving movement that scooped the child smoothly against her breast; her sinuous steps didn't wake the sleeping Turtle. Only when she reached the pile of branches and kindling and shifted her weight to one arm did Turtle wake up and smile at Queenie in perfect love and trust.

She struck a light on the stones around the bonfire and set the flame here and there. In moments there was a blaze that drew them all into its golden warmth.

'Squirrel,' Rowan said, with a sigh.

'I'll get her,' Turtle said, slipping to the sand and starting off for the reef. Suddenly she turned and said:

'Will you come, Queenie? That's a right stubborn bugger, you know.'

'I do,' said Queenie with a chuckle, and took her hand.

Right, thought Squirrel, right then! She concentrated on ignoring them both.

'Can we join you, bonny lass?' Queenie asked, and waited for her nod before sitting down.

'You must have had the best view of the sunset here,' Queenie said, lighting her pipe.

Squirrel hadn't even noticed the sunset. She said nothing.

'Will you come to the fire?' said Turtle. 'You'll get cold out here. And there's fruit, Esther says, better than any fruit we've ever had.'

'We'll need to be up early for the empress mermaid,' Queenie told her. 'I'm hellish for rising early. We're going to need a lookout. Good sharp eyes and wide awake come sunrise. I thought I'd ask you, if you're doing nothing better.'

Well, it was something if Queenie was asking her as if it was a big favour! She scowled and glared at her. One hint of a twinkle and she'd never come to the fire. But Queenie looked very serious, and met Squirrel's glare without blinking.

'OK,' she said and stood up. 'I'm starving. We can't sit here all night, you know.'

She kept it up until they were on the sand, then giggled.

'Do you really need a lookout?' she demanded.

'We do,' said Queenie, forcing herself not to laugh. When you're seven years old you need your dignity. Everyone in the world that matters is bigger than you and they're always deciding your life or telling you to snap out of it. Queenie knew that you'd snap out of it when you were good and ready. Squirrel was good and she was ready.

'Race you to the fire!' she screeched and tore away.

'I don't race anywhere,' Queenie said to Turtle. 'You go on if you want.'

'I don't race anywhere either,' said Turtle firmly and gripped her hand.

Squirrel leapt on Jen as if she hadn't seen her for months. She wished she'd gone fishing, wished she'd seen the sunset, wished the whole afternoon had been different. But now was pretty good, she reckoned, collapsed in Jen's arms.

'I think we have to go along with the mermaid for a while,' Rowan said. 'It riles me, being ordered around, but what else can we do? She's got all the cards. She could wreck the ship, and then where would we be?'

'We'd still have this island,' Princess said.

'D'you think she'd leave us be?' Queenie said. 'Not that one! She'd whip up waves to wash away everything living here. We can't cross her. Besides – tomorrow she shows us Atlantis. That's worth a bit of patience.'

They ate and drank, basking in the heat, but there was an unease curling around them slow as peat-smoke. Esther sucked a star-fruit dry, and leaned forward.

'What we must do tonight is bind ourselves together. Whatever happens, we have to know we're together as sure as breathing. Together in our thoughts and actions, completely at one in our hearts and spirits. There's enough power and magic between us to keep us all safe.'

'What about Sister Mercy?' said Princess, sighing.

'Ah, never fret about her, Princess.' Alice spoke strong and slow. 'She's in no state to be with us the way Esther means, and she may never change. People don't. But she's no threat away from her church and all its wicked sanctifying. Ee, I'd have thought she'd be seeing clearer: the inquisitors, the King's Navy, the mermaid. It'd be enough to blow God and all his saints out of my mind, if they'd been there in the first place. I reckon she's got a sick squint on the world. She only sees what she wants to and if something doesn't fit, why, she pretends it's different.'

'Aye,' said Queenie. 'She'd believe the sun rose in the west if a bishop told her her immortal soul depended on it.'

'And take it on as her duty to convince the rest of the world it was Holy Writ,' said Jen bitterly.

'Do you see what's happening?' Esther asked. 'Listen to us! We're spending a lot of time and anger and disappointment – oh, all those feelings! – on running around Sister Mercy. We've got to stop. We need all our strength for ourselves.'

Queenie looked at her. That was a woman who didn't waste words: she'd never heard Esther say that much before. In the firelight, she could have been a thousand years old with the wisdom sitting serene and serious in her face.

'How do we do that?' asked Princess.

'I have to tell you, daughter of mine,' said Alice. 'Your mother's a witch, bonny lass, not one of your broomstick and baby's blood woodcut horrors, but . . .'

'I know,' said Princess. 'I mean, I thought so. When I used to take Granny Wood her dinner, she told me about the craft and warned me to keep it close to my heart. I started noticing things about our house after that.'

'Why didn't you say?'

'Why didn't *you* say?' Princess repeated. 'When those bastards took me, I was scared they'd wring it out of me and that I'd betray my own mother. Katherine told me what they did to make you talk, and I knew I couldn't bear it. Just couldn't bear it and I'd blabber like a coward. She said they could get you to confess to anything just to stop the pain.'

'It's true,' said Queenie. 'They got a woman to swear she'd put the evil eye on a flock of sheep and dug up dead bodies to feed to her own children to please the devil.'

'Once they put the fear in you, you're gone,' Esther said. 'And they've got the word of law behind them and weapons to make it stick. That's why we took to the woods. We couldn't live under their laws: there was no room for us as we are. And we're not changing. Why should we?'

'I thought I could make them change,' said Queenie. 'Being that I could better any one of them with my gob and my fists. Oh, aye, mighty mouth and the seven seas to strut about on. They acted like they'd changed when I was around, but it was only show. Turn my back and they'd carry on just the same, rape and robbery and all the savage rules they stuck to for running a ship. Ah, they make a ritual out of hurting each other; they call it discipline. Ee, god, I've lashed out in anger many a time. But they store it up, they plan it out, you know? Clap a man in irons and leave the poor bastard sweating and shaking all night. Then lash him up in the morning and flay the skin off his back. And that just for drinking a cup of water more than his due, or sleeping on a watch that's too long after a day's work that's too hard. I couldn't keep my anger boiling all night for tripe like that. Sling some of the cargo and load more water, I say. Go slower and sleep enough!'

'You kept your rage hot for that Italian,' Jen commented.

'I did,' Queenie said. 'He'd ruined a woman I loved. I didn't let it eat me up over the years though, once I'd decided what I'd do with him if I ever got my hands on him. I'm no frigging saint, but I feel cleaner for what I did to him.'

'I thought I'd killed Jethro,' Jen said. 'And I was glad – it felt like I'd rid the world of his wickedness. Then when I saw him again, I was afraid at first. As if he could harm me. But I watched him for a while, I saw the way he was limping and I thought: no, you've no power over me and you just might think twice before you start on anyone else. That I doubt, actually. He'll just pick on anyone weak, like his poor fool of a wife and my drunken fool of a dad.'

'Anger,' said Esther, breathing out a great gust of air. 'We need to harness that anger, wild women! We need to know that we drive the anger, and it doesn't drive us.'

Judith nodded in the shadows, the words feeding her broken spirit. Ever since she'd been dragged from her home, fear had tied her tongue and grief bound her heart. She'd been deeply moved by the things Alice had told her about her husband. Was it possible to be angry with him? She'd loved him, feared him, borne his child, closed her hopeful heart to the pain of his lies and betrayal. Knowing he wanted her dead had left her frozen, in shock; she'd beaten herself up night after night wishing she'd somehow seen it coming, been wise enough to get out with her child long before. All the signs had been there, and she'd not had the wit to read them right.

When Alice told her that she'd had no choices, she clung to that truth and slept a little easier. And she knew the woman Alice had described, her husband's whore. Was she jealous? Yes – but not for her husband: she grieved only for her lost child and the years that woman would have with her, all the growing years that *she* should have had with her.

Isabel slipped her hand around Judith's fists and stroked her wrist. Judith smiled and held her close.

How she loved this silent child: she loved her like little Ruth, oceans away.

They put the tools of anger in the circle.

Queenie's curved and deadly dagger; Alice's scissors; Jen's knife beside its soft woven case; Rowan's slingshot of stone and leather; Esther drew out a sickly-green bottle: pure and deadly poison, she carried it always; Squirrel put her knife down – it was like a toy, she thought, and added stones.

Esther looked at Judith, a question in her eyes. Judith shook her head, then wrenched the wedding band from her finger. She felt calmer and lighter at once. Isobel shook her head with a wonderful smile. Rowan mirrored the smile.

'Turtle?' Esther asked gently. 'What about your anger?'

Turtle wriggled deeper into Queenie's arms. She was her mountain and her strength with rage enough for all of them.

Princess tumbled a heap of things into the circle. Alice looked at her grown daughter in amazement. Tufts of hair, a rusty nail, a gold piece, a horn button, a twist of straw, a cracked jewel, the pieces of a broken clay pipe.

'Tell me,' she said.

'Jonathan who blacked your eye. Martin who threw you against the wall. Simon who killed the cat. Batholomew that came to my bed one night when you were sleeping. Jake who did the same and gave me this gold to keep silent. The button from the witchfinder's waistcoat. That straw from the dungeon. The gaoler's pipe. That jewel was in your ring when Mark tried to steal it. The nail from gormless Gordon's boot.'

'You've got a long memory,' Alice said. 'I've put you through hell, my lass, and I'm sorry.'

'I got rid of them all, didn't I?' Princess said lightly. 'It was Granny Wood told me how to banish what you don't want in your house. And I was angry that you'd always find another wastrel to drag into your bed, always another one and always worse than the last. But that's all over now, Alice. I've a mind to give these to the flames.'

'Then do so, my lass. No. That's mine to do. You've carried it all long enough and far too long.'

Alice picked up the pile of debris and dumped it in the fire. As it burned, she found herself weeping as never in her life before. Princess's arm round her shoulder forgave her; she knew her child was a woman as their eyes met. A woman and her equal.

'No more anger?' asked Esther.

Princess grinned and tossed a string of heavy coins into the circle: Queenie had told her years before about knuckledusters, and she'd made her own in secret and used them to effect on the lechers and riffraff at chucking out time. They were more in awe of her fists than of Jonah the potman for all he was built like a prizefighter.

Sister Mercy woke in a sweat of fever. The moon was red, the stars stabbed her eyes and tore her back to the nightmare plunge into the river when the torches of the mob burned behind her like Hell itself. She hauled herself to lean on one elbow and squinted over the side of the ship. Another vision of Hell! The shore dipped and swayed around a great bonfire and a circle of dancing silhouettes whose shadows stretched to the edge of the waves lapping the unearthly crimson sand. *Help!* Her lips were as dry as stone and her tongue was numb. The sky whirled above her and the line of the ocean was split by a volcano of crimson and rose and lavish streaks of purple and orange. One hand clamped to the deck as she felt herself falling into blackness.

She was out cold.

'Now we've put down our tools of destruction,' said Esther, 'but let us never deny our anger. It's here, and here and here.'

She touched her heart, her brow and her eyes. The others followed suit.

'Feel it,' she said. 'Own it. Be proud of it. A woman's anger is an awesome thing. I feel my anger has driven me to escape, and now I want to use my anger to go where I want to. Right now, my fear of the mermaid's very close to making anger drive me again.'

'My anger always comes – snap! – straight after my first feelings of fear,' Rowan said. 'It scares me. I feel I could destroy. So much of my life has been defence: defending my children, defending my life, defending my lover. Here we are, with every chance to get free and find a safe place, and this mermaid starts treating us like servants! I've never been anyone's servant and I don't want to start now.'

'Why don't we just follow the mermaid? I don't understand,' Squirrel wondered. 'She knows about the map! Why have you all got it in for her?'

'Because she's lying,' Queenie said. 'Either lying or only telling us a part of the truth.'

Squirrel subsided.

'I don't understand why you trust the mermaid, Squirrel,' Jen said. 'Who do you know best in the world?'

'Rowan,' the child said gruffly, 'Esther. You, a bit. Well, all of you really.'

290

'Who do you trust? The mermaid or all of us?'

Squirrel sighed. It made sense, of course it made sense. But caution didn't speak to her wild heart and spirit. She dug grooves in the sand with her toes.

'We need to trust each other without thinking about it,' Princess said suddenly. 'I need to know that any one of you can walk up behind me and I don't even have to think about fear. I need to be able to *trust* that if I fall in the sea one of you will throw me a rope – do you know what I mean?'

'More than that, bonny lass,' Queenie said. 'It's like the storm we were in: I need to know that you'll lash the sails tight and if I reach out a hand you'll grab it.'

'I know that with Esther,' Rowan said. 'I know what she's thinking sometimes, I know what she's looking for. When we had to be silent in the woods, I knew from the look in her eyes what she wanted to do next.'

Alice poured more wine and smiled.

'You always know your own true love that way,' she said. 'And sometimes you think you know your child too. But there's always secrets. There needs to be. Goddess knows I trust Queenie with my life, and I'd die defending Princess . . .'

'That's what this is about,' Esther said. 'We don't usually have to trust people like that, apart from our lovers and children. But *here* and *now* we need to start building that trust between all of us. I'm as private as a woman can be. But it feels to me that I've got to let that go. There's seven grown women here and three children: ten of us faced with a new way of living. We can't trust Sister Mercy, she's brought all her religious rules along with her.'

'We have to be ready to act together,' Jen said. 'That mermaid's not finished with us. We don't know what she'll do next, and that feels like a threat.'

Queenie lit her pipe.

'So how do we do it, Rowan? Ee, I've never thought of it this way. It's a bit like when I first went to sea. The bastards I was shipping with, well, you slept with one eye open. But if there was danger: another ship, a storm, a wild coastline, you'd all pull together. You'd not turn your back on Billy in a bar, but you'd know that if he was lookout you could trust his eyes to see you safe.'

'That's it,' Esther said. 'We don't have to pry. I don't need to read your minds, but I need to know you're there with me. And if my child's attacked, you'll fly to defend her. And I know that. I wanted to say it out loud.'

She wrapped a green ribbon around her wrist and passed it round the circle until all their wrists were bound with the living colour above their linked hands.

'Whenever we're in danger, we know we're not alone,' she said. 'Belle?'

The child cut the ribbon with her silver blade and passed it to Judith.

'Always keep your ribbon,' said Esther. 'Keep it at your fingertips and hold it tight whenever you need to: we'll all be right there with you, whatever the threat.'

'That feels good and strong,' said Queenie. 'I don't know that mermaid's game, well, not a one of us does, but it'll be different when we meet her come morning.'

The children dozed off as the fire sagged down to embers and the last warmth brought sleep to all of them.

The Deep Road To Atlantis

Lametta's night had been less than perfect, and such things are galling to a self-styled empress. She'd combed five wrecks before she found a mast-and-spar large and jewelled enough to put the Shark Slayer in her place. In the second wreck, she'd disturbed an octopus which had taken an instant shine to Spinks and followed them with that fixed look of passion that only an octopus knows how to wear. Worse, Spinks seemed pleased with the attention, and Lametta couldn't work out the languid signals between the two. That was all she needed! She shot to the surface in rage and started to sing.

> 'Say you love me today,
> Let your heart never stray,
> Or there'll be Hell to pay,
> You'd better love me tomorrow!
>
> Swear that you're true,
> And make sure you are too,
> Or it'll be worse for you,
> I'll teach you the meaning of sorrow!'

All that happened was a shoal of luminous snub-headed fish nosed out of the waves and gasped their appreciation. She dived away from the octopus orgy she imagined Spinks was enjoying and swam blindly, her tears unnoticed in the salty galore of Ocean.

Spinks, however, was otherwise engaged. The sleeping octopus had absolutely no interest in her, but was offering her the entire wreck and its treasures in return for Lametta's favours. The initial waving of tentacles could not be ignored without a lifetime's loss of face. Oh, if she could only explain to Lametta! Octopus negotiations are more formal than the diplomacy of ancient Japan: they start with a polite enquiry into the past seven generations of each octopus. Their health, their location, their prosperity. This is followed by the ritual counting of suckers, comparing the colour and scent of their ink, checking that each has eight arms. A demonstration of swimming, floating and diving skills is *de rigeur*. And throughout, neither one must blink or take their eyes off each other.

Only then do they feel free to discuss the matter in hand. Which went as follows.

'Oh, mighty one,' said the octopus of the wreck. 'I honour your family, your suckers, your ink and your swimming. I offer you this humble palace and all its treasures in return for a lifetime's bliss with your mermaid.'

'Oh, mighty one,' said Spinks. 'I honour your family, your suckers, your ink and your swimming. My mermaid is a free spirit who has honoured me with her love, and I can no more think of leaving her or bargaining about her than cutting off a tentacle.'

Formalities concluded, Spinks hurtled away in search of Lametta. The other octopus sank back to her wreck, dreaming of mermaid-love, which is a hallowed octopus tradition, the height of octopus achievement. It was always worth a try.

'Have you seen Lametta the mermaid and her hair like the sunrise?' Spinks signalled to every living creature in the dark waves.

Trills of appreciative bubbles spurred her on. Soon a bitter turquoise taste filled her gills: mermaid tears! Hours later, she found a rock where Lametta was sitting wrenching a comb through her hair, her lovely spine rigid with fury.

'I hope you enjoyed yourself,' she spat, drawing her tail around her. 'I realize I don't have eight arms, silly of me to imagine that two would satisfy you. I will not be trifled with. I can only assume that this is goodbye.'

Lametta looked down haughtily and gasped in horror. Spinks was usually a delicious foxy rose colour, her under-tentacles a miracle of mother of pearl. Now her body was slumped and ashen, deflated, shaking uncontrollably: her eyes gushed a fountain of tears over the rock's surface.

'Spinks!' she cried and caught the icy body to her breast. 'I don't mean it, please, oh, Great Mermother, what have I done?'

Slowly, the body stopped trembling and a little colour crept back into it. *Don't ever doubt me*, thought the octopus, *don't ever doubt me, or I will die.*

For the first time their embrace was all tenderness. Lametta knew for sure that her octopus was just that: hers and hers alone and always would be.

Dawn rose, and Lametta was exhausted. Mermaids *feel* intensely and are unused to trauma. She had her mast and spar, she had her octopus, and she had a whole shipful of split-tails in fear of her groundless threats and waiting on her empty promises of Atlantis.

Wearily, she swam back to the island, one arm around Spinks and certain that she'd never let her out of her sight again, come what may.

Squirrel woke up with the first hint of sunlight. She

remembered banging her head against the sand five times just as she was falling asleep: Rowan had taught her that before they took to the woods, and it never failed. She sat up and shivered. The sand was cold. Ash and silky tatters of charred bark were all that remained of the fire.

She tiptoed past the sleeping women and sniggered at Queenie's snoring. I do not snore! swore Queenie and just wouldn't believe it. How could Alice sleep so deeply, curled up in her strong arms, her ear only inches from the noise? Was that a part of loving someone without loving everything they did? Grown-ups!

At the end of the reef, she squatted and scanned the grey waves for a sign of the mermaid. The sun was halfway over the horizon when she spotted the golden light on her hair. She shot back to the sleepers as straight as an arrow and shook Queenie's massive shoulder.

'She's coming! The mermaid empress!' she shouted.

'Have you got your ribbon safe?' Queenie asked. Squirrel's hand flew to her pocket to check and she nodded.

By the time Lametta swanned into the shallows, planning an imperious and rousing *aubade*, they were ready and waiting. Sacred sturgeon! That was disconcerting enough, and then:

'Good morning, Your Imperial Empressness!' bellowed Queenie.

Lametta pursed her lips: was there just a trace of insubordination in the split-tail's tone? She arched her eyebrows and looked severe.

'It's a beautiful morning for sightseeing,' Queenie went on cheerfully. 'And what a privilege for us poor mortals to see Atlantis!'

The words were just fine, thought Lametta. It was the way the split-tail said them. The mermaid was wary, and held on to her heavily jewelled mast and spar. She felt it lent her some authority.

'Look at her cross!' said Turtle, wide-eyed. 'It's like Sister Mercy's, only much much better. Is the mermaid a really important nun?'

'Ask her,' Esther suggested, smiling impishly.

'Mermaid, are you a really important nun?' Squirrel asked.

Lametta was flustered. What in the name of all plankton did the small split-tail mean? How could you be really important and none at the same time? This was not going well. She had anticipated respect at least – if not downright awe. And all she got was absurd jollity and a shoal of silly questions!

'Don't trouble me with trivia!' she said haughtily. 'I take it you're ready to dive?'

'Certainly,' said Queenie. 'Only we can't stay down for long, Your Imperial Empressness. Being human and needing to breathe air.'

'We'll only be undersea until the sun is high,' said Lametta impatiently.

'That's a good six hours from now,' said Alice. 'Divent ye understand, Miss Mermaid, we cannot breathe underwater? The water goes up our noses and into our mouths and there's an end of us! And you'd not have us drownded, would you?'

Of course! Yet another something that had been nagging at her. Mermother knows her own mother had explained that one over a fresh wreck when she was three meryears old. Split-tails only had a nose and mouth that couldn't keep them alive undersea. Lametta gritted her teeth. She had an elegantly discreet set of gills under her golden cloud of hair; gills that automatically took over undersea. Spinks nudged her and looked intelligent. What now?

'Consider the sea-spider,' thought Spinks. 'A genteel and highly-honoured cousin of my own eight-legged family. Her ancestors are to be found all over the world and some even thrive in water dangerously low in salt. She toils leggily and spins a web so fine it is a delight to her prey to spend their last moments in gossamer glory, a delicious drug drawing them into the next life.'

'What *is* it, Spinks?' Honestly, split-tails who couldn't breathe underwater and an octopus who, despite her many other charms, couldn't speak! Lametta felt that life was becoming just a little more than she could handle. The Shark Slayer was nowhere to be seen, and what had been the point of last night's exhaustingly celibate adventure if not to impress her?

'My exquisite cousin blows an underwater bubble even more delicate than the finest gold dot on your magnificent tail, oh glorious one,' thought Spinks. 'If you will pardon me for suggesting that anything could be more delicate! My cousin then adds tiny mouthfuls of air to this bubble until it's twenty times the size of her own body and she is then able to live under water for weeks.'

'Staring at me doesn't help!' snapped Lametta, only too aware of the crew on the shore waiting for an answer. Maybe it *would* be simplest to drown them, and take her chances with the vulgar curiosity all around her without the fake shark-shadow of their ship! She wished she'd never met them!

'If somehow we could construct bubbles for the split-tails,' thought Spinks, 'the problem would be solved. And if some other wonderful how I could make you hear me, oh love of my every sucker and tentacle, then all this thought would have a purpose.'

298

On the shore, Squirrel was getting impatient. Here was a chance for the mermaid to prove herself! Why didn't she say something and just do it?

'Well?' she called out. 'Do you *want* to drown us?'

Lametta glared at her. She was desperate.

'I shall retire to the reef and consider your problem,' she said, a trace of desperation in her words. She disappeared with an arrogant flick of the tail. Spinks stayed for a moment, beaming her thoughts to the women and children on the shore. Isabel smiled.

'Don't we get to see Atlantis?' Turtle asked. 'Queenie, I want to see Atlantis!'

Queenie hoisted her shoulder high, and looked grim.

'Now we come to it,' she said, 'did you hear a word of power from yon silly scaled bairn? Did you hear a word of three wishes, a tone of command? That eight-legged monster with her has more sense, I'll be bound!'

Isabel pulled her sleeve and looked up at her.

'Well, what do you make of it all, you silent little creature, eh?'

Isabel tugged her along the reef to a scoop of sea water caught and calmed between pink coral arms. She squatted there, pointing at the feathery plants bubbling the surface, anchored by a thread to the rosy outcrop. Queenie grunted as she went down on all fours to look close.

'By all the gold in a Spanish galleon!' she said, peering even closer. 'It's a spider as happy as a hog in shite, built herself a nest round a great balloon of air! Aye, Belle, that'd be one way. Only if we were to do that, pet, the air would keep us afloat. You must have the eyes of an eagle, bonny lass. It's a good thought.'

Isabel shrugged. So the octopus hadn't got that far. If

there was further to go, Queenie would take them there.

'We can wait for Madam Hoity Toity to remember she can grant wishes,' Queenie said, sitting solidly and lighting her pipe.

'We can also do anything we want to,' Esther said quietly. 'You're talking to three women and three future women who flew a raft over the falls with only a twist of twine and a wish.'

'Excuse me,' Jen said, laughing. 'Which was the more effective, my dears, the twine or the wishing?'

Esther looked at her, and her eyes were a thousand years old. Jen wondered at that look. Then at everything that had happened since she chanced upon Esther and Rowan and their wonderful children. Chanced upon? Had that been just a happy accident . . . or was it meant to be? Meant to be? In Esther's eyes she saw the same eternal twinkle as the stars in her granny's eyes: the gentle mirth waiting for her to catch on.

'So it was the wishing?' she asked.

'And the twine, Jen,' Esther said. 'And the skill to tie it, and the need to have it tied. Which came from the wishing to pass the falls . . . you see?'

Jen was startled by a vision of a great circle sparkling into a spiral, busy life leaping and impatient. The picture was tantalizing and vanished like sea foam on the sand. So much for her to work out!

'We've never dived deep and long underwater because we've never had to nor wanted to,' Esther said. 'If we want to enough, we will.'

She started to hum, and to unplait Rowan's hair.

'Oh, that simple, is it?' said Queenie. 'I want to be rich as a lord and live for ever. Now!'

'How did you fly?' Esther asked. 'I don't mean just

last night: that was a wild and witchy showing-off of your power . . . the first time, Queenie, Alice, how did you fly?'

Meldon, thought Alice, thought Queenie, their hands instinctively locked together, and a dusk from twenty years ago so lovely all around them, lifting them high above trees and fields and streams and sheep and hills. Even as it filled the endless space behind their eyes, they felt their bodies lift a hand's span from the warm sand and float there, glowing with the Power, delighted in sheer magic.

'You see?' Esther said. 'It's easy.'

'Can I do that?' Squirrel asked.

Rowan stroked her rosy cheeks.

'If you want to, my Squirrel,' she said.

Out beyond the reef, Lametta was torn between swimming right away from the whole mess, and her natural arrogance, which assured her she could work it out. Or bluff it out. It had been on the tip of her exquisite tongue to boast that she could grant wishes. And she could. She'd learnt how to use that gift on her sixth birthday. You just tuned into the thought/wishes of a mortal and channelled the power of the Great Mermother. But she didn't know how to stop at the traditional three. And that she would only have learnt had she stayed with her choir to the grand old age of eight. The power would simply flow through her, on and on, and *all* their wishes would come true for ever: even if they wished her dead or a thousand miles away. What a backlash that would boil up! An immortal mermaid extinguished through the very power that had brought her life in the first place! She'd have to take a chance on their ignorance.

What choice did she have? She sighed and swam back to the shore.

'I have considered,' she said.

'Ah, divent ye fret, hinney,' soothed Queenie. 'We've worked it out. Ready when you are, Miss Empress! Going down!'

'Not so fast, split-tail!' snapped Lametta. Hinney indeed! 'I have forced myself to remember how primitive your species is. I find it staggering. I spend so little time with my many inferiors. It's a lonely life, but one has no choice. I will grant your wish – undersea breathing!'

'That's reet generous of you, Your Holiness,' Alice said, making the kind of curtsey any titled noblewoman would have blenched at.

'But we don't need it,' Esther said. 'We'd love to take you up on a wish another time – something that would help us all.'

Lametta was speechless.

Only Judith refused to go underwater. She smiled and shook her head but Isabel saw the trouble in her eyes and stroked her cheek gently before skipping over the sand with the rest of them. Judith cupped her hand over the caress, and all at once she felt the long lost warmth of her little Ruth's lovely face in the rushlight, when she was snuggled deep and ready for sleep. She closed her eyes and tried to picture her. She thought of her kitchen table and the fire – but the table was bare, the fire cold ashes and there was no Ruth. Her bedroom, then? All she could see was her little bed, and it was stripped and cold. The yard? Ruth would chase chickens and hide in the tree, giving herself away with giggles. The tree came into focus: one branch was broken and the yard was empty.

Surely Ruth wasn't . . . ? Wait, Alice had been sure

that her husband's new woman would be caring for her. She didn't have any idea of what this new woman looked like or where she lived. All she could do was draw into her mind Ruth's starry brown eyes, the gold and green flecks sparkling there; her feather soft eyebrows; the way her dark hair strayed in wild twists over her brow no matter how long she brushed it, or how carefully she tied it back. She thought of her little nose and its dusting of freckles, her soft cheeks and baby mouth: smiling, laughing, pouting to get her own way. Her lovely lips tight round her thumb, and her chin nothing but a pinch between finger and thumb.

Ruth's face. And it didn't shift and shimmer like dreams: it was so real that Judith almost believed she could open her eyes and Ruth would be there in front of her. But tears blinded her: there was only the dazzle of this strange hot shore and its mad blue sea, and she shut her eyes tight again. Amazingly, Ruth reappeared. All of her. She was smiling and holding her hands out to be picked up.

Judith wrapped her arms round her little girl, and rocked and rocked and rocked.

Squirrel bombshelled into the waves right beside the mermaid. She followed Lametta's every move, careful to keep well away from the octopus with its terrifying fixed glare and its eight fiercely waving arms. She was not to know that Spinks's eyes were beaming undersea welcome to her and to all the split-tails: her tentacles danced an elaborate pantomime of the beauties that lay ahead of them and swore total protection for them all. The protection of Spinks's great great grandmother and all who were dear to her . . . and all who were dear to them . . . and . . .

'Spinks, will you stop foaming around!' Lametta snapped. 'How can I think?'

Spinks immediately forgave her this apalling breach of etiquette, and made a shorthand of three generations of well-wishing sea-dwellers, ending with herself.

'Ee, what a carry on,' thought Alice, delighted by the frill of bubbles streaming from her mouth.

'I've not taken a breath yet without it feeling like air.' To her amazement, she heard Queenie's wonderful voice right inside her head. Their eyes sparkled through the water.

Jen was a delirious streak of streamlined muscle. This was like flying through the air without bothering about landing and balancing. She did back somersaults, tight-roped on a deep current of water, and cartwheeled with the feeling that she need never stop. Spinks was deeply honoured. She had never dreamed of such a graceful tribute to an eight-legger! A minor constellation of starfish rose and applauded with five-toed fervour.

Rowan and Esther swung Turtle between them. Her small body bubbled with delight, and it was all she could do not to bob up to the surface – she felt so *light*! Isabel floated a serene twenty feet deep, nose-to-nose with fish bright as egg-yolk taking the odd curious nibble at the fronds of hair streaming around her head; their tiny lips exploring her eyebrows made her snort with laughter and drove them off in a puff of silver bubbles.

Lametta swirled around and signed for them to follow her deeper. She drifted down past sharp walls of coral blistered with pink spikes, golden bulges like frozen lava, pinnacles and towers in white. Every surface, sharp or smooth, was studded with soft blobs of crimson and lime green that suddenly exploded into living flowers.

Queenie saw a huge mirrored eye in a silvery cleft and made a fish-face at it. Out came a scaled face bigger than her own, with an indignant purple beak that cackled at the sight of her.

'And you're no beauty either!' she thought.

Alice caught her hand and pointed. Just below them, a grey plate two feet across rolled a mournful eye at her and flapped its pie-crust edges to shift itself. It was a gwellup, it was very friendly, and it was very young.

'There's a face only a mother could love!'

'Shite, and here she is!'

The two women swam after the mermaid and away from the heaving puffing fury of a grey plate six feet across, that was now chivvying the smaller plate under its edges.

'I've told you not to play with anyone who's not perfectly round,' scolded the parent gwellup. The baby sulked. An adult gwellup is a solitary creature and can have only one offspring every five years. Infant gwellups are gregarious by nature, but very seldom meet their own kind. Their parent will not let them mingle with reefside riffraff. They are allowed to attend the occasional sole party, but even there they have to be careful. Sole are notoriously nervous and disappear in a cloud of sand at any suggestion of high spirits. And so the gwellup reaches maturity hide-bound by rules, socially inept, and with a command of only the smallest of small conversation: a reiteration of parental platitudes and prejudices. Not even courtship breaks the pattern. There is no courtship. Gwellups are hermaphrodites and maturity brings on feelings and bodily functions so embarrassing that they spend the fertilization period in a puritan coma with their eye tightly closed. The infant emerges from . . . somewhere

. . . and they do their grey and loveless duty by it. The parent disintegrates when the child reaches maturity. Indeed a gwellup can live out its entire life and never meet another gwellup apart from its parent and its child.

Queenie and Alice dived in a delighted arc after the haughty curve of Lametta's ocean-famous tail.

The mermaid looked over one shoulder and motioned that they should follow her through a craggy hole in the coral, where beams of light shimmered aquamarine welcome. One by one they went through, a chain of lithe silhouettes.

The shafts of light picked out clear streamers of blood-red combing the well of water; light played around clouds of sparkle from a shoal of tiny drifting creatures as clear as glass. The tunnel was carpeted with velvety plants the eden green of a newly-stitched tapestry. Taper-thin silver eels tickled and curled around them, like smoke on a lazy summer evening. The tunnel of rock curved very slightly upwards and opened out until they were swimming free again, all the ocean around them as far as they could see. Sunlight tiger-striped their bodies white and turquoise, and they were tantalized by the shadows of strange moving creatures.

Lametta was waiting for something: she brushed clouds of impertinent blue fish from her face; she shook cheerful silver fish out of her billowing fine hair. Then she pointed at a distant shadow and her octopus jetted obediently towards it.

'Sea-slug split-tails!' she thought.

Rowan raised an eyebrow at Esther. Fascinating how they could hear thoughts underwater: the familiar voices of the women they loved, the driving hunger of every fish that flew past them; the fun and frolics that followed eating – and a pulse of passion surging through every creature's living cell, through every drop of rich water. This deep desire swelled and changed tempo: they were amazed most of all by the octopus and how her cells beat a constant desire that became dizzyingly powerful when she brushed against the mermaid.

But it was more than erotic, it was the heartbeat of Ocean herself, the wild endless urge to live out everything every cell allowed – diving, swimming, floating, vanishing into the sand, hurtling towards a rock and hiding in the slimmest crack; every scale and tentacle stroked by the deeps.

And why, in the great womb of all this beauty, were they scorned as sea-slugs and sneered at as split-tails? Ocean surely has room for all life for all life burgeons from her rich waters.

'You just don't swim fast enough!' came flashing back at them.

Spinks twirled back into view, apparently towing a sail forty times her own size. A grey-black creature as big and ungainly as a sodden sail, whose head was a huge soft puppy nose, with eyes small as a blackbird's set high on either side. Her wings rippled like silk and she didn't seem to notice the rows of fish clinging underneath.

'She's a Deepwater Wing – a carrier,' said Lametta. 'Not very clever, but very patient and very strong. She'll speed you to Atlantis. She can swim almost as fast as we mermaids. Just hold on tight. Atlantis is what *you* would call a long way away.'

They found muscled spines under the wide wings and gripped them.

'Is this all right?' thought Esther. 'There are so many of us!'

'Strong, strong, strong!' rippled through the whole body. 'Strong, strong, strongest!'

'Let's go!' cried the mermaid.

Even the octopus took advantage of this free ride and gripped with her suckers. Her face stretched like elastic in the sudden burst of speed and it seemed to Princess that she was grinning like they all were with the joy of speed: as if they were swimming straight up a waterfall without having to lift a finger.

Squirrel screamed with joy and her eyes flashed wide as they just cleared a deep reef and scythed through floating clouds of seaweed. Something gripped Isabel's arm in the middle of the blinding greenness: a minute grip like lizard fingers, and she looked down – it was a piece of seaweed. Or was it? There was no chance of looking at it properly while the Deepwater Wing made nonsense of 'a long way away'.

For, just as their bodies were thrilling with the rush of water and their eyes began to sift out shapes in the racing blur, the creature slowed and her wings rippled gently above them. The seaweed gripping Isabel's arm detached itself and hovered close behind her.

The mermaid was nowhere to be seen.

'Atlantis!' said Esther, holding Squirrel and Turtle's hands. Rowan and Isabel joined them and they flew over the city gates – gleaming mother of pearl, as fine as spun sugar. Along a street, but a city street become undersea, flagstones folded into curved steps after her great fall. No sun would blaze on these stones for all eternity. The houses had shed roof tiles like petals, doors were crumbled to brine-soaked timbers. No wind or rain would ever bother the new Atlanteans.

White fish the size of doubloons were a snowstorm

around gracious marble columns; flame-tailed rocket fish dithered in a window frame, then launched themselves clear across the street to flutter from a stone archway. The flagged street was soft with drifts of sand, and all the traffic was flat fish, leaves of living gold shuffling in a deep-sea breeze. The five earth-walking air-breathers swam along the canyon of the street and came to a square where a fountain stood: no thirst for it to quench down here. Its bronze leaves and satyrs sprouted tendrils and coils of deep-sea plants, and a ferocious fish as small as Turtle's fist had staked out the carved bowl as her home. Hers and her dozens of fish-babes smaller than fingernails. She shot out in purple fury as the women swam nearby and chased them, nipping like a terrier.

Now they floated in a formal city garden, where aquatic anarchy had knocked every statue flat. Fronds of vermilion rioted in sightless stone eyes; irreverent chrome yellow sea-moss placed a soft seal on wordless stone lips. In the world of air and sun-shine, perhaps this park had boasted a massive carved fresco celebrating the victories and virtues of famous Atlanteans: now, deep sea, slabs lay scattered in jigsaw confusion. Or perhaps these were images of defeated enemies, paving the park so that they would be forever underfoot. No matter. Squirrel pointed down. Shell-backed creatures scuttled across the mosaic of gold, lapis lazuli, porphyry and jade, leaving sputters of sand across nameless noble brows and proud lips.

They swam at roof height through the maze of streets, and Esther saw a pattern in the crumpled flags: crimson diamonds that lured them in a sweeping zigzag until they reached a great circle on a hill top. In the centre a massive dome rested on pillars, on the dome a crescent moon, a sea-dragon, a hedgehog, a full moon, a circle of serpents and full-bellied frogs dancing. Isabel tugged them all right down to the foot of the pillars and they tiptoed weightlessly inside.

The dome cut out much of the light, and their eyes were dazzled a moment by the gloom. Light came from somewhere: was it the pure white marble glimmering underfoot? Something huge glowed ahead of them and Isabel let go of Rowan's hand and swam towards it, true as an arrow.

It?

Her.

She stood as massive as a mountain in dreams of prehistory. Isabel landed firmly on the middle toe of one of Her solid feet. Turtle could just curl up on the smallest toenail, Squirrel on the next. Their mothers sat cross-legged on the fourth and the biggest toes. Her leg rose behind them, strong as a wise tree.

'Who is she?' Turtle wanted a name, a story.

Isabel breathed in and drifted serenely up past Her knee, along Her translucent thigh – the length and width of the timbers that curved around the belly of their distant ship. Only this thigh was all of a piece, as if the belly of the Empress of the Seven Oceans had been planed smooth. And it was not wood. The child marvelled at the incredible folds of Her powerful vulva, beautiful curves carved with serpentine mysteries. Her child's hand traced the gracious overhang of Her belly, where a circle of stars glowed and the topmost one lay in Her deep navel. Isabel sat there a while, the glow making her fingers and toes rosy and weird as sea-dwellers – nothing on earth to do with flesh and blood. She sat very still. It wasn't that She was comfortable, or warm, or stone, or wood, or gold or white: although She was all of these. She commanded stillness, she exuded Power.

She.

She was.

That is All.

Goddess, thought Isabel in a spiral of fine bubbles, and the stone/wood/coral/water/goddess seemed to breathe against her back. Breathe deep, breathe with a slow laughter.

Swimming round Her breasts, Isabel was caught in a tumble of water: it was the way the waterfall would have felt if she'd had the nerve to dive into it headfirst! The monster waterfall that had first spoken to her of Power!

She stood on the Goddess's shoulder, and it was a mountain top, the current a mighty wind ruffling her hair and spangling her body with a rushing heat. Far below she saw her mothers and sisters lilting towards her. A gust of water knocked her forwards and buffeted her upwards, away from the Goddess. She didn't – couldn't – resist, and the current stopped and held her still just far away enough for her to see the whole of the Goddess's face.

She looked like no-one Isabel had ever seen before.

No.

She looked like Rowan with her strong brow . . . no, Esther. That was Her eyes. Or was it Queenie? The magnificent web of lines on her brow, at the corners of her eyes. Surely that was Alice's smile, the teasing one where you had to check her eyes since her lips moved so little. And definitely Jen's defiant chin. Or Squirrel's. Both. Her cheeks curved the way Princess's did. And Her whole face said Judith, when Judith was moon-bathing and had a moment when she felt serene. Her eyes were as huge as Turtle's when she needed to leap to safety in Queenie's arms, or leap to joy and mar-vellous danger in the headlong waves.

Isabel wanted to swim to Her face, lie on the curve of Her lower lip, but the water held her still. Into her mind swam a moving picture. She was in it. It was dawn on the river, drawn into the new day from the warmth of Rowan's arms through the trees to a still pool, and the first sunlight mirrored her face. And she loved and laughed at herself.

Her own face? Everything in her said yes. The water drew her towards the Goddess's lips and placed her there as sure as the waves bring treasure to the shore at high tide.

Queenie and Alice watched the wild river witches and their wilful children fly into Atlantis sure as swifts with a beakful of bugs and a nest bursting with chick beaks to satisfy. The lump of seaweed that had fixed on Isabel's arm took off and tumbled after them as if it had a life of its own.

'Well, there's some that know where they're going – mebbes they've been here before,' Alice said.

'Aye, bonny lass,' Queenie said. 'You can see it in Esther's eyes, for one. They've all been on this earth many and many a time. This place means something to them, and they don't seem to want company finding it. Nivver a word from any of them! Not even that scallawag Squirrel. And where's this daft bairn of a mermaid got to, d'you think, her with the big talk and the guided tour!'

'Search me,' Alice said. 'All that bragging about how fast she could swim! I was breathless just holding on to thon great creature that brought us here. Madam Empress-I-don't-think – she's likely got here already and sick of waiting on us.'

'Oh, she'll turn up,' Queenie said drily. 'She'll never

be far from us while she wants something. I wish I knew what it was.'

'Oh, be buggered with the mermaid! Will we go into Atlantis, you and I, my old sweetheart?' asked Alice, twinkling with laughter – ee, they really were here, right on the sea-bed with a world of water above them, and them breathing and blethering just like natural! What a thing!

'I'll even carry you over the threshold,' Queenie said gallantly, and swept Alice off her feet. Inside the city gates they linked arms to stroll and sea-skip along the unpeopled street. Alice was amazed by the white elegance of the houses, the glimpse of a courtyard through sagging archways, the lofty columns.

'This must have been a fine place, Queenie. Can you imagine it? For all the doors and windows are out, can you not picture it? Oh-so-noble folk in their long silk robes strolling down this street, all talking lah-di-dah like foreign lords and ladies. Slaves walking six steps behind and carrying owt in the way of parcels! Lounging round a fountain on a long sofa, eating grapes all day long, and slaves fanning them wi' feathers fine as a sunset. Never an idea of sinking out of sight for ever below the waves.'

'I've always wondered about bells, me. You hear tales of churches drowned deep and the bells ringing clear in the towers a thousand fathoms deep, ringing with the rolling of the tides. Will we hear bells here, bonny hinney?'

'Did they have churches in Atlantis? It was surely long before the Nazarene and the so-called Holy Bible.' Alice thought about it. 'Were they not pagans, with temples and sacrifices and all that carry on?'

'Mebbes,' Queenie said. 'Only I've an idea they were even before that. A peaceful people. I see them working with the earth at the right times and seasons. I divent know where that comes from. I see your Romans as bloodthirsty louts giving pagans a bad name: the musclebound meathead soldiers with their daft leather skirts and ganzies bristling with studs. Spears and throwing folk to lions. War and looting and laws. Some folk say Atlantis disappeared because the people wouldn't have anything to do with blood and guts. If that's true, they'd still be ahead of their time.'

'Or behind it?' said Alice. 'Will those times ever come again, Queenie?'

'If I had my way,' Queenie replied. 'Or if you had yours.'

They wandered off down a side street. All they could see through the gaping windows was rubble, tumbled bowls and statues. Alice didn't want to go inside any of the houses at first, and only when she saw the first skeleton did she recognize why. She hated bones – they made her think of her own death, and she clung fiercely to Queenie's living flesh.

But these bones were neatly collapsed in a doorway: all that remained of a dog. Peaceful it looked too, as if one day it had simply come to the end of breathing and barking and stopped as it lay dozing in the sun. And if a dog stopped just like that, perhaps the end of all breath in Atlantis had been peaceful.

Alice pictured it as an island that had drifted loose from its undersea roots and floated away until waves slopped over its edges, and it sank like a tipping saucer in a washing-up bowl.

Inside, the house was as bare as if no-one had ever moved in. Maybe there had been tapestries, and the salty maw of the ocean had ground away at the silken threads, dusted her sandy belly with gleams of gold. They went through an archway to the next room, and here were signs of a life long gone. Ocean with a playful paw had unset the table: pots were tumbled to the floor; finely traced metal plates were shuffled and dealt out like a deck of cards.

'Well, there's your answer to bells, my lovely,' Alice said, for the current rippled through the plates and set them ringing. Their bodies felt the sound as much as their ears could hear it. Queenie picked up a plate and flicked her finger against the thin metal rim. She smiled as the sound tingled through the water, and let the plate slip to the floor. It sank with a hesitant cadence, playing an old forgotten tune.

Every house in this street was stripped bare, as if after the death of one who has neither kin nor loved ones to mourn or inherit. Each room was empty, apart from plates and bowls – Ocean needs no tableware, for her whole being is a feast.

The street opened into a square paved with egg-shaped stones, laid in patterns of winding serpents and shooting stars. Every building had a balcony.

'Imagine sitting up there a million years ago and watching the world go by! What sights this place must have seen.'

On one of the walls a giant lobster was picked out in shells and mosaic.

'Would you reckon that was the fishmongers?' said Alice. 'And that one, with all the loaves, a baker?'

'Mebbes we've come to a market square,' said Queenie. 'Will we gan in and get the groceries? Let's try this one.'

She strode through a doorway flanked by flagons and grapes faded to a delicate lilac.

'Ee, there's nothing new,' said Alice. 'If we painted it up a bit and hung the walls wi' nets and tankards, we'd be back on the bonny Tyne in the El Dorado. I nivver thought of bars in Atlantis. They always skip owt common like that wi' history. You'd think folk never drank nor ate nor pissed. Trust you to nose your way into an alehouse. Of all the temples and palaces in all Atlantis, you have to come into an alehouse!'

'I'm in good company.' Queenie kissed her. 'But they're ower slow to serve us. D'you think we're dressed wrong?'

Alice laughed at the way their weathered clothes billowed and clung like a second skin.

'Sit yourself down, my fine lady,' she said grandly, and dived headfirst over the bar.

'Ah, you old fool, what would there be worth drinking after a thousand lifetimes under salt water?'

Alice floated back to her, with an armful of bottles – still sealed, and still, when she tipped them, with something liquid inside.

'Ee, I'm mortified. You've forgot the glasses,' Queenie said, mock indignant,

'There's no pleasing some folk. I couldn't see any frigging glasses. Can you not put your lips to the neck of the bottle, Your Highness? Like the common folk do – so I've heard.'

'Ah divent kna. There's nowt common about *me*. But ye can show us how to gan on so's Ah'll know,' said Queenie.

She turned a bottle round in her hands and broke the seal. The neck was thick and skimmed-milk blue like a fisherman's float. She tipped it, dubiously shaking her head.

'The bugger's empty. Dried out. Or salted out, more like.'

'Just wait on.'

A deep red liquid snailed towards the neck, gathering into a great drop on the lip. It oozed apart from the glass and sat solid as a bubble of oil. Then another, and another until a row of them hung clear as rubies.

'Well, shall we?'

'Why not?'

They each put their lips to a bubble and sucked it in.

'And here's me bold enough to call myself maker of fine wines!' gasped Alice. 'There's never been a taste like this on my tongue and I'd have sworn I knew the finest!'

Queenie grinned and dripped the rest of the bottle out into a heart shaped necklace of crimson drops. Whatever it was, time had turned it sugar sweet and as thick as syrup, but after the sweetness came a heat that drove deep into her throat, filled her chest like a roaring hearth in winter and ran along every cell of her body.

It was not to be rushed, this fire-eating liquid. Each drop was to be taken gently on the lips, rolled tenderly across the tongue, then softly squashed between tongue and palate. Then the fine spray could be teased into the throat.

'Here's to us – all. Even the nun!' said Queenie as their lips met on the last drop, and their mouths shared the taste through a kiss.

'And to whoever ran this place. By! Her memory lives on.'

The spirit of Intoxication giggled sleepily through the waters. She may have been resting – a million years, who cares? – but to wake up to a party! She couldn't resist. She'd laid herself down long ago as the waters rose serenely and closed her eyes. Through the zillion moon dreams, she always knew a time would come for her to rise again. She sensed everything about Alice and Queenie and blessed the Goddess for the wonderful wickedness of wild women. Intoxication left to herself becomes morose and maudlin: give her cackling good company and she sparkles like dewdrops on a spider's web in a flaming sunrise.

'Don't look now, but I'm seeing things,' Queenie said, gripping Alice's arm.

'All I can see is your beautiful face, sweetheart,' Alice slurred just slightly and stroked Queenie's nose. 'I'm a happy woman, Queenie. I love you.'

Queenie turned her very gently. 'I love you too, Alice. But d'you see?'

Certainly she saw. But how to describe something you've never seen before, something that changes as you look at it. Someone, she was almost sure. Just as she was clear that this someone had eyes of a shimmering turquoise, even a smile, what seemed to be a face cleared like mist and reformed into a voluptuous shoulder, wisped with silver net. Or an elegant hand curved round a glass fizzing with bubbles that set into a grin, a laugh.

'It's the drink,' she whispered to Queenie. 'What is it?'

'It's wonderful,' Queenie managed.

For her, the shimmering miasma of pastel was something she clutched at from the waking edges of her dreams. It was how her body felt when Alice touched her, when their eyes met. It was carrying Turtle shoulder-high and knowing that she was as tall as any tree.

The shifting shape drew itself together: a smiling lovely woman with seen-it-all eyes and a mouth made for laughing, loving, rolling out words of wisdom and high humour.

'Queenie, Alice,' she said, 'I can't hold this shape for a long time – there's too many other ways to be. But you're welcome, you did very well to come here, you come-hither happy hags. You've woken me, and it's a delight to be awake. Enjoy what's left of my sunberries and golden fruits.'

'Who are you?' said Alice, as the long fingers misted away.

'I'll tell you when I next . . .'

The figure disappeared the way a rainbow does – now you see me, now you don't, and now . . . I'm gone! But maybe, now you think you see me again: the tease of that unicorn-rare blaze of colour.

Queenie split the seal of the next bottle, and scattered a jeweller's dream of wild-honey sparkle around the room. She and Alice caught at the soft jewels, batted them to each other, swirled them into spirals with a wave of the hand. And they watched, mesmerized, as a golden flock rose sedately as if on a thread, and disappeared.

At once, the vision swirled back into being, grinning and licking her lips.

'They were berries I grew myself. We used to call them sweat of the Goddess. We'd gather them after a summer of sweat, we'd gather them in the evening. They were like solid gold beads, and for a whole moon we could strip the bushes every evening. Strong sweat from women's work and the great goodness of the Goddess.'

'Who are you?'

'Ah, where do I begin?' the vision chuckled. 'My name was Dizard. I used to ferment wine for this place and share it with the women. Something changed one day, and we knew our lifetimes in the sun were coming to an end. A great sadness crept in. One day this place was full, the next, no-one had seen Mara. She was a storyteller. So we all learnt to tell stories. After that, Asphodel disappeared. She was a siren. So we all learnt to sing. Julia, the spinner, went next. We learnt to spin. Then it was Arknia, the weaver. We wept and we wove. And Zandra, who made clothes for us. We tore our garments and from then on, called every new robe Zandra. There would be a time when everything seemed to settle. The ones who had gone were still with us because we loved and remembered and honoured their being. Finally, there was only me. And I knew all the skills, as well as fermenting water and fruit into dream-drawing drinks. But there was no-one to share with, and it seemed right to sleep. I remember a night when the water came snailing over the doorstep and I lay down and wished myself sleep.'

'What happened to the women?'

'What, indeed? I don't know. By the time we were afraid enough to wonder, there were only three of us left, and all too fearful to even ask the question. It would have meant: who's next? We'd all lie down to sleep together and then there were two. And then there was me. Oh, you should have seen this place when *we* were.'

'I had a bar,' Alice told her. 'We called it the El Dorado. It was packed to the seams with every kind of scapegrace you can imagine. Buccaneers barely a step ahead of the sheriff's men, pimps, cutpurses, whores, cardsharps, wastrels. Ugly customers I had at the El Dorado. You talk of skills! They could raise a pint pot and drain the bugger dry in one movement. Raise a riot at the twist of an eyebrow, raise Cain seven long days a week!'

Dizard looked sympathetic.

'You must have committed a great crime once,' she said sympathetically. 'Such a crude path back to life! But you served your punishment without despair?'

'Something like that,' Alice said. 'I did my time.'

Dizard shuddered.

'We called this place of evening joy the Well of Loveliness,' she said. 'The water in the courtyard well was the spirit of every wine I ever made. We loved the wine, it gave such a strong feeling of joy. There's bitter sadness when you find yourself drinking all night to dull your feelings. The pain comes back like dragon's teeth in the morning. You drink – it goes dead again. Your life goes with it. And one day, the wine turns on you, forces you into a pit of agony worse than you've ever known. It's a treadmill – here's to leaping off and walking free!'

'I'll go along wi' that!' said Queenie, said Alice.

Dizard showed them how to pour the wine so it hung like streamers, so it coiled like a tender vine. And with every bottle that they spread and supped, she grew stronger, her hair changed hue, the colour and texture of her *zandra* deepened and grew richer.

'Do you dance,' she said. 'Do you love to dance?'

There has never been such dancing as Dizard shared with Queenie and Alice in the Well of Loveliness at the bottom of the sea where time is not.

She was gone when they woke from dreams of late night stories woven by friends, thread spun by a lover, life lived with women, and loneliness only a sad ghost howling somewhere outside with no way in.

When You're In Deep Water, Be A Diver

For Princess, the dazzling gates came from the land-scapes of dreaming: a dream from long ago when she was little, and Queenie had her open-mouthed at stories so wild and wonderful that she was sure she'd never sleep and she didn't want to. Always when she woke she felt she'd been whisked away all night, dancing on exotic shores: stolen away like a faery child to the outlandish cities Queenie tossed in as a by-the-way backdrop for some outrageous feat of daring. The island and the silver monkey would have been enough, and now here she was at the gates of Atlantis.

Suddenly she felt life could only grow richer: life that was hers for the living and loving of it.

She watched Alice and Queenie lightstepping beyond the gates. She would go in soon, but she turned first to see and remember everything about the place.

Extraordinary! All around was a lightless infinity of deep water. The radiance of Atlantis stopped some thirteen feet from the walls and the gate. Above the city, a great clear well of water glowed turquoise and white-gold; the rest of the ocean-bed was held in mysterious darkness. And what's this? Some sea-creature swimming straight at her?

Jen landed beside her, grinning.

'I like to look around before I go sightseeing,' she said. 'Granny taught me to be wary: all that glisters isn't gold, you know?'

'I know. But Queenie says it might as well be, since it was the glister that got people digging it out of the ground in the first place. She's always laughed at me for ower-careful. I'm changing, however.'

'Me too. Are you ready?' asked Jen.

They leapt over the gate and the leap took them to the wave-smoothed top of a column. They clutched each other to stop falling, then burst into a froth of laughter, let go and fell. Only in Atlantis there is no falling: they floated serenely to the ground. Jen darted into the nearest doorway and Princess followed.

Jen was already swimming upstairs.

'I've always wanted to do this!'

She steadied herself on the stone edge of a bench and fell forward and flew around the room and out of the window. When Princess went after her, she was out of sight. No! A whisper of sand gave her away, settling by a doorway over the street and Princess shot through the upper window and froze by the door.

'Boo!' she caught her as she hurtled into the room, then whirled outside and away and flattened herself against a pillar, yanking her flyaway hair over her shoulder and gripping the ridges with her toes. Jen appeared and looked all around – she hadn't seen her!

She grinned to see her swim off up the street and edged round the column in case she turned back. But Jen took steady strokes and turned a corner . . . what now? She darted to the next column. No Jen. The next column then, and she tried to squash the burst of laughter that foamed in her throat like good ale.

Two hands slid on to her shoulders and she turned: there was Jen's face upside down and laughing into hers and what could she do but kiss her?

Dart down as fast as possible, that's what!

Jen held the column for a moment. The way Princess had laughed, eyes dancing with fire! The way her dark hair shot free as she let it go: it was Gentleman Jack Daw and a whirlpool of sensation giddying her body all over again. Steady, she told herself, whoa there! Her self merely raised an eyebrow, thumbed her nose and gave a wicked grin as she swung into the wide street and fixed on a more than tempting foot vanishing through a window frame.

Princess dived through the rooms in a whirl of confusion. She steadied herself at the stairs then moved through the back of the house to find an oasis of beauty: all the houses backed on to a gracious circular courtyard and the gardens were bordered by low white marble slabs like the spokes of a wheel. The hub was a fountain, and centuries undersea had festooned it with coral carvings and luxuriant plants in a majestic riot of bronze and copper and gold. Their leaves waved graciously as if in the slightest of summer breezes, and crimson fish hung there as gaudy as the flowers on Alice's love-quilt.

Jen sidled to the upstairs window and her heart thundered when she looked down at Princess's wild hair streaming all round her. She kept out of sight, waving a frond of weed in front of her.

Sure enough, Princess looked around, scanning every dark frame for a sight of her. Her secret smile – thinking she was alone, and knowing maybe she wasn't? – was it meant to tantalize Jen? To drive her heart all over her body with its mad pulsing? It was the loveliest Jen had ever seen her.

Princess drifted to the fountain and her body made waves that set the plants dancing wildly. She swam round and around in her own dance, a merry-go-round of fandango and back-flip, and stopped still from time to time, then changed her steps as if somewhere a fiddler was playing for her alone.

'Now,' thought Jen. 'What's to do? Here I am at the bottom of an ocean men would give a kingdom to know of. I should be exploring and learning here. And here am I, crazed, dazed, amazed and wanting to see nothing but Princess and learn nothing other than how it would feel to kiss her.'

She looked through the waving plant to where Princess was floating with her eyes closed, like the Lady Who Floats on Air from the freak show – only this was real magic. She stepped back, and the sole of her foot registered something hard: a golden ring fashioned in fine curls and scrolls, the ridges tarnished a brilliant briny green, and a dark stone clasped in tiny claws. She knew at once that it was for Princess. She turned it over in her fingers and she rubbed at the tarnish to make it perfect. It didn't shift, and looking close she saw it was hair-fine sweeps of rich enamel. A sea ring for a sea witch, a witch's ring for a sea Princess. She flattened herself against the window frame.

Princess was still floating, apparently unconcerned. A certain shifting plant in one window had taken her eye; a fizz of bubbles she had at first taken for flowers had her belly pulsing and sure of where Jen was hiding. Her pulse had slowed back to almost normal now, she had collected herself. They were playing hide and seek, that was all. And if it seemed odd that two young women of twenty or so were playing hide-and-seek, well, she had only to think of her own mother and Queenie, a century of living between them and no telling which was worse for daft as bairns.

And lovers. Well, that was them. She wouldn't even think about that. She'd spent more time around children on this strange voyage than ever in her life before, her brain prattled on, trying to normalize and be sensible.

But when Jen swam from underneath her, floated upright beside her, kept a distance and simply stretched out her hand, she lost every word she'd ever known. Her hand met Jen's and was surprised by its firm warmth, the softness of her skin. And a cool hard something in her palm — a scar?

She took the ring and its dark stone glowed on her finger. Her body rocketed her away, but her hand still clasped Jen's, and together they crested the ring of houses and flew over Atlantis.

The sea bowled one boisterous wave after another with never a sign of a human head bobbing up. The sun was a high noon blaze, and Judith felt a flicker of worry. Perhaps they'd drowned? She tried to wipe the words from her mind, and moved into the silky shadow of a tree. Reason said they'd drowned: an unbearable reality. But reality had been turned inside out since the day her husband had damned her as a witch, and she had little truck with reason. Reason would mean Ruth by her side, dry land and everyday: mermaids and spells and mythical cities were reality now. She conjured up Queenie's laugh, Alice's grin, little Isabel's gentle silence. They'd be back . . .

But the sun slipped down the sky and tree shadows slipped ahead of her feet; ragged shapes of darkness scuttled across the sands and the shadows crept towards the spread of foam at the water's edge. Her eyes were an agony of dry heat with searching the darkening sea.

The Empress of The Seven Oceans was a comfortless

familiar shape, a solid black cutout riding the water. That nun was mighty quiet – no doubt wearing her knees to blisters and Aveing every blessed Maria she could think of. Oh, why weren't they back? The thought of the rest of her life with just Sister Mercy for company made her laugh out loud, a sharp cry like a bird in danger.

Her heart jumped at a crashing in the bushes behind her – and her with only the sea to hide in. She made uneasy noises of welcome when the bear lumbered towards her. She'd always steered clear of Miss Walnut, for all Jen swore she was harmless to those who wished her no harm. Now she had no choice, for the huge creature sighed and stretched out beside her, dumping her heavy head in her lap and nudging her arm for a scratch, a head rub.

She'd have to feed the bear. And herself. And make a fire against their return. Heavens, they'd all be frozen, and here she was maundering and feeling sorry for herself. She scolded herself into action.

Suddenly it was dark, and the night sounds began in the trees: busy rustlings, and harsh skreeks of triumph and death. The sparks caught the fire and sulked into threateningly small blue flames. How cold it was once the sun had gone! Oh, sweet relief as the branches caught and crackled and the bear growled with pleasure in the sudden heat.

What if they didn't come back until tomorrow?

She supposed she'd sleep, and if worry kept her from it, well, what's one night lost to wakefulness? She pillowed herself against the bear, and that great heartbeat was a comfort. She swigged some wine to dull the edge of worry.

And what if they didn't come back for a long time?

She couldn't even go looking for them. She was no

swimmer, and not even Queenie would try to sail the ship single-handed. Well, she might. Queenie would do anything. But her and the nun? Between them they had a thousandth of Queenie's skill, and the thought died.

And what if they never came back?

It would be her and the nun and the bear, alone for ever. She realized that somewhere she had been clinging to the lifeline thrown her one day by Alice's words of comfort. Somehow and someday they'd get back to Newcastle. She'd see Ruth again and everything would be all right. Without that, where was the point of living? Keeping herself fed and well and safe – for what? She drank more wine to chase away her fears.

Oh yes, the wine and the fire warmed her, but what then? There were monsters beyond the fire circle, waiting for the wood to turn to ash. Waiting for her to sleep by the cold ash, impatient to stalk into her nightmares shrieking and jeering of endless days and nights alone. Wood blistered into glaring eyes, flames bit savagely into the darkness and the fire seethed with wolves and demons.

This is what he wanted for her: that whoremongering husband of hers. No – he wanted her dead. His cruel and greedy face leered at her from the fire. That look of hatred! If he'd been able to imagine a living Hell for her he couldn't have done much better than this. He'd only wanted her out of his way. And if the fool had told her, she'd have taken Ruth and left him to it. Well, she would *now*. Now that she knew Alice and knew that women could be strong and happy and not give a damn for rules and wedding bands. Then, she'd probably have begged him to stay with her, any man better than no man, any father better than none at all.

Curse it, the thoughts kept flowing!

Everyone in town must have known about him – she remembered the looks she got sometimes when she talked about how good he was, how kind. She'd thought they were envious of her and pitying him for having an ordinary, simple wife like her. She'd been so proud when he picked her, and she'd always done everything to please him. And he was never pleased with her for more than a grunting moment of his sexual pleasure. She would lie awake at nights after he'd shouted at her or beaten her, and try to work out what she'd done wrong and how she could make it better for him tomorrow.

She should have gone when he hit Ruth. That was the only time she'd stood up to him. Had him begging for another chance and swearing on the Bible he'd never do it again. She'd believed him. And things had been better for a few months. She'd actually felt that her marriage would last for ever and only get better – bless the dear man for changing, and thank the Good Lord for the influence of a little child. What a fool she'd been – the next thing was him bringing the bishop's men into the house. He must have been scheming to be rid of her ever since she'd stood up to him. And now she was here. Alone.

'What a poor silly mouse I was,' she said to the bear. 'Put myself into a gold-ringed mousetrap and offering to share all the cheese with the cat. I'm still a mouse, Miss Walnut, a mouse with no house and no babies.'

She settled closer to the bear, for the creature's size and warmth were safe, and she knew in her tired heart that a mouse can die of sheer fright.

She was walking to the sea, her bare feet delighted by

the moist springy turf. Her face glowed in the gutsy breeze, her eyes sparkled at the first sight of the wild foaming ridgebacked waves. The wind caught at her light cotton dress. She smiled and ran towards the whitecaps breaking to an elegant swirl; froth spreading like a sequinned cape, then folding under the next explosion of brine and bubble on the white sand.

The sun went out as a heavy grey cloak of cloud rose from the horizon. She was cold, petrified. The sea washed her ankles, and now it was as gritty and treacherous as the first sweeps of slow ice on the confused feet of a mammoth.

But she tugged her feet free and ran away back to the dunes . . . ran and ran until her toes tangled in roots and the fall knocked the breath from her body.

Sister Mercy, the Shark Slayer, Kerry – she snapped awake from her dream turned nightmare. She could hear the waves, and realized she was on board ship as the deck rolled her on her side. She recoiled from a sharp stench of stale sweat and shuddered when it came with her. It was her smell. Foul! Her skin itched with dirt, itched with heat from the rough woollen robe she was wearing. The sun was an hour or so older than dawn, and it was going to be a scorcher.

She sat up, and looked at the heavy metal cross round her neck. Horrible! There was a near naked figure on it, hands pierced with nails and feet the same. Whoever he was, the look on his face was one of defeat, even acceptance. Poor man! What a dreadful way to be killed. And why on earth was she wearing something so ugly? She took it off and flung it over the side of the ship. Her neck started throbbing, as if the circulation had been cut off for a very long time.

Her whole body ached and she had the mother and father of all thirsts! But when she stood up, even wincing with stiffness, she started to laugh. Some fool had not only put sandals heavy as lead on her feet, but stuffed the stiff leather with grass and shoots. No doubt big brother John was hiding somewhere to laugh at her. She kicked them off and rubbed her feet.

There was something seriously wrong with her feet. And her hands. They were bigger than she remembered – and filthy! Below decks, she rambled through cabins full of strange objects and clothes. Where were her clothes? She shrugged and picked out what must be her brothers' breeks and a shirt.

'John? Martin?'

The boat creaked, but there wasn't even a muffled giggle by way of a reply. Well, they might be away with the fairies, and it was a grand ship they'd got to go fishing, but dirt is dirt and nothing to joke about. She drank some water and went back on deck. The air felt good on her naked body as she dumped the stinking robe. But her skin looked so pale! There were scars on her ribs and she had – breasts? And her hair hung ragged and greasy to her shoulders when she unfastened the rusty pins. She must have been very ill to look and feel this bad.

She jumped into the sea and rubbed her skin – what, no soap? Well, water is water and she ducked her aching head, tugged at her scratchy scalp and wrung her hair again and again. Now that she felt better in her body she started to swim and look around. Those brothers of hers would come rowing back any moment now and she'd have their guts for garters. Making such a guy of her!

She realized that the sea was warm as a bath. It must be a summer like none she'd ever known of. And where was she that the shore was lined with strange trees – the sea glittering as clear as blue glass and alive with fish as bright as jewels? She swam quickly back to the huge ship and hauled herself up on the heavy nets trailing the side.

'John? Martin?'

Where were they? She dressed and went back to the unfamiliar cabins. All at once she froze: she wasn't alone. There was a strange woman staring at her.

'Who are you?'

The figure mouthed at her without a sound. It moved a step back as she moved back. Surely not . . . she raised her hand to her chin and so did . . . Was it a trick or a mirror? She forced herself to walk towards it and it walked towards her, just as slow and shaky as she felt.

Close to, their fingertips met on a cool surface and she looked into her own face. It was awful, it was no doubt her, but nothing in it looked like her apart from her eyes. When had she grown to look so anguished? So old? How had her mouth become so pinched and thin? What had happened to leave lines scored around her mouth, across her brow?

She slumped to the floor and her face was icy on the mirror surface. She looked at her eyes and saw tears drip through the lashes and flood her wasted cheeks. She tasted salt on her lips and her nose dampened to pink, her chest heaved with weeping. What a cruel joke, and why did she remember nothing? She looked as old as her own mother, but her mother had never looked so miserable and mean. A wasted body and a mean and cheated face.

'Kerry, what did they do to you?' she gasped.

She remembered something. A huge gate closing, a comfortless cold bed, and being ill. How long ago was that? She pictured her hands on a thin blanket and they were a little girl's hands.

A long time back.

332

She stumbled away from the mirror and wondered if she was dreaming. Can you be in a dream and wonder if you're dreaming? She went into the bizarre heat and light of this terrifying day. Was that a human voice? She searched the deck and rigging for a human movement. Nothing. The voice came again – from the shore. A figure was standing there waving frantically and hollering at her.

'Help! Help! Sister! Mercy!'

Kerry had no sisters – she was sure of that. But the woman sounded desperate and she dived back into the sea at once and swam for shore.

The tiny clump of seaweed caught up with Isabel, the split-tail she'd clung to when her hiding place was blown to smithereens. She was not seaweed at all, but a cousin to the sea-horse, a creature so shy her fins had sprouted webby leaves like seaweed from years spent among the safe branches and wide leaves of floating forests.

She was a sea-dragon.

The great waves from the Deepwater Wing had scattered her home, and she clutched the nearest brilliant light as it whirled by. The light happened to be Isabel's arm, for sea-dragons see everything living as a light. Isabel was a wonderful pulse of green and white, and the beating of her heart spoke of peace and wonder.

At the gates of Atlantis, the sea-dragon was blinded: the women were a psychedelic dazzle and the city itself was pure white. By the time her eyes cleared, all she could see was a distant whisk of green: Isabel. So she followed.

Now Isabel's viridescent being was still, close to a

huge rainbowed column, scarlet folding on gold, saffron coiling around emerald, aquamarine lapped beautifully into sapphire, heliotrope glowing like amethyst. The Goddess.

What a dilemma for the sea-dragon! She knew this light was The Light, this light was the whole of living. She imagined that she herself shed no light, or just a greyish trickle, a candle stump through a filthy window. She was like a moth, light drugged and drew her. But she had more wisdom than that fluttering flit of passion. The Light energized her and made her full – more, and she would disappear in an incandescent puff of joy.

Isabel's green light was utterly different. It felt like a cave of succulent tender sea-grass. Somewhere she could live with sheer delight. She couldn't – *no* living creature could stay long with the serpentine energy of the Goddess's eternal rainbow.

She hoped.

She drifted along the gleaming streets of Atlantis, sighing hopelessly; hopeful that the green light would come back and walk with her awhile. She hovered outside the gates, wings whirring like a hummingbird.

On the sand, Spinks shifted out of a coma. The flight of the Deepwater Wing had left her breathless, and the end of it had jolted her powerful suckers free. She landed in a grey heap and swam into an unconsciousness where her delicious mermaid stroked and loved her endlessly. She woke and knew at once that Lametta was nowhere in sight or sense; she was alone at the gates of Atlantis, and it should be a fabulous adventure. But how could anything be fabulous without her mermaid? If she'd never met her, she would never miss her or long for her. Having met her and loved her and – miraculous! – been loved by her, nothing compared with her, nothing thrilled the way it did when they were together.

Oh, gracious Ocean, thought the octopus, if it's a lifetime's search, I'll start. But let me know somehow that I'll find her at the end of it. I know I'll die without her.

'I think we should Parlay.'

No-one undersea ignores that word. Parlay. It invites every creature around to comment and consider the comments of others and is only ever used in times of imminent disaster: pre-storm, post-storm, the mafia activities of sharks. Everyone's voice is vital for Parlay leads to decisions: the dispersal of shoals of herring from over-grazed seas, the hasty and complete exodus of moving life when sharks treat grazing grounds like a soup kitchen for the greedy. Parlay is about balance: how to restore it without disaster or casualty.

For Parlay, Spinks would even hibernate her obsess-ive worries about Lametta. She composed her ten-tacles. The sea-dragon turned three times to clear her mind of the light fantastic. And the Deepwater Wing, whose voice had spoken the word, settled slowly beside them. In the deep heart of Ocean, size has nothing to do with importance. The Deepwater Wing spanned at least half the space a shark pack seize as their terror-territorial right. But she was gentle, and used her incredible strength and energy only to carry others on longed-for journeys.

'I was summoned,' she said. 'Summoned to carry strange cargo to Atlantis. Now I have a dilemma. She who summoned me is not here to explain or thank me. I am not able to leave this place while the strange cargo remains, and I have other passengers who have no wish for Atlantis.'

She flapped her wings, where a mêlée of disgruntled

dogfish and squid were drumming their fins. All they had asked for was a ride to pastures new, and Atlantis was so deep that pasture of any kind was out of the question.

'I am here because my home disintegrated,' said the sea-dragon. 'I've seen a light I love – that's all I know.'

It was Spinks turn to Parlay and she sighed.

'Where to begin? I'm in love, in love, in love. It was the voice of my lover which summoned you, Deepwater Wing. She is all things to me. In Parlay, I must admit she is imperious, impossible, unpredictable, indefinable, indefensible. But I love all these things in her. She is a mermaid.'

The Deepwater Wing sighed again and settled, squirting some sweet dream juice over her bickering passengers.

'Mermaids!' The skin over her eyes wrinkled in despair. 'In our lore, there are mermaids. We were once lovers of mermaids. But they're different from us. We know water is life: they use water for life, and then they shoot into the dry space and live there just as happily. It was decided in the time of Fenesha the Goldenwing that, for all our desire, mermaid-love brought a price of danger that would be our doom.'

The sea-dragon spoke.

'Mermaids! For a thousand moons, we forbade the name to help us forget. Forget how they loved us, how they delighted in us – and how they dropped us when we refused the dry space. Mocked us, derided us for our love of deep ocean. Many a dragon died through the casual cruelty of mermaids. Their mouths began to speak in a way we couldn't understand. They did nothing to help us understand, just laughed at our speech. Some dragons were chained and fed only if they spat fire to order at mermaid concerts. Dragons are forbidden to use fire unless their lives are endangered. Some didn't care. Mermaid ecstasy was enough for them: they died as charred dragons.'

Spinks wept.

'It's different for eight leggers,' she said. 'Our nursery tales speak of the love of mermaids, we dream of half-scaled heaven. I have a dream made life.'

'That's dangerous,' said the Deepwater Wing. 'Some of our kind eschewed sense and pursued mermaids. Mockery, as you found, sea-dragon. Rejection, ridicule. So hurt were they that they resolved to be all unto themselves – you know the gwellup. Life continues with the gwellup, but what joy is there? None. They commune only with the sole, she who cannot decide to crawl the sands or swim free. Hopeless.'

'If I can speak? My name is Hauberk.'

They turned to a globular spiked fish who had inched from the outer Atlantean gloom.

'Parlay,' said the Deepwater Wing.

'A myriad moons gone by, we flew from the water and the dry space was heaven,' said Hauberk. 'How we loved it! Came a day when we had to choose: fly or swim. We couldn't. It was the Great Mermother who resolved us. Those who craved flying could do so. Those who feared would swim for ever. But swim so deep that never a temptation of dry space would be near us. Listen to me: a thousand generations bickered and even killed their own kind when they wouldn't go the same way. There were a handful of us left, and ceasing-to-be was staring us in the fins when she came and resolved us. She is the one to resolve this. You have split-tails who can swim deep and long as any of the finned. You have a loved and lovely mermaid who is an infant in undersea wisdom. Who else is to solve it?'

All four deep-sea wonderers pondered. Hauberk's words were unwelcome, though wise. Tentacles, wide wings, delicate fins and the armour of a solitary vibrated in unison. The Great Mermother was needed. And when She was needed, She was always there.

Ocean

Ocean plays the music of sand and rising waves with her seven times seven zillion fingers of foam. She slaps at sea-walls; shrugs at deep-sunk pillars men imagined strong enough to stand for all time against her might. Her sleek jaws crunch a cave out of cliffs too hard for men to mine, too sheer for men to climb. Ooranya sees her coming and stacks up shelves of rock to slow her down: Ocean strokes them smooth with her lace-winged paws. She studs them with limpets, she furs them with sea-moss. She grinds jagged clumps to shallow bowls and scatters purple threads of sea-plants to clutch and cling. Ocean is moving over pebbles, making slow sand. The sea and the earth are fusing and countless living waves away, sand catches on a rock, and maybe one day an island begins.

Tethyz lays swathes of white sand to honour Ooranya and the places where land meets sea. Each gives to each, wild and wary. Sea and her creatures become salt-marsh becomes earth, pulsing with the briny blood of Ocean: earth and rock become sand becomes beach becomes sea fizzing with sand. Ocean arranges her dazzling gift of shells, and her forever song embraces a rattle and ring of tambourines; she heaps up seaweed and her music sighs like wind ploughing through a golden savannah. Her song summons the windwolf who slinks through green

339

wheatfields on a gusty day and no-one can catch her.

Kythara surges in the deeps, caressing the eyeless, the colourless, the spiny batfish, the stonefish, the sea-slugs. She ripples her muscled body along the deadly charge of congers until they shock themselves by giggling. She hugs whales to her breasts, she sits the primeval arawana on her rocking lap and fills their serious ears with stories until their dragon scales hum with joy. She stamps all along her thigh and calf, and a storm drives the barracudas into the jaws of sharks. She chivvies hungry minnows and arctic-starved seals to pick up the pieces. C'est la vie, she says in her grande dame déshabillé voice, and the deeps ring with haggish hilarity and crone cackles.

Tiamat encircles the water world. She smiles as dry-land creatures swim in her shallows and delight in her danger. She frowns as men start drawing pictures of her on paper, raping her of secrets and surprises and saying this land is my land. They have no idea how long it took for her and Ooranya to sort that out. More, they don't care. She decides to show them about land and places and whose is what. She takes back her favourite, Atlantis, where men are planning to stone-wall her. The women don't understand them, but when Tiamat speaks, her words tugging the sails of their being, they understand and mourn: it is time for them to go. They have always welcomed her on the shore, they have returned the gifts of Ocean with cascades of flowers and fruit. They have danced on the silver sands and sung songs and made pictures to honour Tethyz. They have hauled Kythara's lost stragglers back to the waves for all of word-remembered time. They have carved figures of Erda and her creatures, woven cloth the colour of the sea to wave in the breath of Ooranya.

It is time.

Atlantis disappears in a blink of Tiamat's worldly wise eye, a gentle swallow of her foam-flecked jaws. She settles her down gently and says You will rise again at the right time.

A Nun No More

Lametta Moonlighte was cold and fretting. Where were the pesky split-tails? That moronic Deepwater Wing had messed it all up, where she had planned that its incredible speed and panache would be her *pièce de résistance* to silence the rumbles of subversion among her slaves.

There *is* no Atlantis! She had envisaged a pretty grotto of coral confusion where she would mistress it over them. The Deepwater Wing had misunderstood, and had taken them scales only knew where. She shivered at the encrusted extravagance of the grotto. She had no interest in the pink and blue and green dead carapace of creatures, no matter that they were ingenious.

And Spinks! How dare she ride with the rest of them! It was as if she didn't believe Lametta was faster, better, the best. If anything had happened to Spinks! Torn between fury at the chance that she might have been betrayed and terror in case anything had . . . gone wrong? She pictured Spinks annihilated in the cruel jaws of a barracuda, Spinks whirled into the death throes of a split-tail ship. What if a storm had torn her apart, or swept her oceans away?

For the first time since the total ecstasy she had found with Spinks, she stopped and let all the thoughts come flooding back. She wanted her mother! No, she didn't. If she ever asked her mother about anything that really mattered, anything that woke her passion, Marchioness Martina would sit back and give her That Look.

'Well, why, mother, why?'

Martina would sigh, reach over, and comb her hair unnecessarily neat, groom her scales, check her fingernails and then say in That Tone:

'Lametta, you must calm down. Some things just *are*. We have to accept them. It's rather arrogant to think we can understand everything, isn't it?'

Now she was desolate, and claws of sorrow tore at her guts. To lose Spinks . . . what comfort would come from her mother? She remembered when she'd let her pet sea-dragon off its chain. She thought it would stay with her – Martina had told her that sea-dragons adored mermaids. The little creature had stared at her and shot away and she never found it again. What had Martina said then?

'It's not the end of the world. Do stop weeping. Cheer up, Lametta. There's plenty more sea-dragons in the ocean.'

If she could tell her – what then? Martina would roll out some platitude about wordless octopi, as if Spinks was nothing more than an eight-legged curiosity. Indeed, if Lametta told her just what Spinks meant to her, she'd be speechless. Hurt. Disappointed. Revolted. Furious.

She'd have Lametta ritually thrown out of the precious choir on the spot. She'd disown her.

For all that, as Lametta's heartbroken tears ripped at her ribs and deafened her, she cried out with the pain. She roared her need and her loss through the waves and the word was:

'MOTHER!'

'Just what is this all about?'

Lametta looked round wildly. The voice was so big it filled her head. She flinched at its fury.

'Mermaids!' it said. 'You've given me more grief than most. Right at your beginning, you wouldn't decide for Ocean or Air, and we both wanted you. You're too beautiful for Ocean by half. And too beautiful for Ooranya by the other half. So here you are, half scales and half nonsense, luring the luckless out of their element and giving all Ocean a bad name. What have you been playing at this time, and who with?'

Fury? Exasperation? Oh, yes. And with it all, a warmth and love Lametta recognized. Exactly what she'd wanted from her mother and never had; she'd had to dismiss her need as dreaming. She didn't know that Ocean holds every creature in her passionate heat and welcome embrace the instant it's born. Whether egg or seed or polyp – or merbabe. Well, how could she? Most grown mermaids like to lift their heads into the air and pretend it never happened.

She knew at once there was no point in bare-faced lies or even half-truths. She started with her choir, the snobbery, the sea-dragon, the whales, the songs. The voice sighed like air in a nautilus shell.

'I know this story. Tell me.'

Lametta spoke about Spinks, and the voice caressed her cheeks and held her chin high and sent a fleet of silver angel fish to reflect her sad eyes back to her. She mumbled about the split-tails and the ship, and her cheeks flamed scarlet spangles from the angel scales. The voice roared at her like a tempest batting Hell out of a cliff to make caves.

'SPEAK UP!'

She said it all again, and the ocean rocked with laughter.

'Silly child! It's your choir's snobbery that says *split-tails* and *servants*. Those are *women*, mermaids who made their minds up to walk on dry land. And these women are witches who can breathe under water. Immortal mermaid, what a cat's cradle of vanity and sadness you've made! It's time for some unravelling. Back to the island with you! It's time for wait and see.'

When the women met at the gates of Atlantis, something had changed about each of them. There was no need for words; their faces radiated a sea-change, and even Squirrel swallowed her shout of triumphant joy as she saw Jen.

In her wisdom, the Deepwater Wing wafted dream juice over them as she billowed them beautifully away from Atlantis and back to the elbow of sand and coral nudging out of Ocean into the starry brilliance of Ooranya's deep midnight.

On shore, Judith had resigned herself to yet another world-turned-upside down become reality. Reality – for the time being. This change had blown away her nightmare of eternity spent with Sister Mercy and a bear. She had screamed and Sister Mercy – *Sister Mercy!!!* – had dived over the side of the ship and swam straight for shore and come running through the shallows to save her in a sopping embrace.

Sister Mercy with a smile? The hacky nun with a sweet-smelling skin, and able to swim like a fish? Sister Mercy who said she was Kerry and kept asking what the devil sort of illness had made her thin and sick and with no memory at all since gathering kelp and buckies on the beach at home. She of the rosary beads asking how old she was? She of the thousand sorrows and sanctimonious platitudes saying anxiously:

345

'Have I said anything I should be sorry about – for I know that folk with a fever come out with all sorts of hell and nastiness. Why, my own granny shouted at grandad that he was a bloody bastard one night, and all because she had a fever! She told me when I asked her in the morning.'

Judith shook her head.

'I've only known you a short time,' she said soothingly. 'There's a lot of us. Well, there were. I mean. They'll be back in the next few days. They'll be able to tell you more. But I don't think you have a thing to scold yourself with. No-one in their right minds would blame a person for what they say or do in a long sickness.'

The nun – nun-no-more – smiled at her.

'There's one thing you could maybe help me on. When I woke up, I found some fool had put grass and shoots into my shoes. It was murder on the owld feet! And the thing I was wearing! Some sort of woollen robe! In this heat! I stank enough to make a pig sick! There was an ugly chain round my neck with a statue of a sad murdered fellow on it. I thought it was all some lark with my brother John – he was always a prankster. But you say he's not with us?'

Judith smiled.

'I think that was part of your sickness,' she said. 'You wouldn't wear anything but that robe. You called it a habit. We wanted you to change and you wouldn't hear of it! You used to put stones and seeds in your shoes yourself. You said it was for punishment, although you'd done nothing wrong. And the chain was the same.'

'That was frightening,' said Kerry, shaking her head. 'It felt evil to me – I threw it in the sea. I hope it didn't belong to anyone?'

Judith poured her some wine.

'A lot of people wear those chains when they're ill,' she said. 'They think it'll help them get better, like a charm or an amulet. It does seem to help some people – I wore one myself for a while. But when I felt the sickness sweeping over me and I didn't care if I lived or died . . . oh dreadful times! I thought taking it off would kill me quicker. I took it off. Then I found it had been stopping me recovering.'

'Do you think I'm recovered?' said Kerry anxiously.

'I think so. In fact, I'm sure of it.'

'Well, here's to no relapse! If you see any of the signs coming back, you tell me straightaway.'

'I think we all will,' said Judith. 'We'll burn that robe when they come back: it must be rotten with disease!'

They clinked glasses and drank deep.

When Ocean stretched out her gentlest arm to lay the sleeping sea-divers safe on shore, Kerry was showing Judith how to dance. Between the bear and the wine and falling over they didn't notice anything until Miss Walnut honked a hairy hello and lumbered at break-neck bear-pace towards Jen, to JEN to *JEN*!!

Kerry hallo-ed as she danced, her feet beating the sand wildly for all the years she had to catch up on. Judith stopped, breathless. Through the fire-haze and the heartwarming wine and wild dancing, she caught her breath at the sight of Isabel. Isabel flew over the flames and into her arms and danced with her.

A hundred questions fireworked through the darkness. A thousand answers catherine-wheeled them all to sleep.

Ocean woke Lametta.

'Go on. The sun's up and enough days have gone by

347

with those women at your beck and call. Go on.'

Lametta went pale. What could they do to her, these split-tails – these women – these witches? Ocean had rocked her all night with stories of witches and their magic. Magic gifts the same as mermaids practise. But the most devastating thing Ocean told her was this: women and children and witches feel and live and breathe and think just as deeply as mermaids do. And love and weep and dream. She learnt that it was the same for sea-dragons and mullet and seaweed – the same for every living thing.

'It's a lot for a little mermaid to take on,' Ocean told her. 'You're a child. Whoever decided that seven meryears made you grown up should be put ashore between tides!'

'What about Spinks?' Lametta said tearfully. 'If I knew I'd see her again, I'd go and make my peace with the witch-women. If it's only me, then I'll just disappear and leave them to it. They'll be relieved that I've gone.'

Ocean ruffled her lovely hair.

'Just do it,' she said. 'Do you think I can keep my pulse on every blessed octopus there is?'

'No,' Lametta said.

'Make your peace, mermaid. It's easy to swim away and hide. Remember all I've told you. Go on!'

Ocean drove her to shore with a wave that landed her right on the sand in a deafening crash of foam.

'Of course I *can*. My pulse lives through every octopus and eel and sea-anemone. And half of every mermaid, come to that,' Ocean murmured to herself, nudging the somnolent tentacles the other side of the reef. Her waters infused every cell. Spinks waited on her wisdom.

'Well, I'll be buggered!' shouted Queenie, 'it's our

348

mermaid. How are ye, kidder? We missed you at Atlantis. By, there's some city, Your Empressness. When I get home to my queendom, my subjects'll be wetting themselves wi' envy!'

Oh, this was even worse!

'Are you a queen?' Lametta asked miserably.

'I am,' she said, 'if you're an empress.'

'Well, I'm not,' Lametta said.

'Oh, crikey,' Queenie said, sitting solidly on the sand, 'Well I'll not let on if youse don't. Where's your friend?'

Lametta burst into tears.

'I'm not an empress. I don't know where Spinks is. I can't even make waves. I'm only seven. I can grant wishes, but I don't know how to stop. My name's Lametta Moonlighte. *And don't laugh at me!*'

'Who the hell's laughing, Miss Mermaid? I think it's something to be a mermaid, me. Hoy meself down to Atlantis any day of the week. Sing me heart out and bugger the lot of yez! And you've a bonny name. Lametta Moonlighte! See me, Patience Scroggit by birth. Scroggit! I drowned that one and gave it no mercy! Simon Quint by way of freedom, since women aren't free. And now Queenie as any bastard's ha-ha-ha!'

Lametta sniffed and looked up.

'Oh, it's you again,' said Alice angrily. 'What are we supposed to do, bow and kiss your tail?'

Queenie pulled her down on the sand.

'She's had a hard time,' she said. 'Alice Dizard, here's Lametta Moonlighte and she doesn't like to be laughed at.'

'What fool does unless they've said owt funny?' said Alice. 'You mean she's not the storm-raising hoity toity we've been fretting about the past two moons?'

'I'm only seven,' said Lametta.

'Poor bairn's only seven,' said Queenie.

'I can't even make waves.'

'Poor lass! Even the winds and seas won't obey her!' said Queenie.

'I can grant wishes. But you have to know how to stop and I never learnt that.' The mermaid burst into floods of aquamarine tears.

'Ee, life's tough for some,' said Queenie. 'Me, I grant meself a million wishes and none of them come true.'

'Well, I'm honoured,' said Alice. 'Lametta, take no notice of this raucous chorus sitting here. If I asked you for just three wishes, could you do it?'

'I'd have to,' said Lametta. Oh, merciful Mermother, the big one laughing was just another form of her own mother, pretending to be jolly and suddenly turning into vitriol.

'My first one is this,' said Alice. 'I want to find a place that's safe for ever to live with all these women. I want this place to ring with happiness because we're all doing all the things we know and love.'

'She's not greedy,' said Queenie. 'I'll shurrup now. Promise. Ee, do you mind when we made wishes at Meldon – no, no, I swear, I'll glue me gob.'

'My third wish,' said Alice softly. 'Is that you learn how to stop with your wish-granting.'

Lametta looked wildly from her to Queenie. The sneering term 'split-tail' didn't even cross her mind. So this is what witch-women were like! Tough as clams and soft as sargasso moss!

She closed her eyes and felt Ocean, Tethyz, Kythara and Tiamat touch her spirit. Her old vision of the Great Mermother pontificating on a throne looked as ridiculous as the gold brocade and crown her choir had clothed Her in. All of Ocean was the Great Mermother and She was All of Ocean and More.

She opened her eyes to the sumptuous smiles of Alice and Queenie.

'Done!' she said, 'And I can grant all of you wishes – I want to. It's no scales off my tail. I owe you.'

'There's no debts and no payment,' said Queenie. 'What Alice asked for is what we all want. Only I've two more, me.'

Maybe this was it. Maybe this was *I wish you dead*. She clenched her tail.

'I've had a life where if wishes were horses the world couldn't grow enough oats and hay to feed them,' said Queenie. 'I'm not so young as I was so get out your fiddles and we'll all cry about it. Only since all this carry on, I know what's important.'

She held Alice's hand and smiled at Lametta.

'I wish those lovely tears of yours would turn into jewels to make a necklace for the woman I worship. That's one. And I wish for you to get your heart's desire. I've got mine, me.'

Wishes Come True

Queenie draped the sea-sparkling jewels around Alice's neck just as the Queen of Tonga would honour her guests with her finest flowers roped into a lei.

'It really happens!' cried Lametta. 'It really works!'

'Oh, aye,' Alice said, grinning at her delight. 'Magic, you see. You daft great bairn!'

'What about the other wishes?' Lametta asked.

'Oh, divent ye fret about them,' said Queenie. 'Wishes take the time they take. My best one took nigh on twenty years.'

'Mine too,' said Alice. 'It was all to do with heart's desire, you see, and then you've to wait until your heart's desire beats true with you. And that may never happen. Or happen when you've given up daring to hope any more.'

Lametta felt Spinks' orgiastic heartbeat as a stab of pain through her veins. Sometime she could cope with, but *never*? Why had she started this tyranny? So that Spinks and she could be for ever.

'I don't want to think about it,' she said. 'I'd like to give all of the rest of you your wishes – do you think that would make things better?'

'It'll take your mind off whatever's put the sorrow in your eyes,' said Alice. 'Will you have breakfast with us?'

Lametta looked at the circle of women gathered round the deep pool where they had chosen to eat so that she didn't have to be out of water. How could she ever have flexed her pseudo-empress tyranny over them? And where was the Shark Slayer – she, surely, would mete out some punishment?

'Queenie says you're the same age as me,' said Squirrel. 'Are you?'

'Yes,' said Lametta.

'And I thought *I* was bossy!' said Squirrel, 'Did you make it up about the map?'

The mermaid nodded and blushed.

'I knew that,' said Turtle. 'Queenie told me.'

'Seven is bossy,' said Esther, mock-judging. 'Bossy and proud and brilliant. Don't throw that cake at me, Squirrel. I won't give it back. I'll eat it all myself!'

'Will I be bossy?' Turtle asked.

'We have that to look forward to,' Rowan said.

'Was Belle ever bossy?'

'Oh, yes!' Rowan said. 'Just because she doesn't choose to speak! Bossy eyes, bossy mouth, bossy scowl . . . bossier than Squirrel even.'

Isabel giggled. Sprawled on Judith's lap, she snapped her fingers and pointed at the golden fruit and then her mouth. Judith fed her.

'It's good being bossy,' said Squirrel. 'People do things for you.'

'And this is fruit you can't feed yourself with,' said Jen. 'Grown-ups can be bossy too. Only they learn to make it a treat for everyone else as well. This fruit has to be fed to you.'

The mermaid gawped as they each took a piece of fruit and fed it to the person next to them. One of the witches she couldn't remember held her chin and fed it to her, grey eyes dancing. She signed through a chin-dripping mouthful that Lametta should do the same. Lametta found herself feeding Alice.

'What's it like having no legs?' Squirrel asked.

'What's it like having no tail?'

'What's it like having no manners?' said Queenie. 'See, I wouldn't kna. Now I'm mixing with bad company, I have to watch yez all to pick up how to gan on. Am I learning fast?'

'Ye daft bugger!' said Alice. 'Let's have one question each, one at a time. And seeing as she's a mermaid, she can have one for each of ours. I can be bossy too.'

'Will I write that down in case I forget?' Princess smiled at her mother, shy and happy that she and Jen were sitting beside each other and their bodies glowed with delight wherever they touched.

'Grown bairns get cheeky,' Alice said woefully. 'D'ye think I've failed as a mother?'

'Definitely,' said Jen, 'Congratulations on your bad lass.'

'Give us a question, Lametta.'

'What's happened to the Shark Slayer?'

'Who?'

'One of you – I saw her on your ship. She was tall and wore a shark-skin robe and had a great mast-and-spar at her neck. I thought she was the leader of your choir. Where is she?'

The grey-eyed woman next to her laughed aloud.

'Would that have been me? I was very ill, you know. No-one's told me all about it yet.'

'Some things are best forgotten,' Esther said. 'You were so unhappy when you were ill.'

'Did I kill sharks?'

'You had to, to get better.' Esther gazed at her. 'Sharks come in many forms, and you fought plenty. You certainly drove them away, Kerry, scared the life out of them, I'm sure.'

'Did I?' The nun-no-more flushed with pleasure. 'I

have a memory of always being frightened. Always scared of something coming to get me. Well, if I've driven sharks away, I've no need for fear any more.'

'That's the truth,' Esther smiled around the rest of them. 'Who's next?'

'Well, it has to be me,' said Queenie, 'because I'm bigger than the rest of you. Now tell us, Miss Mermaid – you don't have to and you can tell me to shurrup – not that I'll pay you any mind, will you tell us your heart's desire?'

'Well, that's why I made you follow me,' said Lametta. 'I'm in love with Spinks. My octopus. I'm immortal – mermaids are born that way, mother told me, and I thought if I went to the Great Mermother she could make my octopus immortal too. And whenever I sing, every creature in the ocean comes to hear. Can you imagine what it's like trying to swim with a flock of parrot-fish squawking on your shoulders and a pack of dogfish panting along at your fins? The only thing that makes them go away is the shadow of a shark. You know what your ship looks like from underneath?'

'Why didn't you tell us?' said Queenie. 'I'd have volunteered to be bouncer to the blessed ocean in the wake of a mermaid – wouldn't we all?'

'But we'd just found the map . . .' Jen said softly, her fingers drifting into the dark clouds of Princess's hair.

'And I was being bossy,' Squirrel said, giggling as she noticed the caress. Oh, honestly, not Jen and Princess too! Grown-ups!

'And that's still your heart's desire?' Jen scrambled to her feet.

'Yes, only now I don't know if I'll ever even see Spinks again. If I did I think I'd forget about immortality. I don't want it without her if I can't have life with her.'

355

Isabel pointed and Lametta turned round. To a dear, familiar passionate gaze and eight enfolding arms that clung around her.

'And if you want immortality,' Jen sat down again. 'Here it is in a bottle.'

She held out a crystal vial, sealed at the neck and stamped with a hieroglyph in copper.

'Whey aye, and I'm the Empress of China,' said Queenie.

'Tell us about it.' Princess's eyes were a night of shooting stars as she looked at Jen.

'Do you remember when we left the river?' Jen said, 'Before we met Queenie and Alice and Judith and Princess? And a long time before we met you, Lametta. Yes? We knew we were going to sea but we didn't know how. You had to let the raft go and you didn't want to. So you all made a fire on it and sent it downriver, who knows, maybe to the open sea . . . I left you to it, because it was your farewell, your sadness. I had my own. I knew this great bear would come with us. There's no life for a bear in England, just goads and chains from a lickspittle larrikin like Jethro. I had my horse, my granny's horse. I'd known Auntie Clop ever since I was a little girl and she wasn't young even then. I'd die rather than sell her for horsemeat and I don't have the kind of money or trust that pays some farmer to put her out to grass. I thought of shooting her. Either that or waiting until she died before I left those shores for ever.'

'You shot Auntie Clop!' Squirrel was dismayed.

'Shh,' said Esther, said Rowan.

'I walked through the woods with her and talked to her, and suddenly we came on a gypsy camp, a real hatchin tan like Granny had been brought up in. There was an old woman of the craft there, and I told her my story. I think she knew it already. She said she'd take her and look after her. And that she'd have to give me something in return to make it a *kooshti clop*. That's a deal to make us both free and the horse too. I'd forgotten, that's why Granny called her Auntie Clop in the first place. She'd healed a little girl with the devil's fever and they gave her the horse in exchange for getting that dear little life back. I said it would be an honour and she could give me whatever she liked. She hoiked her skirts up and went into her vardo – her caravan, Squirrel, – and gave me this. She said, "Didikai Jen, beware of sleevers and palmers. This bottle holds the secret of immortality. Whoever drinks it will live for ever. And don't dash it into your mouth without you think about it. And don't throw it away ever. If you don't use it, give it to someone who truly has that as their heart's desire." So I said Yn Iach to Auntie Clop and put the bottle away safe until it was needed.'

They all looked at the gleaming green glass.

'So here you are, Miss Mermaid. You and your octopus can live together for ever.'

'But surely *you* want it?' The mermaid was amazed.

'No,' Jen said, smiling. 'I'm here and I'm happy now. Happy now adds up to a whole life of happiness. Anyways, I'll be back. Maybe I'll be a swift next life, seeing as I've done my mortal best to fly in this one.'

'Don't any of you want it?' Lametta looked at all of them. Each smiled and shook their heads.

'It's yours,' Esther said. 'Enjoy it.'

So that was it! Her mermaid wanted her to live for ever! Spinks blushed at the compliment, sighed at the silliness, and took the bottle from Lametta's hand into one delicate tentacle. Live for ever? She knew she would. She sucked the seal from the bottle and dripped the clear liquid into the laughing mouth of Ocean, for her and all the creatures. Did Lametta know what she meant?

The mermaid watched the last drop become one with the sea. Slowly she nodded – she understood.

And Ocean shook her bonniest white breakers with laughing and loving them all.

'It's time for you all to be on your way,' said Ocean. 'I'll show you where the map needs to take this ship of yours. Lametta, you and Spinks are summoned to a Parlay. The Deepwater Wing and the sea-dragon call you. There's a lot of creatures that need to hear from a mermaid how mermaids think. The sea-dragon says you can be trusted: you let one of her sisters go free years ago. You're quite a legend! Come!'

The mermaid was swept serenely out of the calm waters of the lagoon, and she and her octopus waved and waved and waved.

Queenie dropped her aching arm only when her keen eyes couldn't pick out even a speck in the ocean that said Lametta.

'We'll need to get shipshape and out to sea again. Time to find that safe place and maybe settle.'

'Settle?' Alice said, doubling up with laughter. 'The day we settle – any of us – is the day we die.'

'Oh, that won't stop us,' said Esther. 'That's just a hiccup.'

A Scurvy Parcel Of Rogues

'Arr, me beauties!' slurred Captain Petticote, casting a villainous eye over the motley crew slumped around the mildewed hold of *The Unbridled Revenge*. A sorry lot they were, sorry they'd ever clapped eyes on him. Sorrier still that they'd been mesmerized by his wild promises of gold. And sorriest that they still sailed under the insane direction of his one bloodshot eye and the metal patch masking the scar that had once been its twin.

A scurvy parcel of rogues lashed together by a litany of evil that would make Captain Henry Morgan cross himself.

At their head, Captain Nineveh Petticote: three tots of rum and he swore he was first cousin to Captain Blood; five tots made him bastard son and wronged heir to the Czar of all the Russias. When the sun was high, the fumes stirring in the crenellations of his dastardly brain elevated him to first in line for the throne of Beelzebub.

Very few would gainsay the fiery spirit of thrice-brewed sugar cane. No-one but a fool or an angel would argue when the words of the spirits came roaring through a ginger beard bristling six feet above the ground and twisted with scarlet threads, one for each of the hearts that he had stopped for ever. Captain Petticote's hulk loomed over the stinking skulking rabble he called crew, one hand twitching to throttle the life out of them, the other a three-pronged claw of ragged steel itching to rip their guts out.

He trawled the hapless voyagers on the oceans of the West Indies the way a barracuda trawls a shoal of migrating fish; he raked off the finest cargoes and burnt the rest. Between times, his men 'traded' plunder with islanders and colonists too fond of breathing to barter. He stayed aboard The Unbridled Revenge, roaring out orders for repair as she lay holed up in some lushly overgrown inlet. It was never long before his nose had its fill of the scent of frangipan and lotus. His sated belly curdled with fine wines and exotic delicacies. He would cast aside whatever women he'd dragged down to his filthy bed and order his cabin cleared. The crew would busy themselves with all his leftovers.

He strutted on deck, his vulture telescope scanning the horizon for a sail. Now he was greedy for the scent of gunpowder, the rip of sails and masts and crackling flames. His ears ached for screams and pleas for mercy. His claw thirsted to drink blood. It was an awful thing when he smiled and summoned the crew below to unfold his plans.

'Arr, ye swabs!' he growled. 'God rot the day yez ever fell in with me! Not a one of you will live out his old age! What do you say to that, Mister Spainy-Bollocks?'

Jesus y Santa Baptista shrugged. He was one of the newest aboard The Unbridled Revenge, ex-mate of Il Pangoline Rosso, forced to sign on or walk the plank. First to hit the waves was their captain, and none of them were sorry to see him go. Jesus had watched most of his ship's crew refuse to take the oath under the black flag. At which point, Captain Nineveh Petticote gouged his iron claw from shoulder to belly and sent

360

each one on his last voyage, a stagger along the creaking path of death, a plunge into water lashing with the blood-frenzied jaws of death.

'*Va f'an culo, stronzo di cane, capitano,*' he said with a gentle smile. He'd thought Mucchio di Scarto was a wicked captain!

'He says what? Get the bastard to speak English, like a good Christian!' spluttered the captain.

'He says God bless you, you're a brave fine captain,' the first mate said with a chuckle.

Petticote stabbed his claw into the table and up-ended a bottle.

'I've a mind for change, boys,' he said, rum dribbling from his cruel lips. 'We'll be sailing south come morning. These waters are getting a mite hot for my heels. First ship we find, we'll have her and put her crew aboard *The Unbridled Revenge*. We'll torch *The Revenge*. She's been a fine ship, but it's like a woman. And what do we do with women, Samuel?'

Samuel was nine years old and it pleased the captain to make him drunk and have him curse and toss him into bed with a naked woman, well paid to put on a show and frightened for her life if she refused.

'We shag 'em till they cannot walk and throw them into the sea to save us their keep, sir,' he said, gulping rum.

When I'm big enough, I'm going to torture you very very slowly and then I'll murder you when you're begging for mercy. And then I'm going to find an island and hide there and never talk to anyone again.

Samuel escaped to this island in his mind any time he could. The rum made it easier, and the captain never kept him short of rum. Why, a few months back, he could have sworn that one of those women had promised to take him away with her and treat him like her own son. She told him she was sorry for what was happening to him. She told the captain to piss off and let the child – him a child! – sleep! That was when the island dream first came to him, and she was somewhere on it. But when he woke, she wasn't there and he was too sick to even ask where she'd gone.

'You little bastard!' crowed the captain. 'Aye. And *The Unbridled Revenge* is an old whore who's close to her last tumble. We'll torch her and have it rumoured I was on board. That'll throw them off our scent and give us the freedom of the oceans again.'

'Whatever are you doing?' Esther asked.

Queenie looked up at her, face smeared with oil and grime. They were two days out to sea, and sleep had not visited her restless pillow for more than a moment or so. She laughed mirthlessly.

'I'm checking the cannon,' she said. 'I've been a fool with no fire to protect us all, and we've been damned lucky so far. Maybe that mermaid put a spell on us and I've been drifting along with it. Where we're headed, every breaker hides one of the Blood, blast them. The Black Flag rules the waves. I've thought mebbes we'll fly under the dry bones of death for safety's sake.'

Esther sighed deeply and sat next to her.

'When will it ever end?' she asked softly. 'Will it always be like this? Run a little, hide a little, move on and make a home?'

Queenie grunted as she lashed the death-machine tight.

'All very well for Ocean to say she'll guide us. Oh, and she will, no doubt. But if one of those jackals comes slipping across our bows and sees a deck full of women, well, they'll just come alongside and walk in like they'd been invited. I've no need to tell you what happens next.'

'What about magic?' Esther wondered.

'I'd feel a sight better if I was standing at the back of magic with some powder and shot – just in case. Ah, divent ye fret, Esther. It may not come to it. But I'd rather be sure.'

Esther remembered the villagers and how they'd driven her and Rowan and the children almost to death. Ordinary people claiming to be Christian: at least pirates didn't hide behind the skirts of a man of God. And the men of God hid behind the death of a Nazarene, which hadn't *really* been death, and the mystery of a virgin who was not virgin enough to prevent conception and birth. Esther couldn't bring herself to touch things built only for death: neither could she shrink from the fact that they might be necessary.

The afternoon brought a fine mist and clouds the like of which they'd not seen since they'd left the cold northern seas. Dragging like a train behind the grey wisps came the heavy heat of a storm brewing, and stinging handfuls of rain blinding them. The sun set in shreds of furious scarlet and black: night flooded the decks with treacherous waves; winds shrieked like the souls of the lost as they scrabbled at the tightly rolled canvas.

Queenie paced alone, nightmare snapping at her heels. All very well, she fretted, all very well, but what next?

Below decks, Alice hummed as she boiled and simmered and strained. She planned to distil the wild beauty of the island to a brew for them to drink when they finally landed – wherever the map and Ocean

363

chose to take them. She was radiant with the spirit of Dizard. And Kerry had offered to taste everything at every stage as soon as they'd told her that part of her illness had been a horrified aversion to pleasure.

'Moderation?' she'd cried out. 'To hell with moderation, when you've wasted half your life sick as a parrot and bloody miserable with it!'

'Queenie thinks there's trouble ahead,' Esther told Rowan.

'Nothing like fearing it to bring it to you.' Rowan looked serious. 'She has a point. I'd fire a cannon or ply a cutlass to keep you and the babies safe. I hate to even think it would come to that, but if I had to, I would.'

Princess and Jen hadn't even noticed Queenie's anxious preparations. They had flown from rope to rope making *The Empress of the Seven Oceans* ready. Now they were sitting in candlelight, lips and arms locked in love.

Judith was glad of the cannon. She'd helped Queenie shine and prime the pistols and blunderbusses. She'd sharpened the cutlasses, and ground every speck of rust from the long unused surfaces. Isabel sat watching, her child's face as old as the hills. Judith smiled at her from time to time, a smile that said, I'm sorry, so sorry, but chances I cannot and will not take. At one point she looked up and the child was gone.

Isabel didn't want any more words, and everyone was talking or whispering. Only Jen and Princess were wordless, and that was private. Isabel did not want to be alone. So she found the bear well below decks, curled deep into darkness against the screaming abuse of the storm overhead. Isabel put her lantern down and pulled out her knife. She'd got them all to haul a fallen tree on board for her to carve. She wanted to make a

Goddess like the one in Atlantis. And then she wanted to fix her on the front of *The Empress*. No pirate would dare threaten them then. But Queenie was seized with such an urgency, she doubted the figure would be ready in time.

Come morning, she decided, she'd get Jen to help her. And Princess – all of them! But for now she worked on the Goddess's face: that, at least, would be perfect before the sun rose.

The Unbridled Revenge wallowed through the waves like a goaded bull. Heavy weather and a sense of doom made every man jack stumble and fumble and slip and trip until Captain Nineveh Petticote had cursed every curse and threatened every torture known to Satan himself. All to no avail. The skies had promised halcyon days when they set out; the demurely rippling waves had enticed them onwards.

Just as he had begun to relax, an hour or so beyond when it would be possible to turn back, some wild wind had herded up purple clouds and heaped their backs with darkness fanged by lightning. The crew were barely swarming up the rigging to furl the sails and make ready for a tempest when the rain came straight at them: not even falling from the sky. This deluge swept across towering waves like a sabre and cut the legs from under you. The instant you were staggering to grope your balance another sabre thrust from the opposite direction sent you head over heels, skidding across the wave-tossed boards like ninepins.

By nightfall, *The Unbridled Revenge* sagged and heaved, punch-drunk and a squall away from foundering. No use for Nineveh Petticote to rage and jeer his crew to action: four men had already been swallowed in the white fangs of the sea. He could read mutiny in every terrified eye. He went to his cabin and howled with fury at the smithereens of fine china heaped like snowflakes on the sodden and priceless Indian carpet.

For the first time in his adult life, he sank to his knees to pray. The words choked him and, as he spoke, a lightning bolt ricocheted through the cabin windows and split his table down the middle, leaving a triumphant scent of scorched wood.

But the dawn rose, tossing silky scarves of rose around a perfect golden orb. The sea was playful again, and jaunty foam caps sparkled around *The Unbridled Revenge*. Sunlight gave Nineveh Petticote a new bravado, and he lashed the men from their bunks, promising double rations of rum if all was shipshape before noon. For the cabin boy, Samuel, the storm had been wonderful: he had dreamed of his tormentor struck by lightning and spent the night with the crew, at the foot of Jesus y Santa Baptista, the despised Spaniard. He had slept a sleep he'd forgotten possible. The dream of an island stayed with him when he woke, nine years old and sober for the first time in a year.

The sun lost all her gold, and baked them white at noon. The captain called them all on deck and handed out their double ration. They gulped it down before he changed what passed for his mind, and waited.

'Pickings is rich in these parts, me boys! Do you, Mister Spainy-bollocks, get your foreign arse up to the crow's nest and sing out when you spy a sail! Lucky! We've got the devil's own luck to spend a night with the bitch we found last night and come out of it with lead in our pencils!'

He toyed with the idea of an hour or so spent on Samuel's education – no! Time spent thinking about it would give him the greater pleasure . . .

'You go up with the foreign bastard, Samuel. Keep your hands on the eyeglass, Mister. The boy's very delicate and dear to me! What do you say?'

Jesus y Santa Baptista gave his compliments to the captain's unknown parentage and swore that before he died, he, the son of the honourable house of Santa Baptista, would make sure that Nineveh Petticote would eat his own diseased liver. The captain frowned and mumbled, then shrugged. The idiot Spaniard was smiling – damn it! He'd break him.

He paced the deck, his mind on gold and blood. Dame Fortune would play into his unredeemed hands: he could feel it in his bones!

'What do we do when we see a sail, little one?' Jesus murmured softly. 'Do we sing out and let it all start again?'

Samuel glared. What the bleeding Hell was the foreigner on about, all them words – and what was that tone of voice? It sounded like the bastard captain when he did that *be nice to me, Samuel, let me close my eyes and call you Sarah* number. He squatted against the timber of the crow's nest and fingered his well-hidden knife. He knew whose ribs that was for. But old Spainy-bollocks would get it too if he started! The man didn't make a move for all the boy glared at him. Samuel grabbed the eyeglass and stood up.

He spat into the four winds and raised the brass tube to his eye. Nothing east, nothing west, nothing north – maybe something south? The horizon jolted and lurched and he couldn't be sure. He had an idea somewhere that sighting a ship might mean an end to the Hell he had no choice but to call life. Maybe the captain would reward him ... shit to that! His

367

'rewards' had already cost him his dreams. Maybe they'd all be blown to smithereens. He'd seen plenty die, and there was a moment when they twitched and screamed and their eyes bulged – and then it was over. Maybe there was someone wickeder than Nineveh Petticote who'd make them all sign on or die, and he wouldn't be bothered with a kid of nine years old. Samuel's inner voices jeered and leered. He was too old and grey inside to cry.

Jesus took the eyeglass from his clenched hands.

'*Sangre de Cristo!*' he whispered and made the boy look.

A trim galleon less than an hour away and due south. Nothing looking that spruce would be more than a week from land and carrying fresh supplies. And her cargo? Treasure of some kind, for sure. Jesus's mind swam with the thought of enough doubloons to buy his way out of the seventh circle of Hell that meant pirating aboard *The Unbridled Revenge*. He'd take the boy with him and find a good woman and sail to an island where they could live their lives.

'*Capitano!*' he sang out, heady with his dream.

Nineveh Petticote screwed the eyeglass against his one good eye. He grinned.

'To Hell with you, Dame Fortune!' he howled. 'Fuck knows what flag she's under: my skull and cross-bones will master her before the day's out! This is our prize!'

'I knew it!' shouted Queenie. 'There's one of those bastards coming our way. Youse that cannot fire a gun – Goddess alone knows Ah divent blame youse – make yourselves busy with the sails!'

She spun the tiller – the finest Monte Carlo croupier

could not have bettered her three hundred years hence – and kept her fierce grey eye on the sails so near and just a cursed spit of luck so far. Best to close with the fire-eating bastard as soon as maybe! When you're up to your neck in hot water, be like a kettle and sing: Queenie smiled grimly and started to whistle.

Within a heart-wracking hour, the vessels were close enough for hailing.

'This is Captain Nineveh Petticote of *The Unbridled Revenge*! Surrender or be damned!'

Queenie's face twisted into a mask of tragedy. She knew every man on the pirate ship. Not by face, not by name: still less by reputation. She knew the devil-may-care stance of the captain, the hell-mend-us or break us driving lunacy of the crew. One last chance for all of them. She breathed deep and bellowed:

'We have nothing worth your taking. We've had enough storms and robbery for a fleet. Go your way and we'll go our way!'

A ten second pause, then the first gun was fired on *The Empress of the Seven Oceans.* Queenie, catlike, was already lighting fuses and sent a braggadocio seven cannon at the topsails. War was declared. Queenie, Alice, Judith, Jen, Princess, Kerry: all stoked the guns and rolled them back to shatter eardrums with their explosive fire. Pandemonium – and then a slight pause as both pulled back a little to consider their chances.

'Blimey, what's happening down there?' shrieked Eva.

Puffs of smoke exploded in the distance, cannons rumbled and spat flame and sparks. The smoke hung in ugly shreds over the perfect ocean.

'Ah, God, I'm sick of it!' Mad Hattie yelled. 'Men and

murder everywhere you go. Fighting and fury. I'm tired of it. It's been going on too long. Don't they ever learn?'

Panic-stricken seagulls shot past them, not even calling out at the novelty of two women flying, so terrified were they. At least these oversized creatures were flying like any sensible animal, and not fouling the air with gunpowder and the clash of steel.

'We could just ignore it, you know?' Eva glared at Mad Hattie. She'd been trying to get her to land somewhere for the past thirteen days. You have to have cooperation on a double kite, and Mad Hattie was determined to fly on and on until she found the right place. She didn't know where it was, just said she'd know in her guts when she saw it. Eva tried again.

'You're so fond of flying, Hattie. We've seen a hundred islands with trees and rivers and no people around to give us grief, and you've said no to all of them. Why don't we just fly by and give a little wave – you know? You can't catch me! Oh, we're not going to do that. I see. Islands not good enough for you, you've got to find a bloody ship and a battle. Oh, leave me out! I wish you could! Just what's that amazing mind of yours boiling up now?'

Mad Hattie glared and tugged on the ropes.

'Make them shit themselves for a start. Stop them in their tracks. The least I can do is give them a mouthful. I'd like to roll the bloody lot of them up in a bundle and throw them right off this planet. All of them! We're going down!'

'You're sure this thing'll take us back up again?' Eva asked. 'I don't want to wind up on no ship with a bunch of bastards who treat me like the Sunday roast. Which bit do you want, the leg or the breast? No way.

What if they shoot a hole in the wings, Hattie? Think about it.'

Mad Hattie threw her head back and howled with laughter.

'Coming from you! When did you ever think about anything if you knew in your blood you had to do it? I don't have a flaming clue what we'll do down there. But I won't have a beautiful day ruined with gunfire!'

Their wings veered and bore them towards the water. Eva groaned.

'You've done it this time. Look at the flag, Hattie. It's the skull and crossbones! Here's me saying I want to walk again. I wasn't thinking of a sodding plank! Eva does not walk on no planks! Unless they're stuck together and now we're talking floorboards! Jesus, Hattie! This lot are pirates!'

The Unbridled Revenge closed in on *The Empress* with the pall of thick smoke as cover – thick smoke and the deafening roar of cannonfire. Return fire wrenched her topsail loose, and it swung wildly like the broken wing of a giant bird, throwing sparks wide and catching in *The Empress's* rigging. The pirate crew hurled grappling hooks and made them fast. They swarmed along the ropes like cockroaches caught in daylight, and Queenie swung her curved scimitar to slash the lines and send them screaming into the deep.

If she could just wing the pirate captain! Without his bloodcurdling orders, there would be confusion enough to confound the crew for the split seconds needed to break away. Then they'd run before the wind to freedom! He'd be well-hidden – his sort always were, waiting for near-victory to show themselves, deliver a few deadly shots and claim the day.

The Empress shuddered at the impact of a dozen demi-cannon at close range. Jen slashed at the maverick sail with its jagged wooden claw, and it tumbled to the deck.

'Do you surrender? Give it up now, you fools – you've got women aboard!'

That was the captain! Double-dyed rotten sea-leech! Queenie caught sight of his villainous figure through the smoke and aimed for his twisted mouth. Shite and double shite! She missed. She drew dagger and scimitar and stood, a lioness at bay.

'Captain Petticote! God save us all! Witchcraft!'

A high-pitched child's voice from the crow's nest! The captain looked up and howled, reeling back in stark terror. Whatever it was, it had frozen every man aboard. Esther and Rowan with some inspired and crazy bravado? Queenie whirled round to see.

Harpies? Valkyries?

Two tattered creatures flew over the ship and wheeled around, a great wing gusting above them. They swept low over the deck, and Queenie saw that they were women. One flourished a mane of silver hair as wild as lightning, whooping like a banshee. The other was younger and brown-skinned, her hoarse voice fearless and huge. They grabbed a broken spar and shot through the mainsail of the pirate ship. Gaining height, they turned again and skimmed the deck, mowing the crew down and catching the captain solidly across the chest.

They rose over the bows with him dangling from the spar.

'Whatever shall we do with His Ugliness?'

They landed on the deck of *The Empress of The Seven Oceans* and dumped him face down like a broken puppet. He tried to writhe upright, cursing and pleading. The silver-haired woman kicked him flat, and the brown woman gagged him.

'You scum! Stand still where you are – raise your hands and keep them there. I've got the eyes of an eagle!' Alice bellowed from the rigging. The pirates stood as if turned to stone.

'Who the Hell are you two?' Queenie demanded.

'I'm Eva. Nice place you got here – or it would be if these dickheads hadn't come calling.' The brown-skinned woman put one foot on the fallen captain's throat and beat her chest.

'I've always wanted to do that,' she said with a grim smile.

'I'm Mad Hattie.' The older woman grasped Queenie's hand, her silver eyes unblinking. 'Cut from the same bolt of cloth as you, Queenie. And you, Alice.'

Eva groaned.

'Don't ask her how she knows. She knows every-thing, and I've heard most of it non-bloody-stop for the last thirteen days. It would be good if I could say I'd caught you out just once. Love ya, Hattie, right? You're just too flaming much, woman.'

She eased herself out of the flying harness and did a cartwheel.

'Floorboards, Hattie! My feet walking on them!'

'What's to be done with this rabble?' Mad Hattie strode to the side of the ship and glared at the pirate crew.

'What would they have done with us?' said Queenie. 'We'll all have a hand in this.'

The women gathered on the deck.

They locked the crew in the hold and tied Captain Nineveh Petticote to the mast. Mad Hattie stopped Samuel and pointed to a spot on the deck for him to sit.

'Right boy,' she said. 'What's he like, this captain of yours? The truth now!'

'You ain't about to let him free?' snarled the child.

'Never,' Queenie said serenely.

'He's worse than Old Nick hisself,' Samuel spat. 'I've seen bad 'uns, me. But him! He hurts yer real bad and makes you swear on the Bible you like it. He gets that claw of his and digs it in yer neck and makes yer beg him to hurt yer. And then he laughs and laughs. I hate him.'

'What about the rest of them?' said Alice, her mouth twisting with disgust. This nine-year-old was as savage as a starved wolf, his eyes dull with loathing and misery.

'They're all right. No they bleedin' ain't though! Not all of them. Just anything next to him looks like a soddin' saint. That Spainy-bollocks – he's all right.'

'Who?'

'He come off the last ship we done. Don't speak no English and he always smiles. Calls hisself Hayzooss. I reckon he's cursing old Ninny every time he opens his mouth. He's all right. He don't do nothing to hurt yer. Most of 'em do.'

'What do you mean – hurt you?' Eva asked.

'Oh, sod it!' snapped the boy, 'You know, *hurt* yer. You're ladies. I ain't saying what.'

Mad Hattie turned her head to look at the trussed figure, one bloodshot eye glaring over his gag.

'What do you want to do to him, boy?'

Samuel grinned and rocked.

'I want to see him scared. I want to see him wet hisself. Oh, ladies, what I want to do to him! I want to get me knife to his heart and make him beg me to kill him! And I won't. Not that bloody quick, any rate. I want to give him nightmares!'

'Let's get the Spaniard,' Alice said.

Jesus y Santa Baptista looked around at them. Women – but women like he'd never seen before. He toyed with the idea of charming them: but his smile got no response. Even the younger ones had a look about them, a look like his grandmother. She was the voice of God in his family, and even his womanizing father's bluster faltered when she spoke.

Queenie spoke to him in Spanish, nodding now and then, and at one point laughing like a dervish. Nineveh Petticote sweated at the eldritch sound.

'Well, this is the gist of it,' she said. 'This is Jesus y Santa Baptista. He was forced to sign on or walk the plank with a gut dripping blood from His Ugliness's claw. He was shipping with di Scarto. I should have killed that bastard when I had the chance, but he's giving some shark bellyache right now, and good riddance. This here piece of dog's vomit goes by the name of Captain Nineveh Petticote. His entire crew would rip him to pieces given half a chance. What he's done to prisoners and whores and this child here doesn't bear repeating.'

'And what does the Spaniard want?' said Eva, pacing the deck like a cat.

'He wants a boat and supplies and for him and the boy and three others to be set adrift. To find an island and a new way of life.'

'What do you think of that, boy?' asked Mad Hattie.

'Up to you.' Samuel shrugged ungraciously. 'You'll do what you want anyway. I don't want nothing until that bastard's well dead. And chopped to bits!'

Mad Hattie fired a casual shot into the mast so that splinters flew against the erstwhile captain's dripping brow.

'We'll have a think,' she tossed a barrel overboard.

'One down!' she yelled.

They tied up the boy and the Spaniard.

On the poop deck, they sat in a circle.

'Well?'

'None of us has a mind for murder,' said Esther.

'You're lucky if you've never had to choose,' Eva and Mad Hattie said together.

'I know,' Esther said. 'These hands have never had to kill.'

She took Eva's hand in hers. Eva made to pull away, then relaxed. The woman was another loony, but, she thought, what else is new?

'What say we give the Spaniard what he wants? The boy trusts him,' Jen suggested.

'Aye,' Queenie said cautiously. 'A sloop's the last thing to catch up with us. But what about the rest of them?'

'Fuck 'em!' Eva said savagely. 'Throw their arms overboard, rip their sails to shreds, chop their masts down. Leave that festering captain where he is and let them all break out and do each other in.'

Mad Hattie nodded, Alice nodded, Queenie nodded. The nod went round the circle.

They lowered the boat over the side, four men and a boy with as much as they could carry in food and water. Mad Hattie had kept up the pretence of shooting each man hauled on deck; that way, they could make good time before any of the crew had the nerve to try and break free. And Captain Petticote? Samuel spat full into his face and wrenched his talon from him before he left. Rowan blindfolded the malevolent eye with its desperate rolling.

They wrecked *The Unbridled Revenge* with unholy joy.

Then, stealthy as panthers, they tiptoed back on board *The Empress of the Seven Oceans* and cut her free. She sprung away from the distasteful intimacy and her proud bows flew through the might of Ocean.

The Empress Of The Seven Galaxies

'You see, me and Hattie, well, we get twitchy around dry land,' Eva said. *The Empress* was riding at anchor beneath a perfect tropical moon. They sat on the silver decks, sipping at Alice's star-fruit creation.

'This was to be a welcome home brew for all of we,' she said, half ruefully. 'Only after today's nasty little shenanigans, I reckon we can throw out any idea of landing and settling. Welcome aboard, Hattie. Welcome aboard, Eva.'

'You're all mad,' Eva said. 'Stone-mad. Makes me feel at home. I'm going to call you Dizzy, Alice Dizard. Whatever you've put in this, Dizzy, I'll be reeling the night away! And I'm sorry to be a bad guest, but it slipped my mind to bring tobacco.'

Queenie chuckled richly and handed her pouch and pipe.

'Oh, leave me out!' cried Eva. 'Queenie? Queenie's too common for you. Hattie, I love this woman! This ship may be an Empress, but you, Queenie, you're magic, an angel – a spirit!'

'Ah, gerraway!'

'Nah, she's right,' said Alice. 'Ah didn't want to say it, seeing as the doors might get a bit narrow for that bonny head of yours. Angel spirit – give us a kiss!'

'Can I be a spirit?' asked Turtle.

'You are,' Esther said. 'A shell-backed spirit from the womb of Ocean herself.'

'I'm a flying spirit!' shouted Squirrel. 'And so's Jen!'

'OK, OK, I seem to have started something here,' Eva said, grinning in ecstasy through a cloud of smoke. 'Let's all be spirits. I'll be a hedgehog spirit. Guarantees me three whole months of every year fast asleep and snoring.'

'Where do you put me?' asked Hattie, her silver hair iridescent with moonlight.

'I wouldn't have the nerve, Hattie. I put you anywhere you want to be.'

'You're wise,' Hattie said drily.

The waves sang along with the creaking ropes and a voice thrilling with newness curled around them in a joyous chant.

> '*We* are *all spirits*.
> Hattie is the spirit of an owl.
> Rowan is the spirit of a tree.
> Esther is a river spirit.
> Princess is the spirit of a snake.
> Jen is a winged serpent, a dragon spirit.
> Alice is the spirit of a hummingbird.
> Judith is a she-bear spirit.
> Eva is the spirit of a cat.
> Kerry is a dolphin spirit.
> Squirrel is a squirrel spirit.
> Turtle is a turtle spirit.
> Queenie is the spirit of a tiger.
> I am the spirit of Ocean.'

'Belle!' Rowan cried. 'How very lovely to hear you!'

Isabel skipped to her feet and brought the map into their circle.

'Go on,' she said to Queenie. 'We're all spirits, but

you're the boldest, born under the sign of the lioness. *You* say it!'

'Well, it's all riddles to me,' protested Queenie. 'I'm not one for modesty, but I'm out of my depth, Belle!'

'We are thirteen and the moon's full!' the child cried. 'Look!'

Spirit of Ocean, she scrambled to her feet and raised one arm. Her spangled finger made a clear path like a silver wire through the night, and they all gazed along the wonderful beam clear into the face of the moon. Her indigo veins, languorous lady draped in silk shot with hieroglyphs: a perfect mirror of the map that glowed between them on the deck.

Queenie stood and smiled into the pure light. Her ebony and silver mane tore free and blew in a sheet of flame behind her eternal smile.

'Oh, excuse me for breathing!' Eva said. 'What kind of wind can take us *there*?'

'A good question,' said Queenie and started to hum. The canvas shivered overhead, *The Empress of the Seven Oceans* bucked and snapped her anchor chain.

They drew deep breaths of moonlight and scurried round the deck as *The Empress* wallowed through the dark waves. Eva flung her crescent knife overboard. Esther and Rowan slashed the cannons free and sent them splashing out of sight. *The Empress* picked up speed. Queenie's scimitar bit a shining arc through the darkness and she hurled her dagger after it.

A wind wild with unearthly freshness cast the sails into the scudding wake. Lighter and higher, *The Empress of the Seven Oceans* flew across the wave-caps until she lifted from the salty splendours of the seventh ocean and took to the midnight air. She burst through chill tissues of cloud, higher and higher until the clouds were a distant and dazzling snowfield.

Over the hills and far away in the woods near Newcastle, a runaway child called Ruth frowned. Something drew her gaze from the flames of the gypsy fire where she was safe and oh so warm. She caught her breath.

A galleon as small as a child's toy was etched against the perfect circle of silver moon, and Ruth's ears thrilled to the song and laughter of thirteen wild women finally headed for home.

THE END

Rotary Spokes
by Fiona Cooper

Rotary Spokes is unique!

Normal . . . a no horse town in Middle America?

A six-feet-four woman motorcycle mechanic?

Lesbian lust in the sudden dusts and tumbleweeds of a
Christian fundamentalist revival?

Rotary Spokes positively bursts into life in this vivid, often
hilarious account of a young woman's discovery of – and
coming to terms with – her sexual nature. The effect this
discovery has on some of Rotary's smaller-minded
neighbours, and her ensuing search for like-minded
company, is beautifully portrayed in an engaging and
ultimately very moving novel from one of the most
outrageous novelists of the decade.

'A vivacious, audacious, startling debut with a central
character to match'
Gay Times

'Rotary Spokes is the novel for all jaded readers of the
eighties and beyond. A unique style superbly maintained
and packed with laughs'
Sara Maitland, author of *Virgin Territory* and *Vesta Tilley*

0 552 99415 4

BLACK SWAN

Dream Weaver
by Jonathan Wylie

At first they thought it was snow. But it was too warm, too dry, and the white crystals crunched underfoot. There was a tang in the air, sharp and familiar, yet it was some time before anyone realized what was falling on their city . . .

Ancient events haunt Rebecca's dreams, revealing images she would rather avoid. But when it becomes clear that there is a link between these uncanny visions and her present life, she is forced to confront her fears.

As civil war threatens the land of Ahrenia, Rebecca is thrust into a central role in the momentous drama that is engulfing her home. And yet she discovers that war is not the ultimate evil.

The armies of nightmare draw closer, and only the enigmatic talents of the Dream-Weaver can begin to unravel the mysteries of past and future.

Jonathan Wylie, author of the *Servants of Ark* and *The Unbalanced Earth* trilogies, casts an entrancing spell of intrigue, magic and wonder over his most ambitious tale to date.

0 552 13757 X

A SELECTION OF FANTASY TITLES FROM CORGI BOOKS

THE PRICES SHOWN BELOW WERE CORRECT AT THE TIME OF GOING TO PRESS. HOWEVER TRANSWORLD PUBLISHERS RESERVE THE RIGHT TO SHOW NEW RETAIL PRICES ON COVERS WHICH MAY DIFFER FROM THOSE PREVIOUSLY ADVERTISED IN THE TEXT OR ELSEWHERE.

☐	13725 1	EXPATRIA	Keith Brooke	£3.99
☐	13724 3	KEEPERS OF THE PEACE	Keith Brooke	£3.99
☐	99415 4	ROTARY SPOKES	Fiona Cooper	£4.99
☐	13661 1	THE DOOR INTO FIRE	Diane Duane	£3.99
☐	13662 X	THE DOOR INTO SHADOW	Diane Duane	£3.99
☐	13663 8	THE DOOR INTO SUNSET	Diane Duane	£3.99
☐	13627 1	RATS AND GARGOYLES	Mary Gentle	£4.99
☐	13628 X	THE ARCHITECTURE OF DESIRE	Mary Gentle	£3.99
☐	13757 X	DREAM WEAVER	Jonathan Wylie	£4.99
☐	13101 6	SERVANTS OF ARK I: THE FIRST NAMED	Jonathan Wylie	£3.99
☐	13134 2	SERVANTS OF ARK II: THE CENTRE OF THE CIRCLE	Jonathan Wylie	£3.50
☐	13161 X	SERVANTS OF ARK III: THE MAGE-BORN CHILD	Jonathan Wylie	£3.99
☐	13416 3	THE UNBALANCED EARTH 1: DREAMS OF STONE	Jonathan Wylie	£3.99
☐	13417 1	THE UNBALANCED EARTH 2: THE LIGHTLESS KINGDOM	Jonathan Wylie	£2.99
☐	13418 X	THE UNBALANCED EARTH 3: THE AGE OF CHAOS	Jonathan Wylie	£4.99